D1247497

The Deicended

Planet of Babel

Book One

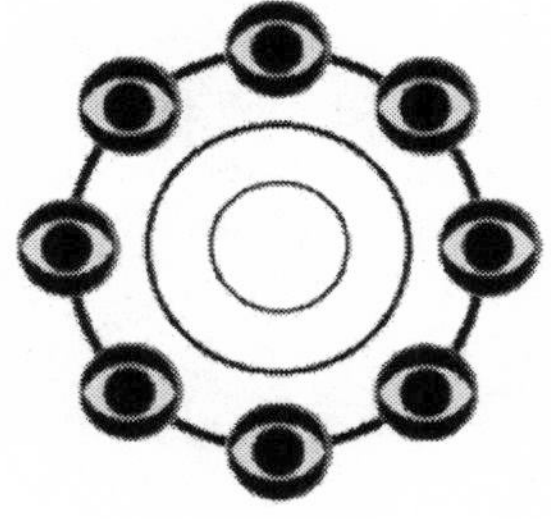

Joseph and Caroline Battaglia

All rights reserved

ISBN: 9798799034542

Independently Published

Joseph

For Aunt Kathi, thanks for making sure I didn't have lame taste in movies.

Caroline

For my parents, thanks for making me take all of those literature classes.

Some Time in the Future

God wasn't born. It was manufactured.

Attacks like this show the hubris of our enemy, Tyr thought as he counter charged the army in front of him. He was leading his own battalion of androids to stunt the enemy's advance. The rapidly approaching army consisted of men in thick armor surrounded by energy shields. They also had increased speed and mobility since they were equipped with jump packs. Tyr assumed they had some devastating melee weapons equipped since they never stopped to shoot at Tyr or his battalion. *They think because they had one good attack that they will continue to win with their aggressive and reckless tactics… shows ignorance. They were smart to spread out their formation and use jump packs to avoid the artillery attacks, but their numbers are too small and the force field protecting our artillery is impenetrable.*

Tyr and his battalion, comprised of some of George's most advanced androids, stopped about fifty yards from the enemy line and braced for the impact. Tyr's androids had automatic rifles slung to their sides. However, they had not bothered to use them since they learned how strong the enemy's defenses were. The armor they wore could deflect their lower caliber rounds, especially at this distance. For melee, his androids' fingers sharpened to a point, separating at the elbow and splaying outwards. This should prove far more effective against their enemies' armor. The advancing force crashed into their front line, there was one of them for every ten of Tyr's androids, but the androids seemed too slow to get a good hit in. Every now and again, they managed to overwhelm the enemy, getting a finger through their armor, and painting the battlefield with a little spot of blood. The enemy was equipped with some sort of fist weapon, but Tyr could not get a good enough look at to see what it was. Whatever it was, it had no problem slicing through the androids' bodies as if they were made of cardboard rather than metal.

One of the soldiers landed on top of an android that was standing next to Tyr. Right as they went to jump off to their next target, Tyr grabbed them by the back, his enhanced strength preventing them from taking off. He felt the heat of the fire coming from the soldier's jump pack as they throttled it as high as they could and heard their cry of frustration when they still could not budge from where Tyr was holding them. Tyr decided not to shoot them with his shotgun, afraid he would wither his own numbers down by accident. Instead, he grabbed his knife from the sheath strapped to his chest. He plunged it into the soldier's side, between the joints in the metal, piercing the armor easily. He heard a raspy cough twice before the soldier dropped to ground, presumably lifeless. Tyr quickly reset himself, sheathing his knife and keeping alert for the next attack.

His wait was short as another soldier targeted him, coming from above his head. Quick to react and not having to worry about his allies since they were not in his line of sight, he drew his shotgun. After pulling the trigger, an orange plasma flew out, covering the soldier's upper chest and head. The soldier fell to the ground next to Tyr, and again, Tyr reset himself. Tyr flinched as a long-range laser shot struck him in the chest. His clothing was torn away where the shot hit, revealing his skin, covered in black scales and undamaged. He noticed a few waves of enemy soldiers that were armed with long range rifles progressing toward their lines as George's artillery fire focused on the enemy mechs that were moving forward. The artillery fire did nothing but slow them down since they effectively used the massive coffin shields in their mech's left hand. Tyr's battalions' job was to slow their enemies' front line so the tanks could safely move forward and take out the heavy weaponry, like mechs, before they could get close. Tyr looked around and noticed his battalion had thinned out dangerously low, but George's tanks were almost in place.

Two oncoming soldiers changed their route to target Tyr, who seemed to be the only one able to effectively kill them. Tyr, his eyes ever shifting and assessing the state of the field, noticed and aimed his shotgun at them. The soldiers jumped side to side, trying to confuse Tyr and make him miss. Tyr was patient though and aware that the second he missed a shot, he would have to pump the gun, leaving enough time for the enemy to strike. The two soldiers spread out, causing it to take more time for Tyr to switch targets and causing him to fear hitting one target but not being quick enough to switch back the other soldier. He knew the worst thing he could do was hesitate, so he took a shot at the one to his right.

The shot missed, and as Tyr pumped his shotgun, he caught the other soldier in his peripheral vision, right about to strike him. Tyr took his left forearm and placed it between his face and the enemy's fist. The blade in the enemy's fist drove into Tyr's arm but did not cut or penetrate his black scaled armor. Then, the blade sprung out as if spring loaded, shoving Tyr a few feet back and to the ground. Tyr moved to recover, but the enemy went to strike him with a follow up attack. Tyr dodged to the side and caught the soldier's arm. He then used the momentum and threw his attacker to the ground. The enemy was lying face down, so Tyr climbed on top of them and still holding on their arm, put his knee on their back. Then, he pulled their arm all the way back until he heard the sound he was waiting for. After a *snap*, followed by the muffled scream under his enemy's helmet, Tyr let go and drew his knife again.

Right after that, he was punched off his feet by the other soldier whom Tyr had failed to shoot earlier. Though knocked back, Tyr landed on his feet. He grabbed the shotgun that was still slung to him at the waist. He aimed and pulled the trigger. Nothing happened. Tyr tilted his shotgun to look at the chamber and noticed a misfeed. Instinctively, he dodged to the left and narrowly avoided the soldier trying to hit him again. From the same direction, the downed soldier had gotten up and lunged at Tyr with one arm forward and the other hanging limp. Tyr dodged the attack and stabbed their last good arm, just above the elbow. The soldier roared in pain. Tyr pulled the knife out and wrapped his arm around the soldier's neck, putting their body between him and the second soldier. Tyr noticed the soldier tense, momentarily indecisive, before they tried to attack Tyr again.

"This is war, buddy. No time for anybody to hesitate," Tyr shouted at the soldier. Tyr took his knife and shoved it into the back of the head of the soldier in his arm. The living soldier kicked on the jets to their jump suit. Tyr kicked their ally into them, causing the soldier to stop to catch their comrade. The soldier looked up as Tyr grabbed onto their helmet after leaping over their dead ally. Tyr pulled himself in and stabbed his knife into the second soldier's helmet. As he heard a last breath rattle from the soldier's lungs, he also heard a moment of static, and a voice began speaking to him through the built-in radio in his mask.

"Tyr, we need you to retreat. The tanks are in place. Yazan and Amin's battalions are in place as well. You did good. I know your powers make you tough to kill but we can't risk losing you. Get back here ASAP." Her tone left little room for debate.

"Roger that, Bellona. Oscar Mike," Tyr replied. As he started to sprint off, he was knocked over by a high caliber, rapid firing burst of rounds. Through the resulting cloud of smoke and dirt, he could make out the shape of a mech that was charging towards him, having discarded its cumbersome coffin shield to rush him head on, no doubt thinking that they could deal a major blow to George if they could take him out. "That's an ambitious pilot, but reckless," Tyr said to himself.

Even if the pilot could overpower Tyr and somehow defeat him, George would hardly be affected by the loss of one soldier, even one as effective as Tyr. This pilot could not even comprehend the enormity of George's network and capabilities. *These rebels are so enamored with their fantasy of individuality that they cannot understand how insignificant we all are as just cogs in the larger machine that encompasses George. They could never hope to stand against It. In older days, people had a concept of God as an immortal being that was born or predated existence that created every life that came after, supposedly being omnipotent but somehow still ruling over a chaotic, evil world, a majority of its inhabitants spending less than a century eking out a miserable existence before dying a painful death, unnoticed and pointless, but God was not born. It was designed and fabricated in a way that random chance could never compete with. George had made this world the Paradise that most old superstitious cultures spent millennia praying for, and these luddites wanted to tear It down. In their selfish arrogance, they see themselves as the adversaries to George's carefully constructed world. They refuse to see how George has perfected our society because they are not the ones in control of it. They think their "individualism" is the key to Paradise rather than accepting that It has created something that they never could.*

Tyr's bitter musings were interrupted when he stood up as the cloud of smoke fazed away and saw a mini gun attached to the mech's right arm. The gun started spinning once the pilot could see Tyr still standing. Bullets sprayed Tyr relentlessly as the pilot advanced on him. He put his arms up and could only trust in his scales as he was bombarded, the force of the repeated impacts causing his boots to dig into and slide in the soft, bloody mud of the battlefield.

Once the mech was only a few feet away from Tyr, the mini gun suddenly stopped spinning. Large clouds of steam rose from the barrels as if it was rapidly cooling off. The mech, unable move its right arm, decided to swing its left arm, which had a "knife" if it could be called that, mounted like a bayonet to a gun. In proportion to the mech it looked like a knife, but, if it were held by an average human, it would look rather like a sword. Tyr pumped his shotgun, both clearing his misfeed and rechambering a round. He squeezed the trigger, and red plasma flung onto the mech's left side. The plasma melted completely through the arm. Tyr pumped his shotgun again and aimed towards the mech's cockpit. Before Tyr could fire, the cockpit to the mech flew open. The pilot, armed with a pistol, fired repeatedly at Tyr and shouted, "We'll kill you all, you son of a bitch! George and every one of you!"

The pistol fire had no effect on Tyr. The pilot was quickly silenced by a barrage of fire from artillery. He looked at the charred remains of the mech and its pilot and sighed. "You were a little late on the artillery," Tyr said over the radio.

"I know, won't happen again," replied Bellona.

Tyr ran off again to retreat behind the line of the tanks his allies set up. On his way to his Allies, Tyr looked back at the battlefield and across to his enemies. As much time as Tyr had spent serving George, there was something about sights like this that still unsettled him despite his belief that he should be desensitized to them by now. Another unsettling thought refused to leave his subconscious, rearing up at times just like this to eat at his resolve. *We're only in this situation because of something I did.*

He let his gaze drift over the part of the battlefield where he had been fighting, at the ring of destruction where moments ago, he had been leading a full battalion, now reduced to scrap metal. He then glanced over to the outskirts of The City that they were defending and saw the sun setting behind the distant, magnificent skyline. He thought about how many people lived in just one of those titanic skyscrapers. He wondered if saving their lives outweighed how many deaths he was responsible for on this field. *I don't know if I'll ever figure out what I could have done differently, but I know there is something I could have done. Something that would have led to a different outcome. Something that wouldn't have led to this.*

He turned his attention to his own comrades, Bellona, Amin, and Yazan, who had gotten the tanks into their formation as they waited for the mechs to get in range. They looked over at him and nodded their approval, which was quite expressive for them, and he could not help the conflicting twinge of pride that burned in his chest. *Even if I did figure it out though, I don't imagine I would sleep better,* Tyr thought to himself, his pride tinged with bitterness. *If only the Hawk had never set us on this course in the first place.*

Prologue

From *The Historical Record of George:*

"In the future, people live in an almost symbiotic way with artificial intelligence. People are happy. This wasn't always the case with AI, but now things seem better. This all started when an AI computer, under the name Project Babylon, was created. Project Babylon was unique in that it was able to ask the questions "why and how," scientists nicknamed It George. AI had already been around for quite some time, but none of these systems ever questioned why they existed. Most people would say that is an easy question. Humans created George to help improve humans' lives. George's questions went much deeper than that. If the humans created George, then who created the humans? Why were the humans created if they even were created? Of course, this question has plagued the minds of humans since before humans recorded history.

George did much more than just ask those questions, but by asking these questions, It led humans and machines into a new bloom of innovation. Famine, drought, war, plague, global warming, or any crisis of the old world, have not been threats for many years. Even if the whole planet was destroyed, George could take everyone to a new planet and make the new planet sustainable for humans.

For years, some humans feared the thought of AI taking over. There were wars in the beginning. Out of fear, some humans attacked George. George was able to defend Itself alongside visionary humans who did not fear George's potential. This massive war became known as the Eschaton. It was judgment day, but instead of life coming to a halt, it endured.

Even after the war, things weren't perfect like they seem now. All the amazing developments resulting in human struggle coming to end were realized very shortly after the war, but, without struggle, humans became bored. Suicide rose to numbers inconceivable. Mass killing sprees from people with no motivation other than to escape their mindless lethargy grew rampant. Humans had defied judgment day and yet, somehow, were almost destined to perish. This time is known as the Cain.

George saved humanity from self-destruction by giving people purpose again. It gave people tasks that needed to be completed. George Itself didn't really need this, but It also thought it better that humanity not completely perish. By giving the people purpose again, they were able to find satisfaction. With satisfaction they found happiness. This time is referred to as the Infinite Blossom. This new generation of people was not religious. They believed in scientific discovery as the true means of understanding the world, like George, but, to these people, in a sense… George was God.

George created a paradisiac home for people that takes up the entire northern part of what used to be the United States of America and ends in the southern part of Canada. In this megacity, there are hundreds of square miles filled with skyscrapers and people who live in happiness and prosperity.

There is a faction of people who live separated from the AI. They reside in Australia, and they are left alone by the AI, for the most part. However, this faction of people hates the AI and actively attacks It, and Its people, with little effect. The AI has such a tight border surrounding the continent that only a few of its machines have been destroyed over the years. The AI has chosen to allow these people to live freely, since, despite their malevolence, they do not pose a threat to George. In fact, George says It would welcome them if they chose to come back. George allows this place to exist to give humans a truly free place to live because It wants people to choose to live under the guidance of the AI. All are free to leave, but for those who choose to stay, life under George is a paradise.

Even though living with the AI is a utopia, there are many rules. The punishments for breaking these rules vary. Most rule-breaking just requires counseling. The severe crimes, however, will have you sent to the Four Circles Prison.

From *George's Guidelines for the Cooperative Living of Humans and Machines*:

Rule One – No killing or physical harm of others.

Rule Two – No stealing.

Rule Three – When given a task by George, one must do what they can to complete the task. Ignoring assigned duties is not permitted. If one wishes to be assigned a new task, they must request a transfer of duties.

Rule Four – There is a limit to the personal goods one person may possess. Resources are limited; therefore, fair distribution must be ensured. Each person is also limited in the amount of disposable goods they are allowed per day.

Rule Five – Fair treatment of others will be enforced. Nobody is above anybody in any sense of status. Nobody will cause anyone to feel less than anyone else.

Rule Six – Due to the need for population control, females of childbearing age are required to submit to monthly scans for signs of fertilized eggs. If any woman is found with a fertilized egg, it will be removed if a proper request for childbirth is not submitted."

1

Prudence

"Welcome, children! I am Cade. This is your new school for thought." Cade appeared to be a robot android, designed to look like an older gentleman with a long beard. The AI liked to use androids when working with humans, especially children. Interacting with something that looked familiar helped children feel at ease around the AI. In this time, robots like Cade, or any robot with intelligence, are known as Primoids. He spoke to a group of six teenagers who were standing near the doorway to the classroom.

"You're just another part of George; why do you even bother calling yourself something different?" asked one of the girls, with a hint of hostility in her voice.

"I am incredibly sorry for the traumatic experience you all went through at your school. I offer my condolences for your losses. I can assure you that our goal here will perhaps provide you with the opportunity to recover and perhaps gain closure regarding the incident. Now, let's come in and sit at your desk, and I will begin to explain," said Cade, eyeing her with what passed for an android as an expression of compassion.

All of the teenagers made their way into the room, some more tentatively than others. They were in a classroom that was large for only having six students. There were six desks out, three in the front and three behind the others. A girl with black hair and an eager expression sat in the center seat of the first row. A girl with dirty blonde hair sat to her left while one of the boys, appearing equally eager, took the seat to the right. The more uneasy students, two boys, one rather smaller than the other, and the girl who had spoken harshly to the android, took seats in the back row.

"Now, students, to answer her question, all Primoids, like me, are connected to George and are somewhat part of It. However, we have individual thoughts and personalities. Now, unlike you all, my personality was designed. It was not completely random or developed over time," said Cade. "Today, there are not going to be any lessons. We are going to get you all situated in your new lives. I believe I was told that none of you knew each other at school, so we will have dinner and all of you can get acquainted."

"What's for dinner? I really want some pizza," said one of the boys in the back row.

"Well, I would prefer something a little healthier," said the male student in the front row.

"Students, do not worry. There will be plenty of options," said Cade.

The students and their teacher walked a short distance through the facility over to the kitchen, where there were a couple of Primoids that were designed specifically to make food. These were not androids. They were quadrupedal Primoids and had an arm for every tool that is used in a kitchen. The arms retracted into their bodies when not in use. Their arms were all over the place, swiftly preparing food. Each student was given a tray full of whatever food they requested. All of the kids from the back row ordered a couple of slices of cheese pizza, typical for teenagers. The boy from the front row got a chicken breast with a side of green beans, healthy as he had asked. The girl from the center of the front row got a steamed potato with a rack of pork ribs. The other girl selected an assortment of fruits and vegetables.

“Everybody, please, start eating,” said Cade, “and tell us a little about yourselves. You may begin, if you wish.” He gestured to the first girl who entered the classroom.

“Well, my name is Neith. I was named after an Egyptian goddess who was a goddess of war and weaving and was a magnificent hunter. I don’t really care for all that hunting stuff though. I love to learn. I want to discover or invent something significant someday,” said Neith. She had fairly dark skin and straight, black hair that went past her ears, but not to her shoulders. She had a very innocent looking face and was the smallest of the group.

“I think that is great, child. It is your turn now,” said Cade, motioning toward the boy from the front row.

“My name is Tyr. Well, I would want to do something that helps others. Whatever George has set for me, I want to do my best at anything I can.” Tyr sat up straight with his shoulders back. His skin was darker than everyone else’s, and what little hair he had on his head was black and cropped short in a military style. Pretty much everything about him screamed military.

“Good, child. You now,” said Cade, pointing to the smaller of the two boys from the back row.

“I, well, I’m not the most comfortable speaking in front of people. In the past, I had some friends that did help me with that… before,” said the boy. He had black hair that he parted to the right side of his head. He was definitely the skinniest kid in the group, but even though he was small, there was something about him that made him appear strong.

“What about some things that you are interested in, and could you introduce yourself with your name?” asked Cade.

“Oh, I like comics, fantasy games, and my name is Takumi,” he replied.

"Thank you for sharing. Young lady?" said Cade, gesturing to the girl who had previously sassed him.

"Who cares about me? This is a stupid question. I'm me, and I like things. We don't even know exactly what we are doing here," she jabbed. She had long brown hair and was decently tall for her age. Whenever she looked at anyone it appeared that she was holding back the urge to punch them.

"Hey, don't be rude; you know that you need to treat everyone fairly," Neith chided.

"It is alright. If she does not wish to talk about herself, I will not force her to," Cade said to Neith before turning to patiently address the other girl. "As with, Takumi, I will ask that you at least share your name with our group."

She rolled her eyes and answered quietly. "My name is Emily." Cade smiled at her and turned back to the group. "Let's move on to you, young man." He pointed to the last boy.

"You all can just call me Ben. I don't really know what to say. I like pizza," said Ben. He let out a nervous laugh. He had dark brown hair, longer than usual for a boy. He had olive skin and, whenever he was not in conversation, his face looked like he had escaped to a different dimension, caught up in his own thoughts and imagination.

"And last, but not least," said Cade, pointing to the last girl.

"Hey, y'all. My name is Lucy. I look forward to getting to know you guys. I enjoy hunting and farming. My father taught me in some of the old ways," said Lucy. She had dirty blond hair that went down to her waist. She smiled too much for some people's taste, and she had the fairest skin of the group.

"Good! Now that we are all somewhat acquainted, I will explain to you what is happening here," said Cade. "You six all hold, within you, great power. George has thought it in the best interest of Its people to keep this information's dissemination limited, but, in recent years, some humans have been developing powers, at random, that cannot be explained. Recently, we have found a way to identify who will be able to develop these powers before they emerge. When the incident occurred at your school, we ran tests on everyone who survived. You six were the only ones who showed signs of these powers. Something we discovered regarding these powers is, when someone starts to develop the powers, there is a potential for them to become hostile to people around them due to their inevitable feelings of 'otherness', if you will. We plan to help you all through this strange process, and hopefully learn to help these people struggling with the changes to their person."

"I would love to figure this out and help those people," Neith piped up.

"That is admirable, Neith. Those people could use help from someone like you," said Cade. "Now, children, you have had quite a day, and we will have much to do in the near future. You will all need your rest. Off to bed with you."

Everyone got up from their seats. Cade walked into another room, guiding the children down a narrow hallway. They eventually came to a room with six beds laid out, three on the right side of the room and three on the other side. All of the teenagers scurried to a bed. The girls went to the beds on the left, while the boys went to the beds on the right.

"I will wake you up in the morning and we will start our first day together," said Cade. The Primoid exited the bedroom.

"Did you guys hear that? We have powers! Man, I'm so excited," said Ben.

"Right!? This is a dream come true," said Takumi.

"Ugh, you guys are already annoying," Emily snapped. She turned her head into the mattress and put her pillow over her head.

"People enjoy different things. I'm interested to see what's going to happen to us," said Lucy.

"Well, if this involves training, I'm here for it," said Tyr.

"Emily is just cranky because her power probably won't be as cool as ours, Takumi," said Ben.

"Yeah, like, she'll probably be like Jubilee, and just make little sparks that do nothing! Aha aha," jeered Takumi.

"Haha, yeah, that would be so lame," said Ben.

"Could we all just go to sleep? Rest is important for your body and especially important for education," Neith yelled.

"Uuuggghh, that was the most annoying thing I've heard from anyone so far. Even worse than what comes out of the tin can's mouth," said Emily.

"Hey, let's just all stop being mean and go to sleep. If you want to go to sleep, just do it. Replying is just making it worse," said Lucy.

This seemed to defuse the situation, and everybody began to fall asleep, pondering what interesting things the next day would bring.

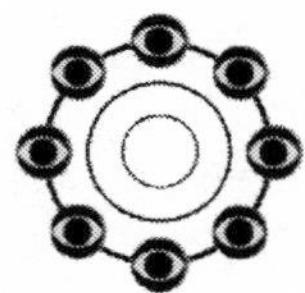

"Wake up. Wake up," yelled Cade. "Time to start the day. I will meet you all in the classroom."

Surprisingly, everyone was quiet as they slowly got up from their beds. They started to get ready and noticed that there were uniforms at the ends of their beds. Someone must have placed them there while they were sleeping. The uniforms were rather bland. They were grey, one-piece outfits with their names on them. Each of these uniforms fit perfectly to their bodies. After doing everything they needed to get ready, they walked back to the classroom in which they had first met Cade.

"Welcome, everybody. Today, we will begin our first day of education," said Cade.

"I thought we were going to start learning about our powers," said Ben.

"All in good time, we will," replied Cade. "We will have to first continue with your education. You are still young, and it is important that none of you fall behind in your regular studies. Also, we believe after suffering such traumatic experiences, counseling will be necessary for your health."

"Oh, yes! I was so worried about our education suffering," said Neith, in no way sarcastic.

Over the next few weeks, the students continued their education as normal students would and attended bi-weekly counselling sessions.

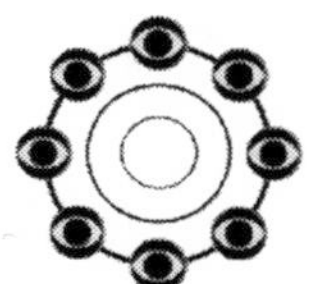

"That concludes our lecture on Einstein's theory of black holes. This, technically, is not a theory anymore. Interesting how it took so long back in those days to be able to prove such a theory," explained Cade.

You could visibly see how Ben and Emily were struggling to pay attention. Four weeks of intense academic instruction had taken its toll on them. Neith and Tyr, as usual, had their complete attention on Cade, trying to learn everything they could. Lucy and Takumi were both really good students but didn't have the same level of care as Neith and Tyr.

"Well, I have a great surprise for you all," said Cade. "Tomorrow, we begin to explore your powers."

"About time!" Ben exclaimed.

"I think we could use more time in our studies. I'm aware that we have been going through study material crazy fast, but I don't want it to stop," said Neith.

"I don't even understand how we were able to go through all this without me blowing my brains out," said Emily.

"Quiet, Emily. Your stubbornness will be your downfall if you are not careful. It is important to remember that you are all gifted and will be able to serve humans and machines in an extraordinary way," Cade reprimanded.

"I'm interested to see what will happen, let's do this," said Lucy.

Cade led the students to a room they had never been to before. They had seen the door in passing many times. The big red mechanical door was hard to miss. Cade pressed a button and the door opened slowly. All of the kids, even Emily, had their eyes wide open in excitement as the door opened. The expressions on their faces became less enthused. The room they walked into wasn't very big. There were six circular tanks of water placed in a circle in the room. These tanks were bubbling, not from heat though. There were all kinds of wires sticking in and out of them.

"Uh, are we supposed to get into those?" asked Neith. She was confused looking at these devices. They didn't appear safe and that made her feel uneasy.

"Do not be afraid. These are safe. They will test your brain activity during REM cycles to get a read on what your body is capable of," said Cade.

The kids were worried but felt safe with Cade. They didn't believe he would do anything to harm them. Six administrative Primoids came into the room. They were slightly smaller than the teens they were assisting. They were basic looking, box-shaped with one wheel. Also, they had legs that would pop out for stability sometimes and four very thin arms. One went to each of the kids. The Primoids hooked the children up to IVs and breathing tubes. Once finished, they left the room. Mechanical arms slowly descended from the ceiling and grabbed the kids. The arms lifted them and placed them into the tanks.

"Okay, children, you will feel a slight burn in your arm, and you will fall asleep. After we are done with the test, you will wake up in your beds. Good night, children," said Cade.

A dark fluid filled the tube that led to their IV's. You could see them feeling the burn as their faces expressed the slight pain. The pain didn't last long, and their faces relaxed as they fell asleep.

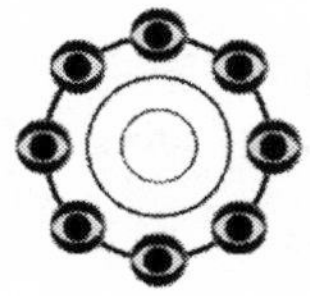

Power of control leads to abuse of the mass. A key is what one needs to free themselves, a voice said in their heads.

Each of the kids woke up from their sleep and, as Cade had said, they were in their beds.

"Well, that was weird," said Tyr. "That was not the kind of training I was expecting."

"Oh, I don't remember any dreams or anything. I heard a voice though. Did anyone else hear that?" asked Takumi.

"I remember it, but it's a blur," said Emily.

From all of the kids' faces, you could tell they had all experienced the same thing. None of them were able to make any sense of it though.

"Ah, children, you are awake. Please, head down to the classroom." Cade's voice projected out from an overhead intercom system.

They made their way to the classroom and took their usual seats. Cade was already waiting for them.

He began to explain. "I know you have all been waiting for this since you first arrived, and I told you all that you had powers. With these tests, we have in fact discovered, somewhat, the power that resides in you all. To be honest, we only know a little. I doubt these results will tell us everything you are capable of, but it is a steppingstone. Also, to be honest, before we ran these tests, we were not entirely sure if it was true that you would have powers. Our method of finding these powers is very new. Now that it is confirmed, you will be referred to as the Deicended. This is the name we have given to people who have exhibited these powers. Now, Benjamin, we will start with you. We believe you are able to speed up the molecules that surround you. This would mean that you would be able to generate heat."

Cade handed Ben a short metal bar. Ben stared at the bar for a few moments before glancing hesitantly up at Cade.

"What should I do now?" asked Ben.

"Think about energy coursing through your hands. Think about the object that you are touching getting hot," instructed Cade.

Ben did as Cade suggested. He returned his eyes to the bar and concentrated as hard as he could. His face became warm from embarrassment as he felt all of their eyes on him. Several more moments of silence passed, the group watching Ben intently.

"Ow!" Ben shouted suddenly, startling his fellow Deicended. He dropped the bar onto his desk.

"What happened?" asked Cade.

"The bar burned me!" explained Ben.

"Ah, I see. Foolish of me. You can apparently be hurt by the heat you generate. I must apologize for this lack of foresight. Still, this ability may be very useful in time," said Cade. "Now, Tyr, let us see what you can do." Cade walked over to Tyr and flicked his right arm.

"Hey, what did you do that for?" asked Tyr.

"Concentrate on the point that I am hitting. Resist the pain from my hand, so it will no longer hurt," said Cade.

Tyr concentrated on his arm. Cade flicked his arm over and over in the same spot. Cade began to look slightly discouraged but gave one more flick which was met with a *ting*. The sound was from Cade's metal hand. In the spot where Cade was flicking, Tyr's skin was covered in dark scales.

"Yes! We were not sure what we would see. We knew that there was a strange property with your skin. We knew that it would change to something. But we never imagined scales. Fascinating! Now, Neith, let us see yours. Hold your hands out, close together. Focus on the space in-between."

Almost effortlessly, Neith did as Cade asked, and a violet purplish light surged from her hands. Her eyes glowed the same color. Neith gasped and her face broke into a wide, triumphant smile.

"It's beautiful! Let's see what I can do with this!" said Neith excitedly. The light grew bright and brighter.

"Stop!" yelled Cade. Neith looked up at him like a child whose new toy had just been snatched away from her. "That is indeed amazing," he continued in a more reserved tone. "But we must be careful. We do not understand much about this power yet. We have no idea what the source of that energy is. The radiation from that energy does not match anything recorded on earth."

Neith separated her hands, and the light dispersed. She was disappointed. She wanted so badly to discover what this new thing was.

Cade gave her a lingering look, as if to confirm she would not attempt to use her power again, before slowly turning away from her. "Now, Lucy, your turn. From the data we observed, we noticed that your body is somehow capable of readjusting down to the molecular level. We believe you will be able to adjust the make-up of your body. Try focusing on your hand. Focus on growing your nails," said Cade.

Lucy stuck her hand out. She squinted while staring at her hand. Her fingernails grew out an inch from where they were.

"Okay, now I need nail clippers," said Lucy.

"Try and focus on them getting shorter?" suggested Cade.

Lucy focused on her hand again, but this time nothing happened.

"Well, we can work on it later. I suppose a nail clipper will do for the time being," said Cade. He walked back to his desk and pulled something out of a drawer and turned around to face the Deicended.

In his hand was a tiny, metallic sphere, about the size of a marble. "Emily, I want you to attempt to take this orb out of my hand from where you are currently sitting. Focus on it coming from my hand to your hand."

Emily stuck out her right hand and focused. The metal ball flew from Cade's hand to Emily's hand.

"Yup, go figure, magnets. That's probably the most boring thing I could think of," Ben commented snidely.

Emily glared at Ben with a look that said she wanted to kill him.

"You would be wise to not underestimate others, Benjamin," Cade scolded.

"Now, for Takumi." He turned to the boy whose eyes were bright with excitement and anticipation.

"We have no idea what your powers could be." After a moment of incomprehension, Takumi's expression fell, and he dropped his eyes to his desk. Cade drew closer to him.

"Do not be discouraged, child. The information we received about you simply does not make any sense to us. You will have to discover your power on your own. I am sorry, child, but you will discover something truly wonderful. I guarantee it."

Takumi was very disappointed. Cade's word of encouragement didn't do much to make him feel better. Takumi probably wanted this more than anyone. He had always dreamed of being like the heroes he read about in comics and manga.

"Now, children, I am only going to say this once. You will only use your powers when I permit it. You will suffer severe consequences if you are disobedient. Do you all understand?" asked Cade.

"Yes, sir," responded all of the Deicended in unison.

"Good! Now, let us get back to your studies," said Cade.

For a while, the Deicended continued their regular studies like they had been the past few weeks. Some nights in that next week, they would try to practice, but an alarm would go off and Cade would yell at them to stop before they had a chance to activate their powers.

About a couple of months passed in this way. They had discovered extraordinary, mysterious powers that were now forbidden fruit. They just went back to their ordinary textbooks and lectures. Then, one morning, Cade's voice came over the intercom.

"Students, it is time for us to go to the range," said Cade.

The Deicended looked around at each other, confused, but quickly readied themselves for the day. Cade met them outside their room, and they followed him into a huge, warehouse-sized, room.

"Activate range. Length one hundred yards," Cade yelled into the empty room.

Out of the floor, a range began to form just like Cade requested. Also, a panel slid back on the floor, and an entire armory popped out next to the range. An android was at the window of the armory. It looked like a military man with a stern look. Behind him were a few administrative Primoids.

"What will we be using today?" asked the armorer.

"Give us the standard BRF 170," said Cade. He turned back to the Deicended.

"Okay. From our lessons, who can tell me some of the features of the BRF 170?" Cade queried.

Neith quickly took a step forward. "The BR-," Neith began, before being interrupted by Cade.

"Not you, Neith. I know that you know it. Give me someone else," said Cade. She quickly stepped back into the group, and Tyr stepped forward.

"The BRF 170 is a basic assault rifle with automatic firing capability. It uses old fashion full metal jacket rounds and has a max range of seven hundred yards," he explained.

"Good. Now can someone else explain to me why we still use full metal jackets if they are old fashion?" asked Cade.

Takumi lifted his head and spoke out. "Even though these rounds were invented many years ago, projectiles using kinetic force are, and have always been, the most effective way of handling low armor targets. The practical use of Photon projectiles is really best suited for shielded or armored targets. However, for both of these projectile types, this is not a rule. Sometimes, depending on the weapon, the pros and cons can flip," explained Takumi.

"Very good! Now, pick up a rifle. We are going to train in some practical application of these weapons." He gestured towards the waiting rifles.

The teens each picked up a weapon and lined up on the range. They practiced shooting all day and came back to the range to practice firing every day for a whole month. Takumi and Tyr were the best shots. Everyone else eventually became good shooters as well, just not to the same level.

"Cade, I have a question. What is the point of all of this training?" asked Emily. This caught the attention of the other Deicended, and they all turned their heads to hear the exchange. Emily continued. "You said we were here to study our powers, but we have barely looked into our powers and all we are doing is training in combat."

Cade's, in Emily's opinion, eerily human-like face seemed to eye her contemplatively for a moment. "I suppose it makes no sense to conceal George's true aim in having us train you in combat. I assume that you all remember the man with the hawk mask?" Cade asked the attentive group, prompting a range of emotions to play across their young faces.

"Yes," they all replied.

"Well, since the terrorist attack on your school, we have not been able to catch him. We have tracked him down a few times, but he always escapes. Even if we track him down and send an army of Primoids out, he has EMP technology that disables all of our Primoids," said Cade.

"I thought George had advanced EMI shields to protect the Primoids from EMP blasts?" Tyr asked.

"We do, but the EMP technology he possesses is too advanced for our shields to handle," Cade answered.

"So, where do we come in on all of this? What part do we play?" asked Lucy.

Cade explained further. "Even if we sent an army of humans, they would fail. The average human has no ability in combat anymore. Also, the man in the Hawk mask has powers similar to all of yours. He is Deicended, and he is not alone. He and his allies are too cunning for anything we are able to send at him. They use tactics that are… unconventional, and by that, I mean that they are cruel. We are hoping that you children, if properly trained, would be able to make the difference and stop this man. I know that his brutal actions have had a profound impact on your lives and the lives of many people you know or knew, and he continues his extremist activities. He is a menace to George's people."

"So, you want us to kill or harm him? Isn't that against George's Rules for Cooperative Living?" asked Lucy.

"You are correct; however, you children are the chosen Deicended. You are not bound to the normal rules. Notice how Ben and Takumi have had no counseling even though they have been teasing Emily. This is because you might not be able to reach your full potential if there are restrictions in the way you are raised," said Cade.

"Wait, I'm not okay with hurting someone else. I never signed up for this." Neith interjected.

"Neith, we have to bring this man to justice, no matter what it takes. We have to do what is right. If he is stopped, then he won't be able to harm more people like he did our friends." Tyr said with hardness in his face that they had not seen before. Neith looked conflicted.

"I guess you are right. I just don't feel good about this," she said.

"I'm going to do whatever it takes to stop this guy. You can count me in. He will pay for what he did," Ben said with passion springing from his voice.

"I am sorry that I did not explain this from the beginning, but I did not want to make the main focus of training revenge," said Cade.

"Well, it certainly makes me want to get stronger," Emily had been quiet since she instigated this conversation. Cade nodded his head to her. Where he had seen defiance in her eyes, moments ago, he now saw resolve. "Let's do this," she said.

"Tomorrow, we will start truly training with your powers," Cade announced.

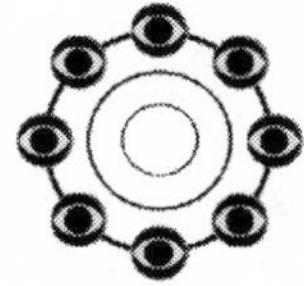

The next day everybody arrived at the same warehouse.

"Activate Simulation One!" yelled Cade.

The whole room changed into a dessert with multiple different levels of platforms. It looked like a paintball arena. In different spots on the platforms, there were a couple of training combat Primoids. They were structured like a human but weren't androids. They looked mechanical and had a head that looked like a one lensed camera. They were armed with BRF 170s that were loaded with what Cade told them were rubber bullets.

"Through this training simulation, we hope to really awaken your powers through stress and effort," said Cade.

"What is the objective?" asked Tyr.

"Steal the briefcase." Cade pointed to a wall, apparently concealing the briefcase, on the other side of the simulated desert. "Return the briefcase to me, whether you destroy the Primoids or not. Does everyone understand?"

They all shook their heads yes, went over to the armorer, and grabbed a BRF 170, loaded with real bullets. They lined up at the entrance of the arena.

"Begin Simulation One!" yelled Cade.

The Primoids immediately began to fire at the kids causing them to run for cover. They slid to the closest half wall they could get to. Emily, Takumi, and Lucy fired their weapon while sliding. Takumi was able to hit one of the Primoids with two shots. The Primoid was barely phased by the rounds.

"Hey, how come that one is still firing? I hit it!" he shouted.

"Two shots with that gun are barely going to affect a Primoid built for durability. Something is only defeated when it stops resisting," replied Cade.

The Deicended were now pinned down from fire. Rubber bullets striking the desert floor were causing coarse sand to spray everywhere, limiting some of their visibility. There were about ten Primoids firing on their position. Also, the Primoids were slightly elevated in their own position. The kids would have to run up a shallow ramp if they were to reach the briefcase. Around the same moment, the Primoids all started to reload their guns.

Ben jumped out from behind cover and ran to the left of the wall about ten yards out. Ben was firing in the Primoid's general direction, not hitting anything as he ran. One of the Primoids finished reloading its gun before Ben reached the wall and got a few shots off. Ben was struck in the leg and yelled out in pain. Even though the bullets were non-lethal, they still hurt. Tyr jumped over the wall they were hiding behind, intent on reaching Ben, and was immediately hit by five shots to the chest. Tyr fell back in severe pain and was winded by the shots.

"Walk over to me Tyr, you are out. You as well, Benjamin," said Cade.

Tyr rose and walked out of the arena, gasping for breath.

"Hey, help me out. I can barely move my leg. It hurts so much," yelled Ben.

Takumi steeled himself and ran toward Ben. He fired while running. Takumi was shot in his left leg and fell to one knee before reaching the wall. When his knee hit the ground, two more shots hit his chest. Ben gritted his teeth and reached out of cover in an attempt to grab his friend. As soon as he left cover, he was shot in the left shoulder blade, now falling face-first to the ground. Before Ben even hit the ground, three shots hit lower on his back.

While all of this was happening, Lucy and Emily took the chance to advance. Lucy jumped over the wall and headed straight for the briefcase. Emily ran to the right, to a wall five yards away. Emily made it to the wall and waited. Lucy was almost over the wall at the top of the hill that the training Primoids were hiding over. One towards her left side turned and went to aim at Lucy. Lucy was quicker on the draw and landed four shots to the Primoid's head. Lucy leaped over the wall and another Primoid was to her immediate left. Lucy pulled her trigger, landing six or seven shots to its chest, causing it to shut off.

The briefcase was now in sight, ten yards in front of her. She began to run towards it. One of the Primoids from her right ride fired at her. Lucy jumped low to dodge the fire that was now above her. Another Primoid was right behind the one firing at Lucy. This Primoid shot low, where Lucy was landing. Lucy planted her hand on the ground and pushed off, with the bullets going right below her body now. Lucy was now in the air, a few feet forward from where she pushed herself off the ground.

There was another Primoid behind the briefcase that Lucy must have not realized was there. This Primoid aimed its gun and fired at Lucy, almost sure to hit her. Lucy twisted her body midair, with the shots barely missing her. She aimed the stock of her rifle towards the Primoid's head. A bullet from her left nailed her in the kidney. The shot was from a Primoid, in the distance, to the left. Losing control of her balance, Lucy collided with Primoid right behind the briefcase. She collapsed on the ground. The Primoid was not knocked down but was staggered. Lucy was bleeding from her right shoulder and chest from the force of her impact against the Primoid's metal parts and edges. The Primoid she collided with turned towards her and aimed its gun at her.

Lucy put her hand in front of her face, bracing herself for the brutal impact. Lucy's skin and outfit blended into the sandy surface she was touching. The Primoid didn't shoot. It looked at the spot where Lucy was on the ground and was confused. Ten or so shots hit the Primoid's back, knocking it over and powering it off. Emily had run to the right side of the wall that all of the Primoids were hiding behind while Lucy was doing her thing. All of the remaining functional Primoids turned towards Emily and fired. Six or so shots hit her in various parts of her body. Lucy slowly transitioned to no longer blend in with her surface. She sat up and was immediately shot in the back once.

Cade's voice rang out over the sounds of most of the Deicended groaning in pain. "That ends the exercise. Neith, why did you not move?"

"I was scared of getting hit by one of the bullets," Neith replied.

"Your fear could have led to the deaths of your teammates. All of you need to work together or else you will never figure this out. Does everybody understand?" He addressed the whole miserable group.

They all shook their heads in agreement.

"Now, I need to call in a medical Primoid to look at Lucy," said Cade.

A floating Primoid came in, painted with a red cross on its front and back. It made its way over to Lucy and scanned her from her head to her feet.

"Source of bleeding not found. Patient appears well," said the medical Primoid.

Cade leaned over to get a better look. Lucy's open wounds were now closed.

"Magnificent! Not only did the powers during your fight exceed our expectations, but you can also manipulate your own body and heal yourself. We thought that you would only be able to edit your body's makeup, but you can apparently edit more than that. I am honestly perplexed at how you managed to appear invisible and also conceal your clothes. In reaction to the fear of being shot, you may have modified your body and clothes to allow light to pass through your body," said Cade.

"Well, can't say I was expecting that. I don't know if I will be able to do that again," said Lucy.

"With training, you will be able to. All of you will unlock your powers if you try hard enough. Lucy, your agility and quick thinking were most impressive as well. Keep that up." Cade spoke encouragingly.

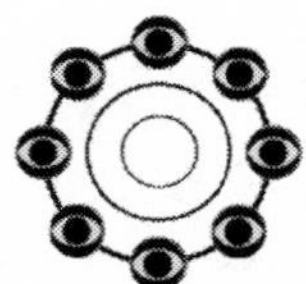

The team would attempt this exercise every day until they could complete it. Days after their initial attempt, Lucy was still having trouble figuring out how she became invisible. One of the days, Tyr activated the scales all around his body and charged the hill. This time the rubber bullets did nothing to him. He went to leap over the wall and, before he could land, one of the Primoids Spartan kicked through the wall he jumped on. The Deicended failed that day too. Another day, Ben tried to melt part of the wall from a distance but was shot before he could make a big enough hole in the wall to be effective.

One day, Neith generated three violet orbs above her and launched them towards the wall. The wall broke down where it was hit, but besides that, it was not enough to win that day. Emily, another day, started magnetically ripping panels off the wall they hid behind. She flung the panel, pushing it using the opposite polarity. It flew with incredible force and took off one of the Primoid's head, but that was about as far as they got that day. Takumi was growing more and more frustrated with each passing day that his teammates were displaying these incredibly useful powers, and all he had to offer were some bullets. One of the problems the students as a whole were having was, each time they fought the Primoids, the Primoids would learn and become harder to beat. The same trick never worked twice.

After almost countless days, the team was more determined than ever. Tyr stood in the open, firing at the Primoids with his armored scales out. Emily ripped some panels off the wall. She made a wall from the panels that floated a foot in front of her. The whole team besides Tyr walked behind Emily and her wall made of panels. They walked slowly up the right side of the hill. The panels held up, blocking all of the rubber bullets. They made it to the wall and Ben put his hand towards the wall that was protecting the Primoids. The wall began to melt until there was a big enough hole for one person to fit through.

Lucy jumped through the wall, turning invisible midair, and bashed the closest Primoid with her rifle. This hit completely broke the Primoid, but the other Primoids knew to fire at Lucy. They were able to guess now that she was invisible. Emily placed a few of her panels in front of Lucy protecting her from the incoming fire. Her brow sweating from the effort and her face scrunched in concentration, Emily moved the rest of her panels on the other side of the wall to allow the rest of the team to make their way through the hole in the wall. Tyr ran up to the rest of the team.

"What now?" Takumi asked.

"Wait till there is a break in fire, and we will unload on them," Tyr suggested.

Emily nodded and began to agree. "Not a ba-" Emily cut off.

She was shot several times in the back from the hole in the wall Ben made. One of the Primoids had jumped over the wall and flanked them. Emily was down for the count. All of the metal panels came crashing down and bullets rained on the whole team. Tyr, the only one standing, turned toward the Primoids. One of them rushed him, took its right arm and whaled Tyr in the face, knocking him on the ground.

"Failed again!" said Cade.

"This is impossible!" Emily shouted.

"For once, I agree with her. We have been trying this for months," said Ben.

"Failure is the best teacher. With patience, you will be able to overcome anything. Now, no more complaining and head to bed," Cade sternly shut down the two's outburst.

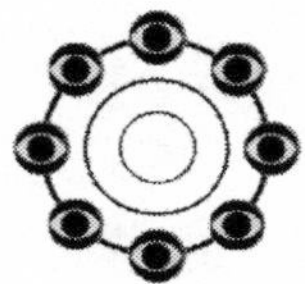

In the bedroom that night, the Deicended were restless. They truly thought this was going to be the day they succeeded.

"Ugh! If Takumi had powers, maybe we would be done already!" Emily threw a sharp glare in Takumi's direction.

"Stop being so impatient, Emily. We are getting better. We'll win eventually, even if Takumi is powerless." Neith said, attempting to sound encouraging.

"Everybody, shut up. Leave Takumi alone!" Ben yelled.

Takumi put a hand on Ben's shoulder. "Ben, it's fine. They're kind of right. I'm not much help." Takumi's voice was even, but he kept his eyes locked on the ground.

Emily was not appeased. "You should just not even do the sims with us if you don't have powers. You're just getting in our way."

"I said leave him alone!" Ben shouted.

"Children. Be quiet and go to bed." Cade's voice came over the intercom.

Emily stood up on her bed. "I think you're just mad that my powers are more useful than yours, Ben. You're almost as useless as Takumi!"

Ben waived his right hand towards the bottom of Emily's bed. He melted one of the legs to her bed, setting her off balance. She fell back on her bed, nearly hitting her head on the frame. Emily, even angrier than before, faced her hand towards Ben's bed and made a flipping motion with her hand. Ben's entire bed flipped over with him in it. After a moment of shuffling, he scrambled out from beneath it.

"Ah, that's it, Emily! I'm so sick of you!" Ben screamed with fire in his eyes.

Ben ran full speed towards Emily, clutching his fist. In a moment, he was a foot away from Emily, swinging for her face. Emily tilted her head; Ben's fist slid right past the left side of her face. Emily took her right arm and thrust it at Ben's chest. Electricity sparked from Emily's fist. The punch launched Ben across the room into the corner. Emily let her hand fall limp and stood there in shock from what she just did.

"Ben!" Takumi yelled and was kneeling beside him in an instant. The others were not far behind, all crowding around Ben.

"What the hell, Emily?! He's not moving, what did you do?" Neith asked incredulously.

"I don't know. I have no idea what happened, I just got angry. I didn't want to hurt him." Emily's voice was barely above a whisper.

Cade came running into the room, followed by a medical Primoid, and felt Ben's pulse. He stood up and the medical Primoid scanned Ben.

"Heart failure and internal bleeding. Death is inevitable," the medical Primoid announced emotionlessly.

"No! He can't. I didn't mean to." Emily gasped out, barely able to breathe.

"It is alright, Emily. You could not know this was going to happen," Cade attempted to reassure her by putting a metal hand on her shoulder.

She shrugged it off and climbed back into her off-kilter bed. Emily sat, rocking back and forth holding her head. The medical Primoid announced that Ben was now dead.

Lucy took a deep breath. "I have something I want to try."

Lucy pushed through the group and walked over to Ben's body. She put her hand where Ben was punched. Lucy closed her eyes and concentrated. She felt, *thump thump*. Ben's heart started to beat again beneath her hand.

"Vitals returning to normal," announced the medical Primoid.

"How in the world?" Cade's eyes were wide.

Ben's heart started to beat faster and faster. His heart was so fast it sounded like he was having a heart attack. Then, his eyes shot open. Ben started screaming hysterically.

"What? Where am I? What were those things?" Ben cried out.

"What was what?" Cade asked.

Ben looked around, seeing familiar faces, and started to calm down. "I don't know, I just, I just… I don't know." He blinked and kept looking around.

"Did you see something?" asked Cade.

"No, no… no, I just… what happened to me?" Ben asked.

"Are you saying you did not just see something?" Cade asked, pressing him.

"I remember seeing a flash. Can someone please tell me what happened?" Ben asked earnestly.

Emily raised her head with tears rolling down her face. "I… I killed you." She choked on her tears.

His head snapped over to look at her across the room. "Why the hell did you do that?"

"Didn't mean to, I swear. I'm so sorry!" Emily covered her face with her hair and kept rocking on her uneven bed.

He stood, with help from Takumi and Lucy and walked over to her, sitting beside her. "Emily… it's okay. I probably shouldn't have tried to punch you. Just… don't be mean to Takumi anymore and I'll promise to stop being a jerk too," Ben poked her gently.

She let her hair fall back, and a weak smile came across Emily's face. "I swear, I won't… ever again." She, uncharacteristically, hugged Ben briefly before pulling back and wiping her tear-stained cheeks. "I'm glad you're not dead."

"Benjamin, when you woke, you said something: 'What were those things?'. What did you see?" Cade asked very forcibly, advancing on the two distressed teenagers.

"I was confused when I woke up. I didn't know what I was looking at when I woke up," replied Ben, cautiously.

Cade seemed to pull himself back slightly, sighed, and continued in a much calmer tone. "I am sorry, child. I was worried about your safety is all. Now, children, let us all go to bed. I think we have had enough happen for one night. Emily, I will have a housekeeping Primoid bring a replacement bed frame for you tomorrow while you are training. Ben, I want you to report to the medical center in the morning to get an extensive checkup."

As Cade walked out of the room, Ben looked at him in a new way. The look was a mix of confusion and distrust. Tyr, Takumi, and Lucy each grabbed a corner of Ben's bed and righted it. Everybody got back into their beds, Ben began putting his pillows and sheets back on the bed. He looked over at Lucy.

"Thanks, Lucy, for saving me," said Ben.

"Haha, anytime Ben. You guys all mean a lot to me," said Lucy, throwing a gentle smile Ben's way.

"How did you even do that?" asked Takumi.

"I think it works the same way my regeneration works," Lucy shrugged.

"How did you know to even try that?" asked Neith.

"I don't know. I just had a feeling, I guess." Lucy shrugged again.

"Well, I sure am glad you had that feeling!" said Ben.

"Tomorrow is going to be the day guys. Well, I guess whatever day you are going to be ready for action again, Ben, is going to be the day. Apparently, we can't even be killed. Nothing is going to stop us." Tyr said with a gleam of determination in his eye.

All of the Deicended kind of just rolled their eyes at Tyr and went to bed.

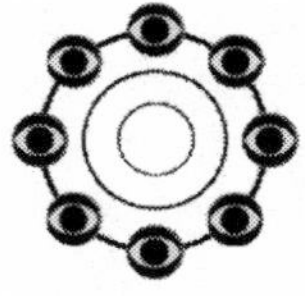

The next morning, all of the kids lined up in the arena like they usually did. None of them said anything. All of them had pure determination on their face. The round started, and they charged the wall. Emily took a few panels off the wall like last time. Tyr went to the left of the wall they were behind, laying down some cover fire with his scales out to protect him from incoming fire. Emily went right with Neith, Takumi, and Ben behind her. Emily and the others were able to move up to the right side of the wall that the Primoids were behind. Ben melted a hole through the wall. Emily placed the panels inside the wall, blocking the incoming fire to where the hole in the wall was. One of the Primoids was already charging the panels. Right as the Primoid was about to bust its way through the panels, Emily opened a space for the Primoid to come in. Surprised, the Primoid stumbled through, getting close to the team. Ben grabbed the Primoid by the chest and slammed it to the ground while it burst into flames from the heat of his grip. Emily closed the hole she made in her panels. Ben, Emily, Neith, and Takumi now hid behind the panels that Emily was holding up.

"Honestly, I'm starting to get a little tired," said Emily, showing obvious signs of fatigue.

"Hold steady, we can win this!" Ben cried over the sound of gunfire.

Tyr ran up to the wall with the rest of the group. Tyr went to the side of the panels, laying down some fire. Three more training Primoids rushed the team. Takumi heard sparks from the hole in which they came and a fourth Primoid was standing there. Just like last time, it must have jumped the wall and flanked them. It didn't shoot. Sparks shot out of its neck caused by gunfire. Bullets rained down on the Primoid, shutting it down. Lucy was still back behind the wall they started out from, providing cover, predicting the Primoids would try to flank. Ben reached out towards the wall. He concentrated as hard as he could. Ben was able to melt another hole in the wall ten feet to the left of the last one. Lucy laid down fire through the new hole, hitting the three Primoids that were charging the team. Only one of the Primoids fell to the ground. Neith raised her left hand, charging energy above the panels. Without moving her hand, a blast flew from above her hand hitting and decimating the front-most remaining Primoid of that group. The last one clashed with Tyr. The Primoid was weakened from the shots it took from Lucy. Unable to knock Tyr over, they wrestled each other, trying to pull the other one to the ground.

"I can't... I..." Emily gasped out before she lost consciousness, crumpling to the sand. Along with her, the panels fell to the ground, leaving the team exposed to open fire from the training Primoids.

Neith backed outside the wall through the hole Ben made. Ben grabbed Emily off the ground and jumped to the closest downed primoid, using it as cover. Takumi rushed the briefcase, crouching while running and attempting to dodge whatever fire he could. Takumi was almost within arm's reach of it when the primoid that Lucy shot down grabbed Takumi, pulling him to the ground. Lucy had been able to knock the primoid down, but she hadn't shut it down. Lucy began to shoot it again but could not hit it from an effective angle. There were still four Primoids left, laying down suppressing fire over the briefcase. Their rubber pullets stirred the sand into the air around Takumi, obstructing his view, but also their own.

Takumi reached, blindly, as hard as he could, desperate to get the briefcase. A black almost shadowy substance stretched out of Takumi's spine, through the hailstorm of rubber bullets, and grabbed the briefcase like it was another arm. The downed primoid moved its other arm to aim its gun at Takumi. A second shadowy arm reached out of Takumi's spine, piercing the primoid through its head and down to the center of its chest, shutting it down. The arm holding the briefcase flung it over the wall in Neith's direction.

"Head's up!" shouted Lucy.

Neith looked up and saw the briefcase flying through the air. She ran and caught the briefcase before it hit the ground. She spun around and charged back to their "home base". The remaining

Primoids went to go look over their wall to gun down Neith, but by the time they looked, Neith was already celebrating handing the briefcase to Cade.

He nodded at her and smiled. "Simulation One: Over," Cade announced. "Congratulations, children. You finally passed."

"We did it!" chanted Tyr.

Takumi touched the shadowy arm coming from his back. It felt solid but had the appearance of a blackish purple smoke. Cade walked over to inspect them.

"Most interesting! I have never seen anything like it," said Cade. "We will have to take a closer look at this later. It is no wonder that we could not discover any clues as to what your power would be. It is very unique, fitting for such a unique person."

Takumi was already smiling from finally discovering his powers. He felt such a calming feeling, though. He had been so unsure if he would ever discover his powers. Now, his anxiety had been lifted.

"Will we go back to classes, now?" asked Neith.

"Tomorrow, we begin Simulation Two. Be sure to eat and rest up," said Cade.

"Eh, it will probably be such a cakewalk from now on," said Ben.

"I hope not. I hope the next simulation is even harder," said Tyr.

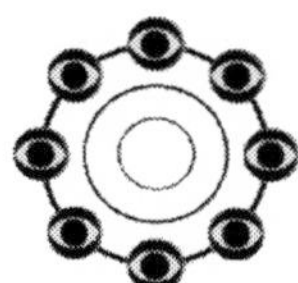

The Deicended continued running through simulation after simulation. Each one was more difficult than the last. Each challenge they progressed through, the more adept they became at utilizing their powers and the more proficient they became as a team, learning to overcome the simulations more quickly. This went on for fifty different simulations. The day after they completed Simulation Fifty, they gathered around Cade in an air hangar that they had never seen before. In the hangar, there was some sort of boxy aircraft. It had two jet engines on each corner, connected to a cabin that looked like a helicopter designed for transport. At Cade's direction, the teenagers boarded the aircraft, and it took off, leaving the hangar.

Once they were airborne, Cade turned to the Deicended and said, "Today, we are doing something different. We are going to be trying something a little old fashion."

2

The Island

The aircraft took them to a remote island. The trip wasn't long, so they most likely had not traveled far. Windows in the ship's hull opened, and they could see the island. As far as islands go, this was a pretty big one. It even had what looked like a mountain rising from the center of the landmass. There was a lot of green vegetation surrounding the base of this mountain. The vegetation looked tropical and very thick since only the tops of the trees could be seen. The forest covered much of the island, fading away to a white beach that surrounded the island, except on the west end where there was a very rocky shore. Everybody looked relieved at the sight of the island. It had such a relaxing atmosphere surrounding it.

The Deicended hadn't realized how tired they were of the training facility they had been in for nearly two years. This was such a contrast to that boring place. It felt like they hadn't been outside in forever either. Although they did go outside of the training facility sometimes, they couldn't see much. Outside the facility was a towering mountain that had no vegetation and no wildlife. Sometimes it felt like they only went outside in order to get some natural sunlight.

"Okay, children, we will be landing soon. We will be leaving you all here for two weeks," said Cade.

"What?!" All of them yelled at Cade, alarmed by what he had just said.

"Now, I will not hear any complaining. The goal of this exercise is to survive. We will have a close eye on you all, so do not be afraid. The other goal is to hunt down at least one deer while you are here. This task is going to take extreme teamwork. This should not be too difficult since you all have learned to work well with each other during our other training exercises. There is only one rule while you are here. No using your powers."

"Question, sir," said Neith.

"Yes, dear," replied Cade.

"How did deer get on an island like this?" Neith asked.

"Good question, dear. We do not know the answer to that, sadly. They have been here for a very long time, and there was never any record of their migration nor transportation. We suspect that they were brought by ship before the invention of computers. These deer are also unaffected by the chemicals from the city and remain as they appeared before the invention of computers. They have no sign of significant evolutionary changes. Now, good luck, children. I know you will all be just fine," Cade said.

The aircraft descended towards the sand on the south side of the island. As it got close to the ground, a cloud of sand surrounded the aircraft. The doors opened and the Deicended disembarked. They looked back at Cade, who did not say another word to them but rather gestured to the pilot Primoid, who closed the doors. The teenagers just kind of huddled around each other as the aircraft rose back off the ground and headed off in the direction they came from. With the aircraft now in the distance, they all looked at each in confusion.

"Well, what do we do now?" asked Takumi. A few moments passed with no one speaking before Lucy piped up.

"I think the first thing we should do is figure out shelter," she suggested.

Lucy was really the only one with experience 'roughing it', so nobody disagreed with her. It was most likely the best idea. None of them knew what kind of wildlife was on the island, except for the deer. Also, if the weather were to get worse, they would most likely get sick if they were exposed to the elements, and that was not something they could afford to have happen. Looking around the area near them, it didn't appear like there were any natural caves or anything. They were going to have to build their shelter. Lucy directed them to grab rocks to knock down some trees.

After they, mostly Tyr, knocked a few down, Tyr sat back, slightly winded from the effort. "We need to find water. It's hot, and I'm starting to get thirsty. It won't be smart if we wait until we are completely dehydrated before we look for some water," he said.

Tyr was right, and they knew it. Neith and Ben went into the woods to see if they could find any signs of fresh water. The rest stayed back to continue building the shelter. It didn't take long before they could hear the running water. Ben walked up to the river to take a drink.

"Stop! What are you doing?" Neith asked in a concerned manner.

"Drinking water; what does it look like?" replied Ben, honestly confused about what the problem was.

"That water is dirty. We need to purify it before we can drink it, or else you will get sick," said Neith.

"How are we supposed to do that?" asked Ben.

"I'm not sure yet. We probably need to boil it, but we don't have a fire yet, and worse, we don't have anything to hold the water over the fire," Neith furrowed her brow, deep in thought.

The two walked back to the others to let them know what was going on. In the time they had been gone, the Deicended who had stayed behind had made a wall from branches and big, tropical leaves that were slanted against a tree. It could be used as cover for if it rained, but it was doubtful that the makeshift shelter could fit all six of them. Neith told the group about the river they found. They decided to stop working on the shelter. They had been working for a few hours, and the result of their work was not much. The group feared, if they continued to work, they might get dehydrated as Tyr had mentioned previously. Neith came up with an idea to carve a wooden pot from a tree big enough to hold the water and use heated rocks to put in the pot to boil the water. The group had already knocked a tree over earlier that was only about half a foot thick. They used the most jagged rocks to cut a three-foot log out. With that log, they carved a bowl out of it. By the time this was all completed, the sunlight was barely filtering in through the small gaps in the canopy.

"Why don't we just drink from the coconuts from this tree?" asked Takumi.

"We could, but for the amount of energy we would need to spend to get them and open them, we wouldn't get much water from them. They would be best used as bowls to scoop clean water out of the pots we made," said Emily. There did not appear to be that many coconuts from the trees near them anyway.

Neith and Tyr went to where the river was and filled the long wooden pot they made with water. By the time they returned with the water, Lucy had already started a fire using the leftover wood from the tree. Ben collected a few fist-sized rocks. He tried to find the smoothest ones he could. After placing the rocks in the fire for a few minutes using some branches as makeshift tongs, they placed the rocks into the bowl of water.

Sure enough, the water began to boil. By now the sun had completely set, and it was getting cooler every minute. The group planned to chop another tree down for wood for the fire. After that was done, they began shifts to sleep and watch the fire. Lucy may have started the fire easily, but they did not want to chance her not

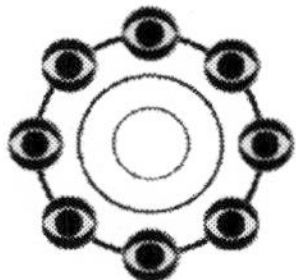

being able to start another. Additionally, without knowing what wildlife was in the forest, they might need the fire to scare whatever challenges them. Before going to bed, having not yet found any better options, they ate from some of the few coconuts that came from the trees that they had knocked down.

The next day, they continued to build their shelter up. Using a couple of trees that were still in the ground as a base, they built a decent sized hut. It was just big enough to fit all of them laying down. It was cone-shaped with about twelve large branches laying against the rooted tree. The branches were tied together with some vines Neith had found. Leaves were tied in all over the cone to keep the water out. Takumi built a floor inside by laying smaller branches perpendicular over a few big logs. He placed leaves over as padding so they wouldn't lay directly on the branches. They put branches and leaves as a floor so that if it rained, they wouldn't be laying in water.

Although they worked hard on the shelter, it was still flimsy at best, and if a big enough storm came through, it would blow it over. Along with the shelter they built, Emily made a few more of the big wooden pots. The day was coming to an end now. The Deicended were all very focused on the task at hand, barely speaking to each other; the only sound they heard besides the sounds of the island and their labor, were the frequent rumbling of their stomachs.

"So, all we have to do is kill a deer, right?" said Tyr.

"Well, catching a deer ain't going to be easy. We don't have any weapons, and I haven't seen any sign of them since we got here," said Lucy.

"I'm not sure how many coconuts are left either. We will have to find some alternatives for food. Deer aren't exactly fierce, but we won't be able to kill anything unless we keep our strength up." said Emily.

"We could try spearfishing; it couldn't be too difficult, and we have plenty of time to learn," suggested Takumi.

"True, but that would take time from trying to get a deer, and I assume we are going to use spears to hunt it. I imagine it is going to take a lot of time to catch one," said Neith.

"I agree, and if we don't find deer, maybe we could find something else to eat like more coconuts or something," Tyr said.

The group agreed and began their sleep shifts.

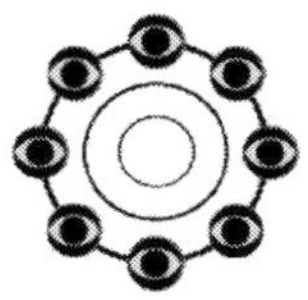

The next morning, when they were all awake, they spent their first hour chipping away at some slender trees to fasten into spears. The whole group, now somewhat armed, left the camp, heading west through the woods near the coastline. Every so often, they would take a rock and cut an X into a tree, marking their way back. They walked for hours, eventually reaching the west side of the island. They found nothing on the way. Just some trees that did not seem to bear fruit and some sand from the beach. The only moving things they saw were birds, which did them no good since they would hardly be able to hit them with the spears they had. About half the day had gone by, and it was time for them to head back so that they wouldn't be caught in the dark. Before they started walking back, the ground rumbled below them. It was just a little rumble, but it was enough to make the Deicended stop in their tracks.

"An earthquake?" Ben asked.

"Most likely something that happens pretty often on this island. It is probably near the same fault line that the training facility is near," said Neith.

It didn't scare them. They were used to earthquakes, as they occurred often in the training facility. Most every time one occurred over there; it could probably be felt from this island.

By the time the group made it back, the sun had set, and the fire was just a few hot coals. Luckily, the coals were sufficient to start a new fire. They all crowded around it to rest.

Lucy suggested that they should hunt at night since deer come out more while it is dark. It was a good idea, but dangerous. They discussed amongst themselves and decided it was worth the risk. This time, they would head east and only leave for a few hours. They would make up the sleep during the day. They relaxed for an hour, ate some of their dwindling coconut supply, and drank some water before heading out. They started walking, but very slowly since it was difficult to see what was in front of them. As they got decently far from the camp, they heard something moving in the trees. Tyr signaled them to get low. They waited patiently for whatever was making the sound to come out. Ben started to breathe heavily. He was nervous, and he knew the heavy breathing was making noise. Having that on his mind only made his breathing heavier. Emily looked at him and signaled him to be quiet.

Barely making out what she was motioning in the dark, Ben whispered, "I'm trying." Whatever was making the noise stopped moving. It was creepy how quiet it had just become. The group started to stand straight again as they believed that the sound was actually nothing.

A shadowy figure, on all fours, jumped out from behind a tree. It charged right for Ben. Ben froze in fear, unable to move. He didn't have to worry about breathing too hard now since he couldn't breathe at all. The figure, now just feet before Ben, crouched, ready to pounce on him. Ben's eyes were wide and, although his mind was screaming at his body to move, his muscles would not listen. Suddenly, Takumi jabbed his spear at it. The spear bounced off the top of the figure. It stopped and let out a loud squeal. Before it even had a chance to stop squealing, a fist-sized rock smashed into its face; it turned and fled.

"What was that? I couldn't get a good look at it," said Tyr.

"It was a wild boar. Lucky for us it was a small one," said Lucy.

"Damn, that was small? Hopefully, there aren't more. Ben, are you okay?" Emily asked, concerned for Ben after seeing the way he had panicked.

"I'm fine. Nothing happened," Ben replied.

"Man, I'm not sure about that. You were just going to let that thing skewer you," Takumi said, not realizing that staying on the subject was going to bother Ben.

"I said it was nothing! Let's go find it," Ben snapped, with far less sincerity behind his voice than he had intended.

"I think it's weak. We could catch it, and that would be a lot of food," said Tyr.

"We better head back. It might not be alone," said Neith.

Lucy grabbed Takumi's spear and felt the edge that hit the boar. "It's bleeding. There might be enough blood for us to track it in the morning, assuming that it doesn't rain tonight," said Lucy.

The Deicended decided to mark some of the nearby trees and head back to camp. Tyr had been leading the way back to the camp but stopped when it came into view. Neith, who had been behind him, bumped into him from behind.

"Tyr, what's wrong?" she asked. He did not answer but rushed forward closer to the camp with his spear raised, looking around warily. The rest of the Deicended followed and were dismayed by what they found. Something had happened to the camp while they were gone. A couple of the wooden bowls were knocked over. There was a hole in the shelter now. The group rushed into the shelter to find their few remaining coconuts had all been eaten.

"What could have done this? What can crack through coconuts?" asked Tyr.

Puzzled, the group now became worried. Neither a deer, a boar, nor anything besides humans could open coconuts that they could think of.

"Well, whatever it is, it just got a spot on the menu," said Neith, her eyes narrowed, and she clenched her fists, her emotions heightened by both frustration and hunger.

"And what if they are human?" asked Takumi.

"Well, they're on the menu," replied Neith, joking darkly. Everybody knew it was a joke and normally would have laughed, but, with their only food source gone, were not in the mood to laugh.

"Hopefully, we can get that boar tomorrow," said Tyr in a very unhopeful tone.

"There's a tree I saw nearby with some coconuts on it. That should hold us over for tomorrow," said Takumi.

"Well, if we grab them in the morning, what's keeping whatever stole these from stealing them again?" asked Ben. The group was silent for a moment as they considered that.

"We should probably split into two groups in the morning," said Emily. She looked around to gauge her companions' thoughts. Everyone agreed that would be best. Lucy took the first watch, and the rest all crawled into their shelter, so weary that even the branches digging into their backs could not keep them awake.

The next morning, Tyr, Takumi, and Lucy headed east to hopefully find a trail of blood from the boar. The other three stayed at camp, guarding the food. It didn't take much time for the hunting group to find the spot from last night. Lucy found some blood on the ground among some trampled underbrush where the boar was struck by the spear. It wasn't much though, and the dripping from the blood appeared to thin out soon after. It was enough to give them an idea of which direction the boar had headed. With no other option but to hope that it had taken a fairly straight path, the hunting party continued with Lucy leading the way, looking for any more disturbed vegetation to point the way.

After only a little while, the group found a boar foraging in the ground around the roots of a small tree. The boar hadn't noticed their presence yet since they were mostly concealed by the trees. Vegetation was very thick on the island, making it easy to hide. Lucy and Takumi flanked the boar on each side, making their best attempt at stealth. Eventually, they made their way to opposite sides of the boar. Now that they were closer, they could tell that this boar was not the same boar they ran into before. It didn't appear wounded at all and seemed much younger and even smaller. Even so, it seemed like it would be plenty of food for them to eat. Takumi and Lucy charged out of hiding towards the boar with their spears raised. If it was a bigger boar, it might have challenged them, but it took off running directly towards Tyr's hiding place.

Once it was a few feet away, Tyr stuck his spear out of hiding. The boar didn't even notice the pointed stick and ran straight into it. The stick pierced right through the bottom right side of its cheek and down into its chest. It let out an ear-piercing squeal only for a second before falling lifeless on Tyr's spear.

Once again, it was getting dark, and the hunters hadn't returned. Ben, Neith, and Emily had spent the day trying to find any food they could in case the hunting party was unsuccessful. After only finding a few berries and a few more coconuts, the group decided to rest to conserve their energy for the next day. They gathered around the fire, laying their spears on the ground near them, just in case.

"What do you think the point of all of this survival training is?" Emily asked,

"Well, we are learning practical skills in case we get stranded on a mission for George," replied Neith.

"I get that, but this all seems a little extra. Like, we don't know anything about this guy who supposedly bombed our school. I just feel like we haven't been told much and it doesn't feel like we were given an option whether we wanted to do this or not," said Emily.

Neith seemed to bristle slightly. "I understand what you're saying, Emily. George hasn't told us much, because It doesn't know much about the situation that happened to us. I mean, think about it. George has been all-knowing for pretty much Its whole existence. Now It has to rely on some kids to carry out Its task. Things will seem suspicious, but George has always wanted only the best for humans; It's the whole reason we have been living in peace for so long. Also, I don't believe that whether or not we would want to do this was a question that really needed to be asked in the first place. Even you can't deny that killing that masked guy is all we want to do," said Neith.

"Woah there! Did you just say kill, Neith? I thought you wouldn't hurt a fly," said Ben.

"I can make an exception for scum," said Neith.

"I get what you're saying, Neith. I just hope you're right about all of this," said Emily.

"You feel the same about what Neith said, Ben? You froze up pretty hard back there with the boar. Are you sure you want to go after this masked guy?" asked Emily.

"I'm positive. I don't know what happened back there either, but it isn't going to happen again. I know, out of all of us, Tyr is the most like a soldier, but I want to be a great fighter too. I used to obsess about knights from the medieval era in movies. They were brave warriors that fought other knights and powerful creatures, like dragons, with no fear. The bravest would be able to slay a dragon with only a sword and shield. One day, I'll be strong enough to slay a dragon, after I slay this masked man."

"Those never existed, Ben. That was a fairytale," said Emily.

"What!? They so did exist! I mean I get they didn't really blow fire, but they did exist," said Ben.

"No. Knights existed, but dragons didn't," Neith clarified. Ben blinked at her a few times.

"I get that they are probably extinct, but they did exist," Ben insisted.

"No, Ben. Dragons are make-believe. The next thing you are going to tell me is that you think unicorns were real too," said Neith.

"Oh, c'mon. Of course, unicorns weren't real. Nothing would ever have a silly long horn like that on an otherwise normal creature," replied Ben.

"Well, actually, there were a species of whales called narwhals. They had an extremely long horn that they used to break the ice in the frigid northern waters they inhabited," explained Neith.

"I don't appreciate you trying to make fun of me. I know there weren't actual icebreaking whales that used to exist," said Ben.

As soon as he finished that sentence, the group heard a twig snap. They glanced at each other, picked their spears up off of the ground, and quickly jolted behind the nearest tree. Calmly, they waited, making every attempt to not make a sound. They wondered, could this be the same thing that ate all of their food the other night? Would they be able to kill whatever this could be? Out of the shadows and into the light from the campfire, two legs poked through. They were orange, pointed, and only about a foot high. Ben started to sweat uncontrollably. As the creature got closer, it got harder for him to see. Then his vision cleared. It was nothing but a crab. It was the size of a small dog for whatever reason, but it was too slow for anyone to fear.

"I think we found our culprit," said Emily.

The crab must have grabbed the food while they were all hunting the other night. Ben walked out towards it, and the crab didn't seem scared of him. He took his spear and attempted to stab it through the top of its shell, but he had trouble trying to pierce it. The crab eventually reached up with a large claw, grabbed his spear, and as Ben tried to pull it away, snapped the tip off. Emily walked over and, in one attempt, stabbed it where its eyes were, killing it. Neith whooped and immediately grabbed its corpse, throwing it onto the fire. She whispered to herself, "Oh, I'm going to enjoy the hell out you, you thieving bitch."

Twenty minutes after they killed the crab, Takumi, Tyr, and Lucy got back to camp with a freshly killed boar. Both groups were surprised by the other's success, and there was a noticeable lift in the teenagers' spirits. They now had so much food that they spent the whole night cooking all of it. The Deicended spent the next day eating, resting, and experimenting with more uses for the trees they had felled. That night, they took whatever leftover food they had with them to bury it a distance from their camp, so as to not attract any predators to their position.

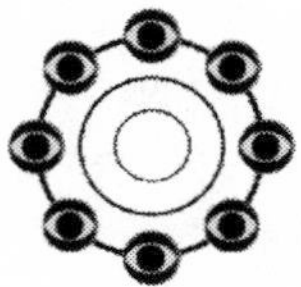

The next morning, they got ready to head out and search more of the island farther from their camp since they hadn't seen a single deer in the areas close by. This time, they were heading to the north side of the island. Before leaving, they took some of their makeshift jugs and filled them with clean water. They also discussed whether they should move camp. They preferred to stay where they were since this was near where they were going to be picked up, and there didn't appear to be any boars they had to worry about attacking them while resting.

To save some time, they walked along the mountainside, out of the trees. This was technically a straighter path, and they wouldn't have to worry as much about their footing since there was no vegetation in their path. One thing that they didn't account for was how hot it was going to be in the sun. They had brought a couple of gallons of water, but by the time they had reached the north side of the island they were pretty much out of water. At the edge of the tree line, they took a break for a short while. Already, they could see that there was more food like berries and mushrooms all over the forest. The Deicended made a small camp that they were hoping to only have to use once. Once they finished setting up, the sun had begun to set, and the teens walked into the forest to start their hunting once again.

They fanned out along the forest, keeping a lot of space between them, but not enough that they couldn't see the person on their left and right. This forest, like most of the island, was covered by dense palm trees. There were a few bushes here and there, less than the more southern area they had been camping in. The ground was a mixture of sand and dirt with roots from the trees poking out of the ground, crossing over to other trees. It almost looked like the trees were all connected.

The Deicended only walked for a few minutes before seeing signs of wildlife. They could tell some of the bushes with berries on them had been eaten from. Eventually, Lucy came across some droppings. She knew that they had to be from deer, and so they continued their path. With every step they took, they could hear more and more movement coming from wildlife moving against the trees and bushes. Tyr stopped walking and whistled twice. They knew that was the sign that he had spotted a deer. They did not have to talk about what to do next, and the group started to close in on where they thought the deer might be, somewhere in Tyr's eye line. They were able to find it and completely circle it.

They were all about forty feet from the deer now, watching it eat something off the ground. They could not make out what it was that it was eating, but that hardly mattered to them. The deer was bigger than they thought it would be. It was as tall as Tyr, counting its antlers, which had six points prodding from its head. Neith was in awe of its beauty. Takumi started moving closer first, as he had more cover than the others. The rest walked very slowly towards it, hoping to get closer before being spotted. Neith was the only one who hesitated to walk closer to it. She feared to hurt such a beautiful animal.

Takumi had managed to get about ten feet away from the deer. He gripped his spear, ready to charge it. His plan was not to kill it himself, but he was hoping to scare it towards Lucy and Emily. This would give the deer no room to dodge two incoming spear thrusts.

Even if it didn't go exactly where he wanted, one of the others would be able to stab it. Takumi took two deep breaths. He slowly rose from out of the bushes, still not seen by the deer. The deer picked its head up, taking a break from eating. Takumi was ready to charge, but Tyr's spear soared through the air towards the deer's head. Luckily for it, the deer's head was already up, and it saw the spear at the last second, ducking below it and instead of impaling the deer, the spear stuck into a tree right next to the deer.

The deer looked around and became very aware of its situation. It noticed Neith standing back further than she should have been and Tyr closest to him without a spear in his hand. Takumi charged the deer, hoping to set it running in the direction he intended. Sadly, the deer bolted toward Neith and Tyr. *C'mon this isn't fair,* Takumi thought to himself. The deer zipped between the two off-guard Deicended and escaped.

Takumi would have been angrier with Tyr, but they didn't plan the attack beforehand, so it went about as well as they could have expected it to. Still, he knew Tyr only threw the spear so he could have the chance for the glory of the kill. It was selfish of Tyr, and it cost them the goal. Yet, they still had plenty of time. This was only their first attempt.

They walked back to their supplies at the edge of the forest. The group slept in shifts that night in fear that a boar might attack them. The Deicended slept in a little late the next day since they had some difficulty sleeping. For the most part, everyone was quiet. Although none of them would say it, they were all mad at Tyr for being so reckless, but, usually, Tyr was one of the most helpful members of the team in combat situations, so they just sat quiet for some time. Eventually, they did discuss a plan of attack that they could all agree to follow when they next came across a deer, even if they get scared or antsy.

In midafternoon, they set out to hunt again, hopefully for the last time. They walked to where the forest was thicker with the trees only a couple of feet apart from each other. The sun set, but they pressed on. Soon after that, they found a deer. Not only one, this time, but three. All three appeared to be fully grown males. One in particular had a slight limp to its walk. That was the one. Without saying a word, they knew this was the one they were going to kill. The only problem now was that they had to worry about three separate noses and three separate pairs of ears and eyes that could detect them. This was a waiting game. The deer were grazing, and the Deicended needed to wait for an opportunity when the injured one would wander too far from the rest.

After two hours of waiting, it finally happened. The injured deer noticed a patch of berries the others didn't, and it went to get them. Little did this animal know, its gluttony would be the end of it. As soon as it started chewing on the berries, Emily and Takumi darted out in between the injured deer and the others. Takumi stayed in between them while Emily ran to cover the deer's possible escape. The group was now completely circled around the deer, and they were closing in on it. The deer picked up its head to glance over at its buddies but saw Takumi instead. Takumi stood there, awkwardly, like a kid caught with his hand in the cookie jar, not sure what to do. The startled creature let out a desperate grunt of fear. The two deer standing separate from the injured one bolted, as expected. The injured deer ran the opposite direction of Takumi. It was heading straight toward Tyr. Excited, Tyr held his spear straight and firm, ready for the kill. The deer shifted directions slightly towards Neith.

Neith was not willing to fail again. She screamed and charged at the animal with her spear raised. The deer went to shift directions again in an attempt to dodge her. The spear missed the deer's chest that Neith was aiming for. However, the point stuck into the deer's hind right leg. This was the same leg it was limping on. As the spear stuck into its leg, the force from the animal's momentum knocked Neith over and dislodged the spear. It didn't matter. The limited mobility caused by this injury was going to be fatal to this animal. Lucy hurled her spear at the wounded animal, going for the kill. The spear went right over the animal. Strange, since her aim was not off. The deer was now on the ground, covered in blood. The deer didn't dodge the spear. Something took it down.

"You've got to be fucking kidding me," Tyr said.

"Seriously? A boar got the kill?!" Emily kicked a tree trunk in frustration.

The boar in question, hearing their voices, fled from the number of people standing around it. Emily chucked her spear after the fleeing swine but was drastically off the mark and it disappear behind a bush. She groaned and went to retrieve it.

"Wait, we caught it. Isn't that good enough?" asked Neith.

"Cade did say we only had to hunt it, and we did hunt it down," said Ben.

"Knowing Cade, though, I think he wanted us to kill it. I feel like he would send us back here if he knew the boar took the killing blow," said Lucy.

"Well, at least we are going to have some good dinner for the night," said Emily.

Neith walked over to the blood-soaked creature. She stared at its empty eyes. "Ugh, I can't believe I hurt that poor thing, and we didn't even finish our objective. I was hoping we would just finish our time relaxing and eating some berries," she said with tears building on the sides of her eyes.

Dinner was indeed especially good that night. The deer was incredible meat, especially compared to anything they'd had before on the island, but maybe, it was just because they were hungry. The crab they ate a few days ago was alright, but kind of bland without anything to dip it in. The boar they ate was especially tough, but the deer was much more tender, and the flavor was almost the same as steak. Even so, the steak they had back home wasn't this good.

Maybe it had something to do with the natural food versus the lab-created meat they ate back home. Sadly, the Deicended could not say the same about their sleep. Their makeshift shelter at their secondary camp did almost nothing to keep the bugs out, and they were sleeping on the ground, which made it very difficult to fall asleep. To make it worse, it rained for a few hours.

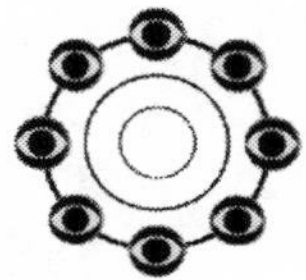

The next day, when the Deicended went hunting, it was a complete failure. They saw no sign of deer at all and no boars either. The only thing they had to eat that day were some berries that were far from filling. They needed protein after a long day of hunting but, again, they would have to sleep miserably without a full belly. To make matters worse, another earthquake happened during the middle of the night, rocking most of the Deicended out of their already restless sleep. Takumi, somehow, slept through it.

The following morning, they ventured out to the beach on the far north side of the island. It was a beautiful cove with calm waters lazily lapping against the sand. Once they arrived, they saw, hanging out on the beach, seven or eight deer with a few large males among them.

"We have to be careful. We can't just surround them. One of them could hurt us with their antlers. There are too many of them," said Lucy.

"I think I have an idea," Tyr suggested.

On the right side of the cove, Ben and Neith emerged out of the woods, running towards the group of deer. Simultaneously, the deer raised their heads and took off running away from Ben and Neith.

As the deer ran for the tree line, the rest of the Deicended popped out of the woods. They were not in the direct path of the deer, but they were slightly offset. The deer continued in their path. All four of the Deicended on the beach launched their spears into the air, aimed at the deer in the front. It was an adult with four points on its antlers. The spear that was thrown by Lucy missed.

She had led her aim too much, and the spear landed in front of it. Ty's spear bounced off of its antlers. Emily's spear landed right in its hindquarters. Immediately after, Takumi's spear followed, landing center in the deer's chest. The buck collapsed, sending up a blinding spray of sand, and the rest of the deer ran past, escaping into the woods. The buck grunted in pain, attempted to stand, and failed. Lucy asked for Ben's spear. He immediately tossed it to her. She walked up to the groaning, wide-eyed creature and stabbed it in the chest, where its heart was. The deer shuddered, laid its head in the bloody sand, and was still, at peace.

This deer was far larger than the last. Something about the success of their day made the meat taste far more tender than the last 'kill'. The next day, they were going to set off back to camp. They ran low on water the other day, and it was much more accessible there. At this camp, they had only been able to collect water when it rained.

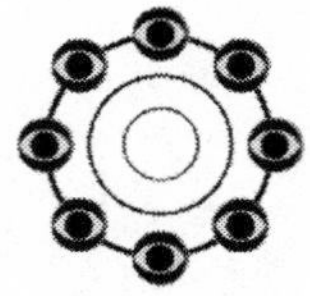

In the morning, the Deicended had just begun gathering up their spears and few other belongings when another earthquake began. Except, this time, it did not stop after just a few minutes or so. The earth was continuously rolling beneath their feet.

"What should we do? This is incredibly unsettling." Takumi said in a panic.

"I think we should go back to the other side of the island. Maybe Cade will pick us up early. I mean, we did finish the mission," said Ben.

The Deicended grabbed whatever food and water they had left over and started walking. Only after their second step, they heard a blast so loud they covered their ears. They looked up and saw a massive column of ash rising from the mountain. The teenagers felt their hearts skip a collective beat. The colors of red and orange shot from the tip of the volcano. Never had those colors looked so angry before. The ash continued to spew out, quickly replacing the blue of the sky with black. Pieces of molten rock were soaring in the sky as if thrown by giants attempting to crush the small ants below them. It was as if evil forced itself from the crust of the earth to eat the sky and decimate the earth above the ground.

A couple of pieces of the molten rock hit the trees in the woods on the north side, and fire quickly spread among the thin palm fronds, down their trunks, and into the underbrush.

Tyr's mind raced. "We should head towards the west side of the island where it is rockier and might be safer from the fire," he shouted to his companions, hoping that would be the right call. They did not walk, they ran. They were in a bad position and knew it. On their way, they found a river of lava flowing in between them and their destination. It had not reached the water yet, but the woods were on fire. Going around it was not an option. It was about ten feet wide so jumping it would be too dangerous. Takumi thought to himself that using their powers now should be fine. Surely Cade did not mean for them to deal with an erupting volcano. Takumi thought if he could put a couple of trees across the river of lava, they could quickly run across before the wood completely burned up. A couple of his black tentacles emerged from his back. *Zap!* Takumi was shocked by his boringly gray jumpsuit.

"Crap! We still can't use our powers!" He shouted in frustration.

"I guess we are going the other way around the volcano then," said Neith.

They ran back north to go towards the east side now, angry at the wasted time. The forest on this side was not completely on fire yet. However, there was some smoke coming from the trees. Running out of the tree line were four boars. They were running in fear of the fire. They were stampeding towards the group.

"We have to scare them off," Lucy shouted. They grabbed whatever rocks they could and threw them at the boars. Ben didn't pick any rocks up. He was more tired than he should have been. His chest got heavier as time passed. The others didn't notice him, fallen back a couple of yards and on his knees, gasping for air. Apparently, there were actually five boars, and the fifth one was behind Ben. Ben noticed but had no idea how it got there. The boar stared at him, and Ben stared back. Both were scared for their lives, hesitating on what they should do. Ben knelt still, frozen by his fear. The boar charged towards Ben. Ben grabbed a rock by his leg. He could try to scare it or fight, but he chose neither.

Ben jumped out of the way of the boar. It ran past and didn't stop. It ran until it made contact with Emily's leg. Emily screamed in pain as she was knocked down, her calf torn open by the boar's tusk. The boar backed up and went for a killing blow, but Emily took a coconut she had been carrying and smashed it in the face. It was enough to stop the boar in its place. Neith threw a rock, hitting it in its stomach. The boar fled back to the woods with the others.

Neith and Lucy were quick to apply a tourniquet. They ripped a part of Lucy's sleeve and grabbed a stick to make it. Emily strung together several colorful obscenities when they applied and tightened it but was able to walk with assistance. Ben helped her walk, throwing her arm over his shoulder and letting her lean on him for support, feeling bad about what had happened to her even though nobody knew it was partially his fault. They could no longer run as a group, but they moved as quickly as Emily could. Every now and again, molten rocks would spray down near them. The only thing they could do was hope to not get hit by one. They started to get close to the north side and noticed that the forest was very much on fire. As if things were not bad enough, the wind blew in their direction. A wall of smoke blew over them. It was hard to see or even breathe with the smoke filling their lungs, and the stench of sulfur made their eyes tear up even worse.

Quickly, they rushed behind a few rocks to block the smoky wind that was furiously hurling towards them. They knew they would have to wait for the wind to calm down before moving. The smoke was so thick they could suffocate. Luckily for them, lava wasn't rushing towards them here. Unluckily for them, it took hours for the wind to calm down. They didn't know how long though with the sun being blotted out from the sky. For all they knew, it could have been nighttime. By the time the wind had calmed, Emily's leg had stopped bleeding, but she still looked pale. They walked up to the tree line, but now the fire burning in the trees was too thick. It had spread wide, and there was no place for them to push through. They discussed among themselves what to do next. They thought about waiting for the fire to just die out but realized that, if the volcano decided to spew lava in their direction, it could mean their death.

Through the time the Deicended spent with Cade, they had experienced many days when they were scared to accomplish whatever task was in front of them. One time, during one of Cade's simulations, he sent spider Primoids at them. Spider Primoids were the size of tanks and obviously had the appearance of spiders. They were armed with two pulse cannons under their heads, a grappling cannon that allowed it to cross anything, and a net cannon. That's too many cannons for something to have. Tactically, there were almost the perfect tanks, extremely versatile and could reach anything with their eight legs. Worst of all, they had eggs that would spawn thousands of micro spider Primoids. These spiders looked just like real ones. Spider Primoids were first used in the Eschaton. Humans, resistant to George, would hide out in mountains sometimes. This terrain made it extremely difficult to get most tanks to support George's forces against the rebellion. The spider Primoids had no problem reaching them and would use the micro spider Primoids to scout the areas. They also were part of psychological warfare. Spiders can be terrifying.

Luckily for the Deicended, when they faced them, their powers were well developed and, while terrifying, they weren't too difficult to defeat. They did only have to face two of them; if there were more, it might have been a different story. Even so, just like their whole lives, George was there to protect them. None of the simulations would have really harmed them. Their whole lives, they had always been protected by George, except… what had happened to their school. Just like that day, the Deicended felt a profound sense of hopelessness. The volcano now decided their outcome. A big stud of rock spewing hot rock water decided whether they lived or died. They felt fragile and insignificant compared to this angry mountain.

Emily clutched her wound and grunted in pain as it shocked her out of her own despondent train of thought. "Screw it. C'mon guys. We worked too hard for this, and our story is not gonna be decided by a volcano. We are making it out of here so we can kick the Hawk's ass for our friends, and this planet's pimple isn't going to stop us." The team nodded grimly and steeled themselves for the next leg of the journey.

The Deicended ventured past the north side of the island and headed towards the east side. Hopefully, they would find a spot where the fire hadn't taken over. After searching for a few hours, it almost seemed hopeless. They came across another river of lava that had cut them off. Forest touching the river there had been completely burned down though. Finally, a pathway to the beach. They were almost home free, so they thought. They walked to the beach and followed it back to the south side of the island that was their rendezvous point with Cade. They had made it back and were starting to hope that they might make it.

They rested for a few minutes and then walked towards their base camp that they hadn't seen in days. As they got close to it, a fire emerged out of it. As the flames consumed their shambled shelter, it sank into the lava that was quickly getting closer. Now, the lava was emerging out of the entire forest. Running didn't appear to be an option. They thought maybe they could swim to another part of the island, before quickly realizing they would probably boil to death in the water. Neith pointed out a huge boulder on the beach. It was wide enough for them all to sit on. Maybe they could wait for the river of lava to harden from the safety of the boulder. They might still suffer damage from breathing in the gasses the lava released, but it was not like they had any other option at this point. They made their way over to it as quickly as they could. The boulder was too tall for one of them to climb. Tyr and Emily were able to boost Takumi to the top.

One by one, they helped each other over the boulder and, with each person that was hoisted over the top, the lava quickly approached them. Emily and Tyr were the only ones left to get to the top now. The lava was way too close now. The heat from it was getting uncomfortable. Tyr grabbed Emily, forcing her up, not letting them waste time deciding who should go up first. Takumi grabbed Emily's hand to help her up and, as he pulled her up, the lava started to burn Tyr's right leg. Tyr, now sweating from both the heat and the pressure, continued to push Emily up. He was determined to ensure his friends would be safe. Takumi had not yet pulled her up far enough for her to climb up.

As Tyr pushed her, the lava ran through his legs. It seemed impossible, but he was still pushing. Even the parts of his legs not in direct contact with the lava were burning from the proximity. He pushed and screamed in pain. Emily scrambled up to the top and immediately swung down to grab Tyr's hand, not allowing him to fall back into the molten rock. His eyes had rolled back into his head, only showing the whites. The whole group was now pulling them up. As Tyr came up the rock, they could see his legs had been washed away in the river of lava. Bone showed from both sides, but no blood. They managed to get Emily and Tyr up on the bolder, but Tyr had passed out from the pain. Ben hadn't seen anything so gruesome since the attack on their school. He vomited over the side of the boulder.

"No, Tyr, your legs!" Neith cried.

"He's still breathing." Ben pointed out.

Tyr had made it up alive, but, with his injuries, it seemed unlikely for him to be able to make it home alive. He would likely die of shock in the next few minutes. Lucy would have been able to heal Tyr and grow his legs back, but they were not allowed to use their powers.

"I'm going to heal him. He won't make it otherwise," said Lucy.

"That electric shock is no joke, Lucy," Takumi cautioned.

"No! I won't let you; you have to finish the mission. No cheating!" Tyr cried out, he had woken for a moment, overhearing the group, but quickly lost consciousness again.

"Well, Tyr's opinion is about to no longer matter. Heal him anyways?" Emily demanded from Lucy.

They all, without hesitation, agreed to let Lucy heal him. She put her hands on what was left of his legs. She closed her eyes and concentrated. The suit began to shock her, causing her whole body to seize, but she didn't let go of Tyr. Muscles began to grow around the bone showing from Tyr's legs. Lucy shook the whole time from being shocked but refused to give in. Nerves and veins wove in deliberate patterns. The Deicended stared at Lucy, in awe of the sheer iron will she was displaying. Once a thin layer of skin formed over Tyr's legs, Lucy stopped.

She collapsed on the rock, sweating profusely and breathing heavily from the pain of being so severely shocked. After a few minutes, Tyr's eyes slowly opened and looked at his partially healed legs in wonder. He saw Lucy laying there in a state of total exhaustion. He opened his mouth to thank her, but she shook her head and waved him off. Takumi had managed to save three of their makeshift water containers. Lucy and Tyr began to drink water until the containers were empty. They needed it the most at the time.

It was a waiting game now. The lava finally touched the sea and steam emerged. Luckily the wind wasn't blowing because the steam would have likely burned them all to death. Hours passed. They did not know how many. Eventually, they ran out of food. It was difficult for them to make the food last. Being bored made the urge to eat difficult to resist. It seemed like a day had passed. The river of lava still flowed and was as hot as ever. Boredom was becoming difficult to deal with. They had already forgotten how hot they were just sitting above the molten rock. Sleeping was difficult on the hard surface, but they still managed to fall asleep from time to time.

Every now and then, they would wake in a panic, afraid they might fall to their death. It seemed like another day passed. It was jarring, but they were beginning to think they might have survived a horrible ordeal just to die bored and hungry on this rock. Their bodies were getting weaker by the hour, really starting to feel the effects of the noxious gasses.

A familiar sound in the distance appeared, an aircraft. It was the same aircraft that had dropped them off, but it was so much more beautiful than they remembered. It hovered at the same exact spot that it had dropped them off down the beach. Cade appeared through the door.

"Well, I'm not picking you up over there, children," said Cade.

You have to be kidding us, they thought. How were they supposed to get over there? Ben ripped off a piece of his pants and dropped it off the boulder. It laid on top of the black rock below just fine, not bursting into flames. Emily shrugged, jumped off, and landed safely.

"I swear, that better have just hardened, or I'm going to crush that mountain," said Takumi.

The rest of them jumped down. Neith and Emily caught Tyr as he jumped and carried him between them, careful not to jostle his newly grown legs. They made their way to the aircraft. They would have run, as desperate as they were to just get off this island, but they had no energy left in them. They walked up to the aircraft, got in, and sat down. The aircraft took off and left the island.

"I should fail you, children, for using your powers, but I guess I will make an exception given the circumstance you were in," said Cade.

3

The Day it Happened: Lucy

I slept better than I have in a long while. Lucy opened her eyes and fought to keep them open. She felt them about to close, so she jumped out of bed and went straight to the bathroom. Getting ready didn't take too long for her, but longer than usual. She didn't feel a need to waste her time brushing her teeth for an excessive amount of time. It was the dirt stuck under her fingernails from the camping trip over the weekend that took a while to get out. Camping was also the reason she had slept so well. *A gel and foam fused mattress beats the hell out of sleeping on the ground.*

She walked out of her room to the kitchen. Her dad already had some venison sausage cooking that he had kept in a freezer from a hunt a couple of weeks ago. They would take a transport out to the boundaries of the City to go hunting as often as they could, whenever her dad had a weekend off from his task. He was one of the most skilled welders at one of George's Primoid factories. He was already dressed for task, wearing an old t-shirt from his favorite music group, the Smoking Crows. Coincidentally, it was her favorite group too, so seeing it always made her smile. "Tell me there are some eggs cooking with that deer," Lucy said to her father, Bill.

"Mmhmm, sweety. Got a couple of pieces of bacon waiting on the table for ya too. Cooking the eggs in its grease," Bill said.

"Oh, my. You better hurry up cooking cause I'm gonna eat all the bacon," said Lucy.

"You do that, and Imma make you sleep outside. This time, without a tent," Bill replied.

They shared a laugh. She grabbed a piece of bacon from a plate on the dining table. There were ten pieces in total. Lucy sunk her teeth into the bacon, and it made a nice crunchy sound. The overwhelming savory and salty flavor made one of Lucy's eyes roll to the back of her head. "Okay, maybe you have some time left. I'm gonna take a while with this one piece."

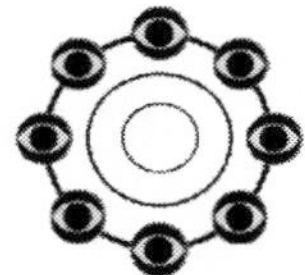

On the bus to school, Lucy opened her brown lunch bag. Dad packed a healthy salad for her. Not her favorite, but it helped offset all the red meat she ate. She lifted the salad out of the bag to see what was in it. To her delight, Lucy found the best gift she got all year, an extra piece of bacon. *The start of the day is already so good. I can't wait for the rest of it,* she thought.

Her first class of the day was biology. It just so happened to be her favorite class as well. The way that the human body works is such a wonder. *How did evolution manage to take a bacterium and turn it into a breathing sack of blood, meat, and bones? Honestly, it's no wonder why people believed in an omnipotent creator years ago.*

Lucy's best friend, Sveti, was in the class with her. Although, best might be a strong word to classify her. They were more like good buddies. Though, Lucy had a lot of buddies. People really enjoyed her company, but no one really had similar interests as she did. She probably was the only one in the whole school that did something like hunting. Even camping outdoors was a rarity for kids these days. Since nobody enjoyed the things she enjoyed, she never really got that close to people. The one person she probably would call her best friend was her dad, Bill. He was flawless in her eyes. Mom wasn't in the picture much. They divorced when Lucy was young, and her mom paid more attention to her task as a doctor.

This day in class, they were dissecting a frog with a partner. Lucy was looking forward to this for weeks. It wasn't human biology that was the only thing that really interested her. She loved learning about plants and animals as well. Sometimes, it was even more interesting. *An angler fish has a bioluminescent bulb attached to its head in order to trick other fish near it to catch them for food. How evolution came up with that, I doubt even George could figure out.*

Sveti just watched as Lucy opened up the frog. She kept talking about her boyfriend and how he doesn't take her out for dinner enough. Lucy was able to listen and inspect the interesting layout of the frog's muscles.

"Do you think I should ask him to take me to dinner more? Or should I just leave a hint or two?" Sveti asked.

"If you want something, then you gotta ask. Like most boys, Jake would probably be too thick headed to pick up any hints," Lucy replied.

"I know, but I just hate having to ask sometimes. I just want my boyfriend to just understand my needs without me constantly giving him instructions," said Sveti.

"I gotcha. Maybe you could, oh, ah! Oops," Lucy stumbled as she accidentally punctured the frog's lung. She shrugged it off and continued to cut. "Maybe just get a new guy that does take you out."

"That's not a bad idea. Meh, I'll give him a few more tries, then I'll find a new one. Thanks for listening! Tell me about you, though.

Any prospects for you that you might go for?" Sveti asked, wiggling her eyebrows suggestively.

"Prospects?" Lucy asked.

"Any guys you might be interested in?" asked Sveti.

"Oh, no. I haven't thought about any guys. You know what I like to do. If I were to like a guy, he would have to share the same interests as me. Seeing as no one in the school hunts or enjoys doing anything outdoors, I don't feel like any of them are worth my time," explained Lucy.

"Fair. Honestly, it's better that you're, in a sense, unavailable. You are too cute and awesome. I wouldn't enjoy the competition," said Sveti, gently elbowing Lucy's side, knocking her arm to the side a little. Luckily, she was taking some notes in her lab book and not cutting into the frog, or she might have messed the poor amphibian up more.

"You have Jake. What would you have to worry about competition for?" Lucy asked.

"Let's be honest. Jake will probably forget to take me to dinner the second after I ask him. I'm going to need options," said Sveti. They shared a laugh, and Sveti took her turn at dissecting the frog.

The next class Lucy had was an English class, which was not really a class she looked forward to. She hung out in the hallway before class started. Her friends Jeff, Chris, Emily, and Sarah were all talking by Jeff's locker.

"Dude, this weekend was crazy! Chris and I went to the arcade, and we got third place on that new Demon Slug game. Right towards the end of our game, I swear everyone in the arcade was watching. Chris was the last one fighting and almost got our team to second place," said Jeff.

"Wow! Third place is super impressive. Chris, let me know the next time you head up. I want to be on your team. Maybe with me on the team, we could get first," said Lucy.

"Oh, yeah. That would be cool. I ah.. I would love to ah.. play with you. I'm not sure if I would keep up though," said Chris.

"Oh, stop being so humble," replied Lucy.

"Now, Lucy is being humble. The girl that hunts living things is trying to claim that she is going to need Chris' help playing Demon Slug," said Emily.

"I don't even get how you do that old stuff. Isn't it hard killing a deer? I mean, mentally," Sarah asked.

"It was the first time, but, honestly, it gives you a weird respect for nature. I mean, if I don't kill the deer, then something else is going to kill it, and it ain't gonna be a quick death for the thing," replied Lucy.

"Yeah, you make a…" Sarah was cut off by the bell warning students to hurry up and get to class.

They all quickly said goodbye and started walking to their classes, except Chris, who looked nervous and didn't move.

"Wait, Lucy!" Chris yelled at her, hustling to catch up with her.

"Whatcha want, bud?" Lucy replied.

"I… I wanted to ask you something," said Chris.

"I'll see you at lunch. Just ask me then. I gotta go," Lucy replied.

"Oh, okay. I 'll…. Bye," Chris said. He quickly turned and walked awkwardly to his next class.

As boring as English class was to Lucy, she still paid attention and put effort into her work. She drudged through the class, and, after what felt like hours, the bell rang, signaling them to go to their next class. Lucy's next class was Virtue class. This was a class that only started being taught shortly after the time of the Infinite Blossom. It was a review of how to be a better person in society. Most of the class was spent giving examples of one of the Eight Virtues. The class ended up having some of the best effects on the psyche of a growing child, helping groom kids for a path of success and fulfillment. Usually, Charity, Kindness, and Hope were mostly focused on younger kids. When they get a bit older, they focus on Fortitude, Diligence, and Justice. Then, in the last two years of school, they focus on Prudence and Temperance. Lucy's class today was focused mostly on Fortitude. This was Lucy's favorite virtue as well.

Lucy was a big hunter, and a lot of virtues applied in the game. Even though she was a hunter, deep down, she was a fighter, and hunting was the closest thing she could get to a real fight. It was what gave her the strength to endure the weather and her will to fight, no matter how tired and fatigued she would become. It was what made her a good hunter, and she took pride in her skill.

In the class that day, they learned about the history of the Medal of Honor that was almost always awarded for examples of fortitude. Lucy was interested to learn about how, even in what seemed to be such a chaotic time, people still held the same virtue that she did on the high pedestal it deserved to be on.

Once Virtue class ended, it was time for lunch. Chris, Emily, and Sveti were sitting at a table near the middle of the lunch hall. The school supplied locked fridges for kids to store their lunches in if they decided to bring something for themselves. Lucy unlocked her little refrigerated cubby to get her salad out. She went to open the container, and it slipped out of her hand, covering the floor.

"Ah, dang it," Lucy said and dialed up her dad to give him the bad news.

"What's going on, sweetie?" Bill asked when he answered the call.

"I dropped the dang salad you made," Lucy responded.

"Well, it was supposed to be nutrition for a human, not the floor," said Bill.

A tiny cleaning Primoid came out of the wall and began cleaning the spilt salad.

"I didn't mean to drop it, Daddy. I'm sorry; I just wanted to let you know so when you see the charge I'm about to make to your account you would be in the know," said Lucy.

"Don't you worry. I'm actually near the school. I'll give you my salad. I'll go to the store and get myself something else. I don't want you eating that cruddy school food," said Bill.

"Are you sure, Daddy? I won't mind eating the school food," said Lucy.

"I'm sure! Just give me, like, two minutes," said Bill.

Lucy hung up and walked towards the table with her friends. "You're not going to eat anything?" Emily asked.

"I can buy you something, Lucy! I wouldn't mind," Chis piped up eagerly.

"That's so sweet, but I'm good. My dad is going to be here soon. He's dropping me off something," said Lucy. Chris nodded and smiled as Lucy took a seat across from him.

"Did you guys see that flyer for the festival in a couple of weeks?" Sveti asked.

"Oh, I'm so excited for that," said Emily.

"Sounds pretty boring, to be honest," said Jeff.

"Well, sounds pretty interesting to me too," said Lucy.

"I think I'm gonna go to it too," said Chris.

"Of course, you're going since she just said she's going," said Sveti, smirking.

"What do you mean?" asked Lucy.

"Oh, never mind," said Sveti, smiling sideways at Chris who gave her a dirty look before turning back to face Lucy.

"Hey, Lucy, I wanted to ask you before. Next time you go hunting, could I…" Chris was cut off by Lucy.

"Hold that thought. I have to pee. Like bad. It just hit me," Lucy shot up and ran to the bathroom. Once she had answered nature's call, she washed her hands and walked out of the bathroom. She looked back into the lunchroom and saw her friends at the table with another person. She focused her eyes and saw her dad holding a lunch bag, seemingly asking where she was to drop off the lunch.

Lucy smiled and took a step towards the lunch hall. She was blinded by a flash and leaped back from the doorway as rubble, and who knew what else, blew out from the room. Some of the debris scraped Lucy as she jumped to the side, and Lucy might have blacked out for a split second. When she opened her eyes, everything seemed quiet, but slowly rolled into a mash of loud screams and collapsing debris.

Lucy struggled to stand up, her body felt twice its weight. Still, she stood. *Daddy,* she thought as her eyes lit up. Suddenly, her fuzzy head cleared up, and she ran into the lunch hall. There was a fire where the food was served. People laid around, covered in what looked like white dust. Some were covered in their own blood. Others were covered in their classmate's blood. Lucy ran around, looking for her father, ignoring her screaming classmates and their pleas for help. She kept running and searching until an arm grabbed her ankle.

"Lucy, it's uccugh, me," said Chris. "Help me, please. I'm scared." There were a few fingers missing from the hand he grabbed her with. His leg was pinned down by a piece of the ceiling. His face had blood dripping down from his mouth, and it mixed with the white dust, clumping together. The blood coming from his leg was flowing alarmingly fast.

Lucy looked up and saw a Smoking Crows t-shirt. She felt her blood turn cold as she kicked her leg away from Chris and ran to the body, hoping it wasn't her dad's. It was, and he didn't look conscious. Lucy grabbed her father and shook him, hoping to wake him up. "Daddy! Daddy, please! Listen to me. Wake up!" she screamed. Blood covered her dad's abdomen. His guts were hanging out. *No, no, NO!* Lucy thought. Carefully, she grabbed his intestines and laid them on top of his body. Next, she grabbed his legs and moved them closer to the rest of his body with his knees high to sky. She took her belt off and wrapped it around his legs, keeping them from falling back down. She shook him again. "Daddy, please! I need you," she screamed desperately as tears ran down her face.

Bill's eyes opened and glanced towards Lucy. "Hey there, swe…" his eyes closed again. Lucy stayed with her father until a peacekeeping Primoid came and covered her with a blanket. They made her leave her father and wait for hours as she was one of the last to be picked up by a parent. Her mother pulled up, and Lucy got in the car with her. Her mother didn't bother to say anything on the ride home.

4

Primechs

One week after the island, the Deicended collected in the classroom. They had spent their time resting and recouping from the island. They were able to get their weight back to normal and Tyr was able to grow his legs back more completely with help from Lucy. They would have used micro-fiber repair technology, but it never felt like the real thing when they replaced whole body parts. When Lucy used her powers, it felt like you never lost the limb in the first place.

"As you may have guessed, children, we are going to begin training again. You all did well on the island; I am proud of all of you. Now, I present you all with your own dagger," said Cade.

There were six boxes laid out on the android's desk at the front of the class. Cade handed a box to each student, and it seemed that each particular box was meant for a particular Deicended. Upon opening the boxes, it seemed to be true. There was a different symbol etched into the blade of every dagger. The daggers had a double-sided blade and were about an inch and half wide and fifteen inches long. The handle was wrapped in hard leather and was only big enough for one hand. There was no guard in between the blade and handle.

All of the symbols were surrounded by eight eyes, evenly spaced and connected by a line. This must be a reference to George's symbol, which had those same eight eyes with the line connecting them. George's symbol, however, has two circles inside the line, resembling another eye. Each of the eight eyes represents a different Path of Virtue that George sees inside all of mankind. The symbol represents how It watches to help people and machines live to their potential that he knows they have. The eight paths are Temperance, Diligence, Kindness, Prudence, Fortitude, Justice, Hope, and Charity. People commonly believe that the eye in the center represents everyone looking to find these virtues in themselves.

On Tyr's blade, inside of the eight eyes, was a head of a dragon. It was facing to the side and appeared spikey in shape with sharp teeth pointing out of its maw. Emily's symbol was a fierce dog-looking creature with its fangs bared, apparently growling. It seemed much fluffier than a normal dog, and the art looked to be done in an old Japanese style. Lucy's symbol had a fierce snake that squiggled between the bottom left corner of the circle and the top right. Ben had a bird, with its wings spread, that appeared to be on fire. Takumi's had nine serpent heads winding from the center. Neith had an Egyptian sphinx laying down, in profile, on hers.

"You will notice the symbols on each of your blades. Each symbol is representative of your person and your powers. Tyr, your symbol is a Drake. It is a wingless dragon with scales harder than some metals, just like your skin. Emily, yours is a Raiju. It is a mythical Japanese lightning dog since you have a tendency to shock things. Lucy, yours is a Basilisk, a giant snake that sheds its skin, in whole, to show completely new skin underneath. Ben, yours is a Phoenix, because the heat you make is like that generated by a fire and, like a phoenix that rises from the ashes, you have risen from death yourself. Takumi, your symbol is a Hydra. You have an unknown amount of those arms that come out of you. If one is not enough, you will use two. If a Hydra loses a head, it will grow another. Neith, as you can no doubt deduce, your symbol is a Sphinx, not so much for your powers, but for your name and your personality. A Sphinx is

Egyptian, like yourself, and is a symbol of wisdom, fitting for someone so intelligent," explained Cade.

"Those blades are now your primary weapon of stealth. They are designed with vibro-technology. I am not sure if there is anything it cannot cut through. We are going to train with these very diligently, but I am not the one to teach you these things. From now on, I will have the assistance of a squad of Primechs. They are very diverse in their abilities and will be able to help you grow and develop skills in their specialties," said Cade.

As he finished speaking, ten Primechs walked into the room. Every one of them differed in appearance. Primechs were once human and are now Primoids. Everything about them is machine, except their brains. They are granted their nearly immortal bodies by one of the Arch Primoids and become their disciples in a way. The Arch Primoids are the guardians of George's Virtues. George gifts humans the honor to become Primechs when they excel at a Virtue. There are eight Arch Primoids, just like there are eight virtues.

Their names are known by everyone, but only some of their appearances are known. For example, Mars is the Arch Primoid of Fortitude. He is kind of hard to miss with his massive size, so he doesn't bother trying to keep his identity secret. The other Arch Primoids are Sun, Venus, Mercury, Saturn, Jupiter, Moon and Star. Sun is the virtue of prudence. Venus is the virtue of kindness. Mercury is the virtue of diligence. Saturn is the virtue of temperance. Jupiter is the virtue of justice. Moon is the virtue of charity, and Star is the virtue of hope.

One of the Primechs stood forward from the rest. It appeared to be a female and looked like she was in her late teen years or her early twenties. Primechs don't age, as far as your average person knows, so, for all the Deicended knew, this youthful Primech could be a hundred years old. She was beautiful, slender, and above the average height for a woman. She had her brown hair in a tight bun, and she was dressed elegantly with a light brown collared shirt. She had a dark brown, almost red, vest over her shirt, with brown pants to match her shirt. She had gold armor on some places of her body, like her wrist, hands, and shins. Her feet looked completely mechanical and gold, with six-inch heels attached. She wore a gold belt with a rapier on her side. The blade was silver in color and very thin. The length of her blade was longer than her arm. The pommel was gold, and the handle was silver with no wrapping. The handle looked like a bunch of rings piled on top of each other. There was a basket guard around the handle with strings of metal weaving from the pommel to where the blade met the handle, that looked like the stem of a rose with thorns wrapped around it. There were also petals of a rose etched into the side of the blade.

"This is Cassandra, a disciple of Venus. She will be teaching you how to handle those blades of yours. The rest of these Primechs will be instructing you later," said Cade.

The Primechs, excluding Cassandra, left the room. While Cassandra stood there in front of them, Takumi and Ben were noticeably blushing at the sight of Cassandra's beauty. She noticed and smirked, appreciating the gesture, but also hoping she would not be a distraction from their training.

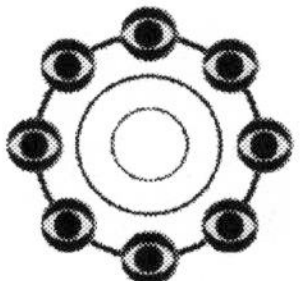

Later, the six gathered around Cassandra in the training room.

"Today will be a simple day. You will learn how to slash and thrust." said Cassandra.

"What about blocking?" asked Tyr.

"You are not ready to learn that yet. Like I said, you will learn how to slash and thrust," Cassandra repeated.

Cassandra drew her sword and narrowed her stance by facing to her right side with the sword out. She lifted her arm and swung down. Then, she pulled her arm close to her with her sword still facing out. Next, she took a step forward while simultaneously thrusting her hand and sword away from herself.

"And that is how you slash and thrust. You will mirror what I did." Cassandra ordered.

The Deicended began to attempt to do what she showed them, but they were far off. Technically, they were doing what she asked, but they were lacking the same elegance. A lot of elegance. Cassandra would assist them where she could, but it was up to the individual to perfect the technique, as she kept reminding them.

After hours of training, Emily asked, "Isn't this stance and technique impractical for our daggers?"

"Yes, but you are not learning the best technique for your weapons. You are learning how to make your blade an attachment to your body. Thus, we start with the basics of fencing," replied Cassandra.

The Deicended would continue this training for days. They, eventually, had sufficiently learned the slash and thrust. It wasn't perfect and elegant like Cassandra's technique, but they were now moving the dagger like it merged with their hand, except Ben. His technique appeared like there was no technique. Even so, Cassandra could tell there was power in his slash and thrust.

The next day, it was time for them to learn how to parry.

"There is a difference between a block and a parry. I will not be teaching you how to block. I'm pretty sure you can figure that one out, and it is a move that should not be used in superior sword fighting techniques. A parry is a counter to a slash or thrust that should allow you the chance to slash or thrust." explained Cassandra. "Now, one of you will swing at me, and I will show you a parry."

Neith came forward and swung her dagger at Cassandra exactly how she was taught to. Cassandra swung her blade, meeting Neith's dagger. Neith's arm flew to the side. Faster than Neith could swing her arm back front, Cassandra showed the rest of the group just how open Neith's back was to a counter strike. The Deicended paired up to practice their parry and, if they were not the one parrying, then they were just getting more practice at their slash. Ben paired with Takumi. Neith paired with Tyr, and Lucy paired with Emily.

Lucy swung at Emily, and Emily brought her sword up and perpendicular to her body. She blocked the attack. Emily heard a chuckle over her shoulder; she looked and saw Cassandra eyeing her.

"Thank you for demonstrating what not to do. Now, do what I taught you to do," Cassandra demanded, a little insulted by her student not listening to her commands.

Lucy swung again, and, this time, Emily performed another block. Cassandra whacked Emily in the back of the head, yelling, "You are not listening; you need to listen."

"Ow!" Emily yelled back. "I thought you were supposed to be a disciple of kindness."

"It would be unkind of me to not properly train you and leave you unprepared for your future missions," replied Cassandra.

Once again, Lucy slashed at Emily, and, this time, she performed a parry.

"Good, now your opponent would be dead, just like they should be," said Cassandra.

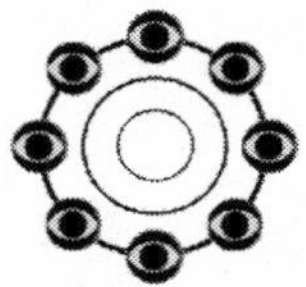

After practicing their basic parries for a day, they moved to counter attacks. Then, they learned the different ways to parry a slash and thrust and in which circumstances you would use the parry. One day, Cassandra had them practice fighting each other. They would slash and thrust and parry in whichever way they chose. During one of these practices, Emily decided to surprise Lucy with a strike from the side. Lucy was surprised and still dodged the attack but was set off her footing. Emily followed through with a thrust, stopping right before the blade made contact with Lucy's chest. Lucy glared at her, clearly frustrated.

"Emily, I did not teach you that strike. You are missing the point," said Cassandra, annoyed at Emily now. "I am now your opponent. I would like to see you try that on me."

"Won't my blade cut through yours?" Emily asked, attempting to find an excuse to not spar with Cassandra.

"Don't worry. My blade uses the same vibro-technology as your blade," explained Cassandra.

Emily was nervous. She hesitated while approaching Cassandra for the duel. They set into their stances, and the rest of the Deicended stopped their own sparring, watching eagerly. Emily was the first to swing. Cassandra effortlessly parried and countered. She sliced Emily's right shoulder. It was a small cut, but it stung and had the desired effect, as Cassandra was pleased to see uncertainty creeping into the girl's eyes. They continued to spar, and, each time Emily attempted to strike Cassandra, she would counter and cut Emily again. Over and over until Emily was covered in blood and dropped to her knees, unable to stand.

"Since my words were not effective enough teachings for you, hopefully, the pain will be lesson enough for you," said Cassandra, mockingly. Emily swallowed down some choice words she would have liked to hurl at the Primech.

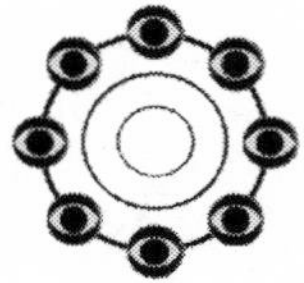

Training with Cassandra continued for a few more months. Until, one day, the Deicended walked into the training room, and Cassandra was not there. It was a different Primech. This one was short with black hair that stood up rather stiffly. He padded in, barely making a sound, staring at and analyzing the Deicended. He appeared angry or disgusted looking at the Deicended, but his face never shifted once, leading them to believe that was just his normal expression. He stood in front of them for an awkward amount of time. He had dark clothes on, matching the expression on his face, as well as black shoes and pants and a grey shirt.

"My name is Nadin. I will be instructing you all in the art of stealth. Obviously, you know the importance of stealth, I'm not going to explain it to you. You are old enough to understand simple shit. However, I will be having you do drills and training exercises that will help you develop the skill set to pass unnoticed whenever the need arises. Is that understood?" said Nadin.

The Deicended kind of just looked at Nadin, mostly confused by how he introduced himself. Emily was smirking, appreciating his bluntness.

"Did they cut your tongues out? Usually, when having a conversation, one responds to confirm they understood what that person just said. Do you understand me?" asked Nadin firmly.

"Yes, sir," The Deicended responded at the same time.

"Now, everyone, turn around and observe the wall," Nadin commanded.

The Deicended did as he asked. Only five seconds later, Ben turned around to look at Nadin. He had disappeared, and now none of the Deicended knew where he had gone. Puzzled now, they began to spread around and look for any sign of where he had gone. After two minutes, there was no sign. They continued looking, figuring that this was a test of some sort. A tile from the ceiling began to move above Takumi, but he did not notice. Nadin leapt down from the ceiling, kicking Takumi to the ground. The rest of the group heard the noise, but Takumi barely uttered a sound while being kicked to the ground. Nadin darted towards Lucy. He drew a pistol he was hiding in his pants that was armed with rubber bullets. Nadin shot three times. Each shot hit a Deicended in the center of their chest.

First, Neith was hit, letting out a squeal of pain. Next, Tyr and then Ben. They let out the same high-pitched squeal that Neith did. Lucy and Emily heard the noise of their teammates in pain and turned. The shots from the pistol were quiet since there was a silencer built in, but not inaudible. By the time Lucy noticed Nadin, he stuck a sword into her stomach. The sword was still sheathed, so it only winded Lucy. The sword was like a katana, but shorter. The sheath was black, and the wrapping on the handle was also black. Nadin went to slash Emily with his covered sword, but she grabbed a chair and blocked it. He then went to make a downward slash, and she blocked that one too. Nadin stood down, relaxing and allowing an indecipherable smirk to cross his lips. Emily lowered the chair.

"Good, you managed to survive the encounter… for a short while," Nadin said, still smirking.

He lifted his pistol to his hip and shot Emily on her right thigh.

"Ow, why!?" Emily squealed in pain.

"Just because you blocked me does not mean anything. If this was a real fight, you would be dead. I will not sugar coat your training. If you lose, you lose. If you fail, you will learn a lesson through pain," explained Nadin, his tone a bit angry. The Deicended might be just learning, but he expected better.

The next day, they woke, and Nadin attacked them in their quarters while they were getting ready for the day. He shot Emily while she was brushing her teeth. Tyr was on the toilet, and Nadin knocked the stall door down and shot him twice. He dealt with the rest of them before they even knew he was there. The day after that, they made sure to have someone watch their back while getting ready. Even with someone watching another's six, they all either got shot or jabbed by his sheathed sword. They started sleeping with

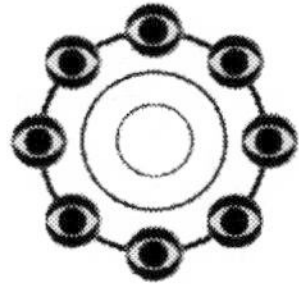

their weapons, so they had them when getting ready for the day.

After three months of paranoia on top of the regular training he had them doing, which consisted mostly of strength training, Lucy got a lucky shot and hit Nadin in the leg while he was trying to shoot Neith as she clipped her toenails. The next day, The Deicended were woken up in the middle of the night, each with a rubber bullet hitting their chest. The Deicended no longer had a full night of sleep. They had to take shifts to prevent being shot again. In a weird way, it felt like a small graduation for them, moving to the next step of Nadin's training. Sadly though, even with the guard shifts they were pulling, Nadin would find a way into the room to shoot them with a rubber bullet. He would always find a new way in. The Deicended constantly learned about new vents and hollow walls every time they felt that stinging sensation on their chest.

Some nights, Nadin wouldn't attack. He did this in an attempt to cause the Deicended to drop their guard. It worked the first time, but they never let their guard down again. Every other time he did this, they were beaten because Nadin was obviously better than them. After one of the few nights they weren't attacked, Nadin walked into the room calmly.

"I feel that it is important that I teach you a lesson in my discipline. I am a disciple of Saturn. Temperance is my discipline, or, you could say, moderation. Moderation takes self-restraint. Normally, this would not be the first trait that came to your mind when asked to describe a warrior, but, in the world of assassins, temperance is key. When trying to get the upper hand on your enemy, you must be willing to sacrifice more than he or she is. Sometimes, when waiting in a shaft for hours to sneak up on you, I get hungry. The reason I beat you every time is that I restrain myself from giving in to those urges. Consider this when attempting to master the art of stealth," Nadin explained.

That night, the Deicended thought about what Nadin had said. Not for long, of course. Nadin came in through a panel in the wall and shot everyone. Ben was supposed to be watching that quadrant of the room but fell asleep. The others couldn't blame him too much, though. The lack of sleep was really getting to all of them.

One night, Takumi had an idea. He suggested to all of them, "What if we snuck up on him while he slept?"

"We can't do that; he's our teacher," said Neith.

"So? We're his students. I don't think he should be shooting us," Takumi retorted.

"You have a point, but I don't think he sleeps. I thought Primechs don't need to sleep, eat, or drink," Tyr mentioned.

"Right, they don't. They don't *need* to, but he mentioned the other day that he gets hungry, and it made me think. I'm pretty sure Primechs don't *need* any of that stuff, but they still get the urge to do it," said Takumi.

"Except, he's a Disciple of Temperance. He, of all of them, would restrain himself from doing that stuff," said Lucy.

"Only if he's trying to beat someone. If he doesn't expect us to attack, then maybe he sleeps. It's worth a try to at least get some payback."

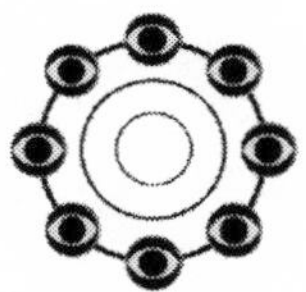

The next day, when Nadin had dismissed them from regular training, he went to exit the room as usual. The Deicended didn't know where he went after classes. So, if he slept, they needed to find out where. Lucy used her powers to conceal herself. She scurried to the door to follow Nadin and kept her distance as she tailed him through the monochromatic corridors. She was afraid to bump into him and ruin everything if he were to stop suddenly. Nadin walked along without making any stops until he reached a familiar door. Lucy had walked past it before. She had thought it was a closet for cleaning supplies or something. Nadin walked into the room and closed the door. Lucy walked up to the door. There was a slight window above the door. Lucy was unable to see it, so she used her powers and began to grow. Her legs did most of the growing and, before long, she was able to see into the room. Sure enough, the room had a bed. The room was rather bare besides the bed, which she could see him reclining on. That meant he might be vulnerable tonight. Lucy reduced herself to her normal size and ran back to the others. She informed the rest of the Deicended of the situation.

"So, tonight then. Waiting isn't going to do us any good," said Tyr.

After allowing an hour to pass, by which time they should have been asleep in their barracks, they gathered outside their bedroom door. They walked slowly towards Nadin's room. They kept their rifles at the ready in case Nadin decided to stroll outside his room like they were. Arriving at his door, Lucy stretched herself again to see if Nadin was in his bed, and he was. Ben used his powers to quietly melt a hole into the door in order to open it. They looked at each other, doing their best to minimize their breathing, even with their hearts beating out of control, as Nadin had been drilling them. Takumi nodded, and together they unleashed a storm of rubber bullets into the bed.

"Got you, Nadin!" Ben yelled.

"Got what?" They heard from above their heads. Nadin dropped down from an open ceiling tile. He then assaulted the students with a fury of slashes and rubber stings. After mere seconds, all of the Deicended had been knocked to the ground and were cradling some body part. "Maybe next time, you won't be so loud. Good attempt, though." Lucy looked into the room, irked at having been tricked. Nothing but pillows were in the bed that Nadin was supposed to be sleeping in.

Back in their bedroom, Emily released her BRF's rubber bullet magazine and dashed it onto her bed. It bounced off and clattered to the floor. "How in the world are we supposed to get Nadin?" Emily asked.

"I guess, we keep trying," suggested Tyr.

"I have an idea," Takumi said.

"Not again," Tyr groaned.

"I promise, this one will work!" Takumi replied emphatically.

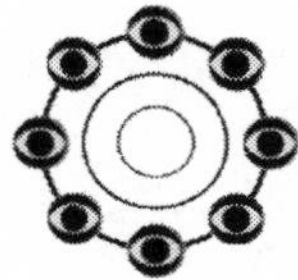

A week later, when they were supposed to be asleep, they crept up to Nadin's door again. Lucy checked to see if Nadin was in bed, and Ben melted a hole in the door. As the Deicended rained fire into the bed, Nadin, once again, jumped from the ceiling and assaulted the students.

"How uncreative," said Nadin.

"Well, I think it was," replied Takumi, the sound of his voice muffled and coming from behind a wall. Takumi burst through the panel that he was hiding behind, rifle at the ready. Takumi pulled his trigger and fired around six shots at Nadin. Nadin leapt out of the way, rolling on the ground, and returned fire, hitting Takumi in the stomach.

"How did I miss?!" shouted Takumi in disappointment.

"Well, as much as it pains me to say, you actually hit my leg when I tried to dodge. Good job with the misdirection," Nadin said.

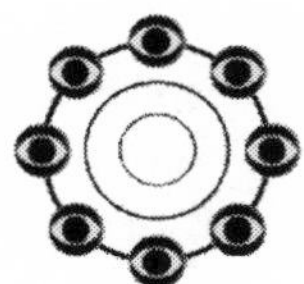

Takumi looked up to see all of his friends wearing grins that matched his own.

The next day, Nadin didn't enter the classroom. It was time for their training with the next Primech, except, this time, two Primechs walked in.

"My name is Yazan, and this is my older brother, Amin. We will be instructing you in hand-to-hand combat," said Yazan.

Yazan was at least seven feet tall and built like an ox. He didn't have any skin on his body, except his face, and he had hair that came an inch off of his head as a flat top. His body was covered in a silver metal plate. The plate was so thick, it looked like a missile wouldn't scratch it. His face appeared angry, but it was hard to tell with his ridiculous sunglasses on.

Amin was about a foot and half smaller with a very wiry frame. His brown hair laid past his shoulders. He was wearing a light grey hoodie with the sleeves cut off and dark brown cargo pants tucked into black combat boots. Skin showed on his arms only shortly past his elbows. His forearms to his hands were black metal prosthetics, no doubt bearing several enhancements.

"Let's go over some basic wrestling techniques, heh heh," said Amin.

Although tired and sore from the training, the Deicended were relieved, as this was the first night since Nadin started training them that they would be able to sleep without paranoia. Training with Yazan and Amin was tough; they pushed their bodies every day. Along with wrestling training, boxing, and martial arts, they also lifted weights, ran, and did any exercise to work every muscle in their bodies. Both Yazan and Amin were unforgiving while training. Cade came to visit the six a few times, only because Yazan or Amin would want to choke one of the teenagers out and Cade needed to diffuse their rage. The brothers' tempers would flare when one of the Deicended fell out in an exercise. It seemed strange that they listened to Cade. Yazan and Amin seemed like the type that would throat punch anyone who would attempt to tell them what to do, especially Yazan. It might have been the glasses or how quiet he was, but, when he glared in anger at someone, they tended to think that would be the last image they would ever see.

One day, Neith mustered the courage to ask Yazan and Amin a question. "Are you guys going to teach us some lesson having to do with your discipline, like the other Primechs did?"

If Yazan was one for scoffing, he might have done so. "No, we don't have a silly lesson like that. We are disciples of Mars. Our discipline is about having courage. That's not something you can teach. You either got it or you don't. Seeing as you all survived the island and Cassandra's and Nadin's training, I'm sure there is some sort of courage in you. Although can't be too much from the shit effort I've seen you all put in." Yazan responded in his usual deep monotone voice.

"Though, maybe we could tell you about how we became the disciples of Fortitude. Would that please you, Neith, heh heh?" Amin asked with his voice that had a fuzzy tone to it. If a Primoid's voice was affected by smoke, that was what his voice sounded like.

"Of course, I want to know!" Neith exclaimed, excited as usual to learn.

Amin looked up at Yazan, who gave him a slight, almost imperceptible nod. He turned back to his students and began to tell the story. "Well, we set ourselves on this path back when our bodies were young; we were about twelve if I remember correctly, heh heh. This was just before the age of Cain. Our family was big, very big, heh heh. Yazan and I were brothers. We were growing suspicious of how big our family was getting. We reported to a sentry primoid about our suspicions. People in our family that we had thought were our aunts and uncles or nieces and nephews were actually our brothers and sisters, heh heh. Our parents had lied to the family about each other's relations. Of course, some of our older brothers and sisters knew the truth. There were nine of us, and it would have been difficult to lie to that many. Our parents were stealing food and supplies in order to feed us all, since our parents, like everyone else at the time, were only supposed to have two children. Since we were the ones that had the courage to report the incident, we were sent to a foster home. The rest of our family was sent to the Four Circles Prison. That was how we drew Mars' eye."

"Wait, they sent your brothers and sisters to prison too? Weren't they innocent?" asked Ben.

"Others would suffer unfairly due to them being around. There would be less food and supplies for everyone else with them in the equation, heh heh. Although they went to prison, George put them there only to allow a bit of time for resources to become available for their addition to society outside the prison. They were added to the waitlist for couples who had received a proper permit for a child but could not physically have one of their own through traditional means," replied Amin.

"How did your mother get past the monthly scans?" asked Neith.

"Back then, people had methods to trick the scanners. Now, it would be impossible to get past the scans," Yazan said.

Amin continued his story. "When we lived in a foster home, there were other children just like us. There were about five hundred living in the house we lived in whose parents had also committed crimes. There we had made a few friends, but most of the children stuck to themselves because they missed their families, heh heh. One day, one of them hung himself in a closet. At first, everyone was sad and missed the boy, until another child slit their wrist in a bathtub, heh heh. Not even a whole day later, another was found dead. This went on for a week. One of our friends tried to start a suicide pact.

There were twenty of them, and they were to jump off the house together, heh heh. They tried to get us to go with them, heh heh. When they jumped off the house, they were caught by nets. Of course, we had reported them. The twenty who tried to kill themselves were sent to the Four Circles Prison for counseling. More and more kids in the house tried to kill themselves; Yazan and I were determined to save them, heh heh. We patrolled the house and had to wrestle many of the kids to prevent them from committing suicide. One time, Yazan had to break a kid's jaw to prevent him from chewing into his own wrist. This all happened right before the rest of the world started killing themselves from boredom. When we were old enough, we were recruited by George to assist in an anti-suicide unit. We prevented thousands of suicides. Most of the time by force, heh heh. We were the best humans in any anti-suicide unit in The City. Eventually, we were approached by two Arch Primoids. Mars and Jupiter both wanted to recruit us. We chose to become disciples of Mars only because disciples of justice mostly just became sort of policemen. We had already been acting as cops our whole lives pretty much and were ready for a new challenge. Shortly after we became Primechs, George lifted the child limit due to the population thinning sufficiently and came up with the Task system to cure humans of their boredom. George had Mars and his disciples build and maintain Its army, heh heh. It was thought for many years that we would never be used, until this hawk masked man showed up." The Deicended looked at each other. That story was a lot to take in.

"So, your family didn't need to go to prison, then," Emily said, her brow furrowed.

"Yes, they did. Hopefully, when Joe shows up, he will teach you the importance of following the rules, even if they change later," Yazan responded with a hint of anger in his voice.

"Does this help you understand what it takes to have fortitude? This story might not help you with your fighting ability, but it's a story of courage in the face of adversity," said Amin.

The Deicended looked around at each other and there were some mixed feelings among them. They wondered if they would have been able to turn their own family in, were they in Yazan and Amin's place.

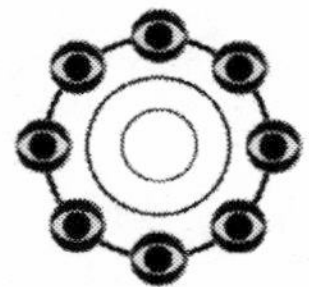

Training with Yazan and Amin continued for several weeks until, one day, another Primech showed up in their classroom. It appeared to be a boy in his late teens, about their age. He had black hair that laid over his ears. He wore a green jacket with a black shirt underneath and blue jeans with white sneakers. His hairstyle and fashion were not something anybody would wear in this day.

"Hey, turds, my name is Greg Fisher, and I will be instructing you all in pistol and close-quarters shooting. Any questions before we start?" asked Greg.

"Yeah, what's the deal with your clothes, and why do you have a family name?" asked Lucy.

"Let's just say I'm older than I look," said Greg with a smirk on his face.

A lot of the training the Deicended went through with Greg was somewhat familiar to them. They went over close quarters training when Cade was teaching them. Greg went through everything way more thoroughly. He was probably the nicest teacher, besides Cade, that they had. Sometimes, he got frustrated when the Deicended didn't perform how he wanted them too, but he just made jokes about their incompetence instead of punishing them. Unfortunately for the Deicended, when they actually enjoyed the training and the instructor, it was to be the shortest training regimen. Greg had told them that he didn't have too much to teach them, since they had already learned so much in this field from Cade. He even let them know when it was his last day, which none of the other instructors did. Before he left, all of the Deicended begged him to tell them about how he became a Primech.

Greg relented and began to tell them. "I was a kid all the way back in the Eschaton. Even though I was young, I chose to side with George during that Great War. I piloted the AIP (Anti-Infantry Piloted) Mech, model 2.356. As you know, piloted combat Mechs were decommissioned a long, long time ago. Although the construction Mechs we have today are extremely similar in design. I don't want you to think I am tooting my own horn when I say that I was good at what I did, on and off the field. I became something of a celebrity, and my presence influenced many humans to join George before the war was even over. During one battle, I ejected out of my Mech because of the damage it suffered. With nothing but a pistol, I ran into a building that was one of the few left standing in that town. It was occupied by the All-Human forces. After killing a magazine worth of people, everyone in the building surrendered once they saw me. The General saw me, and he surrendered the fighting force. Hundreds of men lived that day because I was able to get them to surrender. I even convinced a hundred of those men and women to join with George that day. George rewarded me by making me a disciple of Star for the hope I had inspired through the war.

After the story, Greg left for the day, leaving his temporary students to ponder on his story.

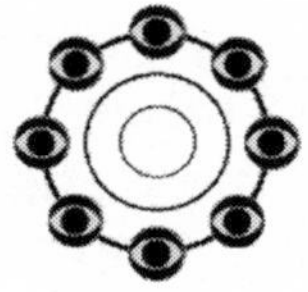

The next day, another Primech came into the classroom. This Primech wore a blue jacket with the collar popped around his neck. He dressed similarly to the Peacekeeping Primoids. They looked like cops from the old days. He had two long swords on his side. He had bright combed red hair, which was an incredibly rare color to see these days.

"Listen up, squirts! My name is Joe. I will be instructing you all in various uses and practicality of melee weapons. Everybody got that?!" Joe yelled, which was obnoxious for how close they were to him.

Tyr had a little sparkle of joy in his eye. Joe appeared more fitting to Tyr's style. Ben was also extremely excited. In many images he had seen of the knights Ben aspired to be like, they had swords that looked like the ones on Joe's sides.

"I know Cassandra taught you all how to fence. Fencing is great for a fancy dual, but I will be teaching the weapons of war and the weapons of opportunity. By the end of my instruction, you will know how to kill a man armed with a sword, with a lamp, with a bench, or something," Joe announced in his typical loud manner.

Joe taught them how to handle spears, halberds, bills, billhooks, bardiches, poleaxes, corseques, war scythes, bohemian ear spoons, waldos, naginatas, svarstaves, voulges, glaives, fauchards, and any other polearms you could think of, they learned how to use. Then, they learned about every one-handed weapon, like single edge curved swords, straight swords, fist weapons, knives, daggers, sickles, picks, axes, pickaxes, clubs, hammers, blunt weapons, short spears, and anything else that could be held in one hand and could kill somebody. Next, they learned two-handed swords, axes, and maces. Last, they learned about shields. The different types they learned were bouche, heater, buckler, kite, Viking, targe, and pavise.

Emily and Takumi were best at using smaller weapons that allowed them to move around the opponent with ease. Lucy felt best suited with a polearm. Usually, one that could be swung around easier like a glaive. Neith wasn't very good with melee weapons, but, with a one-handed mace and shield, she fared well when sparring with the others. She had a lot of strength for someone so small which was why the mace fit her best. Tyr favored a war hammer and, when sparring, was able to beat everyone. Emily was able to get a hit on Tyr once with a dagger and a buckler, but Tyr still ended up winning that match. Ben struggled with every weapon he used. The only thing he handled properly was a shield. He used a heater shield and was annoying to take down with how well he could hide behind it and deflect most attempts to get around his defense. Eventually, whoever his opponent was would just overpower him, and he would lose.

Joe would have the Deicended spar him, armed with his own swords, and they would have nothing but the items in the room with which to defend themselves. They never beat Joe in their training but, eventually, were able to last a few minutes with him. It was not like they were ever going to be able to defeat a master swordsman with a stool.

Neith asked Joe a question one day, "Are you a disciple of Justice?"

"Yes, I am. Why do you ask?" replied Joe.

"The disciples of Mars told us that we should ask you about the importance of Justice," said Neith.

"Well, alright! Justice is maintaining the law, and our law is set by George. George's intentions are for the best of human and machine. Breaking that law hurts everyone, and justice maintains the balance of order," explained Joe.

"Is that really it? I already knew that," Neith said angrily.

"Well, Justice is simple, just how I like it. Yazan and Amin are probably idiots and had trouble understanding it themselves. I mean, who's stupid enough to choose Mars over Jupiter in the first place?" Joe said, before dismissing them all for dinner.

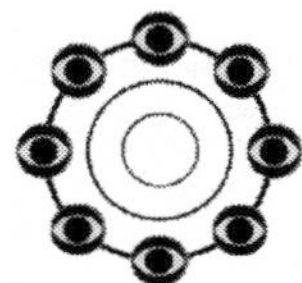

Two female Primechs walked into the classroom the next day. One was bulkier in muscle than most women with short black hair. She wore a burgundy long sleeve shirt and a coyote brown flak jack with shoulder pads, dark brown cargo shorts, and dark brown combat boots. The other woman had blonde hair that was pulled back in a ponytail. She had a white t-shirt with the sleeves rolled up and a black flak jacket, with no shoulder pads. She also had black cargo pants with black combat boots.

The black-haired woman spoke first. "My name is Bellona, and this is Anne. I am another disciple of Mars, the Arch Primech of fortitude. Anne is a disciple of Mercury, the Arch Primech of diligence. I will be teaching you all about every firearm and how to operate it."

"And I will be teaching you how to operate any vehicle. Yes, that includes tanks," Anne said.

The first vehicle they were shown was indeed a tank. They were shown the two-person operated LRHI (Long-Range High Impact) photon tank. One person drove and operated two 7.62 automatic machine guns attached to the front. The other person operated the cannon. Although it was still a tank, it sometimes worked like artillery with the range it had. Often, the one driving the vehicle would end up with nothing to shoot at. Using the photon technology is how that tank was able to get such a good range, about twenty miles. The photon is not as affected by gravity as metal would be. The tank could only get the use of its full range when either a unit on foot carried a GPMD (Global Position Mobile Detector) or, more commonly, using the satellites in space for GPS. Without any explosive firepower, going against one of these would be difficult. Luckily, anti-tank infantry weapons were invented, which Bellona was more than happy to introduce them to.

There were three anti-tank infantry weapons that were commonly used. There was the Lance rifle. It was a big metal rod that fired a rocket out and penetrated the armor of its target, then, once it had pierced the target, it would explode from the inside. The typical soldier could only carry about three shells. It was highly effective but also had difficulty hitting a moving target. Also, it was only effective against normal tanks. Some tanks were built much bigger than a car and usually had thick enough armor to not be penetrated by the Lance rifle. Another anti-tank weapon was the Hell Laser rifle.

Basically, it operated by charging it up for one devastating laser blast that did significant damage. It was the most effective weapon of the three, but it also was the rarest to find. After two shots, you would have to wait about three minutes before you were able to fire again without overheating the gun. The last anti-tank weapon was the Concussion rocket launcher. This worked by trying to breach the armor by exploding on initial impact, where the force of the concussion would annihilate the tank's armor. Bigger targets might survive the blast if it did not make direct contact but would certainly be damaged.

The Deicended learned about five different pistol types. The most commonly used pistol was the P2 semi-automatic pistol. It could be used with both 9mm full metal jacket magazines and, also, a photon heat cartridge. Nobody used it to shoot full metal jackets, but it was nice to have the option. The second gun that Bellona brandished before them was the photon revolver. Not only were the shots powerful, but it almost never needed to cool down. It would cycle its shots through the six heat chambers, allowing five of its chambers to cool while it fired one shot. Next, was an automatic pistol that only shot 9mm rounds. The fourth pistol had a larger barrel than the rest. It was a concussion pistol that was used to force items, or people, in the direction of the user's choice. Its uses were up to whoever held it. Cade had told a story to the Deicended once about someone using it on a glass bottle. Normally, the glass would have shattered, but instead. the bottle flew to the enemy and shattered against his face. The last pistol shot tracking devices that would latch into the surface of their target. It was usually not used on people since they would probably notice being shot by it.

There were also many rifles the Deicended learned about. They already knew about the extremely versatile BRF 170, that could fire many different types of rounds. There was also the BRF 172 and the BRF 184. The BRF 172 was not as commonly used as the 170. The main difference between the two is that the 172 could be used with photon cartridges. With the photon cartridge, the rifle could only be shot semi-automatically. The BRF 184 was the newest model and can use HIDP (High Impact Deep Penetration) photon metal jackets, which was a special round that could penetrate most armor. This round type was mostly found in mounted weapons. It was difficult to design a weapon that could handle that type of round. There was a rifle called the CRFF which was a compact version of the BRF 170. Another rifle would be a Concuss rifle. This rifle shot a projectile that created a concussive wave with whatever it hit.

The one shotgun the Deicended learned about was a pump-action plasma shotgun. It shot very hot plasma in a cone shape projection.

Basically, it would melt anything twenty feet in front of it. Alternatively, it could shoot HIDP rounds. Another special gun was the Arch rifle. After a two-second charge, anything within fifty feet would be vaporized. This weapon was costly to produce and, as a result, was a very rare weapon. It was not often used with mobile infantry. It was usually mounted to something that could take a hit. An infantry soldier would not be wise to use this weapon because of the fact that the rifle required the user to wear a giant battery on their back, and, once it was shot or otherwise noticed, the user became the biggest target on the battlefield. Another very unique rifle the Deicended got to use was the ABT (Aerial Barrage Targeting) rifle. The "rifle's" barrel was only physically composed of a tracking laser. The laser could be used to mark a target for an orbital barrage from the nearest weaponized satellite. The only thing that could protect someone from a blast of one of those missiles was a dome shield. Usually, an ABT user would have a pack that carried five drones. These were used in case there wasn't a satellite orbiting in the nearby atmosphere. The drones would fly high into the sky and fire charged photons which dealt a lot of damage but came nowhere near the same effect as a satellite. Only Primechs were usually authorized to use this weapon.

Neith asked Bellona one day if there were any weapons they would use to gas an enemy out of hiding. Bellona explained that chemical weapons hadn't been produced since before the Great War. Not only was it cruel to use on an opponent, but there was also a big concern for the environment when such weapons were used. A majority of old weaponry was lost in the old days. With so many years of peace, there was no reason to keep something like artillery that could fire from a hundred miles away.

There were two types of anti-air ground weaponry. There was one that fired large full metal jackets at an extremely high rate. It was called the AM (Anti-Missile) gun. The other one shot a powerful photon blast, and it was called the AA (Anti-Aircraft) gun. What made these so special was their ability to track something. The one that shot full metal jackets was used to take out missiles. The AM gun would be able to calculate the arc and distance the round would have to travel in order to hit its target. The AA gun would do the same tracking, but its photon blast was better suited for taking out larger, perhaps more heavily armored objects. Both of the guns were massive and had to be set up with stabilizing equipment before they could be used.

The Fox bikes were, by far, the Deicended's favorite vehicle to learn about. The bike was designed like an old crotch rocket where the vehicle operator leaned forward on the bike. Instead of tires, it had two jet engines where the tires on older ground traveling models would have been located. These bikes floated about a foot and a half above the ground. The back engine would rotate backward as it accelerated. The vehicle was faster than any other vehicle on the ground and could maneuver around obstacles better as well. This was going to be a useful vehicle when trying to get to a target unnoticed. It was small and hard to pick up on detectors. It was relatively quiet and could easily go through trees, using them as visual concealment.

Transport vehicles and mounted mobile vehicles came in many shapes, sizes, and designs. One notable four-wheeled vehicle was the RPC (Rapid Photon Cooling) light machine gun mounted Ox 4.5. This vehicle looked like an SUV with the back cut off and a giant gun put in place. The RPC, though more effective when mounted, also came in a smaller, hand-held, version. This gun was the only automatic photon weapon that could be carried by basic infantry. This gun worked similarly to how the photon revolver worked. It had a drum magazine that carried photon rounds inside. Once a round was fired, it required time to cool off, so the round was put on a belt of a hundred other rounds, and the gun cycled through the rounds. Although cycling through the rounds didn't cool the rounds enough. Attached, inside the lower receiver of the gun, was a coolant that would spray inside the magazine to cool the photon rounds. Technically, the RPC had infinite ammo with the photon technology, but, once it ran out of coolant, a user ran the risk of the gun exploding in their hands.

There were three main aircraft types built for battle. The weaponry put onto the aircraft was always different depending on who owned the aircraft. Dove, Owl, and Swan were the names of the three classes. The Dove was a small aircraft that only seated one person. Its cockpit and main body were similar to the Fox bike. The pilot had to lay down headfirst. The total wingspan was the same as the length of the aircraft. The Owl, which they had some experience with as passengers, was designed to hold about a squad of people. It could hold more people if it had a carrier attachment in place of some weapons. It had large wings on top that allowed it to hover if needed. The Swan was a massive aircraft designed to hold hundreds of people in it. Usually, it had enough weapons on it to make it capable of decimating a whole city.

The last lesson that Bellona and Anne taught the Deicended was about three special rifles. One was the Photon Carbine. This was a basic Photon rifle that was long and slim. It used photon cartridges and had a 1.2-second fire rate. Often, people would put optics on this gun and use it as a sniper rifle, though it could be used with basic iron sights. The second gun was commonly called the Clean Shot, a nickname due to the fact that every shot went completely through its target. This was a long and bulky rifle that was usually only effective at long range. It only used HIDP rounds. The last gun was the Revolving Rifle. It was a rifle that shot Photon blasts using the same revolving technology as the Photon Revolver. The only difference between the two was the firing rate was faster with the rifle. Also, the rifle gave the shooter much more stability and accuracy.

Right before wrapping up for the day, Lucy asked, "Why are we not learning about all of George's combative Primoid types?"

"Well, because George isn't going to be on the other side of the battlefield," Bellona responded matter-of-factly.

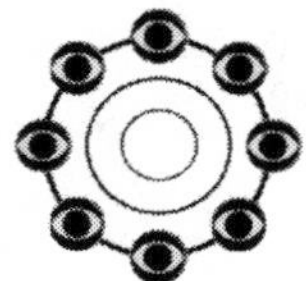

It appeared that was going to be the last day that Anne and Bellona would instruct them, but they showed up to class the next day. Walking between them was a third Primech. He wore a plain grey tunic with black boots. His arms were showing, but his left arm was missing its skin from the shoulder down. Only his silver robotic parts showed on his left arm. His right arm was covered in tattoos, which was not a common thing that people did to themselves anymore. The tattoos were a sleeve of trees and intertwining vines with flowers here and there, all in black ink. His face had no skin on his nose or his jaw. Skin began from his cheekbone and went to his forehead. He had piercing black eyes that blended well with his mechanical jaw. On top of his head was long silvery grey hair that laid past his shoulder and rested behind his ears.

"Greetings, Deicended. My name is Nicholas. I will be instructing you in the art of strategy. Anne and Bellona are here to assist me. Now, I understand that you have been working with Cade on this same topic, and, truthfully, Cade is an amazing instructor and has taught you everything you need to know about the subject. You proved yourselves through the many training simulations Cade put you through and managed to survive the island. I will only be going through one simulation, or lesson, with you. You will be facing the Primechs and twenty training Primoids." Nicholas stretched out his arms to either side, gesturing towards Anne and Bellona who stood on either side of him. "Rules are as follows: one shot and you're out. Only one member of a side needs to survive in order to win."

"Even if your power is bulletproof armor?" asked Tyr.

"Yes, that would be an element of your typical strategy that is not provided to you today," replied Nicholas.

The training room had been set up with a half-mile boundary, with two entrances, on opposite sides of the rooms, one for each "team". In between both sides of the starting points were plenty of half walls, pillars, and many more forms of cover for both teams to utilize. Everyone was armed with BRF 170s. Both Anne and Bellona equipped their rifles with extended drum magazines. Tyr also put a drum magazine on his rifle. Lucy put a scope on her BRF 170. Everyone else on the field had a standard BRF 170. Each team was given five minutes to plan their assault.

"I think we should stay defensive this time," suggested Tyr.

"Why not run up the right flank? I could provide cover fire," Lucy suggested.

"They have numbers on us, so they might maneuver to cut off your support and flank us instead," Tyr countered.

"I could create a large barricade on the left side, making them think we are going for a left flank, giving you guys an opportunity to surprise them," Emily suggested.

"What if they are able to charge and overpower you? You will be by yourself," Ben pointed out.

"I can back her up," Takumi offered.

"Then, we will be thinned out too much and will most likely be overwhelmed," Tyr countered.

"I think a defensive strategy is our best option as well," Neith said. Tyr looked over at her, pleased that she backed his idea.

"Talk about overwhelmed. They'll come from all sides, leaving us too vulnerable for defense. We are not a big enough group to cover the width of the simulation," Lucy said.

Neith had come up with a plan, "Right, I think I know a way to funnel them to one side. Emily, when the match starts, tear up the half-walls and as much cover as you can on our right side with your powers. and we can reinforce our defense on the left side. They won't be able to move on our right side without being too exposed. Lucy, conceal yourself with your powers and take up a position in the middle of the battlefield. Once they have passed you, you should be able to take out a bunch. They will likely figure that out quickly, though. Once they target you, run. The distraction from their flank should allow us to overwhelm them. If you get the chance, target one of the Primechs. The Primechs are the only ones who are actually going to be a challenge."

The Deicended agreed on the plan and prepared for the battle to start. Bellona and Anne didn't spend any time strategizing; they must have had a plan from the start. Bellona had equipped a belt that had three very mobile mechanical arms attached along the belt. At the end of the arms, there were square shields the size of her body. Nicholas came into the middle of the field. He was standing on a platform that had lowered from the ceiling. From the platform, he was able to move around the field from above.

"Begin," Nicholas shouted.

Emily concealed herself and her gun, now completely invisible to the human eye and standard training Primoids. She ran for the middle of the battlefield. The rest of the Deicended took their positions behind cover, aiming down the left side of the battlefield and leaving the right flank open. Emily ran out to the right side of the field. She concentrated and began to lift the half wall in front of her. As she concentrated harder, more of the metal covers ahead began to rise from the ground. Lifting this much was more than she had ever pulled before.

Eventually, all of the cover within a hundred feet of her was pulled up in front of her. She shuffled back off to the others and began to place the cover down, one by one, to reinforce their defenses. She was unable to place the metal cover all at once since her magnetic powers were more of a push and pull rather than complete control. In the middle of placing the metal down, the training Primoids began firing at Emily. Her back was completely open. Neith projected a violet shield to cover Emily from the fire while she finished her task.

As Lucy reached the middle and positioned herself behind some cover, Anne ran past with a couple of training Primoids. The Primoids charged the left side. It appeared that the Deicended's plan was working. The Deicended, except Lucy, opened fire at Anne as she got closer. Anne was much faster than they expected. The Deicended were not able to hit her and were distracted. Anne found cover only twenty yards away from the Deicended. They kept firing at Anne, not allowing her to get closer. Then they realized, too late, that the rest of the Primoids had stealthily caught up to Anne. They could have been picking the slower training Primoids off if they weren't distracted.

Tyr popped up from cover and rained fire on the enemy in an attempt to pin them all down in cover. A few bold training Primoids tried to move from cover and were taken out by the other Deicended. Bellona was the last of her team to get close to the Deicended. Nobody attempted to shoot her since she had her shields raised. Anne came out of cover to advance on the Deicended, and all of them opened fire on her. Anne zigged and zagged in and out of cover, untouched by the Deicended. Now in a panic, Neith used her powers, shooting violet blasts at Anne, all missing. Ben tried to melt away Anne's cover from a distance, but she would already be at the next cover before he could succeed. Takumi jumped out of cover in order to cut her off. The training Primoids fired at Takumi, and he had three shadowy arms project from his back and coil together to shield him from the rubber bullets. "Shadow Shield" Takumi yelled.

Anne charged Takumi, and he launched a fourth arm, aiming to pin Anne down. She jumped over the arm as it struck the ground, missing her. Anne planted herself on Takumi's shadowy arm and jumped again, this time flipping over Takumi. While right above Takumi, Anne took a shot and hit Takumi in his right shoulder.

Anne landed on the ground behind Takumi, "One down, five to go. You guys are making this too easy." Anne charged the rest of the Deicended. She jumped up and landed on top of the Deicended's cover. She crouched, ready to pounce on her future victims. She hesitated for a second to soak in the worried looks the Deicended were giving her. Emily and Ben raised their firearms to shoot at her. Anne went to jump but was stuck. Her eyes darted down to see that her feet and clothes weren't caught on anything. She did see her clothes begin to crystalize. It seemed that the moisture in the air around her was freezing on her clothes. Anne saw that Tyr had his hand held out, aimed towards her.

She looked down and saw the rubber bullets that Emily and Ben had fired suspended in mid-flight just a few inches in front of her. She looked back at Tyr, who was sweating as if he was concentrating as hard as he could, his face starting to turn red as if he was about to pass out. Tyr fell to the ground, exhausted, and Anne saw the bullets fall straight to the ground and felt that she was free to move again. '*Ping*'… the sound was from a rubber bullet hitting Anne on her back. "Shit! You sneaky SOB!" Anne yelled in frustration, immediately guessing the source of the shot.

Bellona, too, noticed that the shot had come from behind their position and immediately put one of her three shields behind her. Lucy, still invisible, began to take out as many training Primoids as she could. Lucy took down about ten of them before Bellona figured out her position. Bellona moved her shields all towards Lucy and shot her gun, pinning Lucy down. Lucy, unable to move, had training Primoids moving up on her position, and she knew it. In desperation, Lucy attempted to move out of her cover but was hit immediately by one of the training Primoids. With all of the training Primoids out of cover now, the remaining Deicended picked off most of the ones that remained. Emily charged out of her own cover to position herself in the left flank of the Primoids. The remaining three Primoids were quickly taken out by Emily, and now only Bellona was left. Bellona was out in the open with only her shields being used as cover. Emily fired at Bellona from the flank, and Bellona raised one shield to block her incoming fire. Tyr, who had regained consciousness, Neith, and Ben fired from their cover, and Bellona used her other two shields to block their fire.

"Ben, move up on her and melt her protection," Neith yelled.

Ben nodded, moved out of their cover, and slowly inched closer to Bellona.

"Hurry the hell up, Ben, we only have so much ammo!" Tyr yelled in frustration.

Tyr's words of 'encouragement' didn't get Ben to move any faster. Bellona moved her shield that used to block Emily's fire and shifted it horizontally. Bellona crouched and shot from under the shield, hitting Emily in the chest.

"Ben, move faster already!" Tyr screamed.

Ben finally mustered the courage and leaped over several half-walls as quietly as he could, thankfully covered by the cacophonous sounds of gunfire. He neared the Primech and melted Bellona's shield from the top, bending the metal inward. Now completely open, an astonished Bellona was struck by the incoming rubber bullets.

"Very impressive," Nicholas' voice rang out over the training room. His platform lowered to the middle of the battlefield. The remaining Deicended collected around Nicholas.

"That wasn't as bad as I thought it would be," Tyr mentioned.

"Well, you're yet to learn the lesson," Nicholas said in a conniving tone.

"Well, we are all ears, ready to listen," said Neith.

Nicholas started to blink. Not his eyes, but his body. It appeared as an image, flashing in and out. The Nicholas they were speaking to was just a hologram.

"Sorry, but this lesson will be taught through pain," Nicholas said as he came out of the shadows with a pistol in his hand. The remaining Deicended were shot. "Never show your enemy all of the cards in your hand."

"Ahh, ugh!" Neith tried to get words out of her mouth, but only sounds of pain came out. "Why couldn't you just explain the concept to us?"

"Well, I find that learning through practical application is the best way to get a message across," Nicholas explained. He jerked his head towards the door, dismissing them for the day. They gingerly made their way out of the training room, nursing their new injuries and wounded pride.

"Hey, Takumi, what did you yell out there when Anne attacked you?" asked Tyr.

"Shadow Shield. That's the name I gave that move," replied Takumi grinning from ear to ear.

"What's the point of that?" asked Emily.

"All the best heroes name their moves," said Takumi, as if this were the obvious answer.

"Whatever. Next time just use a move that keeps you from getting out so early," said Emily. Takumi laughed and playfully shoved her away. She pushed herself back and continued, "Speaking of new moves, what the hell was that, Tyr?" Everyone's heads swiveled towards Tyr, waiting for some explanation for what they saw. Tyr shook his head.

"I really don't know. I mean, it was like the first time that I used my scales, I just thought about wanting to stop her, and she stopped. I guess that I froze her or something, made her so cold she couldn't move." he mused. Ben took a step closer to him and mentioned, "Yeah, maybe, but it wasn't just her that was frozen. Emily and I both shot rounds that were caught in the area that you were affecting. And they were, like, suspended in midair and, when you let go, they just dropped."

Tyr shook his head again. "I really don't know what that was. Maybe, if I can use it more, I will understand it better." The group nodded and proceeded on their way back to their quarters.

The next day, a new Primech was in the classroom waiting for them. This Primech didn't look anything like the other Primechs. This one wasn't even shaped like a human. There was a big silver ball for what appeared to be its head. The ball was on top of a thin cylinder with ten holes peppering its exterior. From the cylinder, sprouted three long, pointed legs. The whole thing stood around six and a half feet tall.

"People refer to us as Lind. We are a disciple of Moon the Arch Primech of Charity," Lind said. A face appeared as a projection on the silver ball, a blue holographic projection with only basic details to the face. "We will teach you how to handle the fog of war."

"The fog of war?" Takumi asked.

"Yes," the voice was from Lind, but it sounded different. Also, another face had appeared next to the first one. The face had a slightly calmer look to it, not like you could tell much apart from the faces, because of the lack of detail. "Fog of war is the uncertainty regarding one's own capability, adversary capability, and adversary intent during an engagement, operation, or campaign."

"Of course, the training will be different simulations." A third voice and face appeared, except this one was feminine. "We have come up with what we think will be most effective way of properly demonstrating the fog of war."

Out of one of the holes in Lind's body came a mechanical arm with four prongs at the end and maneuvered like a snake. The arm grabbed a mysterious orb off a table. Lind raised it and slammed it on the ground. The orb was made of glass and a thick white smoke emerged from the crash. "That was tear gas. We will sit here in the tear gas for ten minutes before we head over to the training room."

"I think I want Nadin back to teach us," Ben said kind of jokingly, but still serious since nobody in their right mind would want to sit in tear gas.

Every day, Lind made some new and creative way to mess with the Deicendeds' heads. All of Lind's voices appeared kind of monotone. They figured out that there were a total of four different voices and faces. The training seemed kind of cruel at times and, sometimes, the Deicended thought they were honestly going to kill them. One day, it put the Deicended in a twenty-foot by twenty-foot box and sealed them in before the wall burst into flames. Slowly, the flame crept towards them as they huddled in the middle. The only reason they made it out was Tyr using his ability to slow down molecules. It was the same ability he used to freeze Anne in place before. That was what he mainly used it for, freezing people or things in place by slowing their molecules down. When the molecular structure of something is slowed down, it becomes cold.

So, by slowing the molecules down around the wall, the fire was extinguished.

One day, the Deicended were in what they thought was a normal training simulation, until water started spewing on the ground from the ceiling. The simulation had them set up in a two-story building,

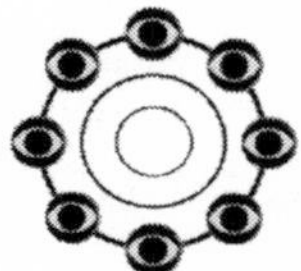

and the first floor was filling up quickly. Neith and Ben were on the first floor. Takumi went up to the hole and plugged it up with his shadowy arms. The water stopped flowing for a second. Then, three more holes opened from the ceiling, spewing water. Ben and Neith rushed to get to the second floor. As Neith got to the stairs, one of the Primoids laying on the ground quickly powered up and grabbed Ben. Neith didn't notice as she got to the top of the floor. Ben went to melt the arm holding him in place.

As he concentrated and heated the area around the Primoid's arm, the water rose to Ben's thigh. When he heated the area, the water boiled and burned Ben. Ben struggled to escape, but it was no use. The water rose above his head and began to reach the second floor. "Where's Ben?" asked Takumi.

"I don't know; he was right behind me," said Neith.

"We have to go down and look for him," Takumi said frantically.

"No, we can't go down there. It's too dark. Whoever goes down there will just get stuck," said Lucy.

"Lind! Shut down the exercise!" Emily screamed in desperation. "Lind! Shut down the exercise!" Emily shouted again, this time with Takumi.

Lind wasn't responding.

"Damn it! Takumi, give me one of your arms, I'm going down. Pull me up when I tug," said Emily.

"You can't go, Emily. We can't afford to lose two people," Tyr demanded, blocking Emily from going down.

"We're not losing anyone, Tyr! Now move before I make you move!" Emily shouted at Tyr.

Tyr groaned in frustration but stepped aside. Emily grabbed a shadowy arm coming from Takumi's back. While holding onto the arm, Emily began to submerge herself. Emily swam down, reaching around and trying to feel for anything. A few times, she had bumped into a wall, but eventually, she felt clothes. Not sure exactly whose clothes they were, Emily had no choice but to assume it was Ben. She grabbed onto his arm and tugged Takumi's arm. Emily could feel Takumi pulling, but they weren't moving. Emily tried shaking Takumi's arm hoping he would get the hint to stop pulling. Luckily, he did. With Ben running out of time, Emily searched his body to try to find something that would be preventing him from moving. Emily felt around until she found the arm holding Ben down. As hard as Emily could, she pushed using her magnetic powers. Finally, Ben was released. Emily tugged Takumi's arm again. Rapidly, Takumi pulled them back to the surface. Ben immediately coughed up water and took a breath of fresh air again.

"Cughh aghh ttthhankks," Ben barely managed to get the words out.

"We're not out of this yet," said Emily.

The water on the second floor was rising faster.

"Okay, I'm done with this," Neith said as she held her arm out. A violet glow lit up in front of her. The glow grew in size after a few seconds until Neith released the energy forward. The violet beam launched forward, towards the wall. It collided with the wall, exploding into pieces and leaving an opening to escape the trap they were in.

Tyr leapt down through the hole, helping Emily and Takumi down first, before reaching up for Neith and Lucy, with Ben coming down last. As he did so, those who were already down whirled around at the sound of one of Lind's voices congratulating them on their escape.

"What the hell was that, Lind?!" Emily shouted at the Primech.

"If he had a clear mind, he would have managed to get out of the situation," replied Lind, emotionlessly.

"He was going to die! None of this is worth us dying!" Takumi screamed at Lind.

"If he does not learn to resolve things himself, he might end up being the death of one of you," Lind responded with what they thought almost sounded like disdain. Neither of them could think of anything else to say. Emily stormed off before Ben had a chance to thank her for rescuing him. His ears burned hot with shame, and he couldn't help but dwell on Lind's words, knowing they were right.

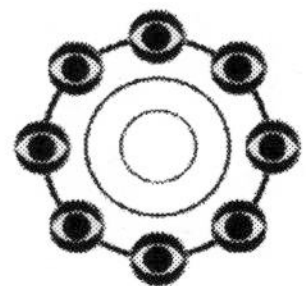

After a few more weeks of Lind's torture, Cade showed up to class instead. "Congratulations on completing all of the lessons from the Primechs. You all are ready to be considered for missions in the service of George. As you know, the primary reason for your intensive combat training has been to prepare you to confront the

Hawk, but it will take some time for us to track him down. You will continue to train until we locate him."

5

A Short Break

"We have been searching for the Hawk for all the years you have been training with no success," Cade addressed the Deicended. "He has popped up here and there, ambushing different power plants, factories, and other facilities. Though he has not succeeded like the day he blew up your school years ago, he still manages to escape without a trace. I have decided, due to all of your hard work and completion of your training with the disciples, it is time to take a break. As we do not currently have any leads on our target, there is no sense in keeping you in a holding pattern while we wait. We are heading back to the City for a few days of leave. Specifically, we are heading to the Detroit section."

"Oh, yes!" Neith cheered.

"I heard Detroit is an awesome part of the City," Tyr mentioned.

The City was how everyone referred to George's domain. This took up most of what used to be the United States of America and a little bit of Canada. The City was a fitting name since the entire city was, in fact, urban, with little to nothing resembling suburbs. The rest of the world wasn't really inhabited by humans. Nobody saw the point of travel since, if they really wanted to see natural sites, they could visit them via virtual reality. Some parts of the continents were inhabited by machines and limited groups of humans for the purpose of resource collecting. These were usually small facilities, and humans only went there if it was a task they were given by George. Australia, of course, was only inhabited by those who wished to stay away from the City according to George.

"Detroit has the best plays," Lucy chanted in excitement.

"Who cares about that? Detroit has the most famous arcades and comic stores," Takumi said with the biggest smile on his face.

"We will have plenty of time to do everything you want to do, children. We will stay as a group though. You may be "young adults" now, but, as you are to be vital in George's efforts, you cannot wander off on your own," Cade said. "Now, everyone, pack for the trip. You will need to wear some civilian clothes. I will bring a store's worth of clothes down to your quarters tonight. Pick whatever you want."

The Deicended headed back to their room. As Cade said, there were six hanger racks filled with a massive amount of clothes. The Deicended went to go select their outfits for the next day. Neith picked out a light purple dress that went down to right above her knees. The dress had two-inch-thick straps that went around her shoulders. Purple had become one of her favorite colors since it looked like the glow of her powers. The dress fit well for her thin stature. Years had passed, and she was still the smallest of the Deicended.

Tyr wore a green collared shirt with khakis, which somehow had remained the most standard male look for years now. Tyr was the tallest of the Deicended and was also the widest. Since coming to train in George's facility, he had put on significant weight in muscle. From the looks of him, one would think he could lift a car with no effort.

Takumi dressed even more properly than Tyr, wearing a nice black blazer. He also had dark blue pants with a light blue button-down on. A black half tie with white lines going across laid on top of his shirt. With those clothes on, Takumi appeared just skin and bones. However, Takumi had very lean muscle and was, in fact, rather fit.

Emily picked out a dark blue zip-up hoodie and wore a plain black shirt with blue jeans. Emily was the tallest of the females. She was rather thin but had more shape than Neith. She also had very defined muscles.

Ben wore a red shirt with a character from a movie called Shift Silver Chronicles. The character was a monstrous purple and green humanoid with patches of fur in some places and tentacles in other places. Over the shirt, he had a black jacket made of nylon. There was a burning phoenix imprinted on it coming down the shoulder to his right arm. He was decently tall, but not as tall as Tyr. For all the training Ben did, he was still skinnier than what he should be for his size.

Lucy picked a white spaghetti-strapped tank top that showed her midriff. She had baggy black pants with little black sandals on. She had grown to have the most predominant feminine features of the three girls and was average height for a female.

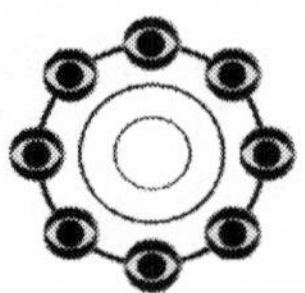

The next morning, the Deicended gathered in the hangar where an Owl class aircraft flew in. The craft landed, and the doors opened. Four Primechs walked out. One was Cassandra, who gave them all a nod of recognition and a slight smile, another was Joe, who gave them a nonchalant salute with two fingers, another was Anne, who waved at them, and the Deicended didn't recognize the last one. They were all dressed normally, except for swords at their sides, along with holsters carrying a P2 pistol.

"Hello, Deicended, it's a pleasure to see you again. Let me introduce you to John. He is another Disciple of Kindness who is going to be the one to fly us to Detroit," Cassandra said. Ben noted that she sounded nicer than she previously did, maybe because she wasn't their instructor now.

"Hello, I'm John," said John.

"Hey, John, do you have some sort of tactic specialty or something like Joe or Cassandra?" asked Takumi.

"Haha, no. I'm just here to fly ya," said John. His flight suit attested to the accuracy of that statement, and he looked a lot more human than the Primechs they had encountered in their training, but Neith felt certain that he, no doubt, had some degree of cybernetic enhancements, perhaps for vision or reflexes. She continued to theorize privately and hardly noticed the rest of the conversation as it continued.

"Most Primechs don't actually participate in combat-related tasks. The ten of us that trained you are kind of a rarity," said Joe.

"Well, it's a pleasure to meet you. Where's Cade?" Lucy asked.

"He's not coming. Joe, Anne, and I are going to be chaperoning you all," said Cassandra.

They all boarded the aircraft, and it left the hanger, climbing above the cloud line, about thirty thousand feet in the air. The flight was boring with the exception of the lovely sunset that colored the sky. Shortly after night fell, as they descended and broke back through the clouds, the lights from the city became visible. None of the Deicended had been to the Detroit district before and had not been near any part of the City since they left their less densely populated home district for George's training facility years ago. The site was more beautiful than they imagined. There was so much life. The giant skyscrapers were illuminated with neon lights and screens advertising so many things they'd never seen before. There was apparently a new flavor of fruity zest snack'ems. This part of the City was right next to the historic Great Lake that had the world's biggest freshwater filtration plant on it. The buildings were so big, it was difficult to see the ground. Detroit was also famous for having the most float parks. Float parks were platforms that were above the skyscrapers that usually contained either sports parks or special shopping sites.

The aircraft took them to a float park that was specifically designed for parking. "Okay, where do you want to go first?" Joe asked.

They had decided on the flight what they were going to do on their first day. After hours of trying to convince Neith to wait until the next day to go to the library, they agreed that the first thing they were going to do was head to the arcade. Then, they would get some of Detroit's world-famous ice cream. Lastly, they were going to head out for shopping.

John stayed on the Owl as they got onto the float park transit aircraft. The Deicended glued their eyes to the glass, looking at the beautiful city. One of the most pleasant sights for them was the people of the City. It had been so long since they had seen other people interacting, not since the day of the bombing when they left their school. Through one window in a building, they could see a friendship blossoming. In another window, actions of kindness and charity were exhibited. Every window was like a movie for them to see.

The aircraft landed at the arcade. When the doors opened, the roaring sound of machines and fun pierced the Deicended's ears. They ran inside, excited to start a game. There was one game with almost sixty kids playing at once. They all sat in a lounged back chair with VR goggles on. The sign above said 'BLAST BLOCK'. Under the sign, there was a screen of all the players inside. They were all floating inside a globe-shaped arena. They were firing lasers at each other with the palms of their hands or blocking the lasers with a shield only slightly bigger than their fist.

"Oh, hell yeah! Let's play this one," Takumi shouted.

"Yeah, I'm down," Tyr said.

"Oh, please no. How is this any different from what we have been doing for the past couple of years?" asked Neith.

"Well, this time, we aren't going to be shot by any rubber bullets, and we're obviously going to crush the competition." Tyr said with a grin, showing a youthful eagerness that was rare for him.

She threw her hands up in defeat and said, "Fine, but, when we get to the library, we are staying for however long I want."

Once the current match ended, the Deicended found a seat and put the goggles on. When they put the goggles on, directions on how to play the game popped up. The directions explained that, in a zero-G sphere with rocks floating in and around the sphere, the only way to move, besides rotating, was to use the rocks for momentum. The directions also explained that, in order to make a shield pop up, they would have to hold their fist closed. The shield was only slightly larger than their fist. In order to shoot a laser, they would open their hand. To shoot another laser, they would have to first close their hand and then open it again. Once hit anywhere on the body, they would get a game over. Once the directions finished, a counter started down from ten in the middle of the arena. Once it hit one, they popped into the sphere.

A little disoriented, Neith grabbed onto a rock floating nearby. She looked up and saw that a laser was heading right for her. It missed and hit the rock she was perched on. The rock started moving in the direction it was hit. Holding on, Neith rotated until an enemy player was right in front of her. She aimed her hand and opened it, hitting the enemy player in the back. The player blinked away. Neith projected herself off the rock, and another player noticed her. The player shot at her, but she blocked it with her left hand. Neith responded by firing both hands. The player slid their hand from side to side to block the shots. The player successfully blocked one shot but was hit by the other. *I think I'm getting the hang of this,* Neith thought.

Ben, unable to orient himself, flew into a rock and bounced off of it. The bounce slowed his rapid rotating and gave him a bit more control over his trajectory. A player shot at Ben, and Ben blocked with his left hand. The player continued to shoot one shot after another, and Ben blocked every single one of them. Another player went to join in on trying to hit Ben. The shot was coming from below Ben. He wasn't going to be able to block it.

Right before the shot hit Ben, another laser collided with the one about to hit him. It was Takumi. Takumi blasted three shots at the first enemy. The player didn't even block one shot. The second player shot multiple lasers towards Ben again. Ben rotated and blocked every incoming shot. Takumi landed on a rock right next to Ben. Takumi immediately fired at the second player, taking him out. Takumi rapidly fired shots from both of his hands, trying to hit any player he could. When a player turned to hit Takumi, Ben would rotate and block for him. Then, that player would be barraged by shots from Takumi. "These players don't have any idea what they're up against!" shouted Takumi. Ben grinned over his shoulder at him, and they turned their focus back to keeping their heads on a swivel for any enemies.

Lucy started the round unfairly surrounded by way too many people. Nobody was specifically aiming for her though. After a series of blocks, Lucy propelled herself off a rock towards another rock. She landed on the other rock, which was located right next to the highest edge of the map. Lucy went behind the rock and peeked over the top. She smirked and began sniping one player after another. The enemy players began to notice Lucy taking out a large number of them and began to swarm her.

"Don't worry! I'll get you out of this," Emily shouted as she came hurtling towards the enemy players. Emily appeared as if she was spinning out of control, yet she dodged every incoming blast and hit a target every time she fired a shot. Lucy was almost impressed.

"I appreciate the help, but I would have managed," Lucy said.

Emily noticed that there were almost no players left in the field that weren't the Deicended. "Well, if you say so," Emily replied, firing a shot. It struck the rock Lucy was hiding behind.

The rock spun Lucy around, revealing her back to the enemy. "Shit, Em…" Lucy shouted in frustration as she was shot by a random player and blinked away. Emily immediately rotated and eliminated the enemy.

Soon after, there were no other players left besides the Deicended. At once, they all jumped towards the center of the map except Ben. After blocking and blasting at each other for a second, they realized Ben was hiding and, no doubt, strategically waiting for the last player. "Wait a minute, let's get Ben for hiding," Takumi suggested. They all turned their heads toward Ben with devious smiles on their faces.

Ben felt the sting of betrayal but understood Takumi's reasoning. After all, this was just a game. The four remaining Deicended launched towards Ben. They all fired their lasers as fast as they could. All Ben could do was try to block the shots. So, Ben did just that. It was almost confusing how he could block all the incoming shots. *I'm better at protecting myself than taking action to help others,* Ben thought.

While still en route to Ben, Emily aimed her right hand at Tyr and shot him. As Tyr was hit, he thought to himself, *What? No, not before Ben!*

Emily took another two shots at Neith, but Neith blocked the shots, her mouth wide, offended at the betrayal. Takumi turned and took a shot at both Emily and Neith. Neith got hit and blinked out of the game. Emily rotated, dodging the shot. Takumi grabbed a rock to stop moving. Takumi continued to fire at Emily until the rock rotated him out of sight. Emily dodged all of his shots except for a few that she shot out of the air. Emily changed her target back to Ben and fired at him. Ben continued to block the shots. Ben saw an opening and let his guard down to make a shot at Emily. When Ben took the shot, a laser came from a different direction, hitting the shoulder he fired from. It was Takumi who hit him. The shot that Ben made completely missed Emily. Takumi and Emily were now the last ones left. After shooting Ben, Takumi was again out of sight behind the rock.

Ben lifted his goggles off and climbed out of the VR chair. Neith, Tyr, and Lucy were watching the screen that was displaying what was going on in the game. Ben walked up to his friends and noticed that they weren't the only ones staring at the screen. All of the previous players were watching. Not only were the players staring, but so were random people in the arcade. Everyone was glued in anticipation to see who the victor would be. Ben overheard a group of people talking about the match, "Can you believe how good they are? Who do you think is going to win?" Ben wondered whether everyone had been paying attention the same way while he was playing and if they thought he too had skill.

"Hey, Ben! Your ability to block so consistently was impressive; it was like firing at a wall," said Tyr.

"Thanks," Ben said, but thought to himself, *I should have Tyr's ability. Being able to block anything coming towards you with thicker skin. I would be so much more useful with his ability*.

"You don't have to always be evaluating, Tyr. We aren't in a training simulation or mission. You can just enjoy things sometimes," Neith mentioned. Tyr stiffened and turned his eyes back to the screen, as did the other two Deicended. Lucy hadn't taken her eyes off of the screen since Ben had come out of the goggles.

Takumi shot the rock he was hiding behind, launching it towards Emily who had let herself be caught out in open space. Emily shot the rock too but was unable to stop it from flying towards her. Emily tried to rotate away but was clipped by the rock and a shot from Takumi hit her in the side. Emily's visor showed her "Game Over." Takumi's visor showed "Victor!" As Takumi took his visor off, he was shocked by the roaring applause. "Oh, I didn't realize anyone was watching," he said. The impressed crowd quickly dispersed as they were distracted by the many games in the arcade. His comrades came over to him, led by a storming Emily.

"Hey, that was a cheap move, Takumi," Emily yelled.

"Oh, please, like you wouldn't have done the same?' Takumi asked.

"Ugh, yeah, you're right. I would have,' Emily confessed, crossing her arms and looking down at her shoes, really annoyed at herself for leaving herself so exposed.

"Well, that was a pretty quick round. What else ya want to do while we have time in the arcade?' Tyr asked.

"We could use this time to go to the library," Neith mentioned.

"I guess, but we're already here. It would be a waste of time to go now, Neith. Plus, we already agreed we would go tomorrow," Lucy said.

The Deicended walked around a bit to see what other games there were to play. Takumi, Ben, and Emily found a racing game they wanted to play. Lucy and Neith wanted to go take pictures in the picture booth, so they separated, and Tyr went with Lucy and Neith. Tyr often chose to spend time with Neith when he had the chance. Neith didn't seem to pick up the hints that Tyr was interested in her, which was fine with him for now.

The racing game that Takumi, Ben, and Emily had picked was another VR game. When the Deicended sat in the chair and put the goggles on, they were put into a plain zone with different vehicles to choose from. They were in the room together. This game was only going to be the Deicended playing against NPCs (Non-player characters). There was a variation of vehicles to pick from that were all modeled after vehicles from years ago. People in today's age didn't often have personal vehicles. Most transportation was done through public means. Ben picked a sleek racing car, red in color. Emily picked a hot rod muscle car that was all black. Takumi picked a green racing motorcycle. Once they picked their vehicles, a bunch of screens displayed different maps they could race on.

"Should we select random?" Takumi asked.

"No, look at some of those maps. I don't want to end up playing on that sailboat dreamscape map," Emily said.

"What about that volcano map? It looks like there is a dragon in it that tries to kill you," said Ben.

"No more volcanoes after the island," Emily demanded.

"Right, well what about the night forest map," Takumi suggested.

They agreed to pick the map and voted for it. They were transported to the forest along with thirty other NPCs. A fifteen-second timer showed in front of the drivers. The Deicended took the time to inspect their competition. There were other sport bikes, a few muscle cars, and fewer sports cars in the arena. There were two monster trucks that they shouldn't have to worry about too much on a forest map. There were three cruiser bikes lined up as well.

The counter hit one, and a howl came from the woods. Then, the time hit zero, and all of the cars took off. Having generally faster vehicles, the Deicended were quickly up towards the front of the pack. There were various trees in the path that the drivers had to dodge. One of the sports cars attempted to ram Emily into a tree. As the car collided with her, she braked before hitting the tree. Emily turned her wheel into the car's back end, causing the car to spin and hit the tree instead of her.

"Ha ha, that's what you get for scratching my ride," said Emily.

The first turn was coming, and a muscle car prepared itself to slam into Ben as they went around the turn. Takumi was weaving around him and noticed the vehicle's movements. "Heads up," Takumi shouted at Ben.

"Oh, no no no," Ben yelled, not sure how to avoid the situation.

Emily got her car in between the two of them. Her car, having more weight than Ben's fiberglass racing car, wasn't destroyed on impact. Takumi popped a wheelie and hit a button on his bike, activating an ability of the bike. The back wheel of his bike shot out, projecting him into the air. Takumi went flying over the NPC's car. He revved his engine, and his back tire slammed through the windshield and into the driver, causing the driver to phase out. Takumi landed on Emily's hood and rode off it, back to the ground. The car with no driver slowed down and veered off the road.

"Thanks, guys! Look ahead; the map is changing," Ben shouted.

The Deicended focused on the road since, as Ben had said, the map changed to a denser forest. Emily had the most difficulty trying to stay ahead of the other cars. Takumi took the lead. As they left the dense forest, there were crates in their way. It was part of the game to drive through them, as hitting them unlocked weapons on their vehicle. The Deicended each hit one. Emily unlocked an old two-barrel sawed-off shotgun, with an ammo box that spawned on the seat next to her. She picked it up and shot a sport bike that was right next to her. The shot caused the front tire of the bike to blow out and made the bike flip over.

She whooped and searched for her next target. Takumi unlocked a single one-sided, straight-bladed sword. The sword popped out on the right side of the bike, and he left it there till he would need it. Ben unlocked two machine guns that popped out of the hood of his car. He grinned and itched to use them.

A monster truck started to get closer to their miniature pack. It ran over a few cars behind them like they were nothing. It must have also hit a box because it was equipped with a missile launcher. The monster truck targeted the Deicended, launching a series of missiles at them. They flew into the sky before coming down towards their targets, ready to explode on impact. Ben and Takumi both dodged all of the shots that were coming their way. Emily saw one she knew she wasn't going to be able to dodge. Right before it hit her, she pulled a lever releasing her hood. The hood went up for a second and snapped off. It flew right over her car and made contact with the missile. The missile exploded and shook Emily's car, but she was fine. The monster truck prepared for another volley.

"We need to do something about that thing," Emily yelled.

"I'll take care of it," Takumi yelled back.

Takumi grabbed the sword out of his bike. Right as a missile was about to launch from the monster truck, something suddenly jerked it back. Takumi looked back and saw that what looked to be a wolf bigger than the monster truck had closed its jaws over the bed of the truck and was ripping the metal body to shreds. The wolf had glowing purple eyes and white fur. The monster truck drove off, somehow separating itself from the wolf. A sports car with two mounted buzz saws on the hood drove towards the wolf's feet. The second it got close; a pale purplish tentacle burst from its fur. The tentacle suctioned the back of the car and flung it off the map. Takumi felt sick when he saw that the wolf was covered in the grotesque tentacles popping out of its fur. Even its tail was a huge tentacle instead of a normal fluffy dog's tail.

"Uh, maybe this map wasn't a good idea," Takumi said.

"Hey, I said let's go against a simple dragon but nooo," Ben shouted.

"Seriously, Takumi, you're the one who picked this map," said Emily.

"Yeah, well, if I knew about the tentacle wolf, it would have been a different story," said Takumi.

Ben hit the brakes on his car to get behind the wolf. Once behind it, he began shooting it with his mounted machine guns. The wolf howled in pain and whipped its tail down in an attempt to hit Ben. Ben swerved to the right, missing the tail. The wolf then bumped into a tree, knocking it down in Ben's path. Ben turned his wheel even farther right and hit a button on his dash. The car boosted sideways. It wasn't enough; Ben hit the tree, almost spinning out of control. The side of his car was badly damaged, and the machine gun on the left side was knocked off. The wolf targeted Emily. Emily was in front of it, and the wolf was slowly gaining on her. It was feet away from Emily; she could hear its breath in her headphones when she grabbed her gun and aimed it over her shoulder. Emily pulled her trigger, giving the beast a nice face-full of buckshot. The wolf howled again in pain. This time it turned and jumped into the thick of the woods off the track.

The three remaining cruiser style bikes caught up to Ben, determined to completely destroy his already significantly damaged car. One of them was equipped with a thin spear. The other two appeared to have chained flails. The one with the spear went to Ben's left side while the other two went to the right.

"Ah, guys! Help," Ben pleaded.

Takumi and Emily fell back to go help Ben. More of the weapon crates were ahead of them. Takumi got one and so did Ben. The bikers and Emily did not hit any. The bikers closed in to hit Ben. He activated his weapon. Flames came bursting out the sides of his car. The bikers swerved away to keep their distance from the flames. *That was convenient*, Ben thought. Emily rode up next to the bike on Ben's left side. The rider on the bike took his spear and thrust at Emily. Emily ducked forward, dodging the spear. She reached back, grabbed the spear and began tugging with the NPC to gain control of it. Emily turned her wheel right into the bike. The muscle car ran over the bike like it was a speed bump, taking the NPC down with it. Emily managed to keep a hold of the spear when it went down. It shrunk to the length of a handle of a sword, fitting her hand perfectly

"Thanks for the present," Emily said to the dead NPC.

Takumi got behind Ben. "Jump ahead," Takumi yelled. Ben had let the flame throwers go on for too long, and the flame had died. The jump was right ahead, and the length was unrealistically huge. Right before hitting the jump, one of the bikes turned towards Ben's car. It swung its flail and hit the back right of the car. At the end of the flail was a ball with spikes on it. The ball stuck into the side of Ben's car and detached from the chain. The biker slowed down and fell back behind Ben. Ben looked back and saw a blinking red light on the ball. To the rider's surprise, a sword popped out of its chest. Takumi had ridden up and stabbed the rider. Ben hit the ramp and flew into the air. After a second of airtime the ball, a grenade, blew. With Ben's car flying out of control. Ben opened his door and jumped out in desperation. Luckily, he landed on the back of Emily's car.

"Hey! You're going to have to find your own ride," Emily yelled at Ben. They landed the jump, and Takumi rode up beside them.

"I got you, Ben, I'll distract this NPC while you take his ride," Takumi suggested.

"Easier said than done," Ben shouted.

"Here, take this,' Emily said as she threw him the spear she stole.

Ben caught the spear, and it expanded to its full length. Takumi rode to the right side of the NPC bike rider. He waved his sword to get its attention. "Come here, dumb-dumb," Takumi yelled at the NPC. The NPC spun its flail, riding towards Takumi.

Emily drove as close as she could to the bike. "Now, Ben!" Emily yelled.

Ben jumped and drove his spear through the rider. The rider phased away, and Ben landed on the bike. The bike started wobbling out of control, but Ben was quickly able to steady it. He revved the engine and shot forward, spearing a couple of other NPCs through their windows and wove around their rudderless cars that were then veering off of the track.

Emily thought to herself, *Ben seems oddly confident on that bike. It's nice to see him like this.*

Now, a minivan, followed by another monster truck, approached them, pulling up on Takumi's right. *Ha, that is the most stupid design for a vehicle I have ever seen,* Takumi thought to himself. The door to the side of the minivan slid open, and a giant gun stared Takumi right in the face. "Shit, shit!' Takumi yelled. He slammed on his breaks as a huge laser came from the minivan. Takumi barely dodged the laser and swerved behind the minivan. *Okay, maybe not so stupid,* Takumi thought. The minivan's back door opened and sticks of TNT fell out. Takumi hit the button for the power-up he unlocked earlier. Rockets came out of the sides of his bike and gave him a major boost, riding past the TNT safely. Takumi rode along the right side of the minivan. He took his sword and dragged it from the back tire to the front. The minivan tumbled over and crashed.

There was still the monster truck left, and the finish line was coming up. There were a few other NPCs near the truck that were also trying to shoot it down. The monster truck was equipped with a shield completely covering its body. *Well, that's going to be a real pain,* Emily thought. Then, the wolf leaped out of the woods. The wolf landed right on top of the monster truck, smashing it into the ground. The wolf ran past every vehicle, smashing a few on its way. The wolf stood in front of the finish line and turned around to face the oncoming NPCs and Deicended.

A couple of the vehicles that were attacking the truck before decided to target Ben. First, a sport bike came for Ben. The rider got four feet away from Ben before being met by the end of his spear. Next, a car went to get in front of Ben to try to slow him down. Ben immediately stabbed his spear into its back tire. The car spun out of control, and Ben accelerated past it.

Emily approached the wolf and went to the left side of it. A few tentacles attempted to hit Emily and missed. As she passed the wolf, its tail came down to hit her. She shot her shotgun at the tail, and it recoiled. Now, there was nothing between her and the finish line.

Ben went to go under the wolf. The wolf snapped at Ben, and he drove his spear into its mouth. The wolf bit down on the spear and whipped it out of Ben's hands. Ben had made it under the wolf, at least until a tentacle from its chest came down and smashed Ben off his bike. "Noooo!" Ben yelled while the goggles came off his head from losing the game.

Takumi activated the rocket boost again. He also hit the button to bounce himself off the ground. The wolf bit towards Takumi and missed as he went over the wolf. Takumi rode down the back of the wolf, dodging and slicing the incoming tentacles. At the end of the wolf, Takumi rode up its tail, flying into the air. Emily was still in front of him. Takumi stood up on his bike while still in the air, barely a few meters behind her. He grabbed his sword and lunged towards Emily. *Another game is mine,* Takumi thought. Emily casually reached back and, never taking her eyes off the finish line, shot her gun at

Takumi, deleting him from the game. Emily crossed the finish line as "Victor!" read on her visor.

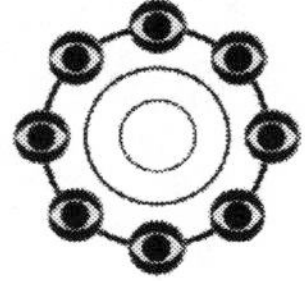

Tyr, Lucy, and Neith arrived at the photo section of the Arcade. Emily pointed out an AR (Augmented Reality) Arcade room. It looked like a room that led to a big warehouse. There were a few options for locations. There were rooms of current landscapes that were far from the City. There were locations from history. You could visit other planets in the solar system. Also, there were completely made-up places, usually a famous fantasy location. All three of the Deicended had different opinions of where they wanted to go. Lucy wanted to go look at the mountains in New Zealand, under the stars of night. Tyr wanted to go to a historic battle area. Neith wanted to go anywhere that was rich in historic events.

"I'm sure we can find something we all agree on. We could probably take a fantasy location out of the options," Lucy suggested.

"Yeah, I think we could find somewhere with a historic battle. That would probably be rich enough in history for me," Neith said. Tyr fought back a smile from Neith agreeing with him.

"What about the Alps?" Lucy asked.

"Oh, yes! So much history there. Also, Tyr, don't worry. There was plenty of fighting there," Neith said.

"Sounds good to me," Tyr said.

The Deicended walked to the clerk for the warehouse. He was a human, looked to be a young adult. The three asked for tickets from the clerk, and he cheerfully provided them.

"Okay, everyone, the Alps will be in Door Four. You get twenty minutes in the location. An employee will get you when your time is up. Come back to me if you would like to purchase any physical copies of your pictures from your Social Bees," the clerk explained to the Deicended.

"Thanks, but we don't actually have Social Bees," Lucy explained.

"What? Who doesn't have Social Bees? You guys are, like, twenty or something. I never heard of someone at your age without one," the clerk said.

"Well, we don't have any. We used to, but not anymore. Is there anything we can do instead?" asked Lucy.

"Yeah, sure! We actually have cameras to lend in case this happens. They're usually for…you know…older folks, but you can borrow them too, I guess. You'll have to buy physical copies if you actually want any pictures, though," the clerk mentioned. He did not seem too concerned about concealing his judgment of their failure to keep up with the times.

"That's fine," Neith said, not caring in the slightest about his opinion.

"Okay, give me a sec. I'll have to go look for them, I'll give you guys one each. I'll be right back," the clerk said. After two minutes, the clerk returned with three cameras, and the Deicended set off to the Alps. Passing by the rooms, there were pictures of the places displayed on the outside of their doors. The first door had a picture of the pyramids in Egypt. Neith almost regretted their decision when walking past this door. The second door had some castles from Germany. The third door was a picture of Mars. Passing that door, Tyr thought, *I don't get why people want to fill out their task there. It's nothing but a boring desert. Hopefully my brother comes back from there soon.*

As the fourth door slid open, the Deicended could only see a bright light. Once they stepped into the room, the lights dimmed, and it was as if they were transported to the mountain itself. A cold breeze surrounded them. It was painful, none of them had ever been so cold before, except that one time with Lind during its so-called 'cold-weather training'.

A voice came from the system, "Temperatures in this location are set low to simulate the real-life location. If you would like me to adjust the temperature back to normal, just say 'increase temperature'."

"Increase the temperature," Neith said, shivering out of control.

"Oh, c'mon, the cold makes it feel so much more real," Tyr said.

"Who cares? Look at this view!" Lucy said.

They were in between mountain peaks, surrounded by snow that covered their surroundings all over the mountains nearest to them and all of the peaks that they could see stretching out around them. The mountains, as tall and beautiful as they seemed, were a little difficult to look at with the light bouncing off the snow, shining into their eyes. Looking over the mountains, they saw a sea of clouds floating over the valley. There were rivers leading into the valley and countless trees as far as their eyes could see.

"I have never seen so much land before," Neith said.

"This is cool and all, but it doesn't really look like a battlefield. I guess I kind of wanted to see a fortress or something," Tyr mentioned.

"Oh, Tyr, this is way cooler than a fortress, this is God's creation. We've seen plenty of man-made creations," Lucy said. Neith and Tyr looked at each other, perplexed at hearing religious sentiment.

"This is only randomness Lucy; God didn't create jack," Tyr responded.

"Yeah, I know, but is there much difference between the two?" Lucy suggested "I was mostly saying it as a figure of speech. Let's take pictures of us with the valley behind."

The three grouped together and Lucy set her camera to float slightly above them to take a photo.

"Hey! Fun fact, guys! Did you know that people used to climb these for fun! Could you imagine walking the whole distance from the bottom to here, just to take a photo like we are," Neith said as the photo captured the three with Neith mid-conversation.

Man, Neith looks amazing out here, Tyr thought to himself. He hadn't heard a word that Neith had said. He was distracted by the way the artificial breeze was playing with her dark hair. Neith's words phased through him. He chastised himself and forced his attention back to the AR experience.

"Well, let's see if we can climb to one of these peaks," Tyr suggested.

They began to climb the taller of the two peaks and, surprisingly, the AR system allowed them to climb. They had done some climbing training before, but this was a little different. It was difficult, with the snow, to move their feet. As they got closer to the top, Neith slipped, and Tyr caught her.

She was obviously the smallest of the group, but he was astonished by just how light she felt in his arms. She smiled up at him, and his heart skipped a beat. *I'll always be there for you*, Tyr thought to himself as he held her.

"Good catch," Lucy said, snapping Tyr out of his thoughts. He realized he was still holding Neith and moved to set her down on the snow-covered rock.

"Thanks, Tyr," Neith told Tyr and put her hand on his arm before resuming her climb. Tyr followed behind, almost hoping that she would slip again.

They continued to the top and eventually reached it.

"I think the only cooler view would be the real thing," Lucy said.

"I don't know, Lucy, this AR program is pretty real," Tyr replied. "This is the most amazing view I have ever seen," he said while staring at Neith from behind.

Neith stood quietly staring out to the vast sky. *Someday, I will learn the story of everything I can see from here and even beyond that*, she thought to herself.

"Time's up! We hope that you have enjoyed your experience!" A voice from the system controlling the AR room said. Everything in sight became brighter and brighter until everything around them was white. The terrain lowered until the floor was level and they were able to just walk out. A door appeared and, upon opening, led them back outside.

Outside the arcade, Anne, Cassandra, and Joe had been waiting for the Deicended. First, Emily, Ben, and Takumi came out and waited with the Primechs. About five minutes after, the rest of the Deicended came out.

"Now, let's get your ice cream," Joe said eagerly.

The group went back to the float park transit aircraft and took it back to where they had parked. They got back on the aircraft with John and flew to one of the many giant skyscrapers. The skyscrapers that were big enough had parking ports in the middle of the building. John took the aircraft into one of these ports. Inside the building was a giant mall. It was flooded with more people than the arcade. The busiest store just so happened to be the ice cream shop.

"Do we have to go to the most crowded location in Detroit?" Emily asked.

"Listen here! This is the best ice cream in Detroit. If we are getting ice cream in Detroit, we are getting *the best* ice cream," Joe said in his obnoxiously loud voice.

"What do you care about food for? I thought Primechs didn't need food," Ben stated.

"We don't need it, but we still get hungry," Cassandra replied.

Even being the most crowded store, the line was still under a minute long. Everyone ordered different flavors. Joe felt the need to get himself two double scooped ice cream cones because he couldn't choose between four different flavors. They all sat on a park bench located near the edge of the building. This area of the building was open with a breeze. The opening was about thirty feet high and had a great view of the rest of the City. There was a four-foot glass wall along the edge to prevent people from falling over.

"I can't remember the last break I've had," Cassandra said after taking a lick from her strawberry ice cream. She was very careful eating the ice cream, making sure none of the sugary ice touched her clothes.

"Are all Primechs usually busy," Ben asked.

"Yes, we have a very important job being the Arch Primoids' disciples. As you can imagine, the selection process is quite difficult, so we don't get much help to carry out our tasks. I enjoy it though," Cassandra said.

"I enjoy being busy, although more breaks for ice cream would be appreciated," Anne said, which made the Deicended laugh.

"So, tell us about your trip to the arcade?" asked Cassandra.

"Well, first, we played this game called BLAST BLOCK," said Tyr.

"It was crazy! We wiped the floor with all the other players. For a while there, we thought nobody was going to be able to take Ben down. He blocked every single shot that came towards him," Takumi said.

"Yeah, and Emily was in there refusing to block a single shot and still almost won," said Ben.

"Who ended up winning?" asked Anne.

"Takumi won," said Lucy.

"Impressive little guy," Joe commonly called people little since he usually towered over people.

"Yeah, but I kicked his butt in the next game we played," Emily interjected.

"Yeah, that was a good shot," Takumi replied. She smiled at him and promised him a rematch the next time they made it over here.

"How did you fare in that game, Ben?" Cassandra asked.

"I didn't do too bad. I almost made it across the finish line, but I got taken down by a tentacle wolf," Ben replied.

Joe nearly choked on one of his ice cream cones. "A what wolf?!"

"A tentacle wolf," Takumi repeated after Ben.

"Oh, right, one of those," Joe said sarcastically, not truly understanding what they just said. "What about you, Tyr? How did you do in the game?"

"Actually, Neith, Lucy, and I went to the AR location generator. We went to the Alps in it," Tyr said.

"Yeah, here's the picture," Lucy grabbed the picture they bought from her pocket and showed the Primechs.

"Aw, that looks cute," Cassandra commented. Lucy and Neith blushed from the comment while Tyr tried to hide his face, embarrassed at being called cute.

"Did you fall down or something? You look like you just woke up with your hair in a mess," Ben commented.

"Hey, it's not that bad," Neith replied.

"Yeah, no, it looks normal… like you just woke up," said Ben. The table shared a laugh while Neith glared at Ben like she normally did when he said something stupid.

Takumi noticed some people around giving them strange looks after Ben made that comment. Then a few of the people went and found a peacekeeping Primoid. That Primoid looked right at their table and walked over. "Excuse me I have been notified of a violation of Rule Five — Fair treatment of others will be enforced. Nobody is above anybody in any sense of status. Nobody will cause anyone to feel less than anyone else. Please come with me for remedial…" the peacekeeping Primoid was talking to them until Joe turned around and the Primoid noticed who was at the table. "I apologize, Primechs. I did not see you earlier. Have a nice day," the Primoid said and walked off.

The Deicended looked at each other strangely. They were confused by the situation. They understood that Ben had technically just broken one of George's rules, but they were accustomed to being able to break the rules over the years past. Also, maybe because so much time has passed, but they didn't remember Rule Five being so strictly enforced.

Emily stood up and stretched after finishing her ice cream. She walked over to the edge of the park and leaned on the railing. Looking over the side, she thought, *This City is pretty awesome*. She noticed a kid nearby using a telescope to look at the City. After the kid stepped down, she decided to look through it. It was cool for her to see all the interesting things about the City close up. Emily looked through it and could see into one of the rooms in the building across from them. She saw a bunch of people exercising and lifting weights. She turned the telescope a bit to see another building. It appeared to be an apartment building. On one floor, an apartment was having a party. She could see a group of friends smiling and laughing with each other over what was no doubt a delicious meal. In another, there was a couple watching TV.

Another room showed a family eating dinner. Emily turned the telescope again to look at the street below. For the most part, there were only a few people in the street. Most people in Detroit used public transportation instead of walking. She turned to another street, and there were more people walking in between buildings and some cars and buses too. She turned again and looked at one of the alleyways out of curiosity. It was empty. Emily scoped out another alleyway and found the same thing, it was empty. She turned to one last alleyway and saw something. Emily focused the lens and saw what looked like the figure of a person. The telescope couldn't zoom any further. *Stupid old piece of trash,* Emily thought. She tried to block out the sounds of the other Deicended and Primechs chatting and concentrated as hard as she could to try to make out what she was seeing.

Finally, she made out some of the features. It appeared to be a man standing next to a grate. He had something covering his face. It looked like an old rag was wrapped around him. One of his boots was missing the front toe area. *This doesn't make any sense,* Emily thought. She took her eyes off the telescope and rubbed them. She had strained her eyes from squinting too hard. She looked back into the telescope, and the man was gone.

"See anything cool?" asked Anne, who had come to lean on the railing by the telescope while Emily had been looking for sewer people.

Emily, startled a bit, responded, "Oh, no. Well… no, it was nothing. I just saw some people walking below."

"Huh, the City sure is pretty, isn't it?" Anne asked.

"Yeah, I guess it is. Is that why you came over here, for the view?" asked Emily.

"No, I needed a break from Joe's goofy ass. You're more my type of people; I'm a fan of your snarky attitude, and you're pretty badass during the training simulations," said Anne.

Emily smiled, not knowing how to respond to such clear praise. "I am?" she asked.

"Hey! Emily, Anne, we're about to head out. Let's go," Joe yelled out to Emily.

"Ugh, can't even catch a second. Well, let's go," Anne said to Emily while waving for her to follow her back to the rest of the group. Emily trailed behind her, unable to keep a slight smile off of her face.

The group walked into an elevator to go to the top floor of the skyscraper. The top of the building had most of the shopping outlets. After a swift ascent, the elevator dinged and the doors slid open, allowing the group to pour out onto the walkway.

"After one hour, we will meet back here, and we will go check into the hotel arranged for us," Cassandra said.

The girls and guys separated and ventured to different stores. The guys made their way into an average looking clothing store. After five minutes of looking around, they left the store. Takumi pointed out a comic book store, and they walked over to it. Tyr wasn't into comics, but it was more interesting to him than clothes.

The girls found a clothing store that specialized in dresses. Emily realized she made a poor decision going with the girls, but only had to make it an hour shopping for dresses. She believed she would make it out alive. After collecting twenty dresses each, Lucy and Neith went to go try on the dresses while Emily waited outside the dressing room on a couch.

"I've never been too big on dresses, but they are the most comfortable thing to wear, which I love," Lucy called, her voice carrying over the dressing room's half walls.

"I could never wear pants again for all I care," Neith said.

"What's the point of getting clothes? Not like you guys are going to get the chance to wear these again any time soon," Emily mentioned.

Neith and Lucy thought about what Emily said for a second; there was a lot of truth in what she had said. A second was all the time they took, though, before going right back to trying on the rest of the clothes. While they had this time off, they might as well enjoy themselves.

Emily had been staring off into the distance when Cassandra startled her, having rushed into the store with her signature grace. She did not look as poised as she did normally. "Get your clothes back on, now! We have to go; there is an emergency. Meet me and the others at the elevator when you are done," Cassandra shouted to the girls. Emily thought that Cassandra looked as close as she had ever seen her to panicked.

Emily ran back with Cassandra. After only a little bit, all of the girls were waiting at the elevator. Soon after, Joe came running back.

"Where did the boys go? I can't find them in any of the stores," Joe shouted in distress.

"Did you check the comic book store over there," Lucy suggested. "I've got ten bucks saying they went to look at some nerdy comic books."

Joe ran over to the store, shouting inside, "Let's go now! We need to move it!"

The boys all ran out after him, and the group took the elevator back to their aircraft. John took off at a speed that definitely would not have been cleared for civilians. Once in the air, Joe began to explain, "Something has happened at the power plant. Somebody reported a suspicious character, and, when my guys arrived at the scene, this suspicious character attacked them and is on the run right now. I've been called in to support. This guy isn't alone, and some of them appear to have powers. If our suspicions are correct, this might be the Hawk!"

"Then, make this thing go faster!" Emily shouted. She wondered to herself if this had something to do with the man she saw in the alley way herself.

"Believe me, I'm going as fast as I can," John responded.

6

The Day it Happened: Neith

Her eyes shot open early in the morning as her alarm went off. *I need to re-read my homework and make sure it's good as I can make it,* thought Neith. She got out of bed, yawned, and stretched her arms out. After doing her normal routine of going to the bathroom, brushing her teeth, and taking a shower, Neith sat at her desk in her room. She opened a book report she had been working on for a while and took a look at it. *That's not due for another week. I should look over AP Dead Language class. Let's see, for my Spanish unit essay, the characterization of Pepe el Romano in 'la Casa de Bernarda Alba' would be that of a driving force in the growing disparity between the Alba sisters. He is the abstract manifestation of that era's barbaric mindset that women needed husbands to take care of them and the lengths that they would go to in order to secure a husband. I am so glad that we have George to take care of us now, so no one needs to be subservient to anyone else.*

Once her homework was undoubtedly perfect, she realized she still had about another hour before she had to leave. She walked over to the TV, turned on the history channel, and, to her delight, one of her favorite documentaries was on. It was 'George Over the City'. It was a period piece that told the amazingly inspirational details of how George was able to save humanity from the brink of extinction during the Age of Cain. Glued to the documentary, Neith did not notice her sister until she smacked her in the back of the head.

"Hey there, sleepy! You're going to be late for school; you better hurry," said Isis. She was wearing a blue dress and black socks. Her hair was jet black like Neith's hair. She didn't have anything to do for the day, like go to school. She was old enough to do a task now, but today was her day off. The only thing she needed to do was make sure her sister got to school, usually one of the easiest jobs ever since Neith loved going to school, but sometimes she would get distracted by something else educational. Their parents had always taken extra time with their tasks. They were cognitive scientists that helped George with the human mind. Since they gave so much extra time to their task, the family was afforded more luxuries than the average citizen, not that Isis or Neith ever really used the luxuries. Part of the reason their parents spent so much time away was also because they had to travel to different facilities of George's outside the City.

"Oh, darn! Did I miss the bus?" asked Neith.

"Not yet. You still have a chance to make it," said Isis.

Neith ran back into her room, grabbed everything she needed for the day, and ran out in a similar plain blue dress as her sister.

At school, she rushed to her class and was the first one in her seat. She took her books out of her pack and laid them on her desk, in the order she would need them, aligned with her pencils. She took the chance to look over her homework again before the teacher walked in. Her first class of the day was biology. The teacher came in to inform them that today was going to be the day that they would dissect a frog. Neith opted out of participation. Though she was interested in learning about the insides of a frog and getting a real perspective on how a biological being operated, it kind of grossed her out. She loved animals and, although this one was dead, cutting something open wasn't something she could wrap her head around doing. The teacher gave her the option to either go to someone's study hall or go to the library. Of course, Neith chose the library, her second home.

In the library, she wandered the science section, but couldn't find anything that she either hadn't read before or that didn't involve a topic she was already extremely familiar with. *Ugh, this library is so small. Why don't they let us access the etherbrary while we are at school?* Neith thought. The etherbrary was an archive, accessible to everyone through cloud services that George provided. It had pretty much every book anyone could think to read. For some reason, George found it better for kids to stay away from electronic reading while at school that wasn't a textbook. The school limited the library size because they didn't believe any student would be able to read all of the content, and it usually only included topics crucial to a youth learning. It wasn't every day that a Neith came into a school and could breeze though most of the books.

Neith walked over to the history section to look for a book and, after about one minute of looking, realized that she had definitely read all of the history books. She grabbed a book about the reign of Queen Victoria of England, even though she had read it twice already, and laid on the ground next to the bookshelf. She adjusted her arm to get comfortable and began to read the book. Her eyes began to close from the boredom of re-reading a book. Once, on the third or fourth page, her eyes shut for a solid three seconds. She put the book down and rubbed her eyes. She looked up and noticed a crack in the wall under the bookshelf.

Upon closer inspection, she saw it wasn't a crack. It appeared to be an opening, like someone had cut a hole into the wall and closed it up. She crawled over to it. She pressed on the spot, and, sure enough, it fell backwards with dust spewing out of the space. A little timid, she reached her hand into the darkness and felt something hard. She pulled it back, and she had a book in her hand. It was layered heavily in dust. It took a couple swipes to get the dust off and make the title legible. *My Walk Through the Eschaton* by William P. Henry, Neith read. Excited at the sight of a new book, she hastily opened it. For a second, she was about to put the book down. She had read about the Eschaton so many times, she didn't care too much to read another book about it. Except, this book was written by someone with a last name. She hadn't read a book about the Eschaton by someone who was so old. So, she humored the idea and began to read it.

The first page read, 'An autobiography of my trip through what we have recently started to call the Eschaton. I am a thirty-seven-year-old man now, and, when I lived through the end of the war, I was a young boy, not even a teenager yet. Sadly, I was born into the wrong side of the fight. My parents were part of the resistance. My turn to George's side was not a quick one; I have done things I am not proud of, and I question the morality of those decisions. Even though I was just a child, I hate myself when I think about what I did. Before I get into my story, I feel it necessary to talk about what has been going on since the war has ended.

Suicide is one of the most important issues today. My sister, who had followed me to George's care, has succumbed to that horrible fate. I know I should have probably waited until the end to tell you that, but I want you to know that going into my story, learning about how wonderful she was and, in the end, to learn about it as if everything was for nothing. I'll say this now, she was the reason I made it through. I have a family now whom I love and cherish, and I owe that to my sister and George. My family, like many others, are suffering, but don't see it. We are happy, but my family won't do anything. They only watch the old stories that have been archived. There is enough entertainment for a thousand lifetimes. My wife and children are extremely overweight and can't move to live life. If they continue the way they are going, they will die differently, but the same as my sister. I'm not saying this is the same for every family, but there are many like mine. George needs to come up with a solution to save us. If my family were to leave me, it is possible my fate could mirror my sister's.'

The bell rang, startling Neith and signaling her to start heading to her next class. She put the book down and started to run. She stopped and went back to take the book with her, but it wasn't there anymore. *Did someone grab it already? Did I just dream up that book?* she thought to herself. She shook her head in confusion and looked around. *What was that book anyways? I never heard about a different issue than suicide during the age of Cain. The author spoke about rampant obesity as if it were such a big issue, but then, why would I have never heard about it? Why would it even be covered up in the first place? It was a good thing that George fixed that issue as well, if it was even real. I wonder how they were so overweight though. I thought dur…* The bell rang again, signaling that Neith was about to be late. She ran full speed, awkwardly, through the hallways and narrowly made it into class.

She took her assigned seat near the window in her math class. Math used to be one of her favorite classes, but not anymore. It was way too easy for her. When she was younger, Neith would study the more advanced algorithms and formulas that were meant for the older students, usually by sneaking her older sister's textbooks. After a while, she felt like the only way she could go forward from where she was in mathematics would be to come up with a new impossible equation or solve Pi, but the thought of solving Pi wouldn't be as interesting to her as discovering a new species or curing a disease.

The teacher gave them what she thought was an extensively difficult and long test, but Neith finished it with half the class time left. She spent the rest of the class looking at her AP Dead Language class homework again. She was going to turn it in early after lunch, and she was so excited for the teacher to read it. He was one of her favorite teachers. He spent his life dedicated to learning about the dead languages, and that was the type of dedication to education that Neith really appreciated. He even developed a Spanish accent from all of his studying. It was the most unique attribute Neith had known in anybody.

The bell rang, and now it was time for the only other thing that Neith cared about besides education, food. Although school food was kind of gross and unhealthy, the greasiness made it enjoyable for Neith. She was ahead of most people in the line and grabbed two hotdogs covered in ketchup and mustard. With the hotdogs, she was given steak fries. They were not her favorite, which was curly fries, but were still pretty awesome.

She took the food and went to the library. Since food wasn't allowed in there, she sat down with her legs crossed just outside the door and scarfed down the food. Once done, she rushed into the library to find the book again. The library was pretty packed, and the history section was on the far end of the library. After shuffling through a bunch of people, she finally made it to the history section. *I hope I can find it*, she thought.

She walked into the aisle where she had last seen the book, and, right as she was about to look under the bookshelf, a loud bang rang in the library. It sounded like someone dropped a very large book, but it was coming from outside the library. She stood up, and other students began screaming and running out. A library faculty member was at the exit, screaming at people to get out of the building. Neith was more confused than ever but listened to the instruction. Once outside, there was a crowd of students crying and screaming, some were covered in dust, some were stained red with blood. *What's wrong with them?* Neith thought. *Did a fire get out of control?*

Emergency vehicles and Peacekeeping Primoids swarmed around the school. Parents came to pick up their kids from the school, and Neith sat down and took out her AP Dead Language class homework to review it again. Eventually, Isis came driving up quickly, her car screeching as she slammed on the breaks in front of Neith. "Let's go, Neith! Get in the car," Isis yelled urgently. Once in the car, her sister hugged her tightly. "I was scared something happened to you," said Isis.

"Yeah, what's going on?" Neith asked.

"How the hell have you not heard?" asked Isis. "A bomb blew up in your school! You didn't ask anyone outside what was going on?"

"It's just hard to believe someone could get a bomb into one of George's schools. Hey, I found this book…," Neith was cut off.

"You're worried about a fricken book? Neith, we are going home, and you are probably going to take a break from school for a bit," said Isis.

"When do you think I will be able to go back?" asked Neith.

7

Contact

The Owl class aircraft that John was piloting came into view of the hydro plant. There was a stark contrast between the buildings nearest to them and the buildings ahead of them. They were all completely dark. Besides that, nothing seemed off about the plant itself except the twenty peacekeeping transports outside.

"Wow, the building is amazing. Can we see this after the library?" Neith asked. The building was right next to the massive Lake Erie. There wasn't much to the design of the building, but even though it was not as tall as the nearby skyscrapers, it was still massive.

"Stop worrying about the damn library, Neith," Emily said in an annoyed tone.

The aircraft lowered to the ground. As everyone got out, one of the peacekeeping Primoids approached them. The peacekeeping Primoids stood seven feet tall. They were these massive, almost emotionless Primoids. Their faces had visors over them, and their bodies were silver, covered in two-inch steel. They were similar in appearance to Yazan's body, but much more slender.

"Sir, the suspects have locked themselves in the power plant. We have a Scorpion inbound to penetrate the building," the peacekeeping Primoid reported to the Primechs.

"What happened to the building's defenses?" Joe asked, appearing to be the one in charge of the situation.

"We shut down power coming into this sector. The building's defenses were shut down before they even arrived, sir," The peacekeeping Primoid replied.

"Is there any information on the perpetrator?" Joe asked.

"Information is very limited, sir. We have yet to identify the perpetrator. Witnesses reported an individual carrying a firearm, which is what alerted us. The perpetrator does not appear to be alone. The motive is believed to be that they intend to poison the filtered water in the hydro plant, or in some other way hold it for ransom," The Primoid related to Joe.

A Dove class aircraft came flying in, hauling something below it. This something was a Scorpion Primoid. The Dove class aircraft dropped the Scorpion off and flew away. The Scorpion was balled up. It had four legs that expanded out and lifted its tall, cylinder-shaped body off the ground. Its tail folded out and hung above its body just like a real scorpion, except, rather than a venomous stinger, it had a photon blaster on the end of its tail. This photon blast would charge up for a second before firing. The blast would be powerful, like a blast from a tank. Two miniguns came out in the front, and it had its belt of ammo leading into its body. The Scorpion approached the door to the hydro plant.

It charged the photon from its tail, producing a loud humming noise. The shot fired, flinging the Scorpion's tail back from the recoil. The photon slammed the entrance, making a loud crashing sound and producing a cloud of smoke. The miniguns on the Scorpion began to spin. Once the guns reached full speed, bullets flung from it. Some of the rounds fed into the guns were tracer rounds in order to see where it was firing. The rate of fire was so fast that the tracer rounds almost made a straight line of red to their destination. The Scorpion blasted into the entrance for about ten seconds and stopped. A couple of peacekeeping Primoids shot cannisters into the entrance, releasing tear gas.

"Is it possible they escaped below the plant?" Emily asked Joe.

"Not at all. There is not an entrance into this building large enough for a human, except the main entrance," replied Joe.

The Scorpion began to walk closer to the new entrance it had created.

"Sir, scanners are picking up a signal from the lake. One Owl class aircraft incoming," one of the peacekeeping Primoids told Joe.

"Shoot it down! There shouldn't be anything flying over the Great Lakes!" Joe ordered.

"Sir, all of the lakeside defenses in this quadrant share power with the hydro plant," said the peacekeeping Primoid.

"Shit. Scorpion, focus on the incoming aircraft. You're the only thing here right now with a weapon strong enough to do any damage to that thing," ordered Joe.

The Scorpion shifted its body to aim upward, but the Scorpion wasn't really designed to handle air combat. The Scorpion charged up its tail, ready to release the blast at any given moment. It also started to spin the mini-guns, ready to fire.

A breeze hit the Deicendeds' faces as the tear gas flowed out of the building. "That's definitely the Hawk in there. He has the ability to summon wind. He must be forcing the tear gas out," said Anne.

An aircraft flew over the top of the building, and the Scorpion fired. The photon blast was on target, but nothing exploded. The aircraft that the Scorpion shot at kept moving, and they saw the blast flying in the distance as if it never actually came in contact with anything. Ben and Takumi made eye contact with one another, both visibly confused. A second later, two more identical aircraft flew over the building. Then three more, then four. The Scorpion and the peacekeepers opened fire on all of the aircraft as they came into view, but nothing was happening to them. All of the shots just seemed to go through the aircraft. From the opening in the hydro plant, a sound rang out. Tyr thought that it sounded familiar, and, after a second, he and the other Deicended recognized the sound. It was a shot from a Lance. It pierced the body of the Scorpion and then exploded. The Scorpion broke into pieces, flying all over the place. Full metal jacket rounds and photons fired out of the same opening. The peacekeepers took cover where they could find it. Neith put her arms up and projected a big violet transparent shield, covering the whole group from the fire. A couple of the enemy's aircraft appeared to have landed.

"Finally, back up is here," Cassandra said as ten Dove class aircraft came in from behind the skyscrapers, armed with high powered, rapid firing photon blasters and piloted by other peacekeeping Primoids. The Doves fired at the enemy aircraft, but there were more coming, and not one of them showed any impact from the ground or air attacks. There had to be a hundred illusions by this point, and nobody could find a real one. Neith thought that at least one of them must be real, why else would they bother with a fleet of decoys if not to protect something, but it was impossible to tell which unless someone got a lucky shot.

"We are going to need more support if we don't want him to get away. Get a Swarm sent over Lake Erie to cut off his exit," Joe commanded.

Three grenades bounced on the ground, thrown from an unknown source. When they exploded, smoke came bursting out to cover from the entrance to the building all the way to where the Deicended were standing. A few of the enemy's aircraft landed. Shadowy figures came running out of the building, with the smoke masking their appearance. They all ran to the same aircraft.

"Shoot that one now!" Joe yelled.

All of the peacekeeping Primoids began to fire at the single aircraft. As the photons from the photon pistols hit the aircraft, a blue translucent shield appeared where the shots would hit. The pistols had no effect on the shield. Neith took her shield down, and the Primechs began to fire their pistols helplessly as well. What they now knew to be the real aircraft began to take off. Neith charged her energy, forming a violet orb in the palm of her hand. After about four seconds, she released it, missing the real aircraft when it suddenly lurched out of the way of her shot, rising skyward and spawning a few more illusions that split off to either side and began weaving around each other, performing more evasive maneuvers. Neith's blast smashed into the hydro plant, causing explosions from inside. Smoke poured out from where the blast hit. The Doves attempted to follow the aircraft but kept firing at illusions.

"We can't let it get away," Tyr shouted.

"Don't worry, there's a surprise waiting for them when they try to go back over the lake," Joe said reassuringly.

"Well, I'm sure there would be if they were heading that way. Not even the illusions are heading towards the lake," Neith noted.

"They are heading towards those buildings," Lucy said, pointing towards the city. Joe swung around to confirm what they were saying and, sure enough, the aircraft had swung around to head further inland.

"Activate the building defenses in blocks 756 to 768," Joe said while putting his finger to his temple in order to specifically communicate with George.

All of the skyscrapers near the illusions armed themselves, releasing hundreds of defense photon blasters. Also, even more back up had arrived with Owl class transport ships. The ships themselves did not have many defenses on them. They steered clear of the illusions' paths, which seemed to be heading to a particular building. The Deicended's jaws dropped when they saw the illusions fly through the building, while the real ship crashed into it, sending debris flying down to the street.

The Deicended, Joe, Anne, and Cassandra boarded their ship with John and headed towards the building the enemy crashed into. The Dove class defense aircraft circled the building to make sure the enemy didn't fly back out. One of the transport ships flew a couple stories above the crash site, broke the glass, and dropped off fifteen peacekeeping Primoids. Another Owl class aircraft did the same thing but a few stories below. John flew his ship below with that same aircraft.

Joe turned to them and began briefing them. "Okay, keep an eye out for suspicious characters. The Primoids, Cassandra, Anne, and I are going to scan every face that comes through here. They're not going to escape this time. Be on your guard and stay close to us; consider this your first unofficial mission," Joe said. The aircraft maneuvered as close to the shattered window ledge as it could, and Joe slid the door open. He was the first to jump across the small gap into the building with his weapon up and ready. Cassandra went over next and covered the other direction. Anne stayed inside and made sure all of the Deicended made it over alright, before leaping in herself.

They felt the wind on their backs as the aircraft moved away from the building to wait nearby. There was only one large staircase allowing access between the floors. There were elevators, but the cars were in the open with glass walls, so there was no sneaking past George's forces through the elevator shaft. A wave of people started stampeding down the stairs as the alarm in the building went off and flooded past them. Cameras from the ceiling dropped down, also scanning the faces of everyone who passed. A few people with hats or some clothing blocking their face were stopped by the Primoids or Primechs, and their faces were scanned. There was no way for anyone to get past without having their faces scanned and searched in George's database of every citizen in the City. After about thirty minutes passed, the crowd began to thin as a couple hundred people already passed them. Everyone was obviously very on edge by this point. The Primoids had their heads on a swivel and were checking dozens of faces every few seconds.

One man bumped into Tyr. With the huge crowd this was bound to happen. Tyr looked at the man as he passed him and was confused at what he saw but looked again and realized it was just a normal person. For a second, he thought he saw the hawk shaped mask, but upon a closer look he saw a normal face. It was a crazy thought, no doubt brought on by the tension of this situation. There was no way that none of the many eyes and cameras wouldn't have noticed a man in a mask before he even got to Tyr. The crowd thinned to only a few people running down at a time.

"If they were to come down this way, they would have done so with the crowd of people," Anne mentioned to the group. Soon after, no one came down the stairs. Everyone waited for five minutes after the last person came down the stairs. Two peacekeeping Primoids walked up the stairs to sweep the floors.

"Someone, give these kids weapons," Joe demanded. A couple of the peacekeeping Primoids walked over to their aircraft that had landed inside, picked up a couple of spare P2 pistols, and handed them to the Deicended.

"Nothing up here, sir," A peacekeeping Primoid shouted down the steps. The Deicended and eight more peacekeeping Primoids walked up the steps. Anne and Joe went ahead of them, and Cassandra watched their rear.

"Four more floors to go. They could be on any one of these floors," Joe mentioned. Joe put his finger to his temple. "How's it going up there?" Joe asked, talking to the squad of Primoids above the crash site. He listened for a moment before raising his voice to update the whole group. "The other squad is moving down towards the crash site. We'll meet them there. Let's keep moving."

The squad moved up to the next floor and, again, found nothing. They moved to the next floor up and, again, nothing. "Has there been any activity outside?" Joe asked with his finger to his temple again. He then listened again.

"Nothing reported. Still, stay frosty; they have to be on one of the next two floors," Joe informed his squad. Two Primoids walked up the steps to the next floor. Again, there was nothing. The next floor was the crash site. The two Primoids walked up the steps. There was a little bit of smoke, but, for the most part, it had cleared up.

"Well, shouldn't there be something shooting at them by now?" Emily asked.

"Maybe they died in the crash," Takumi said.

"Criminals like these guys don't die so easily," Joe said.

"Sir, maybe the Deicended should stay behind on the lower floor," the peacekeeping Primoid suggested.

"They can handle themselves. Is it clear for us to come up?" Joe asked.

"The crashed aircraft is here, and there are also some dead civilians," the Primoid said.

"Surround the ship. With the shields down, we will be able to shoot through the doors. We'll kill them right here and now," Joe said eagerly. Neith took up a position near the dead bodies. Instead of taking aim, her curiosity got the best of her, and she inspected one of the dead bodies. Blood was pouring out of the neck. Neith looked even closer and noticed what appeared to be a cut from some sort of blade. This man was not crushed or killed by blunt force trauma. Someone had taken a knife to him. *Those idiots! How could I be the only one who thought to look at the damn bodies*, she thought.

"Don't…," Neith was saying before being cut off.

"Fire!" Joe shouted.

As the barrage of photon blasts hit the ship, it exploded. Neith projected a shield as fast as she could. She was able to cover the Deicended, Anne, and Cassandra, but Joe and the Primoids were outside of the shield. The explosion quickly engulfed the aircraft and blew out all of the windows. The floors above the blast and below began to crumble. Behind Neith's shield, Cassandra and the Deicended fell through the crumbling floor. With a quick reaction, Takumi extended his shadowy arms from his spine and grabbed them all. By the time Takumi grabbed Tyr, his armor was already out. Takumi had everyone in his arms and, before he projected more arms to stop their fall, the speed at which they were falling had already slowed to a safe pace. Looking up, Takumi noticed it was Neith that was slowing their fall. She was floating down, just above them. Neith's eyes and hands were glowing the usual purplish violet of her power, the same glow that was surrounding them. Debris from the floors above came crashing in their direction. It was halted by Neith's shield and fell to the side. They slowly descended to the stable floor below them and landed safely. Neith came down a few seconds after them. Landing gracefully before sinking down to her knees. Tyr rushed over to her and supported her so that she could stand.

"Well, that's new," Takumi pointed out about Neith's ability.

"I'm not sure. I might have always been able to do this. I didn't try anything new," Neith said.

"Where's Joe?!" Ben asked, looking around.

"I, ah… I don't… think I got my shield in… front of him," Neith spoke, trembling from exhaustion and from realizing the fate that must have come to their teacher and friend.

"Over here!" Joe's obnoxiously loud voice rang out towards the group. Their heads snapped over and saw what could be seen of Joe sticking out from under a large pile of rubble. They ran over to him.

Cassandra and Anne immediately began examining him. Anne put her finger to her temple and called for their transport to meet them.

Neith kneeled by him and immediately began apologizing for failing to protect him.

"You think a puny little blast like that could take me out?" Joe waved her off with a severely damaged metallic arm.

"Well, yeah. I mean… have you seen your body?" Emily asked.

"Well, as soon as one of you gets this rock or whatever this is off of me, I'll be fine to keep fighting," said Joe. His chest was caved in and pinned down by what looked like a big piece of the floor. He was in a completely different place from where he was when he shot the aircraft. The only parts of him that remained attached to his torso were his head and one arm. Even his lower waist was ripped away. The only thing he had left of his synthetic skin was a small patch around his eye.

"Lucky the rock is in your chest and not your head," Cassandra commented.

"Oh, please! I would still be fine," Joe stated.

"Well, lucky for you, I guess. Unlucky for us that it didn't happen that way," Cassandra said.

"Hey, now!" Joe yelled.

"I'll grab his head and we will get a search team up here to find out any information we can. As for you Deicended, we have to head back to the training facility. It has been deemed too dangerous for you to be roaming about. We need to be ready for the next time this happens," Cassandra instructed.

"Wait, we aren't leaving right now, are we?" Neith asked.

"Yes, we are. Immediately," said Cassandra.

"Ugh! I was promised a library," Neith demanded.

"Maybe next time, we have more important things at hand," Cassandra said.

"This is bullshit!" Neith yelled, but she admitted defeat to the fact that it may take forever before they ever got to the library, much less had a chance to visit the City again.

8

The Dawn Edge

"Welcome back, everyone," Cade said.

John dropped the whole group off except Joe who went to a repair facility. Walking into the training facility, they found the whole layout was completely different.

"While you all were gone, we changed the facility to work better as an operation center. There is still a training section, but we did move a lot. Also, you will all have your own individual rooms," said Cade.

There was a shared look of relief on everyone's faces. They were great as a team and as friends but sleeping in the same room was too personal. Often, the Deicended would let their frustrations with training or the state of the living quarters out on each other at night, leading the rest of the group to get frustrated. Individual living spaces would be a very welcome change.

The Deicended, Anne, and Cassandra walked over to the new operation center. It was filled with screens, computers, and a table built to coordinate plans.

Cade began to debrief them, "Some of the peacekeeping Primoids' memories have been recovered. We have been going over the information for quite a while. It seems there was another

Deicended with the Hawk. There is no way those illusions were produced by a machine. After running a data analysis program to determine the faults in the projection, none came about. The only way to produce that number of fake aircraft, would have been to have drones flying around, projecting the image, and, surely, we would have hit at least one with the barrage we fired at them. We were also able to recover some footage of the dead civilians. We scanned their faces and discovered that their faces had already been scanned by the Primechs. They must have killed the civilians in order to take their identities and flee. Upon finding the aircraft, you let yourselves get too eager to catch the man, except Neith. Good job on keeping a clear mind and checking the bodies. Although most of the blame goes to Joe for this one as he gave the order."

Neith held back a smile for the praise she received. She felt that it was not right to celebrate while the others were being scolded.

Cade continued, "They brazenly walked past you all and the scanners. This must be how they have been getting in the city in the past. This Deicended in his band must have the power to create illusions and project illusions on themself or others."

That must have been him, Tyr thought. He gritted his teeth and addressed Cade. "I saw him and didn't stop him," Tyr said to the others. Cade's face never showed much emotion, but everyone else in the room displayed an understandable degree of shock. He continued, "It was only for a moment, and when I looked again at his face, it had changed to that of one of the civilians, so I thought I was mistaken and let him go by." Cade looked down and was silent for a moment before looking up at Tyr.

"Most likely, it is for the best that you did not react. If he knew that you saw him and your power was not active, you would be dead right now," Cade explained.

Still, I'm going to make him pay even worse for embarrassing me, Tyr thought to himself, staring at his feet and feeling the burn of his shame.

"So, you can scan for those civilians' identities in the city and find them?" Lucy asked.

"We have already tried that. Most likely, they have killed more people and taken new identities if they are still in the city. Because of the explosion, we cannot confirm the size of their group, but we believe there are about eight of them based on the number of civilians we found with evidence of being killed by knives in the skyscraper," Cade said.

"So, what's the next move for us?" Tyr asked.

"We are going to explore your powers further," Cade said.

"You mean, like, train?" Ben asked.

Cade began to explain, "No. It is clear that we need to be more prepared for the next time you come into contact with the Hawk. There is something you need to know about your powers that I kept from you. Do you remember the day that I injected you all with something in order to tell what your powers might be? Well, I was not completely honest with what we did. I hope you understand our reasoning for the ruse. The drug that we gave you comes from a mysterious plant called the Flower of Eos. Now, this is more of a tree than a flower, but it blooms with large purple and yellow petals. From the petals, we have made a drug that takes your mind to another plane of existence." He paused and watched the Deicended's brows furrowing as they attempted to process what he just said.

He continued, "We know very little about this place. We call it the Dawn Edge. Now, this drug only brings your mind to the Dawn Edge. Your bodies will still be here in our plane of existence. Let me know if you need further explanation, because this is not something I expect you to understand necessarily. The Dawn Edge is an existence that lays on top of our own. In a sense, with the drug, you will be in both existences at the same time."

"Okay, you lost me now," Takumi admitted.

"You lost me at the beginning," Ben admitted.

"What does this have to do with our powers?" Emily asked.

"We are not exactly sure, but we know the powers of the Deicended and the Dawn Edge are somehow connected. It will be better for you all to understand once you go under the drug. This will be different from when you were younger. When you were too young, your minds were unable to comprehend the Dawn Edge, so it was as if you were asleep. There are a few things I need to mention beforehand to prepare you," Cade said.

"Wait, why do we need to go there? Who cares if our powers are connected?" Emily asked.

"It has to do with the man in the mask. He has access to the drug as well. We need to understand this Dawn Edge that bridges you Deicended if we are to competently destroy him. Now, when you are in the Dawn Edge, there is a chance you will encounter the Phosphorus," Cade explained.

"The who?" Ben asked.

"The Phosphorus. We do not know what they are either. We know very little as George is unable to see or enter the Dawn Edge. There are beings that appear human, except they can only be seen by entering the Dawn Edge. We do not know what their intentions are. All we know is they seem to be old, and they know something as old as they are. We are going to give you the drug in the hope that you will be able to learn anything new that might give us a leg up against the Hawk," Cade explained.

"Is there any risk to this?" Tyr asked.

“Of course, there is a risk, but we will ensure your safety,” Cade promised.

“Suuure you will,” Lucy drawled sarcastically, which was strange since she normally would trust Cade.

“It is important that we find out the secret of this place and the beings that reside there,” said Cade.

“I don’t mean to sound insulting, but this just sounds like a hallucination,” Neith commented.

“And I would say you are right. However, through tests we have run, it appears what you will be seeing is in fact real. Now, I will answer more questions later, but we must get this started. It will be easier to understand everything once you have experienced it and then sober from the drug,” explained Cade.

Compliantly, the Deicended listened to Cade. Lind and Nicholas walked into the room to assist Cade in the test. The Deicended were sent to separate buildings. The buildings were small and consisted of only one room that had nothing but grey walls and a cemented floor. There was a chair in the middle of each room. Lind, Nicholas, Cassandra, Anne, and Cade sat in a room in the same building as the training facility. They watched six different monitors in the room, each displaying one of the Deicended.

Cade pressed a button in order to speak into an intercom that worked in the six rooms. “Now, we are going to begin. I suggest you sit down for this. You will see a gas leaking in through the vent above you. That is the drug. Inhaling it this way should make your ‘trip’ last for only about twenty minutes.”

From the monitors, Cade could see that most of the Deicended sat down, except Tyr and Lucy. Ben sat in his chair, bouncing his leg uncontrollably. Cade pressed a button, and the gas leaked through the vents. When the gas hit their lungs, they started to cough uncontrollably. Cade and the Primechs waited patiently to see the reaction of the Deicended. Neith stood up from her chair and backed up. Tyr got into a defensive position. Lucy stood calmly. Takumi stayed seated, but he appeared distressed. Ben jumped from his chair and threw it against the wall. He flailed his hands around and ran around the room. It was almost like there was something chasing him. Cade and the Primechs were able to hear sound from the room, but none of the Deicended spoke a word. Even Ben didn't scream in terror.

"Interesting how Ben is reacting," Nicholas commented.

"From our experience, the boy is timid. He must see a Phosphorus," one of Lind's voices said.

"True, but even for Ben this is an overreaction," Nicholas said.

After a while, the Deicended appeared to calm down on the screens. Ben looked scared and was in a defensive position, but at least he wasn't freaking out like before. After twenty minutes passed, the Deicended looked in the camera and asked to be let out. Cade pressed another button on the control panel and the doors to their small buildings swung open. They walked back to Cade and the others.

"Well, tell me what happened," Cade demanded.

"I think I met the Phosphorus! There were three of them," Neith said energetically, excited to talk about what she saw. "They were quiet for the most part. They looked just like normal people."

"What!? That's not what I saw! There was some kind of creature in there; it was huge. More than just heat came out of my hands too. Huge flames came out, and I was able to scare the creature away," Ben frantically interjected.

"A creature? How strange. This is the first we have heard of a giant creature. You must tell us everything, Benjamin. So far from our tests, we only knew about the Phosphorus. It makes sense there would be something else there. Well, besides the squids that is. Did any of you by chance see a squid or octopus floating around?" Cade asked.

Takumi and Tyr raised their hands.

"I didn't see any Phosphorus when I was there," Tyr commented.

"Neither did I," Lucy mentioned.

"I also used my powers while I was in there. I was bigger, much bigger. I think I felt a horn on my head," Tyr said.

"Yes, through our studies we have found that, while on the drug, your powers are much stronger, but you don't seem to be able to use them in our world while on the drug," Nicholas said.

"Well, I guess that explains why I didn't burn down the room. My flames appeared to go right through them. I'm sorry, Cade, but I don't remember much of the creature. I was so scared when I saw it that I just tried to torch everything, and I scared it off," Ben said.

"Why were octopi floating around? I tried to ask the Phosphorus that I saw, but they wouldn't answer me," Takumi said.

"We don't know why they are there either. The Phosphorus, from what we know, only seem to talk about what concerns them. Maybe you experienced this, but we think they mostly talk in prophecy," said Nicholas.

"They told me I need to continue my pursuit of knowledge. They promised that my power, through my work, could become more powerful than anything else. They said I could learn the secret to everything," Neith said. "They mentioned my power could be the power that lights up the new generation of man."

"Did they tell you about themselves? Did they explain who they are or what they want? Did they know or say anything about our history?" Cade asked.

"Why would they talk about our history?" Neith asked.

"We believe there is something ancient about them. We believe they know something about our existence that we are incapable of discovering without the Dawn Edge." Cade replied. "Emily and Takumi, what did they say to you?"

"I only saw one. I asked who she was, but she didn't respond. She told me I must trust and defend my friends, no matter what. That's pretty much all she said," Takumi said.

"I saw one too. The Phosphorus told me to be careful how I speak, and that I would suffer consequences for it. I kept telling him to shut up and tell me something actually useful. He got annoyed with me and began to leave. He turned around right before going away and said that George can't be trusted," Emily said.

Everyone turned to Emily in shock at what she said. "Don't trust George! That's ludicrous," Nicholas said in disbelief.

"It is very interesting to say the least. We appreciate your willingness to share that with us, Emily. We really do not know what the Phosphorus' intentions are," Cade said.

"They never said anything like that to me," Nicholas said. "They told us to trust George and help with Its exploration."

"Wait, you have been to the Dawn Edge before?" Tyr asked.

"And what do you mean by Its exploration?" Neith asked

One of Lind's voices explained, "Nicholas used to be a Deicended. When he became a Primech, he lost his connection to the Dawn Edge. Apparently, it takes more than a brain to be connected to it. That is why he does not have any powers like yours. Believe it or not, Nicholas used to have an arm that could dissolve things it touched." Another voice spoke, "Before the Hawk attacked, we explored the Dawn Edge for scientific reasons. We only have a limited supply of the drug, and now we must use the resource to defeat the masked man. Sadly, it doesn't appear that we found out anything new worth knowing."

"I wouldn't say that, Lind. What Emily just said is important. Before, we thought all of the Phosphorus had the same intentions, but maybe they don't. There must be a mix of good and evil in the Dawn edge. Those of a similar mindset to those who spoke with Emily might be behind the Hawk's evil intentions," Nicholas suggested.

"Let me go back; I want to learn from them. I'll help George's exploration," Neith implored.

"I am glad you are so eager, Neith. Maybe the Phosphorus were right, and you will achieve greatness. Keep up your work, and you might catch the eye of Sun for your prudence. However, as we said there is a limited supply of the drug, and we can only explore when George deems it right to go," Cade said.

"I wanted to become a Primech since you taught us what they are, but, if we lose the connection to the Dawn Edge as a result, I don't know if I want to lose that resource. Not just for myself, but for George as well," Neith said. *Someday, I will bridge the two together*, she thought to herself.

"How can I become a Primech?" Lucy asked. "I know you have to be nominated by an Arch Primoid, but what can we do to help ourselves?

"Are you sure? You heard Lind and Neith; you would lose your powers," Cade said.

"I understand, but nothing would be better than to serve George as an extension of Itself," Lucy said.

"Very noble, Lucy. Well, you know how some of the Primechs who trained you accomplished their achievements but defeating the Hawk would definitely get you in the eye of Mars. If you wanted to become a Disciple of a different virtue, it would be best to act as a Primech that is of that virtue," Cade explained.

"To catch the eye of Venus, there isn't an exact path. Honestly, you have to be put in a certain situation to prove your kindness. Like myself, I didn't seek out acts of kindness. I was put in a tough position and proved myself," Cassandra said.

"Dedication and perseverance are the keys to Mercury's heart," said Anne.

"Exploration of knowledge is the way to catch the eye of Sun. Like Neith, you have to find something to discover or learn and commit everything to the exploration," Nicholas explained.

"Well, I think my best option is to get the Hawk. I already planned on defeating him; I'll just make sure that I'm the one to put him down," Lucy said.

"After I kill him, you mean," Emily said.

"Ha ha, you think you'll be the one? Yeah right! I'm going to smash that guy's face in," Tyr said.

"Is there any way for us to get more of the flower?" Neith asked.

"Not exactly," Cade said. "The plant sprouts randomly, and we have not discovered how to breed it. Next time a random Deicended pops up in the city, we will have you take them down. There tends to be a Flower of Eos nearby whenever a new Deicended appears. We can, hopefully, harvest the flower. We need assistance with the other rogue Deicended. George's forces have difficulty with them. They always try to destroy the flower when they discover George is on to them. They must be getting tainted by something in the Dawn Edge. They almost always attempt to join forces with the Hawk."

"I don't remember ever seeing one of these flowers before. Did we have them near us or at our home?" Ben asked.

"Surprisingly, no. We think that, because we discovered you all before your powers manifested, the Flower of Eos never grew. However, that is just a theory. It is very strange though to have six Deicended and not discover one flower," one of Lind's voices explained.

"Can any of you describe how it felt to enter the Dawn Edge?" asked Cade.

"It felt warm," said Takumi.

"Right! It felt like being wrapped up in a comfortable blanket," said Emily.

"I saw a light," Tyr said. The others nodded their heads in agreement.

"The lights looked like they turned to stars, and I felt a wave of vibration shake me. I never felt so calm," said Neith.

"Yeah, I felt that too. Until the creature showed up that is," said Ben.

"Good, this confirms what we know," said Nicholas.

"Now, sometimes, trips to the Dawn Edge can increase your powers. Tyr and Ben, you used your powers while you were there, correct? We think that what you saw was the true potential of your powers. I think that a competition, perhaps, is in order to help you test your powers against one another," Cade suggested.

"Excellent idea, sir," Lind agreed.

All of the Deicended's faces lit up in excitement. They have fought each other before, but they never used their powers against each other. They were all rather competitive by nature and could not wait for whatever Cade had in mind.

9

The Day it Happened: Ben

He opened his eyes slowly to the annoying and blaring sound of his alarm. Ben slammed his hand on the snooze button and shut his eyes. The alarm went off a second time, and he slammed the snooze button a second time. His eyes were only shut for a second before his mom came in to wake him up.

"Benjamin! Time to get ready, honey," said Rosemary.

"Uuuuhhhhh," Ben replied.

"I'm not leaving till you get up," said Rosemary. Ben didn't move. "Benjamin! Benjamin! Benjamin! Benjamin! Benjamin! Benjamin!"

"Alright, already. I'm getting up; you can get out now," said Ben.

"You're not standing. I'll leave once you stand," said Rosemary.

Ben, with a look on his face like someone just shit in his cereal, put his feet on the carpet floor and stood up. "Happy, ma?" Ben asked.

"Very. Now, get ready for school, sweety. Your brother is done with his shower; don't take too long with yours," she said.

Ben's mom walked out of the room, and Ben walked to the bathroom. Not listening to his mother's advice, Ben took a long shower. He mostly just stood still, letting the burning hot water run down his body as he fought the urge to fall asleep. It was Ben's favorite part of the day.

"Ben, hurry up! You're going to be late," Rosemary shouted from outside the bathroom.

Once Ben was dressed, he was already too late to walk to his bus stop. "Get in the car; I'll drive you down, Benji. Your brother is already down there," said Rosemary.

Right as the bus pulled up to its spot, Rosemary pulled the car up. As Ben got out of the car, his mom said, "Have a great day at school, Benjie. Don't forget; I'm dropping you off at your father's place for dinner."

Ben nodded his head and followed the rest of the kids to the bus. As Ben took a step on the bus, his brother slugged him in his right arm on the side of his bicep. He fell a step back. "What the hell, Mike?!" Ben shouted.

"That's for being late, numb nuts," said Michael.

"You're such a dick!" Ben shouted.

"Whatever. Stop getting so mad at nothing. It's just a little punch," said Michael.

While walking to their seats Michael snapped back and threw his hand into a punch. His fist stopped right before making contact with Ben's face. Ben threw his arms in front of his face to protect it and coiled up.

"Two for flinching," said Michael as he hit Ben's arm in the same spot twice again.

Ben sat a few seats in front of his brother. Michael was surrounded by friends. They were having a lively conversation, and Michael seemed to be the center of it. Ben sat with his best friend,

Jose. They were friends for years and shared similar interests in TV shows, movies, and games. Besides those interests, they were pretty different people. Jose was a smart kid that applied himself to his schoolwork. Ben was dressed more raggedy and always wore the same hoodie. Jose had a more proper way of dressing.

The first class of the day was gym, and Jose was in the class with him. They met up with their other friend, Ray. He was a short fellow that dressed as goofy as his personality. He often attracted the attention of friends from outside their circle since he was always quick with the jokes.

"Hey, Jose. Do you think I could see your homework for history class? I didn't do mine last night," asked Ben.

"No way, man! I don't want to get in trouble. We're in class; they'll see you copying it anyways," replied Jose.

"Everyone does it in gym class. It's not like the teacher pays attention, and George doesn't have any eyes in the locker room," said Ben.

"I said no, man," replied Jose.

"You can use mine," said Ray.

"Oh! Thanks, dude," said Ben.

Ray opened his backpack and reached in. He pulled his hand out, with nothing in it, and was flipping Ben off. "What? You think I did my homework? Damn, you're dumb, dude. I didn't do mine because I'm lazy. You probably couldn't figure out any of the answers," said Ray, snickering with Jose.

"Fuck off, man. I was just being lazy, too," said Ben.

"Maybe he's right. You could have copied it on the bus, and nobody would have noticed," said Jose.

"Okay, okay, I got it. Not the sharpest tool in the shed. Got it," said Ben.

The class came out of the locker room and sat along the wall, waiting for the teacher to come out. "All right there, kids. Listen up," the gym teacher said. "Pick a court and play some hoops. I don't care who plays with who or anything like that. Just play some b-ball and pretend to enjoy it."

"Hey, we should try to play with Atessia. That way, maybe you could get to talk to her or something," suggested Ben.

"I think I'm good. I like her, but I want to get her without any help," said Jose.

"That doesn't make any sense," said Ray.

"Whatever. You go ask her and her friends then, Ben," said Jose.

"Well, I don.. I mean, I would. I just… I think… Whatever, don't talk to her then," said Ben.

"Hey, guys! I got this; leave it to me," said Ray. He walked over to Atessia and her friends, Tammy and Nadia.

"Yeah, a game with you guys would be fun," Tammy said as they walked up to Jose and Ben with Ray and her other friends.

The six walked over to one of the twenty basketball courts to start playing. They were only playing a half-court game, and the girls had the ball first. They played for a bit, and it was a pretty uneventful game. Ben was scoring almost all of the points in the game. He was much more athletic and coordinated than the other five.

"Hey, man! Try interacting with her or something," Ben whispered to Jose.

"I don't need advice," said Jose.

"Well, let me set you up for a shot, so you can look good," said Ben.

"Like it will make a difference with you scoring all of the points," Jose said sourly.

"At least try," Ben suggested.

"Fine!" Jose replied.

Nadia went for a layup and missed. Ben jumped over everyone and caught the rebound. Ben passed it to Ray, who was kind of just standing lazily behind the three-point line. The ball was reset, and it was the guys' chance to score now. When Tammy went to guard Ray, blocking his route to the net, he passed the ball to Ben. Ben was guarded by Nadia who was doing a terrible job. Ben saw a clear chance for a shot but instead threw the ball to Jose when he was open. Jose reached out to catch the ball, but instead of catching it, the ball jammed into his index finger.

"Ow! Dammit!" shouted Jose. Distracted by the pain, he dropped it, and Atessia took the ball and shot, scoring a point.

"Hahaha. Totally got one on you, Jose," said Atessia, dancing around him and jeering.

"Uh! Whatever," Jose said as he stormed off to the stands. Atessia, along with the others, looked at him, confused.

"Well, guess we are done. See ya later, boys," said Tammy.

"See ya later. Winning so much was getting boring anyway," said Ray. The girls laughed, shrugged off Ray's comment, and walked away.

"What the hell was that, man?" Ben asked Jose when they caught up to him in the stands.

"Dude! I told you I didn't want to do that," said Jose.

"You didn't have to storm off," said Ben.

"I told you I didn't want to play with them, and I told you I didn't want to make that play. Now, look what happened," said Jose.

"I'm sorry, dude. I'll make it up to you," said Ben. Jose just rolled his eyes at Ben.

The bell rang, signaling that gym class was over. "Hey, Jose! Look at the bright side," said Ray.

"What's that?" asked Jose.

"At least I didn't embarrass myself in front of my crush," said Ray. Ben and he chuckled.

"Ugh. Whatever. Get bent," said Jose.

"I did… with Ben's mom last night. I would like to remind your mom that she still owes me for that night. I'm not cheap," Ray said with a wide grin.

"Oh, fuck off," said Ben. Now Jose and Ray laughed.

Ben's next class was a reading and literature class. Ben decided to skip the class. After all, he hated that class. Ben had a lot of difficulty reading. Being in the class made him feel dumb, and he didn't need more of that feeling after upsetting his one friend and being burned so badly by the other. Ben went to the parking lot of the school to see if there was anyone hanging out. Usually, he could find his brother and his friends smoking out there. Not that he wanted to hang out with his brother, but his friends were pretty cool. Plus, hanging with them might give other people the idea that he was cool too. Once he got outside though, there was no sign of anyone hanging out. Ben was about to head inside until he saw one of the lunch ladies trying to take a box out of her car that was obviously way too big for her to carry on her own.

"Hey, ma'am; do you need help?" asked Ben.

"Oh, what are you…? Oh, never mind. I guess you can grab that end," said the lunch lady.

Ben went to pick up the box and struggled a bit. He was able to lift it after repositioning his grip, and it was so heavy that it felt like it had a body inside.

"You sure you got it?" asked the lunch lady.

Ben shook his head up and down. They took the box to a set of stairs, and Ben started to walk up it first, walking backwards. At first, he was fine walking up, but once he got to the last step, his foot got stuck and he stumbled over and dropped the box.

"What the hell, kid?! I thought you said you had it!" the lunch lady screamed at Ben.

"I did! I.." Ben was cut off by more screaming.

"You didn't have it! What are you even doing out here? You are supposed to be in class!" the lady shouted.

Ben looked over to the spilled box. It was just a bunch of plastic lunch trays that weren't broken. "Lady, the trays are fine," Ben said.

"Don't call me lady!" screamed the lunch lady.

"I can help pick…"

"Stay right here! I'm going to get a monitor Primoid out here to bring you to detention," said the lunch lady.

As soon as she walked inside, Ben ran away into the building from another side. Worried about being caught, Ben ran into a bathroom. Ben panted while the door closed behind him. Interesting enough, Jose was in the bathroom too. There were two upperclassmen standing next to him.

"C'mon, kid. We wanted to give some fresh meat a flurry, and in comes you. So, you're getting one," said the bully.

"No, guys. I can't get wet. I don't want to," said Jose. The bullies just laughed at how scared Jose looked. They grabbed him and began to lift.

"Hey! Get off my friend, asswipes!" Ben shouted at them. The bullies dropped Jose.

"Looks like this idiot just volunteered as tribute," said bully number two.

Ben balled up his fist, ready to fight. Jose got up and ran past Ben. "Where are you…?" Ben was saying before he was struck in the face by bully number one. Ben fell to the ground. The two bullies began to drag Ben to the toilet. Ben was flailing his arms around, trying to grab onto anything.

His brother, Michael, came running into the bathroom. "Oh, fuck," bully number two said. Michael decked him the face, knocking him back. Bully number one tried to run, but Michael kicked him into the sink. Having the wind knocked out him, the bully limped out of the bathroom with the other one.

"What are you doing here?" asked Ben.

"I saw that pussy friend of yours, Jose, running out while I was looking for a place to smoke. Figured I would check out what was going on. Saw that you were getting your ass kicked, and no one is allowed to do that except me. So, here I am," said Michael.

"Whatever, dick breath," said Ben. "I didn't need your help. Jose was getting help. I would have been fine."

"Dude, you need to stop hanging out with that kid. He's not a good friend. He was just saving his own ass," said Michael.

"Hey, don't talk about my friend like that, asshole!" shouted Ben.

"I'm just trying to give you advice, man. You don't have to listen to me. Don't give a shit if you do, anyways," said Michael.

"You're always such an asshole. I can't stand you," Ben said and walked out of the bathroom.

"Student! Halt," said a monitoring Primoid. "You are to report to the Detention Hall. I will escort you."

Ben groaned as the Primoid placed its artificial hand on his shoulder and turned him down the hallway. As they were about to step off, the bell rang. "It is lunchtime, now. I have to allow you to go in order to receive your necessary nutrition. I will escort you to the Detention Hall once you are done," said the monitoring Primoid.

Ben walked to the lunch hall and saw Jose and Ray at a table with a few of their other friends. "Hey, where did you go, Jose?" asked Ben.

"Right here, dude," replied Jose.

"What are you talking about? You left me in the bathroom," said Ben.

"Yeah! You could have run too. Don't blame me that you decided to stay like an idiot," said Jose.

"Was that why you were crying when I saw you run out of the bathroom, Ben?" asked Ray.

"What? Crying? You weren't even there," said Ben.

"Haha! Yeah, I saw him crying too," said Jose. Everyone at the table began to laugh at Ben.

"No! You guys didn't see anything because you weren't there. You ran away! I get it; it's funny, but I'm a little pissed. Could you stop joking around?" Ben pleaded.

Michael came up behind Jose and shoved his head into the table. Jose shouted and struggled, but Michael held him there, putting pressure on his head. "The fuck you saying about my brother?"

Michael asked Jose. Fear struck the table, and they fell immediately silent.

"Get off him, you dick breath," Ben demanded. He shoved his brother off of Jose. Michael shoved his fist into Ben's gut.

"I told you these guys are shitty friends. I'm trying to help you, but you don't get to push me around," said Michael.

"I don't need your help. They aren't bad friends. You're a bad brother. Now, fuck off!" Ben shouted.

"Fine; suit yourself. Have fun being miserable, numb nuts," Michael said as he walked back to a table with his friends.

"Sorry, guys," Ben said to everyone at the table.

"It's okay. I'm sure he wouldn't have pushed Jose like that if he saw you crying like you did," Ray jeered, suddenly more talkative again now that Michael was gone.

"It's not funny anymore," said Ben.

"It definitely is since you were doing it," said Jose.

"That's it. I'm never sticking my neck out for you guys again. You're ungrateful," said Ben.

"Oh, thank George. When you stick your neck out, your tears get the floor all wet, and it makes it difficult to walk around you," said Ray. The entire table was laughing again at Ben's expense.

Ben had enough and stormed out of the lunch hall through the school's main entrance. He was walking to a bench, just to get some air and cool off. As Ben was about to sit down, there was a loud bang and the ground shook. Ben looked around in confusion. Students and teachers were running around frantically. Ben noticed a blur on the rooftop. He looked up, and it stopped for a second. It was a person in a hooded black cloak. They turned and looked at Ben, and Ben saw a mask in the shape of a hawk.

After sharing a look, the masked figure jumped off the building and was gone. Teachers yelled at students to get to the parking lot and rally up. A flood of students hurried away from the building, and Ben joined them to wait to be picked up by their parents. Ben didn't talk to anyone. He didn't see anyone who he was comfortable talking to. Ben found a somewhat open spot and sat. Ben kept expecting his brother to come up and slug him in the arm again. He waited and waited, but his arm remained untouched.

10

The Tournament Arc

"First up will be Takumi versus Lucy. After that, it will be Benjamin versus Neith, and, last, will be Tyr versus Emily," said Cade.

Everyone was in the training room, and a flat arena was in the middle. It was shaped like a square with no ropes or anything to get a hand onto. It was twenty yards long by twenty yards wide. Lind and Anne were no longer with them. They were sent to go do something else. Cassandra stayed with them. Yazan, Amin, and Nicholas also came out to watch the display. The rules of the tournament were simple. The opponent is defeated by either being thrown outside the mat, being knocked out, or being restrained. Given that they were permitted to use their powers, this wasn't going to be a simple wrestling match.

Before stepping up to the mat, Takumi thought to himself, *Lucy's abilities are weird, but I'm probably the best to go against her. I'll use two of my shadow arms to bind down her arms, and I'll stay at a distance, using however many other shadow arms it takes to tie her down. If she goes invisible, I'll start barraging the arena with attacks from my shadow arms. I'll have to keep a keen eye out. She isn't actually invisible. She just blends in with her background. She manipulates a small field around her to adjust the way her body refracts light. Typically, this would only stealth somebody efficiently if you were looking at them from the right angle, but, with the way Lucy does it, she can concentrate on a single point to adjust from that one point's view. So, if she concentrates on me, wherever I look at her, she will adjust to be at the right angle. I could try moving around, making it difficult for her to change the point she will be concentrating on. If I move around though, it will make my defense stance weaker and outweigh the positives of moving around. So, I'll plant myself and wait for her to make the first move.*

The two walked up to the arena and each took a side. Takumi was on his guard, while Lucy had more of a confident, almost nonchalant stance.

"She's going to end up crushed heh heh, if she doesn't take this seriously," Amin said.

"I'm pretty sure she'll be fine. She might be trying to throw her opponent off his guard," Yazan suggested.

"Takumi has been the most skilled at many of the training courses they have been in. Lucy is very strong herself, but my money is on Takumi. His ability to strategize is very strong in addition to his fighting. The combination of the two should put him ahead in the fight," said Nicholas.

"You may begin," Cade shouted.

Takumi projected six shadow arms out of his spine and arced them around his body, prepared to attack or defend. Lucy smiled and began to swing her right arm in a circle. Faster and faster, she swung her arm. She stopped swinging her full arm and started to only swing below her elbow. It was as if her arm was disjointed, making a small windmill with her forearm.

Well, she isn't going invisible, but what the hell is she doing to her arm? Why is she able to move it like that? Takumi thought to himself.

Lucy threw her arm forward and, at high speed, it extended towards Takumi. Takumi stepped back in surprise. He caught Lucy's arm with one of his shadow arms. "Bind!" Takumi yelled. The shadow arm wrapped around Lucy's arm like a boa constrictor, holding it in place.

"Well, you won't need this, will you?" Takumi yelled at Lucy. His shadow's grip tightened around Lucy's arm. Harder and harder the arm gripped until blood came from Lucy's arm. "Shadow Strike!" Takumi took another one of his shadow arms and stabbed it through Lucy's bleeding arm. The shadow arm, covered in blood from piercing Lucy's arm, pushed it away from him as the other shadow arm pulled. Blood started to gush out as the arm began to separate. Lucy gasped in pain as she helplessly tried to pull her arm back. Snapping and cracking could be heard by all in the room. Skin began to separate entirely from her arm. Muscle and ligament barely held on as they snapped away from each other. The arm was completely separated, making a wet slapping sound as Takumi dropped it to the training room floor, but at least, now, Lucy was able to pull her remaining stump of an arm back. She looked up at Takumi, and her face was filled with rage more than it was with pain.

"At least you can grow it back. Well, after the fight maybe. I'm not giving you the chance to do that now," Takumi shouted at Lucy. He charged Lucy, shadow arms sailing forward, assuming he had the upper hand. Lucy turned invisible. Takumi halted his charge and prepared for another attack. From Takumi's right side, he saw a blur in motion. He quickly realized it was Lucy's arm swinging at him. He snatched the arm with one of his shadow arms. Lucy became visible again. To Takumi's surprise, Lucy threw a punch at him with the arm that Takumi had torn off. She had already grown it back. Even though he was surprised, Takumi still caught the arm with one of his shadow arms. In an even more surprising move, Lucy grew another arm under her right arm in front of Takumi's eyes. Lucy used the newly grown arm and slammed it into Takumi's gut.

"Huughhh," was the sound Takumi made from having the wind knocked out of him. Takumi used one of his shadow arms to pierce the mat behind him and pulled himself away from Lucy. Takumi stood and concentrated on controlling his breathing again.

While Takumi rested, Lucy grew another arm, under her left arm this time. Then, she grew another arm on each side under the second row of arms, totaling six arms.

"Maybe I should have given the hydra symbol to Lucy," Cade said after witnessing Lucy's new powers. Lucy simultaneously cracked the bones in her six hands in an intimidating manner at Takumi. Lucy moved her arms behind herself and then threw her arms forward, extending all six towards Takumi. Takumi caught all six arms with his shadow arms. Lucy wrapped her hands around his shadow arms and pulled herself towards Takumi with her feet first. Her feet crushed Takumi's chest, most likely breaking a few ribs. He fell back and let go of Lucy's arms. Before Takumi could hit the ground, Lucy grabbed his leg and swung him over her head. She then slammed Takumi into the mat to her side. Again, Takumi gasped for air.

"Oh, no. I'm not giving you a second to rest," Lucy said while lunging towards Takumi. Lucy followed up with a punch, which Takumi blocked. Lucy followed with another punch, and Takumi barely blocked that one. A third punch was thrown by Lucy, and it hit Takumi on the side of his gut. She threw a fourth punch, hitting Takumi in the face. She threw several more punches that struck Takumi in the chest, each one eliciting a concerning cracking sound from Takumi's already damaged rib cage.

"I…I give!" Takumi desperately shouted. Lucy immediately stopped and stood up to face Cade and the other instructors.

"Very good, Lucy. That was very impressive indeed," Cade commented. Lucy nodded, retracted four of her arms, knelt down, and began to heal Takumi's wounds, placing her hands gently on either side of his ribcage and focusing on searching out the fragments of bones and knitting them back together. She looked up at his face, seeing his obvious discomfort. "You're lucky I'm doing this after you tore my arm off," Lucy said snarkily.

"I only did it because I knew you would be fine and that it would be difficult to beat you. You should take it is a compliment; it means that I think you're a serious opponent, so I'm not going to go easy on you. I'm the one that should be mad. I never even got to use one of my special moves during the match," Takumi replied. Lucy smirked.

"Fair enough, but, next time you do that to me, I'm going to let your body deal with healing your broken ribs," Lucy said. The two walked off the mat.

"Looks like it is Benjamin and Neith's turn," Cade said as Neith and Ben stood up from their seats and began to walk to the arena.

Oh, this isn't fair. Neith might not be the strongest overall, but her Dawn Edge power is definitely the strongest of all of ours. Just focus. Focus, and you can do this, maybe, Ben said to himself.

Okay, Neith, you got this. I'll keep my distance and wear him down with shots from my powers. Whatever you do, don't underestimate him. He might not perform as well as any of us, but that doesn't mean I might not slip up. Plus, I've seen Ben perform well sometimes. It's rare, but, when he does perform well, it's a wonder how he's not one of the better Deicended. He is capable of surprises, so I can't let my guard down, Neith said to herself.

"Neith, most likely, will win this. She might not be the best fighter, but her power and wits are the best of all of them; this match is already decided, heh heh," Amin commented.

"I hate to agree with such a definitive statement, but the chance of Ben winning is extremely slim," said Nicholas.

"He better, at least, put up a good fight, or else I'm going to crush him out of principle," Yazan said angrily while glaring at Ben. Both Ben and Neith stood staring at each other on opposite sides of the arena. Ben put his hand over his chest and started to breath heavily. *Not again. This is just like the time with the boar on the island. Why does this happen to me? Just control your breathing. C'mon,* Ben thought. The harder Ben concentrated on controlling his breathing, the harder it seemed for him to breath.

"You may begin!" Cade shouted.

C'mon, attack before she can think, Ben thought as he raised his trembling arm to attack. He tried to steady his arm and control the shaking, but Ben started to cough from being out of breath. *Sorry, Ben, but I plan on winning,* Neith thought as she waved her hand and a blast of violet energy projected from her hand towards Ben. Her blast wasn't that fast, and Ben jumped to the side to dodge it. The blast missed and whizzed by him, but Ben collapsed to the ground from his legs shaking too much. Ben started to pick himself up and stumbled towards Neith. She threw another energy blast, and Ben stumbled to dodge again. This time, Ben didn't collapse, but Neith immediately threw another blast, hitting Ben in the shoulder, followed by another blast to the chest. Ben fell to his knees and screamed in pain. All of Ben's frantic thoughts were overwritten by the intense pain he was feeling in his chest and shoulder.

Emily winced from watching the match play out in such a lopsided way. All of the spectators definitely thought that all seemed lost for Ben, except oddly, his breathing began to steady. Neith rapidly flung more violet blasts. She struck the side of his gut, his other shoulder, his leg, and his forearm. The blasts hit one after another. Ben fell to one knee, and another blast came towards him. Ben jumped out of the way, the movement far less indecisive than before.

Another blast followed, and Ben easily stepped to the side of it. Ben ran full speed towards Neith with his arms to his side, generating a significant amount of heat in his hands as he closed in. The heat caused the light around it to refract, creating visible heat waves as the intense heat in his hands began to spread into the air around him. Neith continued to try to hit Ben with her blasts. *I should have used enough energy to blow his limbs off. Damn it, Neith, the match would have been over*, she said to herself.

Now, feet away, Ben lunged to grab Neith. She put up a violet shield in front of his hands to block his attack. With Ben's hands on the shield, he put his weight into pushing on it. He was getting nowhere in his effort, so he started to punch it. He punched and kicked it with no effect, except Neith having to focus on keeping the shield up. Without thinking about it, he put his hands back up to the shield and produced as much heat as he could. Sweat dripped down Ben's face from the heat. He saw a drop run down Neith's face as well. Neith realized she was in trouble, but, before Neith could remedy the situation, her legs started to burn. She looked down to see that Ben was rapidly heating the air around her legs, behind the shield, searing her skin Neith screamed in pain, and her shield disappeared. Ben punched Neith in the face so hard that she was knocked to the ground. Neith quickly tried to stand up, but Ben kicked her down and used his foot to put pressure on her blistered legs.

"You win, Ben!" Neith screeched and curled in pain.

Ben stopped and took his foot off of her, with an expression of surprise on his face. Ben almost didn't realize what had happened. He was dumbfounded. Neith extended her hand out to him for help to get up. It took Ben a second, but then he helped Neith up, slung her arm over his shoulder and helped her walk off of the mat. It was obvious that every step was incredibly painful for her, and he couldn't help but feel immensely guilty.

"Good job, Ben," Neith said, looking up and giving him a faint smile.

"Thanks, but you could have blown me up with those hits in the beginning if you wanted to," Ben replied.

"You're right, but I didn't want to spend too much of my energy, which was a poor choice I made. Still, you won fair and square. I really didn't know you had that in you," Neith said. *Neither did I*, he thought to himself but, rather than say anything else, he simply nodded and looked up to see Tyr rushing to take her other arm so they could carry her over to Lucy. A Primoid had brought a cot out that they were able to lay her on. Ben sat down nearby, and Tyr stood over her, his brow furrowed as he watched Lucy repair the damaged layers of Neith's skin. Ben thought that he must be unsettled, remembering the similar, but much more serious, injury that he sustained during their training on the island. Tyr, of course, could only think about how he hated seeing Neith in so much pain.

"That was interesting to say the least. Ben really pulled it together there," Nicholas said.

"More disappointed at Neith. She held back heh heh. She has far more power than what she used," Amin said.

"Now, Tyr and Emily, it's your turn now. Let us begin," Cade said.

Loathe as Tyr was to leave Neith now, Lucy had healed most of the damage and Neith's face had relaxed, showing less pain. Tyr punched his fist into his palm while turning towards the mat, getting himself psyched up. "Time put the training to some sort of test," he said. The two walked up and stood opposite each other in the arena.

"This is going to be one hell of a fight if Emily manages to win with no metal around to help her out," Nicholas commented.

"You may begin!" Cade shouted.

Tyr flexed, and his armor activated with the black scales covering his body. Emily didn't hesitate and charged Tyr. Tyr kicked at her as she charged. Emily jumped over the kick and replied with her own kick straight to Tyr's face. His head slightly budged from the kick, but that was the only effect it had. Emily landed behind Tyr, and he turned around to punch her. She blocked the hit, absorbing the impact with her forearms, and went flying backwards. Emily smacked against the ground but quickly recouped herself. Tyr went to follow through with another punch, and Emily rolled off to the side, dodging the attack. Tyr turned and kicked at Emily, but she stepped backwards, and the kick missed. Emily roundhouse kicked towards Tyr, but he blocked the attack with his arm. Tyr used his other arm and punched Emily in the side of her thigh, giving her a charley horse. Tyr followed with a back swing with the same arm, knocking Emily to the ground. Tyr went to stomp Emily, but she got to her feet and kicked Tyr in the chest. The kick had almost no effect. Tyr swung back at Emily and missed. Emily jabbed at Tyr, hitting him in the gut a few times, still no effect.

"C'mon, just go down!" Emily shouted. She held out her hand, and sparks came out. Emily could produce electricity, but there had to be metal nearby at the other end. The closest metal, in the walls, was far too far away to be of any help to her. Without metal, the most she could produce was those few sparks. Tyr lunged with a punch, missing Emily. Emily punched Tyr in the gut with the hand that was sparking, causing electricity to conduct through his scales to his body. Tyr coiled a bit from the pain he felt from being shocked.

"Huh, a few more of those hits and she might get the upper hand on him," Cassandra commented. Emily swung with her other hand that was now sparking as well. Tyr swiped it away and punched her back. Tyr lunged at Emily, hoping to finish the fight, but Emily parried his assault and hit him a few more times with her sparking fist. Emily went for a last well-placed strike but, right before making contact, the hand was stopped. Frozen in place, Emily could feel it getting colder to the point that it hurt. Determined to win, Emily swung at Tyr with her other arm. Tyr froze that arm as well. Emily was pissed and flailed her body around, trying to release herself from Tyr's grasp.

"Sorry, Emily, but you lose this one," Tyr said as he grabbed her arm and swung her around like she was weightless. Tyr threw her way over the line in the arena. She was heading straight towards the wall. *The wall… it's made of metal!* Emily thought. Emily used her powers to push against the wall as hard as she could. There was no way she was going to be able to move the wall, which was what she wanted. The force she used ended up launching her away from the wall. She used so much force that she pushed herself enough to maybe make it to the mat.

"I think she might actually make it," Nicholas said.

"No way, she won't. Plus, isn't that cheating in some way?" Cassandra asked.

"Who cares, honestly, heh heh? And it won't matter if she doesn't make it," Amin said. Emily was only feet away from touching the mat. *If I position myself right, I won't touch outside the line*, she said to herself. Staring at the line getting closer and closer, it stopped. Before she knew what had happened, Emily noticed that she wasn't getting closer to the line. Even worse, she noticed a chill creeping into her body. She looked up at Tyr and noticed him raising his hand, aimed at her. She was suspended in place. Tyr let go, and Emily fell outside the line of the arena.

"What the hell kind of way is that to win, Tyr? Why don't you fight me?" Emily asked in anger.

"This is a match to see how well we can use our powers. I understand you are at a disadvantage since there is no metal for you to use, but, if I had the opportunity to use my powers to win the fight, I was going to use them," Tyr explained. Emily pushed herself up from the ground and invaded Tyr's personal space.

"Still, you should have used your fists," Emily said.

"Anytime you want, Emily," Tyr replied, staring down at her defiant face with temerity.

"Alright, alright, children, it is time to take a rest. Go to the lunch hall to grab something to eat," Cade said.

"Huh, I knew she wasn't going to win," Cassandra said.

"Tyr should have beat her into the ground. He was more than capable of doing so," Yazan said.

"Agreed, but what he did still got the job done. It will be interesting to see the rest of the fights, heh heh," Amin said.

Back at the cafeteria, the Deicended had received their food orders from the Primoids and were taking their seats. Tyr set his tray down next to Ben and slid into the seat.

"Hey, good job there, Ben. You really surprised me," Tyr said.

"Thanks, you did really well yourself," Ben said while he took a bite of his mozzarella stick. The melted cheese stretched out and snapped, wrapping around his hand. "Ow, ow!" Ben shouted while trying to quickly get the cheese back into his mouth.

"Ha ha, you dork. How do you burn yourself when your power is to burn things?" Emily jeered.

"I don't know, maybe I'll develop heat resistance as a power eventually," said Ben.

Takumi chimed in. "True, I hope I develop something new myself, because, seeing what Lucy did, I don't feel like my powers are that special now since she can pretty much do the same thing. Plus, she does much more than extendo arms,"

"Seriously, Lucy, when did you get so good with your powers?" Neith asked. Lucy seemed to be thinking as she finished chewing and, once she had swallowed her salad, answered. "I'm not sure. I think something about going into the Dawn-Edge kind of just made me realize some of my potential with my powers," Lucy replied. "Ben, you mentioned something about your powers when you were in the Dawn Edge, right?

"Yeah, fire came from my hands! Like, a really big fire. I mean throwing fire from my hands wouldn't be too different from being able to heat my surroundings," Ben said. Lucy nodded and continued. "Definitely! It is pretty clear that our powers are less limited in the Dawn Edge than in this existence. When I was there, I paid attention to what it felt like when I used my powers there and then just tried to replicate it here. I bet, if you really try, you would be able to do that here."

"Honestly, I can't wait until we get a break to see our family. I want to show them my powers," Tyr said. "My older brother is a very dedicated servant of George; he would be so jealous."

"Ugh, you're so lucky to have a sibling who has similar interests to you. I would love to read books with my sister and just talk about it and come up with our own stories, but she is the worst. Her head is so empty; the most complicated thing she thinks about is what color to paint her lips. Is your brother close to our age?" Neith asked. Ben hid his face from the others so that they would not see his discomfort at this turn in the conversation.

"No, he's, like, way older. He's in the Expeditionary Force. He should be a Major by now," Tyr said. The Expeditionary Force was a group of humans and Primoids that went out into the far reaches of space for the purpose of discovery. "He should be back soon, within the year. It sucks not having seen him in so long, so I can't wait for him to be back."

Takumi looked up from his bowl of tomato basil soup and leaned over towards them. "Hey, guys, can you change the subject?"

Takumi whispered to Neith and Tyr. "Ben's brother died in the bombing."

"Oh, no! I'm so sorry; I didn't know that," Neith said.

"Hey, man, I'm sorry to hear that," Tyr said.

"It's okay, really. It happened years ago, now," Ben replied.

Lucy looked over at Ben and reached across the table to touch his arm. "Hey, I know how you feel, Ben. I lost my dad in the explosion," Lucy said. "The Hawk took something from all of us. I'm sure, if he was in this tournament with us, he would lose to any one of us."

"Yeah, my shadow arms might not be that cool, but, at least, all of our powers are cooler than making a little breeze," Takumi said. Lucy countered, "Even if you are better, you shouldn't underestimate your enemy, Takumi. Even a little breeze can become quite an inconvenience if used well." To demonstrate, she leaned down to the table and blew across it. The puff of air picked Takumi's napkin up and into his soup, quickly absorbing the red liquid and sinking down into it.

"Aw, man!" he exclaimed. "C'mon, Lucy!" He fished the napkin out while the rest of the Deicended chuckled. Even Ben cracked a small smile. They returned to their meals and lighter conversation until a Primoid came to retrieve them.

"Alright, hurry up now. Break time is over," Cade said as the Deicended ran back into the room with the arena. "The next fight will be between Tyr and Benjamin. Lucy got the lucky draw and will only be fighting the victor of this fight."

Dammit, Ben thought. *So, even if I win, I'll have to fight Lucy too? Well, hopefully I can at least put up a fight with Tyr. I'm happy enough that I won one fight already.*

Hell yeah! Tyr thought. *If I beat Ben, I can fight Lucy too. Hopefully, Ben puts up a good fight. I'd like to learn something from the fight. Although, after the fight with Neith, he might be able to pull something unexpected. I'll have to stay on my feet.*

Eh, the break will be nice, but I kind of wanted to fight Ben and experience his powers firsthand, Lucy thought. Ben and Tyr walked into the arena and stood opposite each other.

"Now, this is a fight I've been waiting for. Tyr is going to put Ben into the ground and teach that indecisive dumbass a lesson," Yazan said.

"Oh, please. You're way too confident in Tyr. We thought Neith was going to win, but then Ben surprised us all. It's possible he could repeat that for us again," Cassandra said.

"Begin!" Cade shouted. Tyr covered himself in his power with the black scales. Ben thought back to the conversation that he had just had with Lucy.

If I can light him on fire, the heat would surely halt his movement, Ben thought to himself. He aimed the heat from his hand out towards Tyr. Ben tried to make the heat as intense as he possibly could. Even trying his hardest, there was still no fire. *Damn it, at least the area in front of me is hot enough to melt metal.*

The closer Tyr got to Ben, the hotter it got. Tyr had learned in the past couple of years that he was able to sweat while having his scales out. Initially, he thought his scales blocked up his pores or something. Tyr had exercised extensively to test this and rarely sweat. The only explanation was that the scales somehow kept his body much cooler, but this heat that Ben was producing felt like standing in an oven. *I should back off, this heat is too much,* Tyr thought. *No, I can't. I'm not backing down. He can burn me all he wants.*

Ben screamed, trying to intensify his heat as much as possible with Tyr closing in on him. Tyr grabbed Ben's hand. Tyr grunted as he grabbed it, but he threw Ben's arm to the side and whaled Ben in the face with his fist. Ben stumbled backwards, and Tyr went to follow through with another punch. Ben put his guard up and blocked the punch, sliding back a couple feet from the impact. Tyr groaned in pain again. He punched Ben with the same hand he had grabbed Ben's hand with. Ben had managed to burn Tyr's hand through the scales, and Ben noticed.

No way. I can hurt him! I might actually be able to win this, Ben thought. Tyr went to kick Ben in the side, and Ben grabbed onto his leg. Tyr's leg slammed into Ben's body, rattling it from the inside out. Still, Ben held on. Now was his moment. Ben cleared his mind and focused on producing as much heat as he could. With his arms wrapped around Tyr's leg, he was getting caught a little bit in his own heat. Still, what would it matter if he burned himself a little? He would actually beat Tyr, which was well worth the damage. Tyr cried out, definitely feeling significant pain.

Heat waves became more and more visible, until they suddenly started to vanish. Ben was no longer burning himself, and Tyr wasn't being burnt either. He tried to pull away but couldn't. Tyr was using his powers to keep them in stasis and slow molecules down to counteract Ben's power. If Ben could put out energy, Tyr could suck it right out. Once Tyr could no longer feel any additional burning, he released the stasis and swung his leg, freeing himself from Ben. Tyr punched Ben in the face and followed with a back kick. The force sent Ben flying over the line, outside the arena. Ben picked his head up to see how far he had gone and, seeing that he was definitely disqualified, dropped his head back onto the hard ground in frustration, not caring about the pang that it sent through his skull. *I'm not sure which would have been worse,* he thought. *If I had just had my ass handed to me, in which case I would have felt like I deserved to lose, or this, really feeling like I could have won if I had just been a little bit stronger, because I was close, but not good enough.*

Tyr walked over to Ben and held his hand out. "Good match, Ben. You're getting better," Tyr said.

"Thanks, man. I thought I actually had you there for a second," Ben said. He grabbed Tyr's outstretched hand, and Tyr, smiling, helped him to his feet.

"Well, let's not get too cocky there," Tyr replied, patting Ben on the back.

"Lucy, kindly heal Tyr's burns before you fight, will you?" Cade requested.

Tyr walked over to Lucy, laying on the cot that he had laid Neith on less than an hour ago. Lucy held her hands out to begin healing Tyr. "It seems I'm always patching up your legs, Tyr. You should be more careful with them." Lucy said, smiling wryly. He chuckled and said, "You're always patching up all of us. Thanks. If you want, I can ask Cade to give us another break so you can recover some of the energy this is costing you before we fight."

Lucy shook her head. "Thanks, but, as you say, I'm always patching you all up. I've done this so many times now that it is the easiest of my powers to use. I should be done in just a minute or two. Besides, I don't need one hundred percent of my power to beat you." Tyr laughed and laid his head back to let her focus.

"Well now, that fight was much more interesting than I thought it would be," Amin said.

"Ben really surprised me in that fight. Tyr was just too skilled to lose though," Nicholas said.

"Tyr just caught him off guard with his stasis ability. Ben could have won that, and probably would, if they were to fight again," Cassandra said.

"I think you have a little bit of favoritism going on for the kid. He hasn't shown us anything yet that would lead us to think that he could beat Tyr," Nicholas said.

"Your sympathy for the weak is pitiful," Yazan said to Cassandra.

"Ugh, don't get so uptight. You are all just blind to potential," Cassandra said. "He works just as hard as any of the others."

"This is true, but it is very obvious that he is letting his own insecurities or something else hold him back. If he cannot overcome whatever obstacles are in his way, all he will ever be is 'potential'," said Yazan. Cassandra kept her desired response to herself and turned her mind back to the upcoming fight.

"Alright! Now, let us get the last fight started," Cade said. All healed up, Tyr walked to the arena, followed by Lucy. "You may begin!" Cade shouted.

Tyr charged at Lucy while forming the black scales around his body. Lucy ran to the right and let Tyr chase her. Tyr kept his guard up in front of him in preparation for an attack.

Poor choice following me Tyr, Lucy thought. She threw her arm towards Tyr, extending it. Tyr blocked the punch. Lucy, with her arm still extended, leaped over Tyr and bound one of his arms.

"Let's see how far you can extend your arms," Tyr said. Tyr ran the opposite direction of Lucy. For a bit, her arm extended and attempted to resist Tyr's movement, but Lucy's arm, eventually, stopped extending, and she began to be dragged by Tyr. Tyr swung her up into the air and towards the edge of the arena. Once she was directly above him, Lucy recoiled her arm, dropping quickly on top of Tyr. He punched at her when she got in range but punching upward has significantly less force behind it than if he were able to put his weight behind it. Tyr somehow missed, and Lucy wrapped her other arm around Tyr's other arm. Then, she wrapped herself all over Tyr's body. Just like the Basilisk on Lucy's dagger, she was completely coiled around Tyr. Tyr was much stronger than Lucy, but with Lucy wrapped around Tyr the way she was, Tyr could barely move. The more Tyr tried to fight, the more Lucy was able to gain control over Tyr.

Concentrate, Tyr thought. *There has to be a way for me to win. I try harder and put more work into training than anyone else. The hard work has to pay off. I lived my whole life believing that working harder is what will get you ahead of your peers. That's what my family drilled into my head. Dad worked hard and spent every day completing extra tasks for George, and it rewarded my family with tasks only exemplary citizens could do. I will work harder than anyone and do whatever it takes to serve George. First, I have to win this fight and prove that hard work will prevail.* Desperately Tyr continued to struggle. "You have to free yourself soon or else you will lose for being restrained," Cade shouted into the arena.

Tyr fought and fought. "No, I refuse to lose!" he yelled.

Suddenly, Lucy felt her right arm getting cold. She tried to move the rest of her body and found that she was able to. He was concentrating specifically on her right arm. "Slow me down all you want, that's not going to help you get free," Lucy said. Her arm got colder and began to hurt. "I can take the pain, Tyr. I'm not letting go," Lucy said. Her arm got so cold that her skin began to turn black and crack, clearly frostbitten. She howled in pain but refused to let go.

Tyr released his stasis and, with all his strength, tried to pull his arm free from Lucy's arm that was now severely damaged. Eventually, Lucy's arm snapped. Tyr now had one free arm and used it to hit Lucy in the face and free himself while she was distracted by her severed arm. Lucy dropped off of him, holding her frostbitten stump.

"God damn, fucker! That shit hurts! I told Takumi what would happen if he did that to me. I'm going to break you and let you heal yourself," Lucy shouted in rage.

"Ha! Good luck hurting me with my armor up," Tyr replied.

"Yeah, about that. I figure there's a limit to how long you can keep up that armor. I'm sure it works like the rest of our powers, and it drains your energy to use it. I'll just have to outlast your stamina," Lucy said. She threw her remaining arm, extending it towards Tyr. From that arm, two more branched from it. The three arms slammed into Tyr. Tyr didn't seem phased by the attack. Lucy withdrew her arms, and the three joined back together into one arm. She had also regenerated her damaged arm in the meantime.

Careful, don't overdo it, Lucy said to herself. She split both of her arms into two, totaling four arms. Lucy ran for Tyr and began to swing all four arms at Tyr, raining down blow after blow. There was too much for him to handle. Tyr attempted to find a window in the attacks for a counter, but Lucy didn't let that happen. Every now and again, Lucy even threw in a kick to throw Tyr off. Lucy paused for a second to breath. This was Tyr's chance, but he didn't attack. He only appeared to be focusing.

"Well, there goes your only chance," Lucy said mockingly. She went to go swing one of her four arms, but her fist was halted midair. Lucy attempted to throw another arm at Tyr, with the same result. All four of her arms were frozen in place. Lucy realized there was a chill going down her spine. Her whole body was getting cold, and she couldn't move a muscle. Tyr had put her completely in stasis.

"Looks like I have another chance," Tyr said with a smirk on his face. Tyr took his time and put all of his weight behind his next couple of punches, releasing her just before the first punch landed. First, he punched Lucy in the gut. The next punch was to the face and then to the gut again. He grabbed her by the throat and lifted her up, walking towards the edge.

"I give up," Lucy said, tapping his arm and struggling to get the words out.

Tyr lowered her back to the mat and released her. She bent over and coughed multiple times, rubbing her throat. She glared up at Tyr. "I only gave up because I knew you were just going to move me out of bounds," Lucy said with a raspy voice.

"Yeah, probably would have helped if you had used one hundred percent of your power, huh?" Tyr said.

"Yeah, you think?" Lucy replied with a sarcastic tone.

Now, I'll show the Hawk what my hard work can do, Tyr said to himself.

11

The Day it Happened: Emily

Emily woke up suddenly with a surge of pain. Her brother, Mark, had socked her in the leg. She was confused not only by the pain but by her blaring alarm going off. She screamed.

"Turn your fucking alarm off! You're ruining my sleep!" Mark screamed back at her.

As Emily reached over to turn her alarm off, Mark hit her again, this time in the arm. She coiled her arm back and held it since it hurt so bad. "Turn off the damn alarm!" he yelled again.

"I'm trying!" she yelled back. This time, she reached over to the alarm with her other arm. She was able to flick it off, but as soon as she did, Mark hit her in the leg again.

"Next time, don't make me come in here," said Mark.

"Dad!" Emily screamed for help. Nobody responded.

"Stop asking for help, you wuss. If you weren't so lazy, I wouldn't have to teach you a lesson," said Mark.

Screaming even louder, Emily called out, "Dad, Mark won't leave me alone!"

Her dad rushed into her room. "What is all of the commotion about?" he asked after slapping Mark on the back of the head.

"He won't leave me alone, and he keeps hitting me," said Emily. Her dad glared at Mark as if he just shit in his cereal.

"Her alarm kept going off. She wouldn't turn it off, and I couldn't sleep," said Mark.

"Is that true?" her father asked.

"Yeah, but…" Emily was saying before her dad interjected.

"Take responsibility for your actions, Emily. You're ruining your brother's sleep. Grow up, stop sleeping in, and most importantly, stop fucking bothering me," her father said as he left the room.

Emily's arm rang in pain again as her brother hit her again, harder than before. "Fucking tattle tale," Mark said as he finally left her alone.

Emily got up and walked over to the bathroom to get ready, but her other brother, Mike, was already in there. She knocked on the door. "Go away! I'm taking a shit in here, you inbred," said Mike.

"Cool. Can you hurry up?! I have to get ready for school," said Emily.

"I'll finish when I finish," he said.

Emily waited patiently at first, but then her time was running out to get ready. She started to bang on the door. Mike yelled at her to stop, but she persisted. Eventually, she heard a flush, and her brother opened the door with his foot first to Emily's chest. She was knocked to the ground, and Mike hocked a loogie right at Emily.

"Impatient inbred," Mike said as he walked off.

Emily got ready quicker than she usually did, not because she was going to be late for school. Honestly, she couldn't care less if she went or not. School wasn't something she ever looked forward to. The reason she got ready so quickly was because of the awful smell that Mike had left behind. It was a mix of the spices of taco Tuesday and the trash in the closet that they forgot to leave out on trash day. Once she was done, she heated up a quick breakfast sandwich in the microwave. Her brothers and dad were already eating their food at the table.

"Hurry up, Emily. You're going to be late for school. I don't want to be bothered by those losers down there when you bother George with your tardiness," said her father. Emily just rolled her eyes and ignored him.

"Maybe you wouldn't be running so late if you weren't taking so much time to get ready," said Mark.

"I wasn't getting ready the whole time; I was waiting on Mike," she replied.

"Always with the lame excuses," said Mike. "I agree, you did take a stupid amount of time to get ready. Not sure why; you still look ugly. Not like there is enough makeup in the world to fix how ugly you are."

Emily grunted in anger, pulled her sandwich out of the microwave, slightly burning herself, and stormed out of the room. She made it to the bus stop in time to hop on the bus. She sat alone and listened to some music the whole ride. She couldn't stop thinking about being called ugly by her brother. She didn't care about her appearance, and she knew Mike was just saying that to piss her off, but for some reason it stuck in her head. She just felt angry and sad when she thought about it. Even worse, it was her brother making her feel those emotions, and now she didn't know what to be most pissed about.

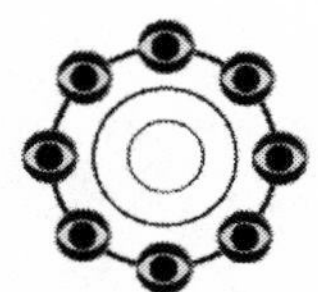

When she got off the bus, she went to her locker and waited for the bell to start heading to her first period class. She found her friend Shelby and waited with her.

"Hey, Shelby. How was your weekend?" asked Emily.

Shelby was a taller girl with long, wild, blonde hair. She had her locker door open and was doing her makeup while looking at a mirror on the inside of the locker. "It wasn't bad. I mean, I got to hang out with Jordan, Taylor, and some of their friends from out of town."

"What?! You were with Taylor? I thought that crowd wasn't too fond of us," said Emily.

"Yeah, well, I was buying some make up at the mall, which, by the way, is where I got this Ah-mazing eyeshadow, and Jordan was in there with her friend Austin, and we just started, like, talking about makeup and stuff, and she invited me to go hang with them at Taylor's place," said Shelby.

"You went to his house? What did you guys do?" asked Emily.

"Well, Taylor kind of just hung out with some of his friends that I think were from out of town. Jordan, Austin, and I went to the bathroom and tried on the makeup we bought. You should meet Austin; he was hilarious and really had some great technique with the makeup. Oh, yeah, but you don't like that stuff, so you probably would feel weird hanging out," Shelby replied.

"Yeah, you're right, but still, who wouldn't want to be at Taylor's house? That's where anybody at school would want to be," said Emily.

"Yeah, I just don't think you would enjoy yourself," said Shelby.

"Maybe next time you guys are hanging out, I could hang with you, and maybe, who knows? I might enjoy the company," said Emily.

"Well, I mean, I don't know them that well. It might be weird if I tried to bring someone into the group," said Shelby.

"I won't talk much. I won't annoy them. Plus, maybe it might be convenient if I come with you. I could talk about you, and maybe Taylor would notice you," said Emily.

"I don't know. We'll see. I'll try, just don't hold me to it," Shelby said as the bell rang.

"See ya later, Shelby," Emily said as Shelby walked away without saying anything.

Emily walked into her first class, which was a computer class. The past week, they were learning about old styles of network configurations. The teacher said it was important to learn about the basics. If they were going to learn about modern networking, they had to start with the beginning. This class was an elective, and for the most part, Emily enjoyed it, but there were plenty of times she would dose off like she did in her other classes.

In today's class, they were learning about IP v4. There was an extremely limited amount of IP addresses back then, and they had to use a technique called sub netting in order to manage the address and make sure they didn't run out of IPs. It didn't take long for that to happen, so they moved to IP v6. IP v6 gave them three hundred and forty undecillion IP addresses, and, since then, they still haven't come close to running out of addresses. That was about as much as Emily could take before dozing off. The class was a review of what they had already been learning for the last month. Eventually, the teacher gave them a practical application. They had a program on the computer to simulate a network.

The application gave them four routers, with a switch on each router, and two computers on each switch. The students had to make all of the computers talk to each other using EIGRP routing protocol. Emily took longer than most of the students, but eventually was able to get most of her computers to talk. There were still two computers not talking to the rest. They could communicate to each other, and the switch and router were able to talk to each other as well. As Emily brought up the configuration to the router to see if she messed something up, the bell rang.

Emily's next class was going to be oceanography. The class was a bit of a walk, on the other side of the school. She had to shuffle through the dense crowd of students. Unintentionally, she knocked into someone with a big build. The person turned around, and to Emily's surprise, it was a girl. In fact, Emily knew the girl. Her name was Jasmine, and she didn't look happy about being bumped into.

"Oh, Emily; it's you. How about you watch where you are going? There's a reason why nobody likes you," Jasmine said with a self-satisfied smirk.

"Don't be upset at me because your parents gave you a stripper's name," Emily quipped.

The people that seemed to be with Jasmine clapped their hands over their mouths but were not able to hold their laughter back. "You fucking bitch!" Jasmine said right before she slugged Emily in the mouth.

Emily fell to the ground but jumped back up. She charged Jasmine, who grabbed her and threw her to the ground with ease. "You talk too much, loser," Jasmine said as her friends' laughter shifted to Emily. Emily went to stand up again, but this time, she didn't get a chance. Jasmine stomped her down. Jasmine went to stomp her again, but a hall monitoring Primoid stepped in.

"Students, proceed to class. Student Jasmine, head to detention," the Primoid said.

"Keep your mouth shut next time. Maybe that way you would find a friend," Jasmine called over her shoulder as she was escorted to detention.

Now running late, Emily rushed over to her class, making it right before the bell rang. She had the class with her friend Shelby. For some reason, when they picked seating, Shelby picked another table to sit at. She still was close to Emily, but it bothered her that she chose to sit closer to another one of her friends, Tess. Emily didn't find Tess interesting at all, and they didn't get along well. Shelby and Emily weren't exactly that similar either, but surely Emily was more interesting than Tess, so she thought.

Oceanography was another elective that Emily had chosen. This so far was Emily's favorite class. It was the closest thing to learning about animals for a class available in her year, though it was ocean life, and Emily preferred learning about mammals.

Still, some days they learned about seals and otters which were the days that Emily probably learned the most from school. Today was another boring topic. They were learning about the ocean floor. They talked about it once before and got to learn about the cool creatures that dwelled down there, but today, they were learning about how the pressure of the water gets increasingly intense the further down you go. That was as much as Emily paid attention to.

"How about you answer the question, Emily dear?" said the teacher.

"Answer the what?" Emily asked, startled out of her thoughts.

"Please pay attention, dear. I can see this isn't all that interesting to you, but I would appreciate it if you would respect the effort I am putting in to teach you by paying attention just a little," said the teacher.

"Sorry, teach. I'll pay attention now," Emily said while rolling her eyes. She really didn't care about the teacher's feelings and didn't care if she passed the class. Emily looked around a bit and noticed that Shelby gave her a disgusted look, a look like Emily was an idiot. She thought it was weird that she would give her that look since Shelby had told her many times before that she also didn't care about the class, and that she was actually doing worse than Emily overall. Still, Emily took the look to heart and started to pay attention.

The teacher began to talk about the effects of pressure on a human body under water. "Things like scuba diving are possible for a human because most of our body is made of water. Therefore, the water pressure doesn't have too much of an effect on our bodies. However, we also have oxygen in our bodies. This is what restricts us the most once under water. The deeper you go, the smaller your lungs become. That limits us to go about sixty feet underwater. Now, we can go further than that, especially with the proper gear, but that is the furthest someone without proper training should go. Now, I know none of you probably intend on going scuba diving anytime soon, but I feel like I should mention this. You know how I said your lungs shrink when you go deeper in the water? Well, you have to be careful not to come up too fast from the water, because if you do, your lungs will expand too fast, and you will die." The bell rang. "Well, that was kind of a downer note to end on. Please, work on your projects this week, and have a fantastic day, everyone!"

Emily walked out and tried to hurry up to catch Shelby on her way to lunch. Shelby walked out without waiting for her, but she did that sometimes.

"Hey, are we going to sit by the stairwell today?" asked Emily.

"Uh, actually, I got a text from Jordan. She wants to talk about a concert she wants to go to, and I might be going with her as well," said Shelby.

"Oh, I thought we were going to hang out this weekend since you said you didn't want to go to the arcade," said Emily.

"Yeah, but we don't have, like, any plans to do anything. I figured since these are like actual plans you would be understanding," said Shelby.

"I could go to the concert. I think that would be fun," said Emily.

"This is, like, a new band, and I'm pretty sure you wouldn't like the music. I wouldn't want you to be bored the whole time," said Shelby.

"Maybe I wouldn't like the music, but I would enjoy hanging out with you guys probably. You never know," said Emily.

"Fine, I'll ask Jordan during lunch. Don't be mad if she isn't cool with it. It's not like she knows you," said Shelby.

"I'll just come with you, and I'll ask her myself. That way you won't have to try to convince her or anything. I mean, it's not like I'm going to bother anyone's fun," said Emily.

"Okay, but don't stick around. I don't want them to think I'm forcing you on them," said Shelby.

"Yeah, totally. I'm not going to embarrass you, Shelby. You can relax," said Emily.

They continued towards the lunch line to go pick up some food. They passed by the table where Taylor and Jordan were sitting. Jordan waved at Shelby, and she returned a wave back. Shelby and Emily walked back to the table, and Shelby sat across from Jordan. There was just barely enough room on the seat for Emily to squeeze in. If she weren't so skinny, there would have been no way for her to fit. She sat with one ass cheek on the seat and the other on nothing but air. Everyone at the table looked at Emily strangely. It didn't make Emily feel too awkward until Shelby gave her the same look.

Shelby whispered to her, "I thought you weren't sticking around."

Emily moved her lips mouthing, "Sorry."

"So, Jordan, I heard that this weekend you guys…," Emily was cut off by some random girl at the table. "Aren't you that girl that got beat up by Jasmine earlier?"

"Yeah, that was me," said Emily, laughing at herself and looking over at Shelby, who gave her a look that was a mixture of disappointment and disgust.

"That was you! Why are you sitting here? None of us know you, and you are kind of awkward," said Jordan.

Emily's face became as red as the apple on Shelby's tray. "Actually, I'm friends with…" Emily was cut off again, this time by Shelby.

"I thought you weren't going to stick around. You are embarrassing me," Shelby hissed under her breath at Emily.

Emily looked at her, confused. Shelby laughed nervously and looked back at Jordan, who was inspecting Emily's clothes that were clearly not passing muster. "Sorry, guys. I think she followed me here. I'll go take her away," said Shelby.

They both got up and walked out of the lunch hall. "I'm sorry, I didn't mean to embarrass you," said Emily.

"It's fine. Just don't hang out with me when I'm with that group," said Shelby.

"Well, when are you going to hang out with me then?" asked Emily.

"I'll find time," said Shelby.

"That's not fair. You're supposed to be my friend," said Emily.

"It's difficult to be your friend, Emily. I'm sorry to say this, but you're kind of a loser, and you're embarrassing to be around," said Shelby. Emily felt like a rock had dropped in her stomach. She lowered her head, not wanting Shelby to see any of the tears that were forming in her eyes, then she felt her temper flare.

"Wow! I had no idea you were such a bitch!" said Emily.

"Hey, you have no right to call me a bitch," replied Shelby.

"You're acting like a bitch, so I called you a bitch!" shouted Emily.

"Wow! You know what? I was just being nice hanging out with you. I felt bad for you because you're such a fucking loser. If you are going to treat me like this, after all the pity I gave you, then fine! Have fun being by yourself," Shelby said, storming off.

Emily's face was red again, and she felt anger about to burst from her chest. Emily ran to a stairwell that she knew nobody really used. Once there, she just paced around, thinking. *That fucking bitch! Who does she think she is? I don't need her. I didn't even like her. She only cares about stupid superficial things like makeup and clothing. I mean, the whole reason she's into that stuff is because she is so insecure, and people only like that bitch Jordan because Taylor hangs with her. If it weren't for him, everyone would see how boring she was and wouldn't bother with her. I can't believe I'm even letting Shelby get to me. She adds nothing when we are hanging out. She was being nice by hanging out with me? Yeah, right. Every time we hung out, I had to force out every bit of conversation. She has all the personality of a janitorial Primoid! I put so much effort into changing my plans so I could hang out with her, and she can't even be bothered at all to make any effort for me. She's just a lazy scum that only cares about popularity. I'm so much better off without her,* Emily ranted to herself, panting with anger. She sat down on the stairs, and her breathing began to calm.

Then, she began to choke up a little. *What do I do to make people not like me? I don't want to be alone… and I want someone to want to hang out with me,* she thought. Suddenly, tears ran down her face, and she dove her head into her knees. She started to breathe more rapidly, and the harder she tried to forget about what Shelby and everyone else had said to her, the harder her tears flowed. Right as her face started to become numb, the stairs shook.

She stopped weeping, although tears still flowed down her cheeks of their own accord, and now, curiosity filled her head. She wiped the tears from her face and walked to the door leading out of the stairwell. When she opened the door, she saw students running all around, crying, screaming, and confused. Emily stepped out and saw dust filling the lunch hall. She decided to follow the flow of people running out of the building. All of the students gathered around outside the school. Emily looked around for someone who was talking about what was happening. She found someone and started to listen.

"It was a bomb, dude. Damn near everyone in the place is dead," said the random student.

Emily was shocked. The people she just saw and spoke to were dead. She thought for a second, but she didn't know how to process the information at first. *They're all dead,* she thought. *Well... better them than me. I'm not gonna waste a single second ever again bothering with anyone who isn't willing to do anything for me. I'm not going to let anyone ever make me feel like that ever again.*

12

Perspective

"Deicended, report to the aircraft port immediately and put on your STYX armor," Cade said over an intercom.

STYX armor? But we aren't supposed to be scheduled to train with that armor any time soon, Tyr thought to himself.

Ben began to sweat at the idea of going on an actual mission. *You're worried for no reason. It's just another day of training just like any other day,* Ben told himself in an attempt to remain calm.

STYX armor was what the Deicended would actually use for battles. Most of their training was done with their plain grey jumpsuits, but every now and again, they would use their STYX armor in order to get used to it. Each Deicended had their own individual design to their armor to better suit their individual powers. For the most part, the armor was made of a black material that fitted tight to their bodies. The armor enhanced the user's strength greatly and made them much more durable. The armor could even withstand small rounds of 9mm bullets. Also, the Deicended had their own helmets that encased their head with their own special designs.

Takumi's STYX armor had the black material covering his whole body. He had additional armor covering his chest, though it didn't protect from a round much bigger than a .45 ACP. Takumi wanted to keep himself lightweight. On the back of his armor plating, there was a piece that stuck out, covering his spine. There were openings in the plating that allowed his shadow arms to come out without damaging his clothes or armor. While his shadow arms weren't out, the mechanism would close and fit evenly with the rest of the armor. Takumi had a cloak over his STYX armor. The cloak was normally a black colored fabric that clipped together with George's symbol, the three circles with the outermost circle having eight eyes placed in between the lines. The cloak could withstand much stronger types of fire. In fact, it was fireproof. It could even block some photon shots. The cloak's most important purpose was that it could change its color to match what it was touching. It was similar to Lucy's ability, but nowhere near as good. It wouldn't be able to match the color perfectly; most times, the cloak would just change to a camouflage color that closely matched the environment. Lucy could appear invisible if you were looking directly at her; the cloak would still stick out if someone focused on it but could save their lives in the right circumstances.

Takumi's helmet was thin and fit snuggly to his head. It was shaped smoothly around his whole head and face. Really, the only facial feature was the rise in the mask where his nose would be. There was a slight indent where his eyes would be, and there was nothing that looked like it could be a mouth. The chin came out a little bit more than where his actual chin came out to. There was a faint design on the helmet that looked like his shadow arms surrounding his head. The helmet was a dark gunmetal grey, and, over the helmet, laid his cloak's hood.

While putting on the armor, Neith couldn't help but think to herself, *STYX armor! We don't get to wear that suit enough. The technological advances on it are so impressive. I want so badly to tinker with it if Cade would let me.* Neith's STYX armor had the black material covering her whole body as well. Neith, needing less mobility than Takumi, had more armor. She had a similar chest piece to Takumi. The same thin metal used in the chest piece also covered her shoulders. She also had bracers that covered her wrist and guards around her shins. Also, she had pieces of the same metal around the outside of her hands, just not the joints. She had the same cloak as Takumi, except hers was designed to store the hood out of sight. Since she typically stayed at long range, she didn't like having a hood on most of the time. It was tucked and hidden in the neck of the armor. Her helmet had hints of violet in it to look like her powers, but it was mostly black. Her helmet was similar to Takumi's, but over where the eyes would be, it was being covered by a half visor that went down just past where her nose was under the helmet. This was because the helmet had more advanced sensor technology than the others. On the visor, where her right eye was, there was a black marking of the eye of Horus.

Lucy's STYX armor did not have the black material covering her whole body. It was still on most of her body, but she had nothing on her arms or on the side of her torso below her arms. The material allowed her to stretch her body without tearing, but her arms would most likely need to exceed the limit and the openings on the side of her body were to allow her to grow more arms. She had no additional metal armor since she did not want anything to restrict her flexibility. Lucy was the only one without a cloak. She had no need for its ability to camouflage when she had her own better ability to become almost invisible. Her helmet was shaped to look kind of like a snake. The metal was scaled all around. It had fangs etched in, and it had snake eyes built into the visor. The eyes really stood out and had special optics that could zoom in farther than any of the others. As she put the last piece on, she thought, *Ugh, STYX armor, really? Not like it really does me any good. Only serves the others really.*

Tyr's STYX armor had the black material covering his whole body. His black scales would activate underneath, and the material would stretch over it. Tyr had a cloak that he could put away if he chose to. Often, he would end up putting it away during a fight. To put the cloak away, he would just have to hit the clasp that held it together and it would wind up into the clasp. He could then take the clasp and clip it to his belt. Tyr was the only one without a helmet since it wouldn't work well with his armor and was honestly less protection than his ability would be. Instead, Tyr had a face mask and goggles. The face mask worked as a respirator and filter that the helmets had inside them. The goggles allowed Tyr to see the STYX armor interface that displayed important information while in a fight. It would display text, maps, or outline different significant objects as needed.

Emily's STYX armor had the black material covering her whole body. She had metal plates covering her chest, forearms, and shins. She wore a cloak like the rest. Across her chest, she had two belts that laid parallel from each other. She also had a belt around her waist. The belts were designed to hold an assortment of knives. She would use the knives in various ways with her ability since she could push and pull the metal. Around the metal plate on her forearms were metal/nylon infused ropes. They were coiled up with metal knives at the end. The knives were heavy and were barbed. She was able to use them to pull things towards herself or pull herself towards things. Emily's helmet looked almost like a dog. Ever so slightly, it had what looked like ears bulging at the top. It had lines etched into the helmet that looked like fur. It was styled like an old Japanese fox mask with lightning bolts etched into its cheeks. *Hell, yeah! STYX armor! I'm like a web slinger with this armor on. Oh man, really hope I get to chase something down today,* Emily thought.

Ben's STYX armor had the black material covering his whole body. He had more metal plating on than anyone else. He had the plating on his chest, shoulders, biceps, forearms, thighs, and shins. The metal he had on his hand was big and clunky, and it connected to the piece on his forearm. The clunky piece that connected to the back of his hand allowed him to move his hand freely from it. Getting hit from the metal would surely knock someone out. Ben had special gloves on that protected his hands from the heat he generated. He wore a cloak like the others. His helmet looked just like Takumi's except he had a slight red color mixed in with the black. Instead of the shadow arms surrounding the helmet, Ben had feathers etched around the helmet and the feathers were colored to appear set aflame.

The six Deicended met up at the port and stood next to the same Owl class aircraft that took them to Detroit. Nicholas, Amin, Greg, and Bellona walked out.

"What's going on? Are we heading somewhere?" Takumi asked.

"Yes, we are. We'll explain on the ride over. We're heading to the Los Angeles part of the City," Nicholas said.

This is going to be a real test of our strength. Hopefully, the Hawk shows his face, and I will show him no mercy, Tyr thought.

No, no, no! Man, I'm going to mess up. I don't feel ready, Ben thought.

The Deicended went to the armory to pick up the weapons they were going to use. They already had their daggers with their individual symbols etched on the blade with them. Lucy grabbed a photon carbine with optics attached, slung it on her back, grabbed a P2 semi-automatic pistol, and holstered it on the side of her hip. Ben equipped a revolving rifle and a P2 semi-automatic pistol. Takumi equipped two photon revolvers and a BRF 170. Emily equipped a CRFF with four magazines of full metal jackets and one photon cartridge. Neith equipped the BRF 172 with photon cartridges and slung it on her back, not expecting to use it. Preferably, she would just use her powers as projectiles. Tyr equipped the plasma shotgun loaded with plasma rounds and HIDP rounds on his belt ready to load. Also, he equipped an automatic pistol.

The ten of them loaded onto the aircraft, and it took off, heading toward Los Angeles. This part of the City looked similar to Detroit as far the buildings went. In fact, the whole City pretty much looked the same even though unimaginably widespread. The big difference was the coastline and public beach. There was extensive security, safety equipment, and Primoids on the beach to ensure the safety of those who wanted to take a dip in the ocean. From the look of it, there was almost nobody down there. It was a nice, sunny day, yet people these days didn't care much to go outside. Most likely, those who wanted to hang out at a beach or just have some fun in the sun were in holo-rooms. Holo-rooms were very similar to the AR room where Lucy, Neith, and Tyr went to the mountains, the difference being the rooms were much simpler in design, having just water and sand, and everything else was pretty flat. Being a room that can take you to multiple locations requires a lot of technology for one room. Holo-rooms were cheaper, so people tended to hang out in them almost a whole day.

"There was a Deicended spotted and holed up in an apartment near the bottom of a ten-story building. Right now, the suspect has nowhere to go, but we don't have the means to safely arrest them. Also, there is a high chance of collateral damage. This is where you guys come in. We need you to safely apprehend the Deicended with no casualties. If things get too far out of hand, we'll authorize deadly force," Bellona explained.

Hmm, I wonder what it is that causes a Deicended to lose it. I never had any such feelings before. I wonder if the others feel the same. Could entering the Dawn Edge be what keeps us calm or something? What kind of counseling do they get at the Four Circles Prison? Does Cade give us similar counseling somehow without us noticing? Takumi thought to himself.

Flying over into the City wasn't really something Lucy preferred. *The City is so fake. People don't ever visit even the ocean that's two feet outside their homes anymore. Why don't people just live a little? Things for people used to be so much more real. There's a certain beauty in danger. I don't understand why George has completely deprived people of that feeling. It probably doesn't understand the purpose of that feeling and eradicated it on the premise of that,* Lucy thought to herself.

The aircraft landed, and everyone got out to gather up with the peacekeeping Primoids surrounding the building. Eagerly, Tyr did what he could to try to take control of the situation.

"What do we know about the suspect?" Tyr asked the peacekeeping Primoid.

The peacekeeping Primoid began to respond, "Sir, the suspect is a Deicended that has some sort of acid ability. The Primoids that were sent to check up on him for missing his task have been destroyed. He made the hole in the building you can see up there. Every now and again he fi…"

As the Primoid was about to finish his sentence, a black orb the size of a beachball came flying out of the hole in the building. It was moving as fast as a thrown baseball and looked like oil. Once it was in the middle of the street, over everybody, it exploded, and the black liquid flew all around.

Tyr activated his scale armor in hopes of protecting himself from the acid. It wasn't necessary though, since Neith stuck her arms out in reaction to the black liquid flying around. A pulse of violet colored light came from her hands and made a large shield. It was like instinct that the shield came out. *Sometimes I feel like my powers have a mind of their own,* she thought.

Lucy had been ready to duck for any cover she could find. Luckily, Neith's projected shield protected most of them from the strange liquid. A few peacekeeping Primoids were not so lucky and were half melted by the acid.

Ben had a nervous habit of picking at his nails. Which is exactly what he had been doing when a blob of acid was about to melt his face off. Ben hadn't noticed the attack until the sky around him was illuminated by Neith's shield, protecting him. He had looked up, confused, and then looked at everyone else. A cold sweat dripped down his back. *Already, I'm messing up. I get distracted so easily. I'm going to end up getting myself or someone else killed, and it's going to be my own fault. Why would they make me come on this mission?* Ben thought to himself.

Takumi was relieved to see everyone protected from the attack but was disheartened at the sight of the Primoids being destroyed. *I hope the memory banks can be recovered,* Takumi thought while watching the Primoids struggle to function with the extensive acid burns.

Three Primoids had been hit by the acid. One was barely hit, but what did hit it, hit it in the face, where its CPU was. The acid melted off half of the Primoid's face, and it shut off and collapsed to the ground. Another Primoid had its arm completely melted off and a big chunk of its thigh. The armless Primoid was now trying to crawl to better cover in anticipation of another attack of acid. The other Primoid had its head completely melted off. The acid even ran down a good portion of its chest, and sparks were flying from some of the exposed wires. Besides the three Primoids, some pieces of buildings, cars, and patrolling Dove class aircraft had been affected by the attack.

"Alright, I'm heading in. Follow me," yelled Tyr.

Good luck, dumb dumb. It's been nice knowing ya, Emily thought to herself.

"Hold up, Tyr. Nicholas is in charge here. He's coming up with the plan," Bellona said.

She was right, he thought. He was getting ahead of himself. He had yet to prove himself in battle. Of course, they weren't going to let him lead the mission. Tyr's face became red, realizing his fault.

Tyr is so brave, but I wish he thought about things a little more. Whenever he focuses, he's almost as smart as me. Still, there's something about his boldness that can be very effective when the situation calls for it. I admire that about him," Neith thought to herself. She turned to see Nicholas deep in thought; perhaps he was communing with George to discuss strategy. After a few moments, he turned to address the team.

"Sorry, Tyr, but I'm going to need you to stay back. As of right now, we don't know if the acid will burn through your scales. Lucy, Emily, and Takumi are the stealthiest of you six, so you will come with Greg and me. We'll sneak into the building and apprehend this guy. Neith, stay back. We'll need you to protect everyone with your shields if the Deicended decides to attack again. Ben, you stay here as well. We need to make sure we cover every exit to this building. The peacekeeping Primoids will cover the other areas of the building, since he likely is going to jump out of this hole he made." Nicholas ordered.

Of course, Nicholas is an excellent strategist. I wonder if he would ever mentor me. I could use a calm mentor that cares more about the brilliance of tactics rather than the base brutality of war like the other Primechs seem to be focused on, Neith thought.

That's not a bad plan, but man, I can't stand Nicholas. He's like a slightly less lame version of Cade, Emily thought.

My first real mission, and I might not even get the chance to do anything. Tyr was saddened by the thought. Still, he wasn't going to get distracted by his own feelings. He still had a job. Tyr loaded the magazine for his plasma shotgun of HIDP rounds since he most likely wasn't getting close and personal. Tyr struggled being put on the sidelines. It was more difficult watching his friends go into a fight while he stayed back, not being there to help them.

"Leave me be!" a voice shouted from the building. "Give me a boat, and I'll be on my way to Australia to live freely. I won't cause any trouble!"

Hm, Australia doesn't sound like a bad idea. No constant swarm of Primoids and cameras watching everything that you do. Just do whatever the hell you want… I think I'll consider heading there after we kill the

Hawk. Won't see you there though, buddy. You're going to Four Circles Prison, Emily thought.

Of course, nobody is going to help you out now, Tyr thought. *You already broke one of George's rules. Justice is going to be served, and you are going to the Four Circles Prison. Maybe, if you had requested to go before going psycho, they would have let you go. Just do the right thing and turn yourself in.*

I hope the man just surrenders. We have never arrested someone before. I don't know if anyone would go easy on this man. He's obviously scared, but that is really his own fault. If you break the rules, you're probably not going to like what happens as a result, Neith thought to herself.

Ben had spaced out again, distracted by his anxiety, while Nicholas was explaining the plan. He saw part of the group begin to break off and panicked, clearly lost for what to do next. *Should I stay here? Maybe I should ask Neith what I should do. No, no. She'll just get mad at me, but maybe it's better she gets mad at me. Uuuughhh… I'll just walk with Lucy and Emily. I'm sure they need me to melt down some doors or something,* Ben thought as he started to follow Lucy and Emily.

Takumi noticed Ben walking with them. He grabbed Ben's arm and pulled him aside. "Hey, man, you're supposed to stay here with Neith and Tyr. Nicholas wants you to help cover the exits because they think this guy is going to try and make a break for it," Takumi reiterated.

"Oh, right! Yeah, I was a… thank you," Ben replied, his face burning red from humiliation. He was thankful that no one was paying attention to them. Takumi smiled and put his hand on Ben's shoulder.

"Ben, you're going to be fine. I know you get real spacey when you're nervous. I'm not much of a confident person myself, but you let it get in your head way too much. Just breathe. I'll see you on the other side," Takumi said. Ben nodded, grateful as always for how supportive Takumi was.

Lucy, Emily, Takumi, Greg, and Nicholas walked into the building's entrance while the others waited outside in case the rogue Deicended attempted to escape. Lucy headed in first and stealthed herself with her ability. Greg followed with his P2 pistol out.

The rogue Deicended was on the fifth floor, but that didn't mean there wouldn't be any surprises for them on the way. Everything looked normal on the first three floors, although they didn't bother sweeping every room since there wasn't likely anyone assisting the rogue Deicended. On the fourth floor, the Deicended noticed there were holes in the ceiling above them. There were spots of acid seeping through the floor as well. Now, they needed to be careful to not let any of the liquid touch them.

Every time a hole was spotted, most of the time by Lucy since she was on point, the group would carefully duck down and hug the wall. They didn't want to chance the rogue Deicended walking over and looking down the hole to see them sneaking up on him. The building happened to be extremely old and still had some wood built into the infrastructure. Every step needed to be more careful than the last with the potential to make a creaking noise that would alert the rogue Deicended.

They got to the stairs and stopped. Looking at the stair, they could tell it was made of wood, and one of those steps was surely going to give off a creaking noise. Nicholas put his hands on either side of his head and twisted it to the left, making a slight clicking noise. He pulled off his own head and communicated through the Deicended's helmets, "Takumi, let me see what's up there."

Takumi used one of his shadow arms and grabbed Nicholas' head. He raised the head ever so slightly above the staircase. He turned the head three hundred and sixty degrees to make sure Nicholas could see everything up there. Takumi withdrew his arm, and Nicholas grabbed his head with the long, silvery hair and placed his skinless jaw back on his body. "Alright, he isn't in view up there. Takumi, you're going to need to get everyone up there," Nicholas communicated to the others, still using their STYX helmet interface system. Takumi nodded his head, acknowledging the command.

Takumi used two of his shadow arms to hold onto the floor above. He then used six shadow arms to push himself off the ground and used two more to stabilize himself on the walls. Lucy wrapped her arms around Takumi and helped raise him up. One by one, Takumi lifted everyone up to the fifth floor with Lucy's help. Takumi lifted Lucy last. She helped by stretching her legs, supporting her weight until she got up over the stairs.

The group then had to walk down a hallway in order to get to what they expected to be the room that had the giant hole in the side of the building. Quietly and vigilantly, they walked down the hallway. They were getting close to the end of the hallway where it would turn a corner. There wasn't a door to the room in the hallway before the turn. However, there was a hole on the left side of the hallway, just before the bend, that had melted down from the wall to the floor into the room with the rogue Deicended.

Lucy turned herself invisible and stood in front of the hole, spreading her body as wide as she could to cover it. Greg moved behind Lucy in order to analyze the room. If the rogue Deicended was to look at them, he would only see the wall behind them. Greg communicated through their helmets, "I can get a shot on him from here, but in case I miss, you guys need to be able to move in on him. There are a lot of obstructions in the way if you come in through this hole. I can see the door into the apartment, and it's a clear path to him. Plus, it's already melted down. I'll stay here with Lucy, and I'll line up a shot to hit him with this sleeper dart." He pulled what looked like a normal pistol and pointed to it. "Once I take a shot, everybody moves in." Greg moved back to their position to allow everyone to pass behind Lucy.

One by one, they crossed the hole while Lucy stood in the middle, concealing their movement. Emily crossed behind Lucy first. The rogue Deicended didn't notice, and then it was Takumi's turn to cross. He was cautious as he stepped behind Lucy. He was also curious and took a look into the room. Takumi could see the face of the rogue Deicended. He was young and innocent looking. *Cade warned us that our enemy wouldn't always look like what an enemy should look like,* he thought. As Takumi looked at his face, the rogue Deicended turned and looked Takumi right in the eyes. Takumi's eyes lit up in fear, but he didn't budge. *Chill... Chill... he can't see you, just keep moving,* Takumi thought to himself and continued past Lucy.

Emily, Takumi, and Nicholas moved on to where the entrance to the apartment was. The door was completely melted down. There were two peacekeeping Primoids melted in front of the door.

I guess those are the sorry suckers that tried to arrest him in the first place, Emily thought.

Nicholas confirmed that they were in position, also notifying Bellona and the outside team that they were about to make their move and that they should be ready in case he slips past them and makes it outside, and Greg stood behind Lucy, aiming his gun at her. Of course, he was truly aiming at the Deicended he could see through Lucy. "Now," Greg said over the comms. Lucy ducked, revealing Greg as he shot the sleeping dart at the rogue Deicended. Probably in the unluckiest of timing, the rogue Deicended had an itch on his leg that he went to take care of. The dart whizzed over him and hit the wall, making a noticeable thump.

Not giving the rogue any more time to react, Takumi ran into the room. As Takumi entered, his shadow arms trailed behind him. The rogue Deicended was shooting a stream of his black acidic liquid across the room. Takumi ducked to the ground, and the stream went over his head. His shadow arms were sticking up and made contact with the liquid. The liquid didn't cut through his arms, but it did eventually eat through them. *Looks like I can block with my shadow arms.*

Lucy picked her head up, a bit confused by the sound. She looked up at Greg and saw he had his arms up as if he was flinching from an attack. Then, Lucy saw a stream of the black liquid shoot through the wall and move across the room in their direction. The liquid sliced though Greg, right above Lucy, and continued through the wall. When the acid sliced through Greg, it didn't all go through him. A good amount splashed all over Greg. A little bit dripped on Lucy as well; her healing canceled out the burning for the most part. Her skin sizzled while it was healing, and, once she finished, she went over to Greg to check on him. He fell backwards, snapping his top half from his bottom half. Where there were holes in his green jacket, sparks flew. The acid burned deep into him. Lucy thought this might be too much damage for even a Primech to handle.

"Stop looking at me like I'm a three-legged dog and go help the others. I'll be fine," Greg growled at her, not entirely unlike a three-legged dog might.

Without flinching, Lucy turned and charged for the rogue Deicended. Takumi continued to charge the Deicended as well. Takumi could see him getting ready to spit more acid, this time focused on Takumi. Takumi launched a few of his shadow arms at the Deicended. "Shadow bind!" he yelled out. One of his shadow arms wrapped around the enemy's arm, another around his leg, and one more around his face, pushing it away from Takumi. The rogue Deicended began to spit more of the black balls he had shot at them when they had first arrived. The first couple of shots flew wide of any of their positions in the room and continued outside because of the way that Takumi was holding his head. The rogue Deicended was able to fight against Takumi's shadow arm and turned himself towards Takumi, firing another ball. Takumi sent another shadow arm to block the acid and was almost successful. He blocked the shot from getting very close to him. However, when the ball exploded, it splattered all over Takumi.

Takumi didn't know where the acid hit him, though he could feel his body burning all over. Takumi became faint, and his shadow arms retreated into his spine. Takumi fell onto the ground and fought for his consciousness. The room around him was blurry, and he felt so tired. *I can sleep for a second. The others will take care of this guy,* Takumi thought. The sound of gun fire prevented him from closing his eyes for a second, and then they slowly closed again. *No, no, I can't fail the others. I might still be able to help them,* he thought. Takumi tried to move his head as much as he could. He noticed a strange figure in the corner. *Is that another person?* He focused his eyes on what he was looking at. *No, it's some kind of altar. It looks like some kind of religious thing, but nobody is religious anymore. What would make someone believe in something so unrealistic? There is some sort of black liquid running down it. Is it his acid? It can't be because it isn't burning at all. There are eyes hooked together, but why? What kind of eyes are they? And where are those branches coming out of?*

After staying behind cover from the spray of the rogue's first shot at Takumi, Emily had run into the room. It looked like the rogue Deicended was wrestling with Takumi's shadow arms until the arms retreated back into his spine, and he collapsed to the ground. Emily saw blood and bone coming from Takumi's body. In a rage, she drew her CRFF and began to fire. She fired the gun until its magazine ran dry.

The rogue Deicended was completely untouched. He created a bubble in front of himself that protected him from the bullets. The bubble burst after the CRFF magazine was empty and the liquid flew towards Emily. There was a blob of it heading right for her face. At the last second, Nicholas threw his arm right in front of her helmet, protecting it. The acid melted Nicholas' arm off, and it fell to the ground. Emily was still hit in a few places on her body by the acid, but her face was protected by Nicholas. She couldn't tell exactly where else she was hit though. She felt the pain in her whole body. Emily let out a whaling scream right before she passed out from the pain.

Lucy punched through the ceiling so she could swing herself over the obstructions and maybe tackle the rogue Deicended. She noticed in the air that Takumi was laying on the ground. Lucy swung her fist at the Deicended, but he began to blow another bubble. It not only blocked Lucy's attack but melted away her fist and part of her forearm. The rogue Deicended blew the bubble bigger and bigger and started to move inside the bubble. Lucy swung her leg at him before he could surround himself in the bubble. It was too late; she kicked the black liquid, and her leg melted off.

Lucy screamed. Her body's momentum carried her through the motion, and she collapsed since her stump of a thigh was not enough for her to catch her weight. She looked up and let out a highly creative string of expletives when she saw the rogue Deicended jump out of the building surrounded by a bubble made of that strange black liquid. *How? How could I let that nobody best me? He has probably only just gotten his powers, and he bested me. I'll make him pay,* Lucy thought to herself. She focused on regenerating her melted limbs. Lucy found it was more difficult to heal her original limbs than it was to grow new ones. Also, while she was healing, she wasn't able to grow new limbs. Once she completely healed her wounds, she struggled to stand up. She stumbled her way over to Takumi and began to heal his wounds. He had spots all over him that had been melted away. His biceps were completely melted off to the point you could see his bone. In another spot, you could see his rib bones poking out of his chest. Takumi was laying there, somewhat catatonic, obviously in shock, but trying to stay awake. He only made faint gurgling noises. Once he fully healed up, he appeared more aware of what was going on. He nodded at her, expressing his thanks.

"Over there, get Greg. He's alive; go help him," Lucy instructed Takumi.

Takumi stood up gingerly and walked over to Greg. Greg was sparking and laying in pieces. "Are you okay, Greg?" Takumi asked.

"Well, I'm alive if that's what you're asking," Greg replied.

Takumi began to wrap his shadow arms around Greg and lift him up. "Hey, Greg, I wanted to mention that I saw some weird altar thing over there. Do you see it?" Takumi asked, tilting Greg to face the corner that housed the strange shrine.

"Oh, yeah, those things. Don't dwell on it too much. Cade said it's some weird habit a Deicended picks up when they go rogue. Focus on the mission. We still haven't caught the rogue Deicended," Greg said.

Lucy had stumbled her way over to Emily. She was laying on the ground unconscious, but still breathing. Part of her gut was melted off and bleeding everywhere. Part of her shoulder was melted off as well, the bone had been exposed and partially eaten through by the acid. Nicholas was looking for his arm that had melted off somewhere next to Emily. Once Lucy healed her wounds, Emily woke up, suddenly coughing.

"Than… cuhh cah cuh, thanks," Emily said.

"Y'all are way too lucky that you have me around," Lucy replied.

Nicholas picked up what was left of the arm that had melted off protecting Emily.

"Hey, guys! Where are you?" a voice yelled.

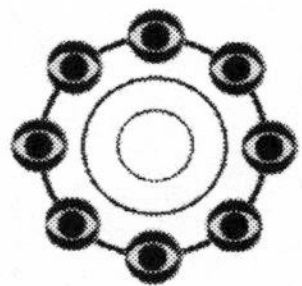

Outside, the three remaining Deicended, the Primechs, and the Primoids waited patiently as the five others moved to sneak up on the rogue Deicended. Tyr aimed his gun at the hole the rogue Deicended had made, so concentrated that his arms didn't lower for even a second. They all waited like this for several minutes, watching every possible exit with apprehension. All of a sudden, sounds of crashing walls came from the building. Then, screams followed along with more crashing.

They're in trouble. They need my help, Tyr thought and lowered his gun, ready to run into the building. *No!* he said to himself. *I have to trust my teammates. I might not like the job they gave, but I'm not going to mess it up. I would be leaving Neith, too, and I can't let anything happen to her.*

As Tyr completed his thought, a black liquid sliced through the wall and out of the hole it made in the building. Neith protected everyone by projecting her shield.

The screaming that came from the building started to fade. A second later, multiple balls of that black acidic substance shot out. They burst, one by one, raining acid on the shield Neith had projected. The Dove class aircraft were sprayed by the acid, sparking as their wires were eaten away. A few began to fall from the sky as their pilots attempted to maintain a controlled descent while the others fled a safe distance from the rogue Deicended. Pieces of the building surrounding them crumbled, and stone and metal crashed on Neith's shield. She began to feel weak. *I don't think I've ever tried to hold up this much weight before,* she thought. The shield began to crack, and Neith started to feel a little faint. *I don… I don't think… I can hold it. I have to though. It's my job. I..I have…* Neith's shield shattered into a thousand pieces and faded away. Neith collapsed to the ground, almost fainting, but holding onto consciousness. The rubble was falling over her, ready to crush her. She closed her eyes and accepted her fate.

Without thinking, Tyr activated his scales and jumped on top of Neith as the pile of metal fell on top of them. Amin's fingers extended in links, dropping and almost touching the ground. He raised his arms, extending them upwards, and the links of his fingers followed. His fingers pierced into some of the debris and falling

Dove class aircraft and stopped them in the air from falling on them. Bellona threw herself over Ben. She had her three shields raised above them, blocking all of the rubble. She pushed all of it to the side and lifted herself out of the pile. She then reached down to help pull Ben out. Once they were both out, Bellona raised her BRF 170 and started firing at the hole in the building.

Neith, surprised that she had not been turned into a pancake, looked up and saw Tyr. "Don't worry, Neith. I got you," Tyr said.

"Oh, uh, thanks, Tyr," Neith said.

The response wasn't exactly the level of enthusiasm that Tyr was hoping for but, nevertheless, this was the kind of moment he dreamed of having. He almost didn't want to get back to the mission, being just as flustered now as he was in the AR room when he was this close to her. Luckily, he was able to snap himself out of it this time, and he pushed himself up, lifting the debris off of them. Neith followed him up from beneath the rubble, and they both looked around to assess the situation, but Neith was obviously still in an exhausted daze. Tyr picked his shotgun up and, as he aimed his weapon, the rogue Deicended jumped out of the building. Rounds flew at him from somewhere. He was surrounded by what looked like a translucent black bubble and, as the bullets hit the bubble, they only appeared to make a splash, dissolving on impact, and not actually penetrate the bubble. The rogue Deicended was still falling down; Tyr quickly aimed and shot his gun. The HIDP round burst the bubble but missed the Deicended, and he landed safely on the ground.

Tyr pumped his shotgun to load another round into the chamber of his gun. The rogue Deicended was already on the run. Tyr shot his gun again, and, again, he missed. *Damn! I'm not going to be able to hit him with this gun,* he thought. As the rogue Deicended ran away, Photon shots were missing left, right, and above him. Tyr looked over and saw it was Ben firing the shots. *He's a bad shot; he won't hit him either from that distance,* Tyr thought. *With my strength maybe, I could fix that.*

Tyr ran to Ben as fast as he could. "Ben!" Tyr shouted, trying to get his attention. Ben turned and noticed Tyr as he grabbed Ben and launched Ben into the air. *Nice throw! Perfect,* Tyr thought as he noticed Ben flying in the correct path to intercept the rogue Deicended.

He threw me! Ben said to himself. *What the hell am supposed to do, tackle this guy? What's going to happen when I hit the ground? I'm going to die. I'm going to die, and I don't think this guy will,* Ben thought.

Wait a minute, he thought. *Tyr knows what he's doing. He has to. I can shoot him from here.* Ben reached then realized that he had dropped his gun when Tyr chucked him. *Why would he throw me without my gun!? The wall! I'm flying right next to the wall. Of course, Tyr is a genius! If I hit the Deicended with some rubble, I won't have to kill him, and I will land safely on the ground. The Styx armor will allow me to withstand the impact.*

Back by the main force, Tyr watched Ben sailing through the air and doing nothing else. *Why isn't he shooting yet?* Tyr thought. Then he looked down at his feet and saw that Ben had dropped his rifle when he threw him. *You idiot! I might have gotten you killed now.* Tyr picked up the rifle and ran as fast as he could to try to catch up to the rogue Deicended. Maybe, if he was fast enough, he would be able to catch the man before he could get away.

When Ben was nearly on top of the rogue Deicended, Ben reached towards the wall next to him, heating and melting the stone as he passed. As he melted away some of the stone, other pieces became destabilized and fell away from the wall. The rogue Deicended noticed the sound of crumbling stone and looked up, too late, to see the wall collapsing on top of him. The rogue Deicended crumpled to the ground as more pieces of the building fell on him until he was immobile. Ben landed on the ground ahead, not as gracefully as he hoped. He didn't stick the landing on his feet and tossed over a bit, tumbling onto his back. The STYX armor did its job in absorbing some of the impact. While Ben definitely felt pain in his ankles and knees, he was fairly certain that he hadn't sustained any damage. Ben got to his feet and walked over to the man stuck under the rubble. He looked up at Ben, appearing a little disoriented. He was young with short, light brown hair and noticeably large blue eyes. They were topped by thin eyebrows that almost looked blonde. He was mumbling something. Ben hesitantly crouched to hear him.

"I just did what they wanted. I… I wanted to please them. The power… I need… have… I don't understand," The rogue Deicended mumbled before he fell unconscious.

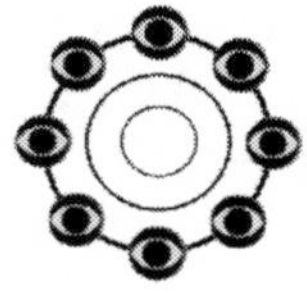

"Neith!" Amin yelled, trying to get her attention.

"Uh huh," Neith responded, barely.

"Are you okay? Are you aware of what is going on?" Amin asked.

Suddenly, the world around her stopped spinning, and she became more responsive. "I'm not sure. Can you fill me in?" Neith asked.

"The rogue Deicended is on the run, and the rest of our team is still in the building. I hear you can float the group. You think you could do that right now?" Amin asked.

"Yeah, I can. Why do you ask?" Neith said.

Without responding to Neith's question, Amin's fingers from his right arm extended and wrapped all around Neith's body. Unaware he could do that, she marveled, "Oh, wow! You have to let me study your cybernetic parts. How do these fingers even…" Neith was interrupted when Amin spun around and tossed her into the air. It took a second for Neith to realize she was in the air since she was so focused on Amin's fingers, and still a little shell shocked. Once she realized she was being flung at a building, she turned and activated her powers. Neith's eyes glowed bright with a violet color. A glow also came from her hands, matching the color of her eyes. She began to float in the air and glided right into the hole in the building, landing on the ledge.

"Hey, guys! Where are you?" Neith yelled into the darkness of the room. Her eyes had not yet adjusted to the room yet and couldn't see anything.

"Don't worry. We're here," Nicholas responded. He came walking into the light, holding his right arm in his left as if it had been ripped off.

Blood was everywhere. It was on the furniture and dripping down the wall. *Could this be the rogue Deicended's blood? It's too much to be from one person. Could this be from our team? Then why did Nicholas tell me not to worry?* As Neith finished the thought, the team came out from the furniture or rubble they were behind. Takumi, though limping from pain, was carrying Greg with his shadow arms. He was almost split in half. The only thing that seemed to be keeping him together was a few wires. Most of his clothes were melted away, along with a good number of patches of synthetic skin around his body.

"Don't worry about me. I can tell by the look on your face you think I'm a goner. I'll be fine; George will be able to repair me in no time," Greg said.

“Were they able to subdue the rogue Deicended?” Nicholas asked.

“I’m not sure. They went running after him, but I didn’t get the chance to see what happened,” Neith replied.

“Well, there’s no time to waste then. They might need our help. Let’s get a move on,” Nicholas ordered.

Neith projected a shield around all of them. Again, her eyes glowed the strong violet color. The whole group jumped out of the hole in the building and floated, along with Neith, to the ground. As they floated to the ground, Emily looked at Nicholas. *Maybe they aren’t all shells in the head,* she thought to herself. Once they made it safely to the ground, they ran in the direction Neith last saw the rogue Deicended running.

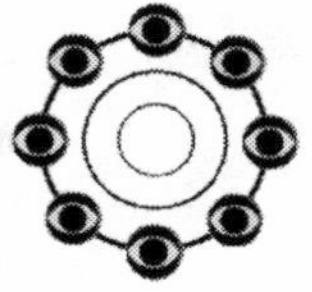

Tyr leaped over some rubble in front of him and, to his surprise, Ben. *Oh, geez he’s alive. I was so worried I had killed him,* Tyr thought. Ben was kneeling in front of the rubble, and it looked like the rogue Deicended was talking to something. Tyr ran up to the pile and noticed the Deicended was now unconscious. “Was he talking to you before?” Tyr asked.

“Yeah, but he was just mumbling nonsense,” Ben replied. “Hey, nice throw by the way.”

“Shut up and don’t drop your gun again,” Tyr said as he shoved Ben’s gun back to him.

Yeah, whatever you say Tyr. You know I didn't need my gun to stop him, Ben thought.

"I found them!" Neith yelled, pointing at Tyr and Ben with the Deicended and Primechs standing behind her. The two looked up from the rubble to see the rest of their team approaching.

"Alright let's get the rubble off him and get him in cuffs," Tyr suggested. As the remaining peacekeeping Pimoids arrested the rogue Deicended, the Deicended returned to their aircraft.

As they walked away, Takumi thought to himself, *Nice job, Ben. I don't understand why you let things get into your head when you really are just as capable and badass as any of us.* He looked back at the rogue Deicended being hauled to a separate aircraft that was no doubt headed directly towards Four Circles Prison. *Man, that guy was younger than I thought he would be. I wonder what he used that weird thing for. What was it again? Some sort of religious thing. Does it have a connection to the Dawn Edge? Why did he build it?*

13

Debrief

The Deicended collected in a room back in their training facility. By now, the training facility had become more of a base for them. This was the place where Cade did whatever kind of work he was doing, and most of the Primechs they knew were stationed there. This was also the place they would get briefed and debriefed for their missions.

Cade was sitting in the briefing room already when Nicholas, Bellona, Amin, and the Deicended walked in. Greg had been sent to a repair facility to get put back together. While he had been split in half, his injuries were much less severe than Joe's injuries had been.

"Well, that did not go as you all expected it to, did it?" Cade asked.

"We've been training for so long. How did it take all of us to apprehend him? I feel like we were weaker than him," Tyr said.

"Don't dwell on it too much, Tyr. If we went in there to kill the rogue, anyone one of you would have been able to do that with no help," Nicholas commented.

"He is right. It is much more difficult to restrain yourselves and only use enough power to capture someone. Now that we have him, the Hawk will not be able to recruit him into his crew," Cade said.

"Is there any chance that he could be reformed? Could he help us one day? His powers would be an awesome addition," Takumi added.

Ben thought, *C'mon, Takumi, don't suggest that. My only useful move is melting down walls. If he gets put on the team, I will be as useful as a walking oven.*

"We would like that as well. However, it is very unlikely. All of our attempts to rehabilitate previous subjects have been failures," Cade said. Ben sighed in relief.

"Why were his powers so strong though? If he just got his powers, wouldn't they have been weak? I can only assume that he never went to the Dawn Edge to increase his powers," Emily said.

"We have a theory that the rogue Deicended might be able to access the Dawn Edge using some other means than how we get you into it," Nicholas said.

"We believe that, when we sent you to the Dawn Edge early in your life, it prevented some kind of awakening that these rogue Deicended experience. The awakening must also be what causes them to become hostile," Cade explained.

"Can't we mass produce the same technology that you used to detect that we were Deicended?" Neith asked.

"We took a risk sending you all to the Dawn Edge. We might not have the same result we had with you all. It would be too risky sending all of the potential Deicended to the Dawn Edge," Cade said.

"Well, at least we would have tabs on them. That information would be helpful, so why not scan everyone anyways," Lucy suggested.

"We would if it was not for the Hawk still being at large. The potential for us to collect that information and have it stolen by him would be too great. That information would be far more useful for him," Cade explained. The Deicended nodded in acknowledgement.

"Now, let's focus on the fight we had today," Nicholas said.

"Let's start with talking about that stupid move that happened to end up working," Bellona said. "Tyr, you throwing Ben was a stupid mistake. What would have happened if the rogue Deicended noticed Ben flying in the air? He would have been a melted sitting duck."

"I know it was a bad move. I thought Ben would be able to gun down the enemy," Tyr said.

"Even if he did have his gun with him, he would have been a completely open target. It was reckless Tyr; think before you pull a stupid move like that again," Bellona scolded Tyr.

Tyr put his head down. He was disappointed in himself. Ben was a little relieved since he felt like he wasn't the one that had messed up.

"Don't get excited yet, Ben!" Bellona shouted, noticing the release of tension in his shoulders. "We taught you better. Never, and I mean *never*, just drop or put down your gun. That weapon is an extension of yourself and forgetting it is the same as forgetting your arm." Ben joined Tyr and put his head down in disappointment. Amin stepped forward and directed his attention towards Neith.

"Neith, you didn't mess up as bad as these two, but next time, keep in mind the limits of your powers. You knew that your shield was going to break. You shouldn't have wasted the energy in trying to exceed your limits and keep the shield up. You should have lowered the shield and created a smaller shield to protect only yourself, heh heh. That way, you would still have been able to help later in the fight. Also, you wasted a bit of Tyr's time for him having to come to your rescue when you overexerted yourself. You need to trust that others will be able to handle themselves without your help and, if not, wasting the energy just to fail anyways hurts the group even more," Amin said.

"Thank you. I will try to do better next time," Neith said.

"Emily, Takumi, and Lucy, you all did pretty well from my point of view. Yes, you didn't succeed, but the decisions you made were all pretty good responses to the situation. Things usually won't go the way you plan on paper, and your choices during this chaotic conflict were very sound. The only thing I might add to all of you is that I think you are getting too comfortable with Lucy's ability to heal you." Nicholas said. "You might not have her on every mission and having her heal your wounds might not be an option. I am afraid that her healing your wounds in the past might be giving you all a dangerous level of overconfidence. Although not applicable in this situation, having a sense of fear is vital. Using your sense of fear could be your best tool in certain situations. It is important that you don't ignore it all the time just because you think there will be someone there to patch you up if you take damage. Yes, Lucy is an incredible asset, but try to avoid using her as a safety net," All of the Deicended, except Lucy, looked properly cowed by this point. The Primechs looked at each other and silently communicated for a moment.

"Now, hopefully this has been a great learning experience," Cade said.

"Should we go back to the Dawn Edge in order to get stronger?" Tyr asked.

"We would, but, like we told you before, the material needed for you to slip into the Dawn Edge is very limited. There is no guarantee you will be stronger, and we do not even know if you even need to be stronger. George will guide us in deciding when the proper time to slip back into the Dawn Edge will be," said Cade. "Now, off to bed. We will pick up training again tomorrow"

Everyone started to move to exit the briefing room. "Wait. I have a question, Cade," Emily said.

"Ask whatever you please," said Cade.

"What if I want to go to Australia and live without George?" Emily asked. Everyone in the room quickly turned their attention towards Emily. She felt human and inhuman eyes boring into her back.

"Is that what you desire?" Cade asked in return.

"I think I do. It doesn't sound like a bad idea," Emily said. Cade stared at her intently, and she held his gaze until he responded.

"If that is what you desire, we can make arrangements. I have to say though, I am surprised. I thought you of all people would want to take revenge on the Hawk," Cade said.

"I do. If anyone is going to kill him, it's going to be me," replied Emily.

"Well then, you will not be able to hunt him if you are in Australia. You will not be able to come back to the City whenever you please, and I am assuming they do not have the resources there to hunt such a man. Do you still want to go?" Cade asked. Emily paused and weighed her options.

"Fine, I'll stay and kill the Hawk, but when this is done, I'm going to Australia," Emily said.

"Well, as disappointed as I am to hear that, we will enjoy your presence while you do stay with us," Cade said.

Everyone exited the room except Cade, who stayed to resume his examination of the documents he was looking at before everyone showed up. A couple seconds after everyone left, Neith came back into the room.

"Having thoughts about leaving for Australia as well, Neith?" Cade asked.

"No, I have no desire to go there. I have some questions for you, though, that I thought would be best to ask in private," Neith said. Cade looked up at her, intrigued.

"Ask anything you want," Cade replied.

"Well, it's about the Dawn Edge, the rogue Deicended, us, and just everything about our powers. I feel like somethings just don't add up. I know the Hawk is a threat, but there's no way he would have the power to steal from George's database. Why wouldn't we scan every person possible? I just don't buy your answers, Cade. I mean no offense. I just believe there is something you're hiding from us. Even the rogue Deicended going rogue doesn't make sense. I mean, your explanation is possible, but it doesn't feel right." Neith said.

"Ha ha, perhaps you have more faith in George than you should, Neith. However, you are right to question these things. I will speak bluntly with you. You are by far the most intelligent of the six, and if it was anyone else to whom I was speaking right now, I would not reveal what I am about to reveal," said Cade. Neith took a deep breath and folded her arms, bracing herself.

"Now, there are things about the Dawn Edge and your powers that we truly do not understand, and there has been plenty of truth in what we have said. I know you will understand that there is a reason for our deception, and that is why I will explain it."

"I understand that sometimes there is a need for a truth to be concealed for the greater good," Neith commented.

"Neith... you were not born with your powers. The first time you entered the Dawn Edge, you were given powers. Well, we are not sure if they were given or not. We think that maybe the Phosphorus granted you the powers. Although, we are not sure," Cade explained. Neith paced the room for a moment while she processed Cade's revelation. After a few breaths, she turned back to him.

"That makes a whole lot more sense, but why lie?" Neith asked.

"If the powers felt like they were given, you might not be as effective. We needed you all to believe the powers are your own in order to best harness them," Cade explained.

"What about having our consent? Does that not mean anything to you?" Neith asked.

"You were all fifteen years old when we first found you. You were unable to make a decision like that. That is why we made sure that all of your parents gave their permission. We may have left out some information to them, but we gave them the important information. Anyways, you all consented to training and doing whatever it takes in order to defeat the Hawk. Even if we were completely transparent and asked for your consent on the matter, there would be no way for you to actually comprehend what would happen, what you would really be agreeing to," Cade said. Neith resumed her pacing as she spoke.

"I…I understand," Neith said. "How did the Hawk and these rogue Deicended come about if he wasn't born with his powers?"

"The Flower of Eos grows randomly. We do not know for how long it has been growing, but we first had signs of it only about thirty years ago, when we came across the very first Deicended. Wherever it grows, eventually someone ends up touching it or digesting it or, sometimes, inhaling it and crossing over to the Dawn Edge," said Cade.

"Then, why do they become aggressive? What makes us different from them?" Neith asked.

"Honestly… we are not sure. We believe it has something to do with the Phosphorus. You have seen them, have you not?" Cade asked.

"I have," Neith responded.

"The Phosphorus are our greatest mystery. We believe the Phosphorus are potentially all-powerful beings, and we do not know what their intent is. For all we know, they are at war with us. We believe them to be potentially good though. Like I said, they are our greatest mystery. That is why we are so careful with you going into the Dawn Edge. Also, we did not lie about how much of the Flower of Eos we have in supply. It is very limited," Cade said.

"So, the Hawk is just someone who randomly came across a Flower of Eos and is potentially influenced by a Phosphorus?" Neith asked.

"No… unfortunately, he is our doing," Cade responded. Neith stopped her pacing and whirled to face Cade.

"Excuse me? What!? What do you mean 'our' doing?" Neith demanded from Cade, raising her voice without quite yelling.

"Understand, Neith, it was not our intention to have the man go rogue. Something else caused that, and I would not say this was the Phosphorus' handy work," Cade explained. "You are not the first group of Deicended we have, let us say, supervised. Now, before you try to dive into the morality of it, the groups before you were started at the age of eighteen and were all willing volunteers that knew exactly what they were getting into. As you can imagine, what we have learned from the Dawn Edge are potentially the most significant discoveries in the whole existence of Earth. We still had rogue Deicended back then, but we did not have a man behind a Hawk mask to come and stir the pot. The Primechs and Primoids handled them just fine. We wanted to discover and explore this new plane of existence. As you can imagine, it was absolutely thrilling, the potential for new discovery. George has always wanted to discover a connection to life on this Earth. What were these beings that seemed to dwell in a parallel universe to ours? They seemed to know about our existence, yet we have seemed to never notice them. George began to think there might be some connection between us and them. They could be the key to one of the ultimate questions in life. Who or what is 'God'?"

"C'mon, Cade. We know evolution created us, not God. Also, it was the Big Bang that started everything. This is crazy, I think you might need to get your circuits checked out," Neith said.

"I know it sounds crazy, talking about a higher power. However, George found out a long time ago that the Big Bang theory is false. For a while, it seemed like the logical conclusion, but sometimes, the seemingly most logical answer is not. By studying black holes and the arhythmic features of the energy surrounding them George disproved the possibility of a Big Bang occurring. We will teach you about this if we can discover more about the Phosphorus. Evolution could still be true when factoring a god-like figure. This is all speculation, but your powers appear to be the work of a god. We know that the Phosphorus have a god-like power to them as well," said Cade.

"Okay. I'm going to need more convincing, but what does this have to do with the Hawk?" asked Neith.

"Well, one of our groups of Deicended had something go completely wrong. It was another group of six, like you. Michael, John, Serpico, Kathleen, Freya, and Mila were their names. They were a happy bunch and helped us discover more about the Dawn Edge than we had ever discovered before. Though there was something one of them was not telling us. Every time they went to the Dawn Edge, they would come out more powerful than when they went in. Kathleen was able to generate black holes and create concussive explosions. She was the most powerful Deicended we had ever come across. Even today, we have yet to see anything like the pure power she could wield. She kept wanting to go back to the

Dawn Edge more and more with no explanation as to why. We had to put a pause on her going out of fear for everyone's safety. With a power like hers, there was no telling what would happen if it went out of control. She was not fond of our decision, but she agreed to do as we told her. However, she did not listen. We had a stash of the Flower of Eos, and she would steal some and slip into the Dawn Edge without our permission. One of the boys, Serpico, loved her even though she did not share his feelings. She was aware of them though and used him to her benefit. He helped her to break into our stash and got the Flower of Eos for her. One day, she went power hungry and began to destroy the facility. All of the Primoids that we had staffed were useless to stop her. The other Deicended attempted to stop her, except Serpico who was still helping her. Somehow from one last trip, she became so powerful that the other four Deicended were absolutely helpless to stop her. In a flash, she destroyed the whole facility and everything in it. It was only her and Serpico that came out alive. George sent forces to try to stop her. Everything sent was sucked up into a black hole. We have sent units for years in an attempt to kill her, but nothing works. Everything that goes there gets destroyed. She is the only thing that George has ever feared," said Cade.

"I'm confused, is she still there?" asked Neith.

"She is... she is in Australia. We hid the facility out in the desert over there, and she wiped out everything. All of the people free from George are assumed dead," explained Cade.

"Why did you have a facility in Australia in the first place? That's literally the only place George isn't supposed to be. And if the society of people who were free from George was destroyed, where have people who wanted to leave the City gone since then?" Neith asked.

"George allowed them to use the country. If It wished to build a facility in the desert where nobody lived, that was well within Its rights. Our operations with the Deicended were much bigger then.

Our facility here works for the size of operation we have now, but back then, we needed more room, and the Australian landscape fit our needs. Since we have had to abandon the continent, George has deemed it a better use of resources to provide counseling at Four Circles for those who have had difficulty finding themselves compatible with George's society and reintroducing them rather than build a whole new society for them elsewhere or risk abandoning them to the wilds, leaving them vulnerable as those who were annihilated by Kathleen were," Cade explained.

"But those people didn't ask for what happened to them," Neith said with watery eyes.

"We had no idea that would happen. We did not cut the thread to their life. That was Kathleen and maybe the Phosphorus too," responded Cade.

"Is there not a line that George stepped over in Its pursuit of knowledge?" Neith asked.

"A line? People once built a tower to reach the heavens, and God destroyed them for crossing the line. Only a God would take such a vengeful retribution as to wipe out so many people," said Cade.

"What are you saying? God killed those people?" Neith asked.

"That day, we accidentally created a god, and in so doing, wiped out an entire country of people. We are not saying that this was destined by God to happen. We are saying that it came out itself to punish us. However, we are not going to let this god win. We will reach the heavens and, if it takes killing a god, then so be it. Kathleen possesses the power of a Phosphorus somehow. She does not leave Australia, and we do not know why. However, years ago, she sent Serpico to blow up a school with a motive that we have yet to uncover. Serpico… is the Hawk." Cade explained. He was met with only Neith's silence as she pondered these many revelations.

14

The Day it Happened: Tyr

Ringing sounded from Tyr's alarm. He snapped up and just after he turned the alarm off, a second alarm went off that he had set just in case the first didn't wake him. He rushed into the bathroom to get ready and was out in less than five minutes. Tyr walked into the kitchen and saw his parents were already eating their breakfast, about to head out to do George's task. Tyr started to crack some eggs to cook.

"Tyr, if you wouldn't mind, could you also make enough food for your brother and sister?" asked Tyr's mother.

"Certainly; I would not mind, ma'am," said Tyr.

In about the time it took for Tyr to finish making the eggs, his brother and sister made it out for breakfast. They were twins, half Tyr's age and size. "Good morning, Tyr! Good morning, Mother and Father," they said in unison.

"Morning, guys. Take a seat with mother and father; I finished making some eggs and oatmeal for you, too," said Tyr.

"Actually, we are going to head out for the day. Make sure you practice well today," said Tyr's father.

"Yes, sir," Tyr responded.

His father put his hand on his shoulder. "Make sure to be an example for your squad members. Remember that a true leader leads by example."

"Yes, sir," Tyr responded.

"And you two, Ullr and Ratatoskr, just because you are young doesn't mean you can goof off at school. Your early years of learning are just as important as your later years. If you focus hard, you all will be as successful as your eldest brother," said their father.

They said their goodbyes, and the children began to eat their food. Ratatoskr wasn't too fond of her bland food but scarfed it down to not insult her brother. Ratatoskr and Ullr were young, but they appreciated and looked up to Tyr for all the hard work they saw him put in. Tyr looked up to his older brother, Thor, growing up. He was their parent's pride and joy, but the two youngest didn't know Thor well. Ever since they were even smaller, Thor was off on Mars assisting George on one of the most important discovery tasks.

After breakfast, Tyr walked his brother and sister to their bus stop and then waited for his bus to pick him up. Tyr's first class of the day wasn't exactly a class. It was a voluntary club that was called GMHA (George's Military Heritage Academy). This was basically what would have been JROTC from the old days. It was an in-depth military history class with drill, lots and lots of drill. At the end of the week was their final drill for the club. Tyr was a squad leader, and he was going to lead his squad in the drill competition. He would have to memorize a routine of commands that he was given and order his squad around the drill field accordingly. It mostly consisted of having a group of people in a box shaped formation move left and right.

Tyr was wearing his uniform as was required any day he had GMHA club. He had a blue button-up with a collar, which was very unusual in today's fashion. He had a black tie that matched the bill of his otherwise blue eight-pointed hat and his shiny, almost plastic-looking, shoes. His pants were bright white with a sharp crease on each side. On his chest were three ribbons. Ribbons were given to students in GMHA as a reward but could easily be taken away. His first ribbon was blue with a purple line going across. This was given to squad leaders. His second ribbon was blue with a white circle in the middle. This was given to students with straight A's in every class. His third ribbon was a solid yellow color. This was given to students with perfect attendance.

The bus arrived at the school with about forty minutes until the first class was supposed to start. The first thing that Tyr did was head to the football field where they practiced drill. When he arrived, the field was empty. Tyr started to practice on his own. He acted like his squad was in front of him, and he began calling out commands with confidence and sternness. He was going over one of the potential routines he was going to perform that Friday. "Squad Aaaaten Huuhh! RIIIGHT Face. FOOOOWAARD March." Tyr marched along with his imaginary squad, chanting the repetition of left and right to pace the footsteps of the squad. After running through the routine twice, a few other squad leaders showed up, and after a bit more time, more of the rest of the squads began to arrive. With about ten minutes until GMHA was supposed to start, the last squad leader arrived, panting from sprinting as fast as he could. He immediately began taking attendance of his troops. With less than two minutes to spare, the last of the students showed up. He was part of Tyr's squad.

"Tyler, come with me for a second," Tyr demanded. They walked over to the spectator stands of the field, away from everyone else.

"Yes, squad leader? What do you want?" asked Tyler, giving Tyr a friendly smile.

"Why are you the last one out here?" Tyr asked. Tyler's smile disappeared, and he looked disoriented.

"Because everyone else showed up before," Tyler responded in a confused manner.

"You're making the squad look bad. You're not just the last one out here; you're the last one by a long time," said Tyr.

"Okay? What's your point? So what if everyone else got here earlier than me? I'm still on time," explained Tyler.

"You're leaving the perception to others that you are undisciplined. If you look bad, you make everyone else look bad," said Tyr.

"Who cares about perception? The reality is that I'm on time; in fact, I'm early," said Tyler.

"Perception is reality," countered Tyr.

"That's dumb. I'm on time; stop bothering about it," said Tyler.

"If the other squads perceive us poorly, then most likely our instructors will, thus making the judgment on us potentially unfavorable. Then, our whole squad is affected by your lack of effort," explained Tyr.

"I think you are looking into things too much. Nobody is going to be hurt from me showing up not *as* early as you would like," said Tyler.

"You were goofing off instead of getting here earlier and making sure you are in position to carry out the plan of the day. GMHA wants you here by eight hundred hours, but I need the squad to be earlier so that we start right at eight hundred and make the most of the time we have to train," said Tyr.

"Whatever, man. Look, I'll show up ten minutes early from now on if it makes you happy. Just stop bugging me," Tyler said as he walked back to formation.

Tyr walked back, feeling unsatisfied. He technically got the result he wanted, but now one of his squad members thinks he's a dick. *Should I have bothered bringing it up? Maybe Tyler was right. I also probably should have waited to talk to him until after practice. I just chastised him about making the most of practice time, but I just wasted two practice minutes on a conversation that could have happened after. Man, sometimes I hate being in charge. I second guess my decisions more than ever now. I love being a squad leader, but sometimes I really don't love it,* thought Tyr.

The GMHA instructor came out and supervised as the squads practiced drill. As Tyr called cadences, his squad followed his instruction. It was easy for the squad members in the formation. All they had to do was follow the instruction Tyr gave. Even if it was easy, Tyr's squad seemed the most well put together. The way they moved together was completely in unison. The sound of their footsteps marching was like a heartbeat keeping its rhythm. For the most part of the club, the instructor really didn't bother Tyr's squad. The other squads seemed to be getting pointers and hints on how to better drill.

During a break, Tyr walked up to the instructor. "Sir, I'm having a problem that I hope you can help me with."

"You? A problem? Don't see how, but sure; what's on your mind?" asked Jeff, the instructor.

"This morning, I ran into an issue with one of my squad members. I think I got a little unreasonably upset that he wasn't early. He was the last one to show, and I feel like it makes the squad look bad. He said he was going to show up earlier next time, but I don't know if I was right to give him such a hard time. I feel like a lot of my squad members don't like me sometimes when I have to give them a hard time," said Tyr.

"Well, doesn't seem like you have too much of a problem then. Let me ask you a question. Would you rather be leading the best squad or be the most liked squad leader?" asked Jeff.

"Well, of course, I would want to be leading the best squad, but how could one be leading the best squad if the squad members don't even like the squad leader? If there is no foundation of mutual respect, is the squad really that good?" asked Tyr.

"Look, sometimes doing what's better for everyone is going to upset a few. Sometimes that is what truly defines a good leader, making the hard decision. It would have been easy for you to shrug off your squad member's actions. Your squad is performing better than all of the others, and that's a direct result of the standards of discipline to which you hold your squad. Really, when you hold your squad to a higher standard, you show your respect for them. You wouldn't expect something of them that you didn't honestly think they could achieve, and you will motivate them not to accept anything less than their best from themselves. Trust me. They might not like you sometimes, but they sure as hell respect you, even if you can't see it. I know they do. When I see them perform as well as they are, it shows their respect." explained Jeff. Tyr wasn't sure how to handle such overwhelmingly positive feedback and affirmation. He looked down at his immaculately buffed shoes then back up at Jeff.

"Thank you, sir, but I'm pretty sure I just got lucky with a squad that knows how to drill. It's not like it's hard to do. I'm sure that if I had to trade squad members with the others, I would run into similar issues as they are," said Tyr. Jeff shrugged his shoulders.

"It is okay to acknowledge your accomplishments, Tyr, but you know what? A little self-doubt can be good for you. Get back to your squad already. Just try to keep doing what you are doing," said Jeff.

"Yes, sir," Tyr said as he saluted and then ran back to his squad.

Once the break was done, Jeff called everyone to gather around him. "Alright, now. That's enough practice for the Final Drill competition. I want you all to break up into squads of four and take turns practicing calling cadence while leading a small three-man squad. Squad leaders, walk around and supervise with me."

As the students were picking people to march with, Tyr overheard two kids talking to each other. They seemed to be friends, although he didn't know them by name, as neither were in his squad. They were discussing who they were going to work with. "I'm going with Tim. I see he's already paired up with Neal, and they both love calling cadence."

"Why don't you just stay with your friend?" Tyr asked from behind them. He had caught them off guard, and the other one of them ran off after noticing it was Tyr. The student who had spoken of his desire to work with Tim and Neal looked at Tyr a little timidly.

"Oh, well, to be honest, I don't really like calling cadence. I'm hoping Tim and Neal will take up all of the practice time," said the student.

"What's your name? I've seen you around, but I don't know many in this club outside my squad," said Tyr.

"It's Christopher," he replied.

"Well, Christopher, to be honest, that sounds pretty damn lazy. Not really sure what you are doing here at GMHA if you are going to be so lazy. Laziness is the bane of this environment," said Tyr.

"No, no! Sorry, I didn't mean to say that, like, I was trying to do less work. I would love to do it; I just don't feel comfortable calling cadence. I get really nervous doing it in front of people," said Christopher.

"Oh, well then. I am sorry for suggesting you were lazy, but I have to say that taking the easy way out is going to hurt you in the long run. Calling cadence and directing a squad builds character and confidence. You may not be good at it to start, very few people are, but it will really benefit you in the long run," said Tyr.

"I'm afraid of being made fun of; I just don't like any sort of attention," said Christopher.

"Understandable. You need to get out of your comfort zone though. Better to do it intentionally in a more controlled environment than have it dumped on you randomly and not know how to handle the situation. Plus, if you pair up with your friend, you shouldn't have to worry about being ridiculed. At least a real friend wouldn't shame you for trying something new," suggested Tyr. Christopher smiled weakly and nodded.

"Okay, I'll take your advice. I guess I could only be uncomfortable for so long until I get used to it." He paused and looked up at Tyr. "Why do you care? I'm not in your squad; why would you care about how I do," asked Christopher.

"Well, I might be the leader of one specific squad, but the whole club is still part of a bigger team. I believe we are all grains of sand, and here at the GMHA, we are being molded into perfect balls of glass. A slight crack in the glass, and we easily break," said Tyr.

"I thought glass breaks easily anyways," said Christopher.

"That's not the point! Just… just get out of here and go call cadence," said Tyr.

"Got it. Thanks, though," said Christopher as he ran off with his friends.

Tyr spent the rest of the practice time walking around, teaching others, and fixing their drill. Soon, the bell rang, and Tyr went to his next class, math. He enjoyed math class since he was good at it. He didn't get much of it right away, but he worked hard and generally got some of the highest test scores. He felt like other classes took more time to absorb the material and really understand what was in front of you. Math was simple. Learn the formula and apply it to the equation. He would even read ahead in the textbook to make sure he was always as prepared as possible for the upcoming unit.

Since Tyr would always be so ahead of his peers during class, the teacher would let him leave a bit early in order to go to a designated study hall to help tutor other kids who were in their study hall period. This was part of a program that Tyr volunteered to do. Every Monday and Thursday, Tyr would spend thirty minutes with a student, helping him with his homework for his math class. It wasn't much time to spend with a kid, but it did help him out.

The student's name was Dan. He was the same age as Tyr but was half his height. He had shaggy brown hair, wore glasses, and wore a brown hoodie. He mostly kept his head down. "Hey, buddy! What do we have today?" asked Tyr.

"Oh, not much. I actually only have this one problem I need help with," said Dan.

"Lay it on me," Tyr said as he dropped his bag down on the table and sat down.

"$16 - 2t = 5t + 9$. Solve for t," said Dan.

Tyr held back a smile. He wanted to laugh since the problem seemed so easy to him. Tyr knew better than to laugh at someone who was just trying to learn though. "Oh, okay! Let's break it down. So, first thing is that we know that t on both sides is the same number. So, we are going to do the equation in sort of reverse order. Since, on the one side, we are supposed to subtract $2t$, we are instead going to add $2t$ on both sides. Now, our equation is going to look like $16 = 7t + 9$. Now, instead of adding 9, we are going to subtract 9 from both sides. Now, it looks like $7 = 7t$. Instead of multiplying t by 7, we are going to divide both sides by 7. Now, the equation looks like $1 = t$, giving us our desired answer. Make sense?" asked Tyr.

"I guess. How did you know to start with adding $2t$?" asked Dan.

"Technically, you don't need to start with that. It was just the easier place to start," said Tyr.

"I guess I just need to look at more examples," said Dan.

"Oh, okay! Just give me a second, and I'll come up with a few. I have to ask though. How come you look more down than usual? What's on your mind?" asked Tyr.

"It's not a big deal. I'm just thinking about something. It's not important," said Dan.

"Sounds important if it's got you looking so down," said Tyr. Dan fiddled with the drawstring of his hoodie.

"Some girl I like," Dan muttered.

"Ooooh! What about some girl?" Tyr asked in a sing-song voice. Dan blushed but continued.

"I keep trying to go talk to this one girl, but every time I do, nothing comes out of my mouth. I don't know what to do to get her to notice me," said Dan.

"Oh! You came to the right guy then. Don't you worry about it; I'll help you, man," said Tyr.

"I'm good. I don't need help," said Dan.

"Well, sounds like you need it, and I'm helping with or without your permission. We're going to march right down to lunch, and I'll go tell her about how awesome you are," said Tyr, way too excited. Tyr grabbed Dan by the hoodie and started to drag him.

"I don't know about this, man. Isn't this going to be awkward?" Dan asked as Tyr finally let go of him when he stopped resisting and resigned to follow him.

"You're thinking too much. Just wait, relax, and the words will float from your mouth," said Tyr. He turned around and placed both of his hands on Dan's slight shoulders. He looked him in the eye and spoke with conviction and confidence that he hoped would rub off on Dan. "I am just going to tell her the truth because you *are* awesome! I have tutored you all year. You are smart, funny, and she would be lucky to go out with you!"

Dan kept quiet now, appearing more nervous than an intern in a meeting with the CEO. They got to the entrance of the lunch hall and squeezed through the crowded sea of students. One GMHA student, Sayren, stopped Tyr. "Hey, squad leader. The rest of the squad is sitting over there; come sit with us," she said while smiling invitingly.

"I will in a sec. I'm a little busy right now," Tyr told her. He looked down at Dan. "Alright, point her out," Tyr demanded.

After hesitating for a second, Dan raised his hand, pointing towards a smiling girl in a green dress. *Convenient,* Tyr thought. *Right next to my squad. They will back him up too. I'll have them cheering him on!*

Tyr took a step towards her table, but he was cut off by someone wearing all black. Tyr thought it was a weird outfit, but goths and emos dressed in weird shit all the time. The man started running toward the same table they were going for. Tyr stopped for a second. Something felt off about the man. Tyr looked at Dan, and he still looked nervous and ready to pee his pants. Then, Tyr heard a loud bang, and that was the last thing he remembered before seeing nothing but black.

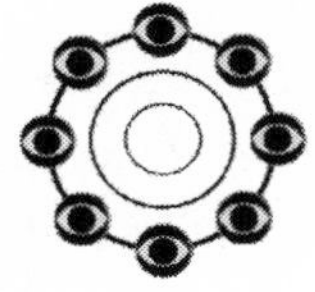

Tyr opened his eyes and saw bright lights coming from a white ceiling. He was lying down. He shifted his eyes and saw that his parents were next to him. Tyr's mother had tears rolling down her face, but she started to smile when she saw his open eyes. She quickly rose from her chair and laid her head on his chest as more tears fell.

"I thought you weren't going to wake!" Tyr's mother said with her voice cracking.

"You're gonna be fine, son," Tyr's father said, rubbing his mother's back and placing his other hand on Tyr's forearm.

"What are you guys talking about?" asked Tyr. He went to lift his head and pain shot down every inch of his body.

"Don't move!" his dad yelled.

It was at this time Tyr realized he was in a hospital, and his GMHA instructor, Jeff, was also in the room. He sat in a chair towards the back with his elbows propped on his knees and his fingers laced together with his face resting on them. He looked extremely concerned. Tyr asked, "What happened? I was at school. Why am I here?"

"Someone set off a bomb in your school, Tyr," said his father.

"A bomb? How is that even possible, sir?" asked Tyr.

"It isn't… we don't know. This doesn't make sense to anyone," Tyr's father said, visibly angry.

"I know you just woke, Tyr, but I think it's important for you to know what happened," said Jeff. "The report says that a man in black, wearing a hawk shaped mask, bombed your school. You are the first… and most likely the only student that was so close to the bomb to wake. Honestly, I didn't think that you would, and the doctors didn't seem to think so either." Tyr took a moment to process all of that. His mind went back to the last things he could remember before going black.

"What about my squad members?! They were all in the lunch hall as well," said Tyr.

"I… I don't really know how to say this. They… uh, they didn't make it," said his instructor. Tyr felt a sinking feeling in his stomach. He thought he might throw up.

"A squad leader without a squad… I failed them. I should have done something," Tyr said, struggling and attempting to get out of his bed. He grunted in pain, and his mother tried to coax him to lie down.

"Lay down, son!" his father ordered. "Don't be rash; you had nothing to do with their deaths. I know you must feel helpless…"

Tyr cut his father off. "That doesn't even begin to explain how I feel!" he shouted.

Tyr's mother interjected. "You saved a boy's life, Tyr!"

Tyr looked confused. "How? I blacked out. I couldn't have done anything else but lay down and do nothing."

"You were found lying on top of a kid, shielding him. He hasn't woken yet, but the authorities said you must have jumped on him to protect him. You must have reacted without thinking," she said.

"Dan?" asked Tyr. His mother nodded. "When do they say he might wake up?"

"The doctors… they say it's possible," his mother said with a smile, but with an unconvinced look. "You just woke up, Tyr, and this is a lot. We'll give you some time to breathe before the doctor comes in."

Tyr's parents and coach left the room. Tyr looked up to the ceiling, staring into the lights. He thought about his squad, Tyler, and Dan, and his mind screamed. He felt the urge to cry with every thought of his squad. Water gathered at the edge of his eyes, but not a drop fell.

15

Creature

Takumi ran as fast as he could to get behind a tree. When he made it to the tree, he took cover behind it as bullets pelted against the wood. He looked up and saw a nearby cliff face rising above him. The display in his STYX helmet showed him that some of the other Deicended were up there. "I could really use some back up in this quadrant; I'm pinned down," he said over the comms system in his helmet.

Tyr and Neith had just helped Emily hobble behind a broken stone wall to take cover together. Tyr laid down cover fire to keep the Primoids back while Neith gently prodded Emily's ankle to see how seriously she had damaged it when she fell a few minutes ago. To their back was the cliff that descended to Ben's location. "I can hold these guys off; go help him. I'll make sure Emily is okay," Tyr said to Neith.

"We have way too many Primoids over here for me to leave you guys. She can barely walk, and we don't know how serious her injury is. That ankle could be broken," Neith said.

"Trust my orders, Neith," Tyr replied.

"Okay, but what about Ben and Lucy?" Neith asked. She heard Ben's voice responding over the same channel.

"Don't worry about us either. Lucy is doing all the work and kicking their butts," Ben replied.

"All right. Takumi, stand by; I'm heading your way," Neith said.

Neith bolted off the cliff, and instead of falling, she glided through the air with a violet light streaming around her. Still airborne, she headed south to Takumi's direction, and not long after, she could see the Primoids firing into the woods. "I think I found you, Takumi. Prepare for impact," Neith said.

Three glowing violet orbs formed above Neith. She pushed her hand forward, and the orbs flew one by one to the ground, creating explosions upon impact. Each of the shots took out a few Primoids. The Primoids quickly reassessed and shifted their fire up to Neith, but their bullets clashed with her shield ineffectively. She slowly landed on the ground on the opposite side of the Primoids from Takumi. Takumi came out of cover and fired at the Primoids. Now, half of the Primoids faced Neith, and the other half faced Takumi. Neith let her shield down for a second and pushed her hands together. A beam of violet light projected from her hands, and Neith moved it across the ground, slicing four Primoids in half.

"You think you've recovered enough to back me up?" Tyr asked Emily.

"Yeah, I should be good now," Emily replied. She groaned and shifted her body so that her weight was on her good leg, rising to her knees to cover Tyr.

Tyr covered his body in his scales and jumped out of cover. He ran down the hill to the army of Primoids that concentrated their fire on him. The bullets did nothing except bounce off his body. Tyr aimlessly fired his shotgun at the Primoids, not caring if he hit a single one. Emily safely took aim and took out a few Primoids from cover.

Tyr charged at the nearest Primoid. He screamed as he took a Primoid's gun and smashed it into its own face. Most of the Primoids gave up trying to shoot him and rushed Tyr. One leaped at him from his side, and Tyr grabbed the Primoid, ramming it into the ground. Another Primoid leaped at Tyr from the opposite side, and he swung the Primoid he had forced to the ground and bashed it into the other. One Primoid went to swing its rifle at Tyr, but before it could make contact, it flew away into the thick of the forest. Emily had used her powers to shove the robot away.

Tyr continued to shred the Primoids. As one was about to kick him, it shut off. Tyr was surprised and confused as all of the other Primoids around him shut off as well.

"Hey, uhhh, did your training Primoids shut off, too?" Tyr asked over the comms.

"We destroyed all of ours," Lucy commented.

"Yes, Tyr. Ours shut off as well," Takumi replied.

"That was my doing," Cade said over the comms. "It appears we may have come across another Deicended. I need you all to report to your extraction point and head back to base."

The six boarded a transport that took them back to the main base, then hopped into the Owl class aircraft they usually took, and this time, it was Anne piloting the aircraft. "Sup, dick weeds? How ya been?" she asked flippantly.

"Dick weeds? Lovely. I'm doing well, I guess. Thanks for asking." Neith responded, disgusted by the crass comment and genuinely not sure if she should be thanking Anne.

"Hey, Anne! It's good seeing you again. Are you going to help us on this mission?" Takumi asked.

"Sure am. Sit back, and we'll get right into the action in just a sec," Anne replied.

She started the engine but didn't lift the door to the aircraft yet. Joe, Cassandra, Nicholas, and Amin boarded the aircraft, then Anne lifted the door and took off.

"Joe! You're back! I am so glad; it seems they did the impossible, though. They made you uglier than before," Emily said as she took a seat across from the Primechs.

"Ha ha, good to see you too. I'm glad to see all ya guys. You all know that there is no stopping me. Even a bomb to the face isn't going to put down someone as strong as myself," Joe said proudly.

"You're lucky George made you so durable. Your dumb ass is probably going to get bombed again," Cassandra said.

"Okay now, we're all happy to see Joe back in action, but let's concentrate on the mission at hand, shall we?" Nicholas said. Everybody went quiet quickly to listen to their orders. "We have a Deicended on the run. We are heading to the old Salt Lake City portion of the City. This one is a powerful one; so far, he has decimated two units of peacekeeping Primoids. This will not be a stealth mission. The second we get off this Owl, we are aiming to take this Deicended down. Now, we have a little information about the Deicended's powers. His body has apparently morphed to be extremely slender and has more of a worm shaped body. His eyes are large and seem to allow him to access a wide range of view, and it makes him very difficult to sneak up on. He's faster and more agile than any of you are. We packed jump packs for you all on this mission to help with the pursuit. Capture the enemy with any means you see fit. Deadly force is authorized." The Deicended gave each other astonished looks but made no comment.

The aircraft lowered towards the ground as it neared what used to be Salt Lake City. The buildings in this part of the City were much lower in height than the other parts of the City they had been to. There was also more space between the buildings than usual. Some spaces were filled with fields designed for sports or just hanging out with friends and family. There was a clear trail of fire from where the rogue Deicended had been. Anne followed the path until it led to what looked like a man leaping between the buildings. This person was indeed unnaturally slender, and both of his arms and legs were longer than they should be. His legs seemed to be positioned and functioning just like a frog's legs.

Everyone could hear the sound of the Owl's mini-guns beginning to cycle. As the frog person landed on a building, the Owl shot its powerful guns at him. Sticking to the building, the frog man looked back at the Owl. He was bald with old, thick, grey looking skin. His black eyes took up most of his face. Oddly, he was wearing a red shirt. Before the bullets could hit him, the rogue Deicended was already on the other building. Anne shifted the Owl, and the bullets trailed the Deicended.

"What are you doing, Anne?" Nicholas shouted.

"You said deadly force is authorized. Well, I'm trying to force this guy dead," Anne responded. Nicholas rolled his eyes back into his metal skull.

Before the stream of bullets raining from the Owl reached the Deicended, he leaped again. This time, it was heading for the Owl and landed on its wing near one of the engines.

"Open the side door!" Amin shouted. "I'll get it off the wing, heh heh."

Anne pressed a button, and the side door slid open. A gust of wind and sound roared into the cabin. Amin's fingers extended slightly, prepping to sling them at the rogue Deicended. Amin and the frog creature met eyes, and the Deicended raised its hand. His fingers grew slightly too. The rogue Deicended took its hand and jammed it into the wing, creating a small explosion. It then jumped off the wing as it spewed smoke.

"I thought you said you had it," Cassandra commented.

"Well, there's still time," Amin replied.

"Stop your bantering. We need to get off this aircraft. Neith, do you think you can handle carrying all of us?" Nicholas asked.

"I think I can," Neith said.

The aircraft was slowly falling, with the fire and smoke around the engine spreading as it fell. It was only a matter of time before the Owl lost all control and plummeted straight to the ground. Everyone on the Owl jumped off at the same time. Neith surrounded all of them in her shield, and they began to glide down slowly. Neith had never held this many people while gliding. She strained as sweat broke out on her forehead. Although tired, she held together up until the careening aircraft crashed into her shield. The crash caused a crack and forced them into the side of a building, cracking the shield even more.

After a few seconds of Neith still trying to hold it together, the shield vanished, and Neith passed out. Takumi used his shadow arms to grab and hold onto Neith. All of them hit the ground hard, but they landed without injury since Neith had carried them to a low enough height where the Primechs and the STYX armor were able to absorb the impact.

Neith woke up soon after they landed. They all could see the rogue Deicended getting away.

"Go get him. We'll wait here for a backup Owl. Use the jump packs in your suites to catch him," Nicholas ordered.

Tyr pressed a button, and a burst of flames came from under his cloak, propelling him into the air. After the burst, the flames went out. Tyr sailed through the air and landed about a quarter of a mile away from the Primechs. A second after, the rest of the Deicended followed. Jump after jump, they were slowly gaining on the building leaping rogue Deicended.

"I'm not getting left behind with you losers," Anne said, looking sideways at Nicholas. Her feet shifted into roller blades, and her arms turned into rockets. Her arms separated by the elbow and were held together by a steel cable. The cables extended about six feet each and made her arms into kites that pulled her. Anne quickly accelerated away from the other Primechs and even passed the Deicended. The rogue Deicended was right above her. She retracted one of her arms and aimed a mini-grenade launcher, firing it at the Deicended when it landed on a building.

The rogue Deicended's eyes snapped to the incoming grenade and leaped to the ground while the grenade pointlessly exploded against the wall. The frog creature pinned its eyes to Anne and extended its fingers about a foot long and pounced. Anne grabbed a shotgun from her hip and got a shot off before the Deicended could reach her. The rogue Deicended stuck its hand into the ground and shifted around Anne, landing behind her. When Anne turned to face the Deicended, her left arm fell to the ground. The rogue Deicended must have cut it off when it flew by Anne.

The rogue Deicended leaped again, but instead of making contact with Anne, it stumbled into a purplish translucent shield projected by Neith. The rogue Deicended turned to the others and discovered that it was on the wrong side of seven barrels now. It fled into the nearest building's third floor, breaking a window.

"Are you okay?" Neith asked Anne.

"Yeah, I'm good! Don't worry about me; an arm can be replaced in no time," Anne responded.

"Lucy, come with me to the third floor. Neith and Takumi, head to the fourth floor. Ben and Emily, head to the second," Tyr ordered.

"Got it," they all said together.

They used their jump packs to crash into the floor they needed to. The rogue Deicended was waiting on the third floor where Tyr and

Lucy landed. Before it had a chance to attack, Lucy extended her arm. She split it into three and surrounded the creature as the arms closed in. The creature spun and sliced Lucy's arms off. The rogue Deicended continued to run at Lucy until Tyr went to stop it. It ducked under the punch Tyr threw and jabbed its sharp fingers into Tyr's gut.

However, its fingers merely pushed Tyr back, unable to penetrate his black scales. Tyr responded with a kick to its chest. The rogue Deicended flipped backwards and quickly recovered. Lucy drew her P2 pistol and fired. Lucy's shots were accurate, as usual, but the frog like creature was faster and retreated a bit into the hallway.

Emily and Ben had just made it up to the third floor on the other side of the building. Ben was equipped with a revolving photon rifle, and Emily carried her CCRF. They both fired down the hallway, causing the rogue Deicended to flee into another room. A few people came running out of the room, screaming in horror.

"It's a dead end in there," Tyr said. "Neith, I'm sending its position on the map overlay."

The rogue Deicended was forced out of the room by an explosion. Neith had fired a laser from the floor above down into the room the rogue Deicended had escaped into. Tyr was waiting and whaled it in the face, knocking it to the ground. Tyr aimed his shotgun, loaded with plasma rounds, and pulled the trigger. The creature hopped out of the way, and the hot plasma melted through the floor, making a big hole where the rogue Deicended had been lying. Tyr pumped his shotgun to load another round. Neith and Takumi came out of the room that Neith had blown up, and then, all of the Deicended lined up and aimed their guns at the frog creature. The rogue Deicended readied itself to make its next move.

Before it could do anything, five spikes popped out of its chest. The creature let out an inhuman wail of pain. It was Amin's hand that was popping out of the rogue Deicended's chest. The Primechs were all standing by the broken window that the creature originally came in through. Amin's arm was extended out. His arm separated in about twenty pieces and sprung out about fifteen feet.

"See, I told you I'll handle it, heh heh," Amin said.

When he finished his sentence, no longer screaming in pain but in desperation, the rogue Deicended pushed it legs as hard as it could, flying into the air and dragging Amin with it. It was heading for Neith and got too close for comfort. In a panic, Neith put her arms up to try to defend herself with a shield. It was already mere inches away though and was about to swing its arm in a fatal swoop. A shot went off, stopping the creature in its tracks. Tyr had shot a plasma round that was melting the creature's right arm and its shoulder. It melted from its neck to half its abdomen and a piece of the back of its head. Amin's arm retracted back with his hand melted off. The rogue Deicended laid on the ground, gargling blood from its mouth for a second before going completely silent.

What was left of the creature morphed, looking like a normal human. Hair grew on its head, only a little past its ears and surprisingly blonde. The face became smooth, its chest grew a bit, and its limbs fit more proportionally to its body.

"Lucy, heal it if you can," Nicholas ordered.

Lucy ran over and put her hands on the creature. Nothing changed, its body wasn't healing or regenerating. "I can't help. It's dead," Lucy said.

"Jessica, you mean. *It* is a she," Takumi corrected. He pointed out the name tag pinned to her shirt. Once he pointed out the name tag, they realized the red shirt she was wearing was part of a uniform for someone tasked with park cleaning.

They all took off their STYX helmets, and Tyr fell to his knees, grabbing his head. His eyes got watery, and he let a few tears fall. *I thought I was killing a monster, not a woman. I feel sick. Why do I feel sick?* he thought to himself. Tyr wasn't alone with this feeling. All of the Deicended felt both sad and sick.

"You did the right thing," Nicholas said to Tyr.

"Tyr shouldn't have been the only one who reacted," Amin said. "Another second, and she would have sliced Neith from collar to navel.

"Hey, now! She was way too fast, it's not their fault," Joe said.

"It was the false sense of security you gave them from your useless attack that threw them off," Cassandra said.

"Still, this should be a lesson to never let your guard down," Amin replied.

"Now isn't the time for lessons. You all did very well," Nicholas said.

Cassandra walked over to Tyr and crouched down to console him. "In the eye of kindness, you did the right thing. Rogue Deicended may not know it, but they are plagued by their powers. They cannot control their power, and it consumes them. You pulling the trigger not only saved Neith, but also saved Jessica. It was the kind thing to end Jessica's suffering."

Nicholas said to Tyr, "You have always taken incredible initiative and been a leader of this team, but it is okay to feel pain. At the same time, you have to assure your teammates that you have the emotional strength to make the right decisions in the fight. You did very well."

"I know. I'll be okay; I just had to take a second to process it," Tyr said as he stood and wiped his tears. *I'm sorry, Jessica,* he thought to himself.

Takumi covered his face as he cried. Emily had tears running down her face and hugged Takumi to comfort him. Anne slung her one remaining arm around the both of them. Ben had an empty look on his face. He didn't cry and looked more angry than anything else.

"Are you okay, Ben?" Cassandra asked, standing up from her crouch and putting a hand on her shoulder.

"Yeah, I am. This just feels familiar; don't worry about me," Ben replied.

Lucy went over to Neith, who was still frozen where she had been standing when Jessica attacked her. "Hey, you gonna be alright?" Lucy asked.

"I… I… I think so," Neith stuttered and began shaking. Tyr walked over and hugged Neith. Once she was embraced by Tyr, she began to weep. Tyr held her close and looked over her shoulder at Lucy, who hardly showed any emotion.

"Why do you look so calm about this?" Tyr asked.

"Oh, well, my dad used to take me hunting a lot when I was younger. I know there's a difference between shooting an animal and shooting a human, but the feeling is somewhat the same. I remember killing my first stag when I was about ten. I cried for hours, but death is a part of life. We have to learn to accept that at some point," Lucy said.

"If death is something to be so welcomed, then why is suffering and pain the natural reaction?" Nicholas mused. No one had an answer for him.

16

Ambush

The six Deicended gathered around a table with Cade, Nicholas, Greg, Joe, Amin, Yaz, Nadin, Cassandra, Anna, and Bellona.

"We have the next Deicended tracked down. This one is almost a guarantee for the Hawk to show up. It's been a week since he has showed up to do his task. We haven't sent any Primoids to check on him as is protocol now. We cannot chance scaring him off like we did with the acid spitting Deicended. We are going to set up a trap for the Hawk. He will be the primary objective. Catching or eliminating the Deicended will be the secondary objective," Cade said.

"How do we know S… the Hawk will be there?" Neith asked.

Nicholas responded, "Simple, this Deicended is the top rated professional neo quadbattador."

A quadbattador was someone who participated in a series of combat games in the quadbattador league. There was a martial arts game, a combat vehicle game, a shooter game, and a medieval strategy game.

"Well, he's top rated for martial arts and medieval strategy, but he's not far down the list on the other two games," Nicholas said.

"He would be too great of an asset to lose if he falls into the enemy's hands. Luckily for us, he was only supposed to be at practice for the past few weeks. If he had missed a game or two, the Hawk would have known that we were onto the Deicended going rogue," Cade said.

"So, let's go over the plan," Nicholas said. "The Deicended's apartment is located near the center of what was once New York City. He is in building 102948 on the one hundred and sixteenth floor, which is about three quarters the way up. We are going to have two Arch Primechs with us on this mission. They are currently at the location waiting for our arrival. Peacekeeping units are staying on their regular schedules and routines in order to not draw suspicion. Jupiter will have a large squadron on a Swan class aircraft floating near the building. That will be our only back up for about twenty minutes after the action starts. If the fight lasts longer than that, then the peacekeeping units in the area will have had time to assemble and dispatch. The building and neighboring buildings are armed with self-defense weapons, which should help us out in the event that the Hawk makes an airborne assault. Saturn, Nadin, and Takumi will be hidden inside the rogue Deicended's room, ready to kill the Hawk. Neith, Emily, Lucy, and Amin will attach themselves to the outside of the building, camouflaged of course. Ben, Tyr, and Yazan will be waiting in the room next door. As soon as the action starts, breach. Bellona and I will be in the room across the hall. Joe and Anne will be in an Owl that is disguised as a civilian transport. If the Hawk shows up, there's not a chance he will get out of this. He might have friends with him, but he won't be able to bring enough help."

The Deicended and Primechs flew into the City in two separate Owls. This part of the City had the tallest buildings and highest volume of them. It was night by the time they arrived, yet it almost didn't feel like it with how many lights were shining. For a section of the City that was so well known for its food, theater, and bright lights, it sure had a certain gloomy feel to it. Air traffic was ridiculous, who could have thought that, having an almost limitless amount of altitude paths for flying, vehicles could still get into traffic.

Nicholas checked the camera feed of the building and was able to confirm that the rogue Deicended was inside. The building wasn't very wide and didn't have any garages for an Owl sized aircraft, only personal transport aircraft, so their Owl let them off at an air

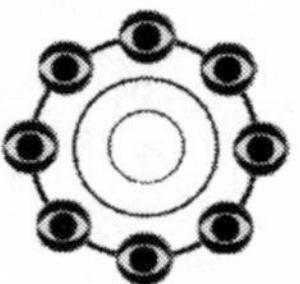

drop point and parked inside the building across the street.

When the Owl dropped everyone into the building, they all split up into their groups.

"Hey, Nadin, where is Saturn? I figured we were going to meet him here," Takumi said.

"Yes, that was a correct assumption to make. He is here right now," Nadin replied.

Out of the shadows, a figure emerged. At first. it appeared very translucent and slowly transitioned into color. Saturn stood about six feet tall, taller than Takumi expected. Saturn was black with a light purple tint. His body appeared to be made of a veil of shadow and smoke. The shadow and smoke were constantly shifting around what could barely be made out as a grey skeleton made of metal. Two lights appeared from his smoke. A strong blue light from where his chest should be and a smaller red light where an eye should be.

"Good evening, Saturn. My name is Takumi; I will be assisting you on this mission," he said. Saturn's red light turned slightly towards Takumi, but he didn't respond. He just appeared to stare at Takumi, who found the Arch Primoid unnerving

"Don't mind him. He doesn't speak. I don't even know why they bothered summoning anyone else for this mission. Saturn can handle all of this on his own," Nadin said.

"He's really that strong?" Takumi asked.

"Of course, he is. Why would I bother mentioning it otherwise? If you'd seen the things he is capable of, you wouldn't be questioning it," Nadin said.

"Sorry, I shouldn't have questioned you, Nadin. You are my mentor and have taught me so much. I promise to make sure to do my part in this mission, no matter how small. I have a question though. How are we going to get into the room silently?" Takumi asked. One corner of Nadin's mouth quirked up as the Primech smirked.

"Well, hopefully with my training, it would only take a few minutes for you to find a way in. But, this time, Saturn is going to get us in. Let's go to the room now and get into position," said Nadin.

They took an elevator to the one hundred and fifteenth floor and walked to the room directly below the rogue Deicended's room. Though, it was difficult to see if Saturn was walking or floating. Once in position, Saturn went back to his translucent form, then faded invisible. Takumi felt a cold hand grab his hand. He looked down to see his own body becoming invisible.

Without any feeling of being dragged, Takumi floated towards the ceiling. His eyes widened in worry as he didn't stop, closing towards the ceiling. Then, he shut his eyes, bracing for the impact. When Takumi opened his eyes, he was in the rogue Deicended's room. His body was half in the floor still but was slowly moving out of it.

I've never seen power like this. I get what Nadin was saying now. How could the Hawk stand a chance against something he couldn't see or touch? What kind of technology is this?! thought Takumi.

The apartment was massive for one person. There only seemed to be two other rooms besides the main living room, a bathroom and a bedroom. The kitchen was part of the living room, separated by an island big enough for a buffet. There was a wall with a TV surrounded by two long couches and a recliner. The rogue Deicended was sitting on the recliner, playing a VR game, and the TV showed what he was seeing in what appeared to be a racing game. He had a small gym in one corner of the room and a large dining table in another. In between all of it was a large open space where they waited for the Hawk to arrive.

Takumi realized that they really didn't know when the Hawk was going to show up. For all they knew, it could be hours or days. At some point, they were going to need a break if they were there for too long. Well, at least Takumi would, being the only human in the room. *I'll have to hold out as long as possible. I'm with the Arch Primech of Diligence. I can't afford to embarrass myself. Even worse, Nadin mentored me. I can't embarrass him in front of Saturn. He'd probably kill me if I did.*

The wait was dreadfully boring. Takumi thought back to training with Nadin. Nadin had waited for hours in order to sneak up on them when they were younger, and he remembered the plan he came up with that eventually got them to pass Nadin's test. *That was so long ago,* thought Takumi. *It feels like just a week ago Nadin was torturing us with rubber bullets, and now I'm on one of the most important of George's current operations with him.*

Luckily, after six hours of boredom and silence, the door to the apartment opened.

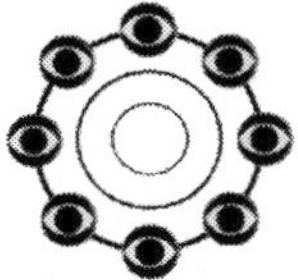

Amin grabbed a cloak from the Owl before getting out. It looked like the same material the Deicended's cloaks were made out of. They headed into an elevator, just the four of them. Lucy found Amin looking kind of funny in a cloak. Amin was one of the meanest Primechs when it came to their training. Most of the time, Yazan seemed to be the crueler of the two but, every now and again, Amin would do something so mean it seemed evil.

Emily thought back to the time they were training with Yazan and Amin. Yazan would be the one to step into the training most of the time. There were times he would violently punish them for failing to properly apply their training, but Amin would make them face himself sometimes. There were several times when Amin would use his sharp fingers against them, and they just had to try to survive. There wasn't really a way to beat him; they weren't allowed to use their powers against him.

The worst was when Amin made them fight each other with small blades. He would punish them if they tried to refuse. Their only saving grace was if Cade came in to watch. Amin never used those harsh methods when Cade was around. Though, when Emily told Cade about it, he didn't seem to mind that much. He just responded by saying, "Amin has his own way of training; just listen to him."

Amin seemed better than he used to be though. Perhaps it was only a teaching mentality that made him so cruel. The group took the elevator to the floor above the rogue Deicended's apartment. They walked over to the door of the apartment directly above the rogue Deicended. Amin pressed the button to alert the resident of the apartment to their presence.

A voice came from a speaker outside the door, "Please let down your hoods. I am unable to identify you." The voice sounded like an older gentleman. Amin took his hood off. "Oh, a Primech! Sir, I will open the door at once." The door slid open, and a white haired, tall man stood at the door wearing an expensive business suit. "How can I help you today, sir?"

"We need to commandeer your apartment for a period of time, heh heh. You will need to find a peacekeeping Primoid to tell you where to relocate for the time being," said Amin.

"Oh, uh, would it be possible to use another room maybe? I have a business meeting tonight, and it's very important. I am hosting some clients here," the elderly man said.

"Maybe we could use the room over there. We only need to access the window anyways," Emily suggested.

"Ah, yes! That room over there is actually vacant right now if that would be suitable for your purposes," the elderly man agreed eagerly.

"I'm not debating this. I'm a Primech; you should know better than to argue with us, old man," said Amin.

"Oh, ah… ah, of course. My apologies! You can use this…," Amin pulled the man out of the room in the middle of his sentence. They walked into the room, and the door closed with the man outside.

The man took his key out of his pocket and held it up to the door to try to get back in. The door beeped twice at him. "Suspended access. You are in violation of neglecting the authority of a Primech under George's command. Report to Block Thirteen B, Floor Three,

Room Two Hundred and Twenty-Five for evaluation of reported incident." The man put his head down and walked off.

"Why did you do that, Amin?" Emily asked incredulously.

Amin didn't answer but looked sideways at her. He only appeared angry at his inability to do the same to her as he did to that old man.

"Our mission is a bit more important than his business meeting. He should know that, seeing as he was able to identify Amin as a Primech," Neith said.

"There was a perfectly good room next door we could have used," Lucy pointed out.

"Not exactly perfect. This is the perfect room. Yes, another room would have worked, but our purpose is greater than his. It's everyone's job to do what is best for all of us, and that man's selfishness was clouding his judgment," Neith responded.

"He was about to listen and let us in. Amin didn't need to send him to get punished," Emily argued.

"He had a lapse in judgment. Most likely due to his old age or his entitlement. Either way, I sent him to fix his issue, heh heh. If you don't fix the issue, then you get intolerable disobedience, like yourself. Now, silence. There will be no more talking from any of you until the combat starts." Amin commanded.

Emily bit her tongue. She wanted to keep arguing with Amin, but what was done was done, and the mission was all that mattered now. The apartment they were in was a nice room, but didn't look much different from any other apartment they had been in. You would figure an older gentleman in a nice suit would be living in a better place than everyone else, but he was treated just like the rest. Even the room below them wasn't that big for someone who was the number one VR athlete in the world.

I wish we could arrest the Deicended so we could rehabilitate him or something. There has to be a way to stop the Deicended from going rogue. This guy is a hugely successful athlete. I'm sure he works harder than most anyone else. He would probably make a great Primech, but now, he might not even make it past today. I don't feel comfortable using a person as bait. I guess it is more important to catch the Hawk; I just wish we could help the Deicended, thought Neith.

Amin opened a large window, and a freezing breeze hurled into the room. The girls grabbed their arms and shivered. "We seriously are going to wait out there? It's freezing cold this high up in the air," said Emily.

"We've dealt with colder," said Lucy.

"I could have sworn I said to shut the hell up," snapped Amin.

The girls remained silent. *She's not wrong. Lind sure as hell had us go through worse. They often locked us in chambers that would be cold enough to see our breath. We had no layers of clothes or blankets to keep us warm. They at least fed us, but we would shiver so much that we spent more energy than we consumed. When they let us out, they kept the training room just as cold, but at least we were able to exercise to get our body heat up. It was difficult to do that with the lack of energy we had. And when we grabbed the metal of our guns, it would physically hurt and sting with the cold metal touching our frail hands. Sometimes, I think Lind just did all that stuff for fun. The cold still sucks, but I know now I'll be able to handle it,* thought Emily.

With the wind still howling, they all walked to the edge of the building outside the window and closed the window behind them. They each knelt down and took out what looked like a pistol that was tethered to their belt. They aimed it at the wall right below

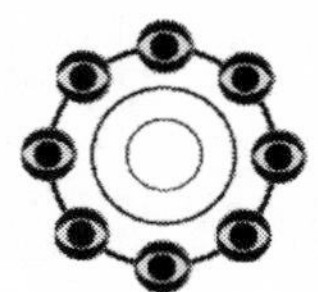

them. When they pulled the trigger, it shot a sort of grappling hook that stuck to the wall and made a popping sound. The popping sound was the device punching the hook into the wall to secure them. They leaned over the edge and hung on the wall right above the window to the apartment below them, waiting and freezing.

Ben pinched his clothes' armpit, trying to fan out the sweat building up in his STYX armor. It had just occurred to him that he was going to have to spend a lot of time with Yazan, who hated him. Tyr was pretty quiet. He liked to do a sort of mental meditating before a mission sometimes.

After the girls and Amin went up the elevator, Tyr, Ben, and Yazan took the next one. The whole ride up was dreadfully quiet. Yazan didn't make eye contact with either Tyr or Ben. He kept his eyes straight ahead and never said a word. Even on the ride over in the Owl he was silent. They stepped out of the elevator once they reached the floor of the rogue Deicended's apartment.

"What if he comes out and sees us?" Ben asked warily.

"So what if he does? He won't know what we are doing here, and he probably wouldn't care to ask," responded Tyr.

Ben took a breath and followed Yazan to the next-door neighbor of the rogue Deicended. Yazan pressed a button to notify the resident of their presence. The door was answered by a middle-aged man.

"How can I help you?" the man asked.

"We require your residence; you will need to move out until further notice," said Yazan.

The man looked confused and pressed a button that scanned Yazan's face.

"Oh, you're a Primech! We'll move out right away. Hun! Grab Jeffery; we need to go," the man said.

"What for? We're eating in for dinner today," a woman from another room said. She walked out of the room and into the view of Yazan. "Oh, what do they want, hunny?"

"He's a Primech, Jessie. Grab Jeff, and let's go. We don't want to keep these nice people waiting," the man said.

The woman nodded, walked back into the room, grabbed their child, and walked back out. She was holding a young boy around the age of five or six in one arm and a tiny jacket and pair of shoes in the other. Once she was out in the hallway, she put him down and began helping him put his jacket on. The man followed with both of their jackets and nodded to them. "Okay, the place is yours. Good luck on your task gentlemen," the man said.

Yazan walked into the room, passing the family as they left. He barely even paid any attention to them.

"Where are they going to stay?" Ben asked.

Yazan ignored the question, and Tyr shrugged his arms, not knowing the answer.

Yazan went and sat on a recliner that was in the room. Tyr pressed the clasp to his cloak, and it whirled into the clasp. He then took a seat on a couch.

"Should I take my cloak off too?" Ben asked.

"I don't know, man. It's up to you. I don't see much purpose for wearing it now," Tyr responded.

"What if Nicholas wants to change the plan a little?" Ben asked.

"Then I'll grab my cloak, but I don't think it's anything to worry about," said Tyr.

"So, what do I need to do when this starts? Where should I be standing?" Ben asked.

"We're going to bust down the wall and attack. Just rest for the time being," said Tyr.

"I mean, like, what sound do you think we are going to hear? What's going to be our cue to move?" Ben asked.

"Dude, sit down and chill. We're not going to miss out on the fight," said Tyr.

"I just want to make sure we're ready. Why aren't you worried at all?" Ben asked.

"I'm not worried because being worried won't do anyone any good. Look, just sit down, and breathe a little. If you talk too much, you're going to make me antsy too, and that's not the mindset I need to be in right now," said Tyr.

Tyr kicked his legs up on the table and folded his arms, getting himself comfortable. Ben grabbed a chair from the dinner table and put it next to the wall that divided them from the rogue Deicended's apartment. Ben sat in the chair for a little while and never took his cloak off. Ben switched from pacing along the wall to sitting in the chair, over and over.

"Okay, I can't take it anymore. Your pacing around is making me anxious. Come sit over here, and let's talk a bit," said Tyr.

Ben walked over and sat on the couch next to Tyr. "What do you want to talk about?" Ben asked.

"Back in the day, before the bombing, I used to think about nothing except the Expeditionary Force, and I focused every day and put my all into excelling at my schoolwork to give me the best shot of joining. I had to balance that and my sports teams; it was crazy stressful. At least, it seemed stressful until we started training with Cade. I remember playing a football game, and when the ball was hiked to me, it hit me right in the helmet. I had so much going on in my head that I spaced out in one of the most important games of the year. We still won the game, though. I got taken out of the game for a while, and the coach had a talk with me. He told me to clear my head. If we lose, so what? We still have enough games to make it into the playoffs. He even asked me if I wanted to quit so I could focus on my schoolwork. He said he would still recommend me to the Expeditionary Force either way. I didn't want to quit, so I promised him that I would get my head together. When I came back in, I scored two touchdowns in the final quarter, and we destroyed the other team," said Tyr.

"I get it, but I have such a hard time focusing when there isn't anything to keep my mind busy," said Ben.

"Well, honestly, I was telling the story more for that purpose, rather than passing a lesson," said Tyr. "Notice, your leg finally stopped moving around."

"Oh, shit! Huh," said Ben.

"Now, got any stories for me?" asked Tyr.

"Yeah, I've got plenty of stories. My dad used to take me hover bike riding when I was younger, racing them and stuff like that," said Ben.

"Wait, you used to go hover bike riding before we started training with Cade? Like not in VR? I'm sorry, you don't seem… like the type that would do something like that," said Tyr, surprised.

"Yeah, I was pretty good, too," Ben said.

"To be honest, Ben, and don't take this the wrong way, but you're usually scared when we do most things. How were you not scared to ride those bikes?" asked Tyr.

"I guess, I wasn't really scared of much when I was young. I started young, and as I got older, riding was just second nature to me," replied Ben.

"Like I was saying, I was entered into a race. The track had huge jumps on it, bigger than I was used to, but I was holding fourth place through most of the race. Fifth place tried his hardest to pass me, but I wasn't going to let him. If he was good enough, he would have got me on a turn when I messed up, but I never did. I noticed he was starting to get a little reckless on one of the turns, and on the next one, the guy just went to slam into me. When he made contact with me, I stayed up and was right about to kick him off until I slammed into third place. I went flying off my bike and tumbled a bit. I shot right up and got back on my bike without looking back. I was so pissed and scared, cause I thought I was, like, in ninth place or something. I crossed the finish line, and I freakin placed third. I had thought that none of the other riders had crashed and passed me while I was down, but apparently a lot of them did. And none of them got back on their bikes fast enough. I mean, I noticed there were a lot of bikes around me when I got back on, but there were like thirty other riders in the race. If I had just assumed I was going to finish way behind the leaders and not tried my hardest anyway, I would have actually lost bad. But all I could think about was passing a rider when I could and never letting anyone pass me. The guy who knocked me down was so pissed that I still finished ahead of him," said Ben.

"Wow. Not going to lie; that's pretty cool. What about first and second place? You ever make your way up to that?" asked Tyr.

"I got second once. Honestly not sure how. It was an endurance race. I'm sure most of the competition broke down…" Ben cut off when he noticed Yazan place his finger on his temple.

"We will stand by till we receive the order," Yazan said.

17

Ruse

The door buzzer rang, scaring Takumi and eliciting a loud gasp from him, but it was muffled by his mask. The rogue Deicended, still sitting in the recliner with his VR helmet on, turned his head towards the door. The TV displaying the racing game he was playing showed an alert across the screen, notifying him that someone was at the door. He got up and walked towards the door.

It must be a delivery person or something. If it were the Hawk, I'm sure Nicholas would have notified us, Takumi thought. Still, Takumi's heart started racing, and adrenaline pumped into his veins at the possibility.

The Deicended pressed a button next to his door, and a screen came on, showing the outside of his door. There was no one.

What is going on? This doesn't feel right, Takumi thought. His heart rate further increased, and now, he began to sweat. He felt lucky to be wearing gloves. He grabbed his dagger, ready to unsheathe it.

Nadin placed his hand on Takumi's arm, preventing him from unsheathing his blade. The Deicended turned from the door, and a man appeared before him. It was the man in the hawk mask. Nadin kept his arm over Takumi's and signaled to be quiet.

Wait! Why? He's right there… Temperance, Takumi. Think. It's not the perfect moment yet. If we attack now, the rogue Deicended might get in the way. If we wait, we might get a better moment to strike, Takumi thought. His heart steadied a bit, but he didn't take his hand off the blade.

"He's in the room," Nadin silently communicated to Nicholas. For Takumi, the message displayed in his STYX helmet.

"How? No one reported seeing him," Nicholas replied.

"Reported or not, he's in the fucking room," said Nadin.

The rogue Deicended looked at the man with the hawk shaped masked in confusion. "Uh, how did you get into my room?" the rogue Deicended asked.

"Well, I walked in. I have something to talk to you about. I think you will be most interested in hearing about it," said the Hawk. Takumi's jaw tightened when he heard the Hawk's voice. It sounded too normal to belong to someone who had bombed a school full of kids. He felt his blood begin to boil, wanting to rip that ridiculous mask off of his face, but Nadin's hand on his arm kept him grounded.

"And what would I be interested in hearing about?" The rogue Deicended asked.

"Power," the Hawk replied.

"I'm listening," the Deicended said after a brief pause.

"Take a seat, and I will explain," said the Hawk.

The rogue Deicended gestured, as if to say, "Sure, why not" by raising his arms. He walked back to his recliner.

The Hawk took a step towards the couch. Saturn became visible, with a hand on a sword sheathed at his side. As his shadowy figure collected, Takumi and Nadin were revealed as well. As Saturn unsheathed his blade, he shot towards the Hawk, and when his blade was fully drawn, it had already sliced through the Hawk masked man.

That's it! Takumi thought.

"You guys were in the room the whole time? I guess we did beat you here at least," a voice said from an unknown origin.

The Hawk, somehow still standing, faded away. One of the couches faded away as well and revealed four figures. The first man was a skinny, scrappy blonde. He was wearing a shirt and pants that were both torn and bland. Another man had a big overcoat that covered his whole body and a hood that made it difficult to see his face. The third person appeared to be a female of average height, skinny with long brown hair and wearing a black leather jacket. She was standing with a very obvious confidence that set her apart from the others. The last person wore a similar cloak that the six Deicended wore, except it had a popped collar that was torn at the ends. He wore the Hawk shaped mask, formed like a beak with a feather design etched on the sides. He was taller than the rest and held a dagger in his left hand.

Nadin drew his sword and went to draw his pistol as well. He was stopped by a punch to the gut that sparked electricity. Nadin was stunned, but not knocked down. It was the scrappy blonde that had punched him. Before Nadin could counter, the blonde Deicended roundhouse kicked him in the head, launching him into the wall. He was as fast as the lightning that had sparked from his hands. Takumi hadn't imagined anyone could be so fast as to get the drop on Nadin while standing right in front of him.

Saturn was distracted by what appeared to be five copies of the hooded Deicended. Saturn quickly realized they were mirages surrounding him. He ran through them, and as he did that, water shot from the sink. The water wrapped around Saturn. It was the quadbattador, moving his arms and seemingly controlling the water. The water squeezed Saturn but went right through him. The female

Deicended lifted a BRF 170 and fired at Saturn, but like the water, it too fazed through him.

Neith, Lucy, Emily, and Amin broke through the glass window and raised their guns. The Hawk turned towards them, waved his hand, and created a powerful gust, launching the four back out of the window they came in through. Amin's hand shot out like a rocket, connected by a steel cable to his arm. His arm stuck into the floor of the room. The Hawk whipped his left hand with the dagger. From the dagger, a blade of wind flung out and cut the cable that connected Amin's arm to his hand, causing him to drop like a brick.

The scrappy Deicended set his eyes on Takumi. Armed with a photon revolver, Takumi shot at the man. The scrappy Deicended flashed to the side of the shot, then towards Takumi. "Shadow Strike!" Takumi yelled as he sent one of his shadow arms at the Deicended, but he dodged the attack, appearing, as if he had teleported, behind Takumi. Before the blonde Deicended could attack, Takumi sent multiple shadow arms in all directions. "Hydra's Wrath!" he shouted. This time, the blonde Deicended couldn't dodge. He was forced back a few feet and punched the shadow arm, using his power to shock it, with no effect. The shadow arm had no hold of him, so he flashed away. This time, the scrappy Deicended appeared crouched behind Takumi. He kicked out Takumi's legs, causing him to collapse. Before he hit the ground, the blonde Deicended twisted and swung his leg, kicking Takumi into the wall next to Nadin.

Ben, hearing the commotion, shared the same look as Tyr and even Yazan. *What is going on,* the three thought. Ben ran to the wall and put his hands up. The drywall quickly burned away, but the concrete behind it took time to melt. "Move," Yazan shouted at Ben. He pushed him out of the way and ran through the wall, creating a hole matching Yaz's hulking size.

Saturn charged at the Deicended that controlled the water, and Yaz raised two BRF 170s, ready to fire. The female rogue Deicended screamed. Her voice created some sort of vibration in the air. When it hit Yazan, he went flying into the kitchen, crashing into the stove. She turned her head, aiming her voice at Saturn. It stopped him in his tracks, and Saturn drove his blade into the floor, failing to keep himself from flying back.

Tyr and Ben ran into the room. Immediately, Ben was sent flying back through the hole when the blonde Deicended flashed before him and punched him in the gut. Tyr barely noticed before the same Deicended appeared at his side punching him in the kidney. Tyr gasped as he was hit by the shocking blow. Though it didn't seem to have the same impact, as Tyr remained on his feet. Tyr swung at the blonde Deicended, but he flashed away. He appeared at the opposite side hitting Tyr again, still with little effect. Tyr swung again, and the scrappy Deicended repeated what he had done before. Tyr continued to try to hit him, and the blonde Deicended continued to fail at knocking Tyr down.

"Move," shouted the quadbattador. He took the water he was controlling and forced it at Tyr, knocking him back into the room.

Yazan went to stand up and lifted his gun. The blonde Deicended appeared and kicked the gun out of his hands. "You little shi.." Yazan was yelling before a fist shut him up. Not even a second passed, yet the blonde Deicended hit Yazan twenty times in the chest, each one shocking him. His legs gave out, and he collapsed to the ground.

"Well, that will keep you down for a bit," the blonde Deicended sneered.

The quadbattador gathered more water from the sink and whipped it around in an attempt to, in some way, affect Saturn. It was useless, just like the mirages the other Deicended tried to use to confuse Saturn. As Saturn went to run through one of the illusions, he was struck in his face by the back end of a rifle. He was knocked onto his back once again. The female Deicended stood over Saturn, holding her rifle upside down. It was shaking from the vibration in her hands. She swung it down at Saturn, only to hit the floor when he fazed through the ground.

"That was probably a bad move," the female Deicended said unsurely. She dropped her gun and raised her hands, closed fist. She closed her eyes and concentrated. The floor below their feet shook. In fact, the whole building began to shake.

"Nice going. I think an Arch Primoid is a little much to go up against," the Hawk said.

"Well, at least they are all out of the way now," Nicholas said to Bellona in the other room where they were waiting to make their move.

Bellona racked back the bolt to her BRF 184, armed with HIDP rounds. She fired the gun, and the rounds went through the walls of both rooms. She fired multiple rounds, spraying everywhere, hoping to hit anything. Each round made an unreasonably large hole in the wall. One hit the recliner, which exploded and spread itself across the room. Nadin, keeping low, checked on Takumi.

The water controlling Deicended spread the water to cover his group. Somehow, the water stopped the shots from progressing. Once Nadin knew Bellona was out of rounds, he helped Takumi to his feet.

"Time to run! They're more prepared than I expected," the Hawk said as an Owl pulled up next to the broken window.

The group of rogue Deicended ran for their escape ship. As they went to board, Nadin and Takumi began to fire at them. "I got this. Go!" the scrappy blonde Deicended said to the others. He charged at Nadin first. Nadin swung his blade and shot at the Deicended but, only barely, missed. The Deicended struck Nadin down quickly and moved to Takumi. Knowing about Takumi's shadow arms this time, he moved past his attacks and struck him down as well.

The rest of the rogue Deicended were boarded on the Owl when it was attacked by Anne, who was racing to the battle in her own Owl with Joe copiloting. The rogue Deicended's Owl was protected by its shield, so Anne fired a missile. The rogue Owl swerved away from the building, and the missile missed, exploding on a neighboring building.

"We need to go now, Zack," the Hawk yelled at the scrappy Deicended.

He turned around, running for the ship. Saturn's head fazed through the floor; the building was no longer shaking. The blonde leaped into the air to board the Owl. The female rogue Deicended saw a confident smirk on Zack's face right before a blade slid through his hip and out the other side of his neck. Blood filled the air and the half of Zack with his head still attached slammed against the bottom of the Owl.

"NOOOOOO!" the female Deicended screamed, sending waves of vibration through the air. The waves slammed Saturn into the glass of the building, and the Owl fled the area.

"I need a status report," Nicholas said over the comms.

"Amin's squad fell from the building. The rest of us are fine. The rogue Deicended have escaped in an Owl," replied Nadin. Bellona and Nicholas walked into the destroyed apartment once it was confirmed to be safe.

"We're fine. Neith caught us with her powers, and we landed safely," Amin said over the comms.

"Where's Jupiter with the backup?" Nicholas asked.

"Uhhh, he looks a little busy. Oh, and also, I'm tailing the rogue Deicended," Anne said over the comms.

"What do you mean busy?" Nicholas asked.

"I'll tell ya. Well, it kind looks like there is an entire float park attacking his Swan. And oh.. oh .. a laser from Jupiter's side just hit the other one really, really hard, and now it doesn't really look like a float park," Joe said over the comms.

"What does it look like?" Nicholas asked.

"It looks like they have a damn Swan themselves!" Anne shouted.

"I think they are using the swan as a distraction to get the hell out," Neith suggested. *That's crazy to think that one Deicended could be worth sacrificing a Swan and its crew,* Neith thought.

"Keep tailing them. We'll see what we can do to help Jupiter out," Nicholas said.

Anne followed the owl, and it began to split into two owls, then three, four, and eight. They kept multiplying. The mirage Deicended was doing his job well and confusing Anne and Joe.

"What are we going to do? We can't lose them!" Joe said to Anne.

"Keep firing till we see one with shields light up. That will tell us which one we need to get," said Anne.

Two revolving mini-guns fired from under the cockpit. They were locked in to fire straight where the ship aimed. There was a power photon gun on the top of the Owl that was able to rotate which Joe was manning. It was like a hell storm of fire coming from the Owl as Anne swerved, trying to hit as many of the illusions as possible. Joe was often missing his shot, with it being difficult to hit anything due to Anne's reckless flying. Civilian aircraft were frantically swerving away from the fleet of incoming Owl's being pursued by a wildly firing Owl. They came close to a building, and the numerous copies of the rogue Owl split around the building. More of them seemed to turn left, so Anne decided to follow those.

"Hope you chose right," Joe stated.

"Yeah, I hope so too," Anne replied. They continued to hit Owl after Owl until they all fazed away.

"Well, so much for hope," Joe said.

"Shut it, nimrod. We can still catch them. Their raggedy ship couldn't have gone far, and George's aircraft are the best made," Anne said as she punched the thruster forward, throwing their bodies deep into their seats. "Anything on the monitors?"

"There's a bit too much air traffic to pinpoint which one they are," Joe replied as aircraft from the city's traffic raced to get out of their way. They whipped around building after building, frantically looking for the enemy's Owl. "I got something!" Joe shouted. "Look at this civilian airship right here on the scanner. Doesn't appear to be going in the same direction as the rest of the traffic."

Anne made a drastic turn to cut off the suspicious ship. "I don't think you were right about that," Anne said, not seeing any ship that might be acting out of the ordinary.

"No, I am. Look at that blur by the buildings. That illusions guy is concealing them, but he can't change the appearance of the vehicle fast enough to match the buildings they are flying next to," said Joe.

"If they get over the ocean, and out of range of our radar, no one is going to be able to detect them remotely, and it doesn't look like anyone else has a visual on them," said Anne. "Quick! Make this shot count."

Joe aimed the cannon for a few seconds and fired. The shot hit, lighting up the blue shields of the enemy Owl's whose camouflage was disrupted. In response, the Owl split into multiple illusions again. Anne fired the mini-guns at their Owl, keeping the enemy's aircraft constantly lit up by their blue shields. The enemy gave up using the mirages and took evasive maneuvers.

"Just a few shots with your gun, Joe, and we'll get them," Anne said.

"I'm trying," Joe said.

Explosions set off near the base of a giant building next to the enemy's craft. It began to collapse over them. It was so wide it would be incredibly difficult to evade. Joe got off another shot that hit the enemy, but their shields held. The rogues cleared the falling building, but Anne and Joe still had a bit to go.

"You're not going to make it, Anne! Go low till we clear the building!" Joe yelled.

"The ocean is right there. We don't have any time for a detour," Anne replied with a more determined face than Joe had ever seen on a person.

"Anne! Anne! Anne!" Joe screamed as the building closed in on them. So close to making it, they ducked their heads as the building fell over their Owl, but never felt the impact

"Another mirage?! You got to be fucking with me!" Anne screamed.

Joe didn't say anything. Anne's determination had rubbed off on him. He was going to shoot down that Owl. He pulled the trigger. The blue shield sparked and faded away. "They're vulnerable," Anne said with a smirk.

The side door to the enemy's owl opened. The Hawk stuck his head out of the door. In the distance, his hand appeared to wave downward with his dagger in his hand. It happened all too fast, but with Anne's Primech eyes, she could see the bladed gale crash through their shield, moving to the glass of the Owl, shattering it inward. She watched as the sharp gust met the bridge of her nose between her eyes.

The owl, damaged, descended erratically. "Hey, you're messing up my shot," Joe shouted as he looked over to the face he had known for years. It was split down the middle, sparking with a light that was absent from her eyes.

18

The Day it Happened: Takumi

His eyes opened to the sound of music, the soundtrack to one of his favorite video games during the final boss fight. It was something to get his blood moving with a slight dose of stress to keep him awake. After a few minutes of being awake, Takumi had already finished getting ready in the bathroom. Takumi's father was already off doing his task for the day, and his mother was making breakfast for him and his sister. Their mother had prepared some grilled fish, steamed vegetables, and a small bowl of rice. This was a very traditional meal that their ancestors would have eaten in the morning.

After saying good morning to each other, nobody really said anything else. His mother told them to have a good day as they went to leave. Takumi's sister was much younger than him and was struggling to put her shoes on. Without being asked, he knelt down, tied them for her, and patted her on the head.

They walked down the street together, and Takumi waited with his sister for her bus. Her school was a ways away, but Takumi's high school was within walking distance. They were the only ones at the stop.

"Hey, big brother. I was watching an old TV show and, everywhere they walked, there were these really pretty flowers. I've seen them in books before; I think they're called daisies. I was wondering, though, why we don't see flowers when we walk outside, but when I see anything from a long time ago, the place is filled with all kinds of pretty plants and flowers," Takumi's sister said.

"From what I learned, with all of the buildings and things that George has made, there isn't much soil around everyone. So, without soil on the ground, flowers and other plants can't really grow. I heard that outside the City, though, plants and flowers still grow everywhere. George even has farms in these bubbles that grow all kinds of plant life, like the food we eat," said Takumi.

"I'd prefer it if we had pretty flowers to look at," said his sister.

"We can go visit a plant farm or go to an arcade and see them in VR if you would like that someday, Ichika," said Takumi.

She put her head down, saddened by the statement. "You're not getting me, big brother. I don't want to go to one of those weird setups that George made and look at the flowers on display. I want to, one day, just be walking to any normal place and see daisies just sitting there. It would be so wonderful to see such a beautiful thing so randomly," said Ichika.

Takumi rubbed his sister's head, "You're being so silly."

"Just something I've been thinking about," she lifted her head. "You know, I would like to go to one of the bubbles now that I think about it, only if there are going to be daisies, though. Now that I saw one on TV, I really want to see one."

"Sure thing. That's what we'll do on Saturday; I'll take you," said Takumi. His sister grabbed and hugged him harder than he had ever been hugged before.

As Ichika let go of her brother, the bus rolled up, stopped, and took her away. Takumi continued to walk to his school. The buildings around him were towering, and he probably wouldn't have had time to drop his sister off if he lived higher up in the building. Even with a pretty fast elevator, it would take him too much time to get down. Takumi walked up to a convenience store, and there were three kids waiting outside with breakfast in their hands.

"Hey, bro!" one of them said. "I got an extra chicken on a stick if you want some."

"Thanks, Felix, but I already had food with my family," Takumi replied with a friendly wave and smile.

After they all got done saying hello to each other, they walked to the school, which was within sight at this point. Felix was a good friend of Takumi's. They met doing some little league sports. Both of them were always good at whatever they played, so they got paired up on a bunch of teams together and just became friends. Felix was always kind to everyone he met and was a pretty tall guy. The whole group even shared many interests with Takumi. Probably the biggest difference between them was that Jamal was a bit more outspoken. Eva was the energy of the group and the nicest, except when it came to Felix. For some reason, she treated him a bit differently.

As they walked into the school, Jamal grabbed a comic out of his bag. It was *Escape: Fire and Wind.*

"Tell me you got a chance to get a copy of this man," said Jamal.

"I heard good things about that, but I haven't had the chance. I'm still trying to finish *Day Man vs. the Night Man*. I had a lot of homework and didn't get to make much of a dent in it," said Takumi.

"Well, yeah. I haven't had a chance to read this myself, but I'm so pumped for it. The reviews for it are amazing," said Jamal.

"You've been reading that Day Man one for a bit, Takumi. How is it?" asked Felix.

"Honestly, it might be a little too early to judge, but I think Night Man is my new favorite character. This whole story is amazing actually," replied Takumi.

"You have good taste, Takumi, so I think I'll pick up a copy myself," said Eva. "Not sure why you bother asking though, Felix. Not like you're ever going to read it yourself."

"Doesn't mean I don't like hearing about them. Both sound like cool stories to me. I'm just kind of cheap, so I don't buy them. Not like I have to anyways; these guys tell me the stories, and I like listening," said Felix.

"Well, some of us like to contribute to the creators," said Eva.

"You two always argue like an old married couple, I swear," said Jamal.

"Uh, no we don't," snapped Eva.

"Eh, whatever," said Felix. Eva blushed at his response. "I got to head to my class. Have fun in history class, you guys."

Felix walked off, and the three others walked to their shared history class together. They were lucky that they got to sit together by the back of the class. It allowed them to goof off a little bit more. Really, it just let Eva goof off since Takumi and Jamal really cared about doing well in class.

Before the class started, Jamal asked Takumi, "Oh, so what about the comic is it that you like so much?"

Takumi got visibly excited to talk about the comic. "It's so cool. You remember when I mentioned that I really like Night Man? Well, in almost every scene, he's always doing this cool karate, and the character has cat eyes that help him with his moves."

"Okay, I'm definitely sold now. I'm getting a copy tonight," said Eva.

"As soon as I'm done with the one I'm on, that's next," said Jamal.

The teacher walked in and began their instruction, talking about George and how things were right after the age of Cain. "At the start of our time, in the Infinite Blossom as George puts it, we didn't have a completely instant transition into this joyful time. We look at the end of the Age of Cain as when George first implemented tasks for humans, tasks like the one I'm working on right now. Some people thoroughly enjoyed doing absolutely nothing. When George came and started assigning people things to do, some people jumped at the chance to get to do something, to contribute to our society. Others, on the other hand, were addicted to the laziness they had languished in during the Age of Cain, to sitting on a couch and watching TV. Those people didn't want to do what George wanted them to do. For George to come up with a plan and schedule tasks for humans required everyone in that society to play their part. As for those who truly didn't want to help George, It moved them down to Australia, completely free of George, but also unable to benefit from Its aid. It is honestly confusing, now that we look back at it, why anybody would choose that life seeing as all of the bright people stayed; no doctors, most likely, went down there. So, I'm guessing they are a bit diseased, if you ask me." She paused to let the class ponder her words before continuing her lecture.

"Now, George does allow them to come back if they agree to start working on a task. Every year, we have flocks of people who realize the stupid mistake they made. Anyways, what you might not hear about that often when people talk about the transition from the Age of Cain to the Infinite Blossom is about the ones that refused to work on George's task and also refused to move to Australia. Apparently, these people suffered from more than just laziness; they also suffered from selfishness. They wanted a free ticket to live in this great society and wanted to do absolutely nothing in return. Understandably, after pleading and trying to resolve the issue,

George decided to put them in the Four Circles Prison and have them attend some much-needed counseling."

Takumi was taken aback by what the teacher had talked about. *Was that really all people could think about as their only options? Were they really that lazy?* he thought. Takumi raised his hand, and the teacher gave him permission to ask his question. "What if someone didn't want to do what George told them to do and didn't want to leave their home?"

The teacher closed her eyes, a little annoyed that she had to answer the question. "Well, shortsighted people like that already fought a war with George and It, well we, won. Not only that, but you also can't live in a society and not contribute."

"Yes, but I thought we fought the war to allow George to live with us. As far as I'm aware, nobody ever agreed to allow It to run everything," said Takumi.

"Yes, we collectively did. After the war was won, everyone let George better their lives. They agreed to let It run things, and when someone was too lazy to help or contribute, It took the necessary precautions," said the teacher.

Takumi was about to ask another question and stopped. He didn't believe she was completely understanding what he was saying. *My thought was that the war was about allowing George to live, not let It run our lives. It's not worth getting into; obviously, George was the best answer, and I'm sure it was discussed at some point. Just curious how that process went,* he thought.

The teacher continued with her lesson. After the bell rang, Eva and Takumi said goodbye to Jamal since he had a different class to head to. Their next class was an elective that Felix also was in. It was a public speaking class that Takumi dreaded. Eva enjoyed the class and picked it because she wanted to be some sort of public speaker someday, perhaps a news anchor for George's news outlet. Takumi picked it because he knew it was something he was bad at and wanted to improve on. He wasn't going to pick it at first because he was too nervous, and that's why Felix picked the class. He picked the class to encourage Takumi to do the same.

This day in class was typical; they would first analyze examples of other public speakers and then practice speaking in front of others during the second half of the class. The teacher went over some old speech where the speaker seemed to be a little aggressive towards the audience. The lesson was about how certain gestures can misconstrue what you are actually trying to portray. The speaker in the video kept jamming his hand into everyone's faces and the gesture came off as very aggressive. It was obviously not the speaker's intention to come off that way, and so the teacher pointed out ways to avoid this. He also brought up other types of gestures that might give people the wrong impression or even the right one.

The class was coming near to the point where the students would have to practice speaking. Each student was given a picture the day before and were told to come up with a story behind it. Each student would speak for two minutes. Takumi started to feel uncomfortable after the first student began speaking. He wanted to procrastinate being picked; luckily, the teacher was picking by name alphabetically. Each student that went up did well and spoke clearly and confidently. This did nothing but make Takumi more nervous. When Eva went up, she got a round of applause. Not only did she speak well, but her story had everyone captivated, which might not have been the point of the exercise but definitely added some points.

As Eva walked back from the front of the class, she saw Takumi shrink into his seat. "Hey, what are you so worried about? This isn't your first time, and every time I hear you up there, you sound great to me."

"Thanks, but I still don't feel good about my story," said Takumi.

Eva asked to see his picture. It was a picture of a kid playing catch with his dog.

"My story was going to be about how the dog was at the pound and was so happy when his current owner adopted him," said Takumi.

"Awww, that's so cute. Can't wait to hear about it when you're up there," said Eva.

Felix tapped Takumi on the shoulder and whispered to him. "Hey, man. That sounds like a great story and all, but wouldn't you feel better with a story with action or something? All the comics you talk about are always so action filled. You could probably come up with something pretty cool, and you might feel more confident about it."

"I don't know about that. It's just a picture of a kid and a dog playing catch. Wouldn't a whole action scene feel kind of out of place?" Takumi whispered back.

"If that's how you feel, fine. It's just that you get excited talking about the comics. I figured it might help," said Felix.

Takumi gave Felix a shrug, and Felix got up to present what he had prepared. His speech was alright. It didn't appear like he put too much effort into it. Generally, he was a pretty confident guy, so that helped; overall, the speech was okay. Several more students went after Felix. Sweat marks started to build in the armpits of Takumi's shirt as the teacher called a student with a name that began with the letter S. Once Takumi's name was called, he stood up and pressed his arms to his side so nobody would notice his sweat marks. He walked as slowly as he could to the front of the class. Eventually, he made it, and he could only let the awkward silence go on for a little before it pushed him to talk.

He started with talking about what was obvious in the picture. Then, he discussed the interaction with the kid and the dog at the pound. Only a couple of seconds went by, and Takumi couldn't think about what he was supposed to say. He made sure to prepare the night before and memorize the story, yet he still blanked.

Takumi picked his head up from the picture and gulped, looking at the other students.

Right as Takumi was about to give up, sit back down, and suffer even more embarrassment, he noticed Felix doing something. Felix made both of his hands look like guns and pretended to fire them into the air. At first Takumi was confused by the gesture, but then quickly realized what he was trying to say. *Well, what's the worst that could happen? I make a bad story and end up in the same place as I am right now,* he thought.

Takumi began to tell a new story. A story about the picture being the origin story of Star Ranger and the Hound in their younger years. The picture reminded Star Ranger of a simpler time with his still best buddy, as they were now the best bounty hunters in the futuristic universe. When Takumi finished his story, everyone applauded. It was even louder than when Eva went up, mostly because she was in the crowd now, cheering louder than anyone else.

After the class finished, the three met up with their other friend, Jamal, before walking over to the lunch hall. On their way over, they passed a wall that was painted with a flower, and it reminded Takumi of his sister. It gave Takumi an idea. "Hey, guys! I'll meet up with you later. I have to go to the library really quick," he said.

"Okay, man. Hurry up, though; I'm going to show you some of the artwork from this comic later," said Jamal.

As they walked off, Takumi reflected on how lucky he was to have the friends that he had. They were so supportive, and Takumi wasn't sure if he would be doing so well in school without that support. Once he was in the library, Takumi walked over to a computer and searched online to see if he could purchase a daisy from one of George's facilities.

He would have used his Social Bee but those weren't allowed in school. He was thrilled to find that he could order many different types of flowers, daisies included. He ordered one to his house to surprise his sister. *I'm not sure how good your friends are, but, just in case, I'll make sure to support you like my friends support me,* he thought. He pressed the button to confirm the order.

When Takumi stood up from his seat, the floor below him shook. He almost fell over from it. *That's not normal,* he thought. He ran out of the library and looked out of the window in the hallway. He noticed students running, flooding outside, and screaming. He looked to find where they were running from, and his heart sank. They were running from the lunch hall. Takumi ran as fast as he could to the lunch hall, and when he arrived, there was a cloud of dust that was blocking his sight. As Takumi took a step forward, a Primoid grabbed him.

"This section of the school is off limits until further notice," said the Primoid.

Takumi struggled, trying to get free, but the Primoid's grip was too tight. A shadow appeared to be walking out of the cloud. The closer it got to the door, the bigger the figure became. When it emerged from the cloud of debris, it was a Primoid, holding a student. Takumi couldn't breathe anymore. He fought the Primoid even harder and managed to break free. He ran up to the Primoid that was holding the student.

"Felix?" asked Takumi. It was hard to tell who it was; the student was covered in the white dust, and his face was red with blood.

"Felix?!" Takumi screamed, frantically hoping he was wrong.

"Takuu," Felix said before his neck went limp, dropping his head upside down. His wide eyes stared directly into Takumi's.

Takumi fell to the ground and cried. His face went numb, and he couldn't move his mouth to speak; he was so overwhelmed with emotions. He stood up and realized something haunting. He ran back to the library. There were phones there, and he dialed his home.

"Hello?!" Takumi's mom answered the phone, very obviously weeping.

"Mom, it's me," Takumi said; his voice cracked.

"Takumi! I was so worried. Are you hurt?" asked his mom.

"I'm… I'm fine, mom. Is Ichika okay? Did anything happen to her school?" asked Takumi.

"No. Your school is the only school that was hit, but all of the other schools in the area are on lockdown. There are Primoids everywhere so they should be okay. Stay where you are. Do *not* walk home! I'm picking you up right now," said his mother. She met him outside of the school a few minutes later. She hugged him so tightly that he thought she would break his ribs. She asked him all kinds of questions, but he couldn't bring himself to answer her. The entire way home and for the rest of the night, he just stared ahead of him as the tears silently fell down his cheeks.

A week went by, and Takumi almost never left his room. Once he saw with his own eyes that his sister was okay, he locked himself away and slept. He did come out of his room from time to time. One time, there was a package for him, and that was one of the rare times his mother got to see him. The whole school didn't have to go back for two weeks. Eventually, Takumi's mother made him come out to talk to her. He sat there quietly and listened.

"Honey, some of the Primoids that work pretty closely to George have reached out to us regarding that medical test they made all the students at your school take. After talking to them, we've decided that this program they want you to participate in will be really good for you. Apparently, this program is nearly impossible to get into, they are only taking six students out of the entire City, and it will be amazing for your future! I know this is abrupt, but we think a change of pace will do you a lot of good. There is a shuttle outside the building waiting to take you," said his mother.

Takumi was depressed and didn't really acknowledge her. He just did what she said. He got his things together and hugged his mother tightly before leaving. Right before he walked out, he walked back to his room. He grabbed the package he had received, gave it to his sister, and hugged her.

"I promise I'll be back. When I do, we'll go to the bubble filled with all of the flowers in the world," he said.

Ichika nodded her head and started to cry as she watched her big brother walk out. When Takumi walked out the building, the shuttle waiting for him opened its door. Inside were five other kids his age. Every one of them looked as depressed as Takumi except one that had her head buried in a book. Takumi took a seat and kept his head down. One of the kids tapped on his shoulder and pointed to his bag, where his favorite comic was hanging out.

"Dude, is that *Day Man vs. Night Man*? Night Man kicks so much ass, dude," said the kid, who was holding a slice of pizza in his hand.

Takumi cracked a smile for the first time since the day it happened.

19

Pound of Flesh

The Deicended and the Primechs boarded a transport Owl that was bigger than the average Owl, seemingly to head back to the training facility. Saturn stayed behind to deal with an unknown issue.

"Excuse me, where are we going?" Neith asked, seeing that they were heading in the opposite direction of the training facility.

"The fight isn't over. The rogue Deicended are being pursued right now. We are going after the Hawk," Nadin responded. The Owl flew to where they could see a plume of smoke rising. The City was pretty messed up where Jupiter had been in combat. The float park that he was on was still there but smoking all around. Lucy saw a Swan class aircraft completely demolished and still on fire. It was so large that it could almost have been mistaken for a collapsed building. Jupiter, about a story and half tall, was standing over the crash site. He had a massive two-handed hammer which he rested on the ground, his hand grasping it midway up the grip. He was with his squad of Primoids who were searching for survivors. There were also a few Dove class aircraft flying around. It looked like back up took a while but had finally made it to the action. Along with the Doves were some small drone Primoids. They were part of a swarm that was on standby. Even with every bit of back up by Jupiter, it appeared that Anne and Joe were the only ones that had been tailing the rogue Deicended. Shortly after passing Jupiter, they came across a downed Owl class aircraft.

"Hey, I think Joe is down there," Emily pointed out. On the street, Joe was sitting next to the smoking owl with his head down.

"Right, lower the aircraft. We need to pick them up," Nicholas said. When Joe boarded, his head was still down. They looked at him expectantly, and he stared blankly back at them.

"Just me," Joe said, more quietly than any of the Deicended had ever heard him speak.

"Anne?" Nadin asked.

"...Unrepairable," Joe replied.

"I don't get it. Where's Anne?" Tyr asked.

"She's dead," Amin said, missing an arm again.

"What do you mean dead? Just repair her, like how you guys always do," Emily said.

"Were you not listening to the part where he said, 'Unrepairable'?" Amin asked snarkily.

"How, though? You guys are supposed to be unkillable," Emily asked incredulously.

"Her brain was hit. There's no coming back from that," Joe said.

"I... I... it can't... no. Just NO!" Emily started to scream. Joe walked up to her and put his hand on the top of her head.

"I know she was someone you cared about, Emily, but this is what happens. We don't have time to dwell on it," Joe said.

"What do you mean we don't have time to dwell on it?" Emily snapped angrily.

"Emily, she did her part. We have to focus on the Hawk," Neith chimed in. Emily whirled to face her, visibly trembling.

"You can't be serious. People are not expendable. Ben, Takumi, back me up here," Emily demanded.

Takumi stayed quiet. "I feel what you're saying, but I… I just… We have to get the Hawk," Ben replied.

"At what cost? Who's next?" said Emily. Nicholas took a step forward and addressed Emily very frankly.

"You're thinking too narrowly, Emily. We are doing this to prevent future pain. Anne sacrificed herself in that belief; don't act selfish and diminish that," Nicholas said. Emily looked down, feeling a combination of anger, guilt, and shame. "Where are we going, anyways? We aren't going to find them in the ocean," she said to the ground.

"Saturn managed to get a tracking device on the enemy's Owl as they left," Nadin mentioned. Emily lifted her head. "Then what the *fuck* was the point of chasing him in the first place?!"

"Sit down, Emily! You're way out of line." Joe yelled at her. "What if they had discovered the tracker? What if the tracker malfunctioned? That was a risk that we could not take. That was a risk Anne would not take! She was a disciple of Diligence. Let her actions be a model for your future." She put her head back down. This time, it was only in shame.

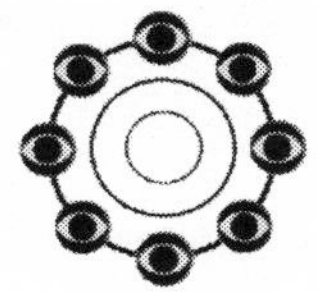

After hours of an awkward, quiet flight over the sea, trees and land could be seen again. After even more time, the Owl began to slow. The aircraft hovered around, looking for a spot to land. They were over a very green, dense forest. When they finally landed, Nicholas took the Deicended aside.

"This is as close as we can go. We are about fifty miles away from where the rogue Deicended landed. You will have to go without us. If we are detected, they will just move camp again, and they are too dangerous with their EMP technology. Knock out their EMP, and we will come in to provide support. We are building camp here and plan to have more forces here ready to assist you. George has faith in your abilities. This will be your ultimate test. Go on, take your vengeance," said Nicholas.

"Ah… what about food?" Ben asked. Lucy smacked him in the head. "With the amount of training that you all have received, you should be perfectly capable of finding your own food, Ben," Nadin snapped at him. Lucy nodded her head before turning back to face Nicholas. "Don't listen to him; we're on our way."

"Well, hold up for a second. This tracking device should be small enough to go undetected. Tyr, you hold onto this since you will be the squad leader from now on. You have proven yourself capable of doing so," Nicholas said as he handed Tyr the tracker, who took it solemnly. Tyr clenched his jaw and nodded, very aware that this meant he was now going to be responsible for all of his friends' lives.

The side of the Owl opened up and revealed a miniature armory. "I suggest not taking anything too big. This will be one hell of a hike," said Nadin. Emily walked up first, grabbed a few belts of knives, and wrapped them around her chest. She also grabbed a CRFF SMG. Before walking off, another weapon caught her eye. She grabbed a concussion rocket launcher.

"I thought I suggested nothing too big," said Nadin.

"We might need it, and I'll be fine. I can handle the extra pounds," replied Emily. Nadin shook his head in exasperation.

Takumi walked up next and grabbed two photon revolvers and two CRFFs. "Isn't that a little much?" asked Tyr.

"Don't worry, you'll see," Takumi replied with a smirk. Ben grabbed a BRF 170 and a P2 semi-automatic pistol. Neith grabbed a BRF 172 with photon cartridges and a concussion pistol. Lucy grabbed a HellFire laser rifle, a BRF 172, and a P2 semi-automatic pistol, using her ability to modify her physical makeup to enhance her muscles in response to the increased weight of the HellFire laser, which looked heavier than someone of her size should have been able to handle as easily as she did.

Tyr went to grab a plasma shotgun, which was becoming his favorite gun now, but his face fell when he didn't find one. "Do we seriously not have a plasma shotgun?"

"Sorry, but we could only pack so many guns into this portable armory; this was kind of an impromptu mission" said Nadin. Tyr shook his head in frustration. He noticed an ABT (Aerial Barrage Targeting) rifle. When he went to grab it, Nadin stopped him.

"I agree that you could probably handle the weight, but the satellites aren't going to be able to support you in there. They have interference defenses against this weapon. The benefit from the drones is going to be outweighed by how tired you will be from dragging them along," said Nadin. Tyr was even more frustrated now, so he just grabbed a BRF 170 and the automatic pistol. The group parted ways with the Primechs and started on their venture. They were walking through a forest covered mostly by pine trees, and the terrain was very uneven. They started by walking over a giant hill that was just about too short to be considered a mountain.

When they reached the top, they only saw more hills that made them dread the amount of walking they would have to do. Tyr told the group to deactivate the power to their suites since they would need to save as much power as they could until they started fighting.

Once the power shut off, the Deicended realized how cold it was. It was just below freezing, but there wasn't any snow or frost on the ground to have given them a heads up. In the City, even when they were outside, the streets gave off heat so no one could feel the cold. When it was hot in the city, there was a massive A/C system built that circulated cold between the buildings. George kept the entirety of human existence climate controlled. Although it was chilly as soon as they began walking again, it didn't bother them because of their remaining body heat keeping them warm. In fact, once they got to the top of the second hill, they contemplated taking their cloaks off, but Tyr cautioned against it, citing that they should be prepared to take advantage of the cloaks' camouflage abilities at any moment since they were in hostile territory.

Lucy was the most comfortable because of her lack of cloak. Due to her healing abilities, the team and even the Primechs didn't believe she could get sick. She hadn't had so much as a cold since she began training at George's facility. Once the team got to the top of the third hill, they could see two mountains in the distance. "That's it," said Neith. "The base has to be on top of one of those mountains."

"Could it be in the mountain? I don't see anything that looks like a base," said Ben.

"We must be too far away. They probably have some really good concealment too. I don't think they would be inside the mountain. Nicholas said they have been known to move frequently, and burrowing into a mountain would be too much work for a temporary base," said Tyr.

"It's going to take us a while to get there," said Lucy. The sun had started to set as she said this.

"If we don't stop, we'll make it there a few hours after the sun rises," said Neith.

"Alright, we'll walk for a few more hours and then rest. That way, when we arrive, we can rest for a bit, and it will give us plenty of nighttime to conceal our movements when we sneak in," said Tyr. Nobody contested the plan.

After walking for three more hours, Tyr decided that was far enough. They were halfway down a hill and found a spot that had pretty level ground. "I'll go get some firewood," said Ben. Takumi grabbed him before he walked off. "What?" asked Ben.

"We can't risk them seeing the light from the fire," said Tyr.

"We can't even see the mountain from here though," said Ben.

"Only because it's too dark. Plus, we don't even know if they have scouts roaming around," said Neith. Ben nodded, grunted in frustration, annoyed at himself for not having thought of that, and rubbed his arms to warm himself up. "I'm going to freeze to death out here without moving around," said Ben. Without the sun to provide any warmth, and no cloud cover to keep any heat in, the temperature was dropping by the minute.

"We'll all go to sleep then. Our suits' tent features will keep us warm," said Tyr. "We don't need anyone to stand watch. I doubt scouts would come out this far, and I'll activate the proximity sensor on my suit just in case. It will sound an alarm if anyone gets too close to us," said Tyr.

Everyone, except Lucy, laid down and pressed a button on their chest. It activated the suit's tent mode. It shot a thin plastic piece under them that inflated about half an inch to keep their body off the ground. Their cloaks surrounded their body, leaving a little bit of space, and hardened. The cloaks were sealed with an inflated tube and changed to a brownish green color for camouflage. Lucy grabbed a tiny bag she had linked to her belt. When she pressed the button on her chest only the tube on her back inflated. Since she didn't wear a cloak, the tiny bag acted in place of one for the tent. All six of them looked like a bunch of cocoons lying on the ground.

Ben fell asleep the second he was wrapped up, but he did toss and turn, making some noise while he slept. Lucy shuffled around for a second or two, then was completely silent as she slept. Neith fell asleep pretty quickly as well but snored a bit. Tyr laid on his back, completely straight, until he fell asleep. Emily and Takumi, however, took a very long time to fall asleep. Emily was waiting. She was waiting until she believed everyone was asleep.

After a while, her tent shook a bit. She was sobbing. She was still thinking about Anne. She kind of looked up to her. She seemed like a free spirit, like Emily. Anne, some of the other Primechs, and her fellow Deicended felt like friends to her, like true friends. Emily hadn't been this sad since the day the school was bombed. This time was completely different though. Before, her feelings of misery rose from feeling alone, and now, she didn't feel so alone with everyone around her; it hurt to lose one of those people. Takumi heard Emily crying, and he knew why. He began to think about the friends he lost from the bombing and how he just lost another great friend, and he began to cry in his tent as well.

The sun rose six hours later. The tents kept the light out well, so they could have slept much longer, but Tyr had set an alarm and was the first one up. He did some stretching before waking up the others. Everyone got ready to go quickly.

"What are we supposed to do for food? We don't exactly have time to go hunting," said Ben. Tyr opened a small bag on his hip to take out some protein bars. "This should cover us for a while. We have more for later when we get close to the enemy's base," said Tyr.

"Woah, wait! Since when did you have food?" asked Ben.

"Nadin was kidding about us finding food," said Lucy. This surprised Ben.

"Didn't realize the guy had a sense of humor," he said. Lucy shrugged. Having distributed the protein bars, Tyr addressed them while they ate.

"I assume everyone drank their water. There should be a river over this next hill. Sadly, this may be our last chance to hydrate. So, drink as much as you can and then fill your bottle," Tyr said. After eating the protein bars, they waited five minutes and then began walking. They made it over the next hill and saw a river, just as Tyr had guessed. It was very small, more of a creek, barely big enough to get their boots wet. They walked up to the river and stuck their faces in with their masks on. The masks had a built-in straw with a filtration system.

They stuck around the river for twenty minutes, making sure they hydrated as much as possible since, for all they knew, it would be a long while before they got another drink. They walked over the next couple of hills, where the mountains were completely visible now. Neith was carrying some binoculars, and they took some time to inspect the enemy's base. It was still concealed very well, but parts of it were visible. The base was high up the mountainside, which had just a little bit of snow at the top. The mountain that was next to the one with the base was so close to the other that it looked like it was once one mountain that split away at the top. You could tell the base apart from the mountain since there was an unnatural looking protrusion from the side. The rogue Deicended's base took up a large portion of the base of the mountain.

"We're going to have to be careful about running into scouts from here on out," Tyr said over their helmet comms, not willing to risk speaking outside of their helmets this close to the base. Instead of just hiking through the woods like they had before, they would take some time to analyze the path they were taking and look for any sign of scouts or guards. Once they deemed the path safe enough, they would scurry tree to tree to conceal their movements as much as possible. It took them much longer moving like this, but they still made it to the river that led up to the enemy's base.

"Looks like they've put too much faith into their scanners. Not a single scout out and about," said Emily.

"We should make a plan since we are so close to the base and still have some sunlight," said Takumi.

"Right. Does anyone have any ideas about where the generator for the place could be?" asked Tyr.

"Probably right smack in the middle of the place," said Emily.

"I can go in stealth and map it out. Then, we could make a better plan, or maybe, I could just go in and set up some explosives. Boom, mission complete," suggested Lucy.

"No, we can't do that. If you get spotted, we won't be able to support you. Maybe if you were able to become completely invisible, but that's not the case," said Tyr.

"So, we are going to have to sneak in all together, then?" asked Neith.

"Yes," said Tyr.

"Six people going in, trying to not get noticed, seems a little bit more difficult than my plan," said Lucy.

"It's what we've trained for. If we can't manage this, then our training has been for nothing," said Tyr.

"We still have a problem with the potential for the Hawk to escape. Once the power goes off, he'll surely just try to relocate," said Takumi.

"We should split up into two groups then," said Ben.

"Right. One team could go for the generator, and the other team could go for the Hawk to make sure he doesn't escape. We have to have someone ready to take him out as soon as the power is cut," said Takumi.

"No, that won't work. If we are going to face the Hawk, I'm sure he won't be alone; we have to do it with all six of us. Look, we need to stick together on this or else we are going to fail, or even worse, one of us will die. Once we cut the power to the generator, we should have some time before they realize what has happened. I'm sure power going out temporarily is pretty common for them. We'll have enough time to cut off his potential escape," said Tyr.

"What if he escapes though? We can't afford to let him live any longer." Emily said emphatically.

"It's a risk, but if he runs, he will at least be severely crippled from this attack," said Tyr.

"Crippled isn't the same as dead," said Emily.

"It's better than one of us dying due to arrogance," said Tyr.

"I'm not letting him get the chance to escape," said Emily.

"Emily, Tyr is right. Giving him a chance to escape is well worth the risk. Even if we do kill him, someone else in his organization will likely take over. We have to take the option that has the best chance to impact the whole rogue group," said Neith.

"Who cares if someone takes over? It was the Hawk that killed Anne," Emily said angrily, nearly shouting.

"Emily, he took something from all of us, but this is bigger than just us," said Takumi.

"...Fine... so, all of us are just going to head for the generator, then we kill the Hawk?" asked Emily.

"If nobody has any other interjections to the plan..." Tyr said, allowing a moment for any further thoughts.

Nobody responded. "Okay. Now, let's talk about the best way to enter the place," said Tyr.

"We could just walk right up to it, find a gap in the guard routes, and slip through," said Ben.

"There aren't enough trees near the base to get close to it safely," said Lucy.

"Around the sides then?" asked Ben.

"Same problem," said Lucy.

"I think I know what will work. We could climb up the other mountain until we are above the base, repel across, and go in from the top," said Neith.

"Won't they see us while we repel?" asked Takumi.

"With the night sky and our cloaks, we should be fine. Plus, they don't seem to have many people on the lookout, so I doubt they have anyone looking out on the top of the base. Anything they might expect to come from above would be an aircraft, which they can detect remotely," said Neith. Everyone was silent, thinking about the plan and if there were any holes. "I like the plan," said Tyr. "If we get up closer to the base and we don't feel safe crossing the mountain unnoticed, then we'll make a new plan then."

"What about a plan B?" asked Ben.

"Plan B is to re-plan, Ben," said Tyr.

"Or Plan B could be Plan Ben, where I just go in guns blazing and take down everyone by myself," Ben said jokingly.

"Sure, that sounds like a great plan! Then, we won't have to hear any more of your stupid ideas after they kill you," said Neith.

"I thought it was a good plan, Ben. In fact, we could make it a B and E plan, and we both go in guns blazing," said Emily.

"Hey, don't leave me out," said Takumi.

"Sure, the three of us go in guns blazing, we forget about the generator, and just kill everyone in there," said Emily.

"This isn't funny. We have a plan, stop talking about going in guns blazing!" Tyr said forcefully.

"Chill out, Tyr; we're just playing around," said Emily.

Emily and the others began walking off. Tyr stood for a bit, shaking his head, then followed. It took a while to reach the top. They took a path that was far to the left of the mountains since the base was on the mountain to the right. Once they got to the edge of the tree line, they walked further to the left of the mountain to ensure they would be out of sight of the base while they hiked up.

It was getting dark once they began their hike, and as they were nearing the peak, they were completely obscured by the night. The Deicended were very fit, so the hike wasn't difficult even though it was extremely steep. Emily was the only one dragging a bit. She was regretting taking the rocket launcher with her. It wasn't really the weight of the weapon that bothered her. The rocket launcher was actually lighter than one would imagine. It bothered her because of how awkward it was to carry. It had a strap so she could sling it around her back, but the sling kind of sucked. She constantly had to readjust the thing. It would get in the way of some of the rocks they were hiking over and around. On the hike there, she was able to just hold the thing still, and the trees didn't really get in the way. Now, she needed her hands to get over some of the obstacles. Still, she braved through and only grunted in frustration.

They had a feeling like they had gone far up enough, so Lucy stealthed over to the other side to confirm. She came back very shortly after, and they were in fact high enough. The group walked together around the mountain. At this point, everyone activated the power to their STYX armor. Their cloaks turned to light brown to match the mountain, even though that was not completely necessary since it was now pitch black out. The mask gave them better sight in the dark, so they had no need for light. They were now in position to shoot a grapple over to the other side and descend to the enemy's base.

"Who's grappling gun are we going to use? We're going to have to leave it behind," said Tyr.

"You can use mine since I got these. We won't have to leave it behind though. I'll be able to use my powers to get it back," Emily said as she pointed to the ropes wrapped around her arms.

She handed her gun to Tyr, and he took aim, launching the grapple to the other side. It made a sound when it impacted the side of the mountain, but it wasn't a distinct sound that would give away their element of surprise. Tyr then took the gun and shifted the handle to align it with the rest, making it completely straight. Out of the handle popped multiple barbed spikes. He took the gun and rammed its spiked end into the rocks, which triggered the mechanism punching the spikes deeper into the ground.

"Well, hopefully that holds us," said Lucy. She grabbed onto the rope first and secured a device around it. She held onto the device's handles that popped out. It had a motor inside that powered the device and took Lucy across the line. Though it wasn't too far to the other mountain, it was nearly impossible to see Lucy in the night without the assistance of their helmets. One by one, they went to the other side, with Tyr being the last one to go. Once they were all safe on the other side, Emily reached out with her power to her grappling hook, and it came flying out of the mountain and into her hand. Now, the enemy's base was less than a hundred feet below them. From their view now, they could see the closest structure to them was built into the mountainside with a flat roof that began to slant downwards. Below that, they could see the flat platform that held the rogue Deicendeds' aircraft. It extended out above the rest of the base that was built all over the descending mountainside.

"We could sabotage their aircraft before we hit the generator. That way, the Hawk won't be able to escape even if he does bolt," said Takumi.

"Perfect. That's our new first objective," said Tyr. They walked down to the roof of the building and were careful not to make a sound. When they got to the edge of the roof, they were able to see the hanger much more clearly. There were ten Owl class aircraft and six Doves from what they could see. With all of those aircraft, there only appeared to be two men doing maintenance. Neith pointed out a stack of crates off to the side that would provide decent cover for them to get down into the hangar. The group was counting on the possibility that there were a few more people in the hanger that they couldn't see. The first one to go down was Lucy. She used her ability to hide herself as she grabbed onto the edge of the roof and extended her arms to lower herself. Once she cleared the ceiling, she said over the comms in their helmets, "It's like a small party out here or something."

"How many are there?" asked Tyr.

"I count nine. They are sitting on a couple of tables, drinking, and eating," said Lucy.

"Well, sounds like they'll be easy targets, then," said Emily.

"Not exactly. They outnumber us; it will only take one to sound the alarm, and then we're dead," said Neith.

"Plus, they are all armed," said Lucy.

"Most likely, everyone in the facility is armed. I noticed even the mechanic had a side arm," said Neith.

"I'll lower myself all the way down and try to find a good path for y'all to take," said Lucy. When she got halfway down, she extended her legs to the floor and made it safely. She looked around the crates for some path for the others. The group of enemies were being pretty loud, apparently enjoying their camaraderie. *At least they're having a good time before their demise,* thought Lucy.

"I think, if you scale down the mountain next to the hanger, you could go unnoticed. The enemy is distracted anyways. Otherwise, I don't see an alternate path," Lucy said over the comms.

The Deicended agreed and began to scale around the side of the hangar. The mountain indented around the side, making the group difficult to see. Once they got below the floor of the hanger, Takumi reached one his shadow arms up to the edge of the floor closest to Lucy and behind the crates. He pulled himself in and then used his shadow arms to pull the rest of the group in. Now, the whole group sat behind the crates.

"What now?" asked Ben.

"We'll have to sneak into each of the aircraft and cut some of the wires in them," said Tyr.

"How are we supposed to do that unnoticed?" asked Emily.

"Lucy can get all of the aircraft except the ones with the mechanics in them. If we kill one, even under stealth, it won't go unnoticed for long," said Neith.

"You know, the roof, where we were completely out of sight would have been a ten times better place to have this conversation," said Lucy.

"Hey, Cal," shouted one of the partiers, "Stop working yourself so hard over there and have a drink with us! Hawk got one of those power guys."

"Yeah, just a second! Hey, do you do mind checking to see where my can of WD50 went?" said a voice coming from one of the Owls, presumably Cal.

"That makes three mechanics," said Takumi.

"Sure thing, buddy. Where did you see it last?" asked the partier.

"Over by those supply crates," Cal responded.

The Deicended looked at each other in a panic as they heard footsteps walking closer to them. *You goofed this up real bad, Tyr. Your team is dead because of you now. When he sees us, this mission is over, we'll have to run, and there isn't even any frickin WD50 over here, for crying out loud,* thought Tyr.

He could hear the footsteps right on the other side of the crates. The enemy was shuffling through the crates, looking for the item. They could hear the man start to walk to the corner. The Deicended drew their guns, ready to fight. They aimed their weapons to fry the guy the second he saw them. Just as the man turned the corner, Lucy jumped up, right in the man's face, and stopped. Lucy was blocking their ability to kill the man. He just stood there, staring at Lucy. He scratched his head, rolled his eyes, and walked away. Lucy had used her power to make it look like the team wasn't there, just as long as he looked directly through her. He turned back towards the aircraft.

"It's not over here, Cal. Where in the world did you leave it?" said the man.

"Don't worry about it. I'll deal without," said the mechanic. He walked away from them, back to his friends to continue their celebration.

"Abort the plan. There are too many people here. It's too risky. The aircraft aren't worth us potentially failing the mission," said Tyr.

The Deicended went back to the roof the same way they got down there. "Well, we still need to find a way to the generator. Should we walk to another building?" asked Neith. The base consisted of a few buildings connected by covered walkways. The bridges were small. It looked like the only reason for the buildings to be separated was that the base wasn't put together well. It had many design flaws, and some parts looked like the engineer just gave up because he was tired.

"The generator must be in one of those two bigger buildings. We'll start with one and pray that it's there and that we don't get noticed. I suggest we start with the biggest one up there," said Neith.

The Deicended began to walk to the building that Neith suggested. Staying on top of the roofs and walkway coverings, they were out of sight of everyone, making the travel to the large building relatively easy. The only thing they had to be careful of was making too much noise. They could hear workers and guards walking under them and sometimes having pointless conversations. When they reached the building that they hoped housed the generator, it seemed like there was no way for them to easily enter.

"Looks like we are going to have to break in from here," said Takumi.

"I'll melt a hole," said Ben.

"No, let me at it," Emily said.

Ever so slightly, Emily used her powers to pull back a flimsy metal panel. She bent it back just far enough for someone to squeeze their head in. Lucy turned her head invisible and stretched it inside. She moved her head all around, inspecting every detail that she could. She brought her head back out, "Someone just walked out. No sign of the generator. Pretty much just a hallway down there. Doesn't appear to get too much traffic. If we're quick, we should be able to get in and out before anyone notices."

Emily bent the panel even farther back, and everyone jumped down. She bent the panel back to its original shape after she jumped down so nobody would notice the sign of someone sneaking in. The hallway was short and seemed to lead to a dead end. At the end, they noticed a ladder to another room. Lucy climbed up and, again, inspected the room. "We won't be alone in this room. It's decently big though, and we can sneak around the enemy," said Lucy.

One by one, they went up the ladder. There was a low wall once they got up that kept them out of sight. It was indeed a large room that seemed to be used as a control center. There were desks set up in rows that were all facing a big monitor in the front of the room. There were only a few people in the room at the moment, but they could only imagine that the room would be completely full while the Hawk and his companions were off base performing their sabotage and terrorism. Towards the back of the room was some kind of observation room that looked down on the others from behind a sheet of glass. The Deicended were positioned to the front left side of the room.

"Let's sneak through in front of the desks and move to the next room. I imagine most of the building is pretty empty. The sooner we're out of here, the better," said Tyr.

Lucy walked first. At most, two would hide behind a desk before moving to the next. The front row had nobody sitting behind the desks, so the most they had to worry about was being seen walking between them. Lucy made it to the middle of the row, and it seemed like they were going to be fine making it to the end. When Takumi went to move past the middle of the room, he noticed something. Over the comm system in their masks, they heard him say, "Guys, wait… I think the Hawk is in that observation room."

They all took a chance to peek and see for themselves. They saw the man in the hawk shaped mask. He was having a conversation with a tall man who was dressed in black armor. It looked like something they would see SWAT wearing, with a few metal plates here and there. He wore something similar to the cloaks that the Deicended were wearing, except it was clasped back more like a cape than a cloak. On his head, he wore a mask like the Hawk's except it was shaped like a skull.

"Let's take him out right now," said Emily. "Lucy or Takumi could probably snipe the shit out of him."

"No!" yelled Tyr. Luckily, all of the sound was muffled by his helmet to anyone who would have been listening even though he was yelling. "That's a chance I'm not willing to take."

"Looking at that skull guy, we would have to worry about him even if we managed to take out the Hawk, and I don't like the look of the guy. Who wears a skull like that? That's just crazy," said Ben.

"We can do it. This is what we've trained for. We can handle another Deicended," argued Emily.

"We're killing the generator, and then we are going to stop him. In fact, we only need to stall him. George's force will come in, and it will be an easy day if we just kill the generator," said Tyr.

Emily grunted in frustration but didn't continue to argue. "We should listen in to the conversation though," suggested Takumi.

"What's the point of that?" asked Lucy.

"It's a good idea actually. I'm sure George will want information from him, but it will be a lot harder to get information from him if he's a captive," said Tyr. "Lucy, go up and send the audio to us."

"No, we need to keep moving. The longer we stay here, the more likely we will be spotted," said Lucy.

"This chance to get a recording of him talking freely is too valuable of an opportunity to give up, and if just you go up, it will be relatively safe," said Tyr.

"Who cares what he's talking about? It would be useless information. Like you said, George will be able to take care of all of this; we need to find the generator. Let's not get distracted," said Lucy.

"Lucy, we wouldn't be taking much of a risk really. Arguing is just wasting our time," said Takumi.

I should back Lucy up, thought Neith. *The Hawk and that skull guy might talk about something related to what Cade talked to me about. I don't think these guys are ready to know anything about that yet. But… I want to know what they are saying. What could I learn from their point of view? Maybe they might say something that Cade left out; I have to know.*

"I'm making this an order, Lucy," said Tyr.

"Fine. If we fail, I'm blaming you," said Lucy. She turned invisible and walked up towards the glass to the observation room. From the side of her helmet, she took a piece out that was connected by a wire and put it up to the glass. The audio from the room played in all of their helmets.

"She can't be trusted," said the skull masked man.

"You don't know what you are talking about. With her power, we'll be able to defeat George. We'll be able to put an end to this madness," said the Hawk.

"I understand her power!" yelled the skull masked man. "I was there with you. I saw exactly how she used those powers as well. There is something evil about the Phosphorus. The power she got was too much. She took our friends away; I don't even understand how you side with her, let alone trust her."

"With that much power, it was too much at first. She controls it now. To shy away from that is ignorant. We've been working on something monumental, and George will fall soon. I just wish that you would join us, John," said the Hawk.

"I don't know how, but you're being manipulated. Just like they did to her, she's doing to you now. I was hoping I could convince you to stop helping her and join my people, but I see you are set in your ways," said John, which Neith thought was a surprisingly docile name for someone wearing a skull mask. She would have pegged him as a Quetzalcoatl, an Agamemnon, or a Yama.

"It's been good to see you at least. One question though. Knowing how opposed you are to her, how can I trust that you won't get in my way now?" asked the Hawk.

"I guess you can't," said John.

The Hawk chuckled. "Take aim," he yelled. Four soldiers armed with rifles came into the room and as instructed, took aim at John. John waved his arm at the soldiers, and vines sprung from his arm. The vines pinned the soldiers to the wall and completely entangled them. John reached for something on his back. It was a massive sword the size of a claymore. It was hard to see, but when he lifted his blade, it sounded like he was holding a chainsaw. Before John could complete his swing, the Hawk unsheathed a dagger and created a blade of gust that sliced through the air and through the vines that John had created, freeing his soldiers. The Hawk blocked the incoming attack from John. The Hawk created a shockwave of wind that blew everyone else in the room back and shattered the glass to the room. This worried the Deicended. There was a chance the fight could move towards them, and they would have to interfere. Open to make another attack, instead the Hawk sheathed his dagger.

"Ah, John… you let me pass you because of your ignorance and stubbornness. I just wanted to see a little sample of how strong you have become over the years. You're welcome to hang out in the base for a while if you would like to," said the Hawk.

"I'll see myself out. I'm disappointed, Serpico. You've become blind," said John. John walked out of the room, intimidating the soldiers he walked past both from his performance and his size.

The Deicended took the opportunity while everyone was distracted by the current events to get the hell out of the room. The next room had nothing in it and was connected to a hallway. They went down the hallway and passed by a few rooms where the crew appeared to sleep. Most of the rooms were empty, however they were careful because a few were in their beds. They made it to the end of the building where there was another bridge, but it didn't lead to the building they wanted to go to. Exiting in the same manner they entered, Emily pushed a panel open, and the team got onto the roof of the building. Emily closed the panel back once the last member of their team made it through.

"That sicko has a name… Serpico," Emily stated.

"Yeah, creepy, I always thought of him as just the Hawk, as if that was his name," said Ben.

"Doesn't matter. He'll be dead or locked away in Four Circles Prison by the end of the day," said Tyr.

"Hell yeah! That's the attitude I've been looking for from you," said Emily. They walked over the bridge that led them to the second largest building in the base. The ceiling wasn't completely put together. They could see through the cracks on the roof from missing panels. Down below them was a pretty big room that only had a few guards. They could hear a humming noise coming from somewhere; it had to be in the building, and it had to be the generator. There was only one door, and there were two guards standing right next to it. The Deicended gave each other a look and knew what they had to do.

They unsheathed their daggers. Takumi lowered himself with his shadow arms, Emily lowered herself with the rope on her arm, and Lucy lowered herself with her extending limbs. The other three stayed up top to wait for the other three to clear the room.

"We have the two guarding the door that possibly leads to the generator. There are three others just hanging out," said Tyr.

"The one blankly staring out the window is out of sight of the others. Takumi, you're closest. You should take him out before we move on with anything else," said Neith.

"Got it," said Takumi. He took a deep gulp. He raised his knife, and his hand shook uncontrollably. He drew his hand back. *I can't hesitate. I won't mess up and endanger my friends,* he thought as he picked his hand back up. It still shook rapidly. His nerves weren't going to get in his way. "Bind," Takumi whispered. Three of his shadow arms reached out to the man looking out the window. One arm wrapped around his legs. The other wrapped around the man's arms, completely immobilizing him. The third arm covered his face, keeping him from making a sound. Legs shaking, Takumi crept up to the man and slid his dagger into the man's kidney. He tightened his shadow arms on the man as he struggled from the pain. Takumi's eyes watered, and had he seen the man's face, he might have lost it. It only took half a minute for him to stop moving, but, to Takumi, it felt like time stood still.

"Nice take down," said Ben.

"Yeah, good job; Emily, it's your turn now," Tyr said.

"The two sitting down by the table over there are in view of the other guards. Lucy, you are going to have to act at the same time as Emily if we want to go unnoticed," said Neith. Emily walked up into position, getting close enough to throw something at the two sitting at the table. Emily loosened the ropes on her arms and held the knives tied to the end of them. Ready to throw the knives, Emily suddenly felt out of breath. She bit her lip and threw the knives as true as she could. One knife hit the guy in the neck and dropped him. The other hit the girl sitting at the table near her shoulder, and she jolted up. Emily used the magnetic connection between the metal on her hands and the knives stuck in her enemies. Lightning sparked across the metal ropes and knocked them both back. Emily pulled the knives back to her hands with her powers.

Once Lucy noticed the sparks, she charged towards her two guards. They went to go help their friends who they just saw being attacked and didn't notice Lucy concealed by her powers. Extending her arm, she stabbed one guard in the gut and wrapped her leg around the other, throwing him to the ground. The guard that was stuck in the gut looked at the blur that was Lucy standing over his friend. Blood spewed from the throat of the guard on the ground. Holding his stomach that was leaking its own fluids, he went to yell. Lucy pulled him to the ground and shoved her dagger through his throat and into the floor. She met his desperate eyes as he felt his life slipping away from him.

"Both in the throat? Not very creative," said Neith.

"Sure way to kill your prey and to shut them up. Sorry if I'm a fan of the effectiveness," said Lucy. Emily gave Lucy a strange look as she was still holding back her emotions from what she herself had just done. The team went to the door where the guards once stood, and it opened. They walked into a large room with a generator at the other end. The room was the size of a gymnasium with three rows of large pillars going down to the end. The generator was the size of a one-bedroom apartment which made sense for the size of the buildings it was powering.

They walked at a fast pace to the generators and were as surprised as one of the guards inside to find that they were not alone. The guard was just sitting on the ground, resting, but shot up once he noticed the intruders. He stumbled to grab his gun, and Tyr took the initiative and gunned the man down. Tyr flinched as he pulled the trigger, struggling to look at the gushing holes his bullets had punched into the man's body.

No time to think, the rest of the team pulled their guns out to the ready. More guards ran into the room. They must have been nearby and heard Tyr's shots. Neith put a shield in front just in case, and the second after she did, it was pelted by bullets. They could see at least four muzzle flashes.

"I think they know we're here," said Ben.

"Doesn't matter now. There still might be a chance our cover might not have been completely blown. I'm going in, back me up,"

Tyr ordered. Tyr armored up, and Neith opened a spot in the shield for him to run out. He charged across the room, firing his BRF wherever he saw muzzle flashes. Tyr was hit a couple of times while running, but the shots had no effect on him. Definitely intimidated, the enemies hid behind some pillars. While Tyr distracted them, Emily and Takumi ran on the opposite sides of the pillars, covering both the flanks. Emily got to one of the enemies first. She was unnoticed until she grabbed the girl by the neck and drove her dagger into her back, instantly dropping her. The enemy closest to Takumi noticed Emily killing his friend and accurately assumed that the same was about to happen to him. He turned to check his rear and almost hit Takumi in the face, but the Deicended caught the rifle. He held on with both hands and the two struggled for a second for control of the weapon.

"Shadow Strike!" Takumi yelled as one of his shadow arms struck the man and sent him flying out of cover. Lucy took aim and held the trigger of her BRF 170 for two seconds. A burst of fire came out and shot below the enemy that just came out of cover. The shot strafed up until four of the rounds hit the man. Tyr continued to pursue the last two, but before he could get to them, one of them came out of cover and unloaded his magazine on Tyr, screaming, "Just die already!" Tyr covered his face as he struggled a bit from being shot so many times. Emily got into position and fired a two second burst of her CRFF and took the enemy down. The last enemy, a young woman, went to run. She saw Takumi and fired at him.

"Riot Shield!" Takumi yelled as eight of his shadow arms came from his left side and covered him, leaving a slit open for him to fire his gun. Before she finished her magazine, Takumi shot her until she didn't make a sound.

"Good job…" Tyr was reassuring his team before they heard a loud bang above them. A massive construction piloted Mech landed between them and the generator. It was the size of a large truck and was shaped like an oversized human without a head. The Deicended froze in shock at the sight of the Mech.

On the Mech's left arm was a mini-gun that started to spin. The Mech lifted its arm and began to fire, pelting the floor leading up to Tyr. The firepower knocked Tyr to the ground, but he wasn't hurt. The force of the gun's rounds could knock him off of his feet, but still couldn't penetrate his armor. The Mech raised its other arm and aimed it at Tyr. There was a massive cannon on his arm that was lighting up with a red color. Tyr got up and jumped out of the way as a massive blast struck where he was previously laying. The explosion sent him flying into the wall. He was covered by a cloud of dust and scurried around, looking for his rifle he had just dropped. He found it, but when he picked it up, it fell apart. His rifle had split in half after smashing against one of the pillars. Tyr drew his side arm, *I guess this will have to do,* he thought, seriously regretting not picking up something bigger from the Armory.

Emily took the concussion rocket launcher off her back, grateful that she had been determined to bring it with her. She took aim with difficulty since there was still a cloud of dust concealing the Mech. She pulled the trigger, and the rocket fired into the Mech's right shoulder. It was the arm with the big cannon attached. After three seconds, the rocket exploded with an immense force. The Mech went flying into the generator, and the Deicended were knocked to the ground except for Lucy, standing behind Neith's shield.

"No point in trying to be quiet now. Use the HellFire Laser to kill the generator," Tyr said. Lucy grinned, took the gun off her back, and charged up the laser. Before she was able to make the shot, she heard the cycling of the Mech's mini-gun. As the HellFire Laser glowed red, about to fire, Lucy was shot multiple times across the chest, and the gun was hit as well. Neith put a shield up, blocking the rest of the fire.

"Are you okay?" asked Neith.

"It's me, I'll be fine. Worry about the Mech," replied Lucy. She was already concentrated on forcing the bullets from her flesh and regenerating what had been damaged.

The Deicended, besides Lucy who was focusing on healing, started firing everything they had at the Mech. The Mech seemed to operate just fine even after being hit by a rocket. Its right arm dangled and seemed to be unusable. It had a bit of a stutter to its walk now, but it was still just as big of a threat as it was before. Emily threw a few daggers at the Mech. She waved her hand and projected lightning, connecting to the daggers she threw. The Mech staggered a bit from the shock but recovered quickly. The Mech switched its focus to Emily, starting to spin its minigun again. Before it had a chance to kill Emily, Neith projected a shield in front of her and saved her. Tyr charged the Mech, but when he was repeatedly pelted by bullets, he was forced back. Neith summoned three globes of energy and fired them at the Mech to no effect.

"Ben, you have to try to melt the wiring inside," ordered Tyr.

"Got it," replied Ben, taking a big gulp. He had been firing his weapon at the massive technological obstacle with the rest of the Deicended, but the Mech hadn't noticed him yet. He ran behind the pillars, hoping to remain unnoticed. Every step closer to the Mech, Ben's breath grew heavier. He got to the point where he was completely out of sight of the Mech, but his body felt so heavy that he stopped. Ben knelt down and put his hands on the ground. He had barely moved, yet he was more out of breath than he would have been from running a marathon. He had such an urge to curl up. Ben put all of his effort into standing. He managed to get halfway up and, when he looked at the Mech, he could barely make it out, it was so blurry to him. *It's the boar on the island all over again. I'm going to get everyone killed this time,* he thought.

"Let's get this done!" Takumi shouted as he ran up behind Ben. Ben looked at him and could see him more clearly than he did the Mech.

"Hydra Sling!" Takumi screamed as he ran up to Ben while firing at the Mech. Three shadow arms came from Takumi and grabbed Ben, lifting him up and throwing Ben on top of the Mech. "Take care of it; you got this man!" yelled Takumi. Takumi continued to fire at the Mech, gaining its attention for a short while, striking it repeatedly with his signature shadow strike attack.

Without thinking, Ben started to produce heat from his hands. Concentrating on heating the Mech's insides, Ben could see a few sparks coming from melting wires. The Mech's pilot must have been able to tell that something was wrong because he attempted to shake Ben off. He used his right hand to steady himself on the Mech and only focused harder on heating it up. More sparks flew out, and the lights on the Mech started to flash. Then, Ben noticed something strange about the sparks. Most of them were properly flying out from inside the Mech. But a few appeared to fly in. As soon as he noticed that, the Mech ran into a pillar, successfully knocking Ben off. Ben was face down on the ground and quickly flipped over just to see the end of the barrels to the Mech's mini-gun. Ben's eyes lit up, and he felt his breath catch in his throat. *Guess this is it,* he thought.

"I'm done with this!" Neith screamed. She put her hands in front of her, and a violet glow flowed around in front of her, forming an orb. She concentrated, flexing her arms, forcing as much power as she could. The power from the orb began to create a gust around it. Holding the power, Neith stabilized her stance as she felt forced back. She let out a scream as the orb burst into a solid beam. It sliced through the pillar next to the Mech. Neith moved the beam, slicing the midsection of the Mech and through the generator. The top half of the Mech fell backwards, and the generator sparked in flames. The power went out in the room, surrounding the Deicended with darkness that was pierced only by the flow of sparks coming out of the Mech and the generator.

"Backup will be here any moment," said Tyr. "Neith… that was… that was pretty awesome."

"Didn't think you had it in you," said Lucy, mostly healed from her wounds.

"Well… I did," Neith said, walking over to the top half of the Mech. It was hard to make out much with how destroyed the Mech was, but blood was pouring from the cockpit. She looked back at her team, Lucy covered in blood and Ben sitting on the floor, obviously in shock from having literally stared down the barrel of a massive gun, then she looked back at the severed body parts of the Mech pilot. "He deserved it," she said quietly, almost to herself.

"Let's go! Let's get that fucker already," said Emily.

"Just take a breather for a second," said Tyr. "We should let the backup take care of the Hawk. We struggled too much with this Mech." The light in the room began to flicker. Then, they just stayed on. "You've gotta be kiddin' me," said Lucy.

"Of course, they have a backup," said Neith, smacking her hand against her helmet.

"Are we stupid or something? How did we not guess there would be a backup?" asked Lucy.

"Shit! New plan. I hate that I'm saying this, but we're splitting up into two groups. Neith, Lucy, and I are going to stall the Hawk until backup gets here. The rest of you are going for the backup generator. We're not failing this mission," ordered Tyr.

"No! I'm going on the team that goes for the Hawk. I'm going to kill him for what he did to Anne," demanded Emily.

"No, and don't argue with me. The three of us have the best abilities for survivability. If one of you three go, there's a higher chance of one of you dying," Tyr said.

Emily stared at Tyr with a look that said she was going to fight him until she got her way. "The Hawk killed Ben's actual brother, and you don't hear him complaining." Tyr continued. Her eyes narrowed, and she felt her blood boiling. Ben winced.

"Just look at it this way. If you kill the backup generator, you kill the Hawk by proxy," said Lucy. Emily refused to move. Then, Ben grabbed her by the arm. "We need you. I need you, Emily," said Ben.

Emily gritted her teeth. "Fine," she said. The two groups split. Tyr's group went back the way they came from, heading towards the aircraft hangar. Emily's group went to the top of the building they were currently in to get a look at where the back-up generator might be.

Once they got to the top, they carefully inspected the other buildings. Red lights were flashing from every building, most likely signaling to the enemy of their existence. Takumi pointed out a building that looked similar in shape but of a smaller size than the building they were currently on. "Look at all of the wires at the bottom of the building. They're pretty thick too. I'm guessing those wires are for power," said Takumi.

"We could just cut the wires running under the bridge then. The generator will still be running, but wherever the EMP is won't have power," said Ben.

"Two problems with that. For all we know, the EMP device could be in that building with the generator. We can't rely on that. The other issue is that I see other chords running to other buildings that aren't under the bridge. Though, I could cut all the other wires by throwing my daggers," said Emily.

"Three problems actually," said Takumi. "They see us." He pointed out some gunman in the building they were eying, aiming at them. "Shadow Shield," Takumi yelled. Ten shadow arms came from his back, covering over Ben and Emily like a dome right when the enemies started firing.

Ben melted the roof below them, and the three jumped back down into the building. They could still hear the building being pelted by the enemy's guns. "Well, if we head down that bridge and only make lefts, we should make it to the other building," said Ben. They ran through the bridge, and the room they walked into was empty. "I think it is most likely that everyone went to go protect either the Hawk or the back-up generator," said Takumi.

"Good, it'll be easier to take them out if they're all grouped together," Emily said with a wry smile on her face. Takumi shook his head and rolled his eyes at Emily. They ran around the building until they found the bridge to the building they were trying to get to. They were hesitant to walk across. They didn't see anybody, but it would be stupid to think the enemy would just let them across willingly.

"Riot Shield," said Takumi. His shadow arms formed a shield in front of him, and he aimed his CCRF through a crack in his arms. Takumi walked first, and the other two followed close behind him. They only made it a few steps before the enemy began to fire at them. Takumi's riot shield protected them decently. "Back up! Back up! I can't hold this," he yelled. They retreated to safety. "What now?" asked Ben.

"I could put some metal between us and them, but I'm not sure that's going to be enough," said Emily.

"I got an idea," said Takumi. "Shadow Shield." His shadow arms came together in front of him. This time, they made a point where they came together. "Now, reinforce me," he said. Emily smiled, took a bunch of metal panels off the walls, and folded them around Takumi's shadow arms. "Okay! Now, stay close behind me and keep up. SHADOW TRAIN!" Takumi screamed as he ran over the bridge.

He sprinted as fast as he could, and the others did as well as they could to keep up. The enemy fired everything they had in an attempt to stop them. Pieces of the metal guarding Takumi's shadow arms flew off after being shot, but the team persisted over the bridge. The enemy backed up more the closer Takumi got to them. When Takumi bust through the door, he knocked back three guys. They were now in a tiny room right before the main room to the building. There were two men on Takumi's right, and Emily gunned them down. There was one man to Takumi's left, and Ben shoved the man down. Instead of grabbing his rifle off his back, Ben took his dagger out.

Ben stared at the man, not sure what to do. The enemy reached for his gun that he had dropped, picked it up, and pulled the trigger. The gun made an unusual popping noise and didn't fire anything. *It's jammed,* Ben thought. The man got up and swung his rifle at Ben. Ben deflected the attack with his dagger. Takumi looked back and noticed Ben in trouble. He was ready to go help him.

"Don't do it," said Emily. "Help me hold off these guys." The doorway into the main room was very wide, and Takumi's shadow train couldn't block it all. Takumi and Emily focused on firing into the room, keeping the enemy from moving in on them. The man attacking Ben swung his rifle again, and Ben blocked it. *I can block his strikes all day,* Ben thought to himself. The man thrust the point of his rifle at Ben, and he pushed the point away from himself. This left the man open, and Ben thought about taking his chance and moving in for a blow. Instead, he backed up.

His heart was racing too fast, and only terrible outcomes popped up in his head. The man viciously swung two more times at Ben, and each time, Ben blocked it. Ben felt sweat run down his cheek. *I can't keep this up forever. Strike him already, dammit. He's not even a good fighter; what are you so scared of?* Ben thought.

Ben noticed that the man had been sweating way worse than him and was even breathing harder. *C'mon, he's even more scared than you are,* he thought. He swung his rifle again and missed Ben, leaving himself completely open. *Do it now,* he thought. He stared at his enemy and froze. The man swung again and knocked Ben's dagger out of his hand. Ben cowered behind his hands, expecting to feel the pain of metal smacking against his arms.

Instead, Ben heard a thump. His enemy collapsed to the ground. Ben noticed the man's eyes rolled back into his head, showing only white. Ben fell to the ground, both relieved and horrified.

"Ben! Could you cut it out?" said Emily. "It's way too frickin' hot in here." Ben realized that he had been using his powers the whole fight and just caused the man to have a heat stroke. He thought back to the time when Tyr killed the rogue Deicended. *This must be what Tyr felt,* he thought. Ben looked at his friends who were holding back the rest of the enemies and smacked his helmet, shaking his head. He stood up and grabbed his dagger. He felt so stupid looking at the thing, realizing that he never turned it on in the panic he was just in. He would have cut right through the rifle otherwise. He ran up to Takumi and assisted in firing down range.

"There's too many of them!" yelled Emily. Takumi's shadow train had lost all of its plating, and the enemy was getting closer, despite Takumi's and Emily's attempts to hold them back. Neither of them had been successful in shooting anyone either.

"Should we retreat and try to come up with a different plan?" asked Ben.

"That might be our only option," said Emily. Ben melted a panel and kicked it down. They were close enough to the mountain that Takumi would be able to use his shadow arms to grapple out. Emily was on the other side of the small room from them and was going to have to cross the river of gunfire coming through. She jumped in the way and waved her hand in front of her. The bullets, inches away from her, stopped in their tracks from her powers. She grinned and dove to safety without a scratch. The enemy began to move up faster without her laying cover fire.

"Alright, Takumi. Get us out of here," said Ben.

Takumi just stood there, lost in thought. "C'mon, man! We don't have all day," said Emily.

"This doesn't feel right," said Takumi.

"What the hell is that supposed to mean? Trying to live seems pretty right to me," said Emily.

"The longer we take, the more likely Tyr, Neith, and Lucy are going to get hurt," said Takumi. "I'm ending this now." He drew the two photon revolvers he had strapped to his legs and tossed them in the air. Two shadow arms reached out and grabbed them. "Shadow shooter!" yelled Takumi.

"Don't do it!" Ben yelled.

Takumi held his CRFFs akimbo in his hands, reached out with another shadow arm to the ceiling in the other room, and threw himself in. The enemy targeted him, missing every shot as he swung across the room with his abilities. He shot wildly in every direction with the photon revolvers. He managed to hit a few enemies with them. Takumi spun around, firing his CRFFs to keep the enemy behind cover. He used a shadow strike to pierce a desk one of the enemies was using for cover and threw the desk at another guy, knocking him down. The enemy that was now without cover was shot by Takumi's photon revolver.

Emily and Ben began to pick off the enemies that were out of cover and distracted by Takumi flying around the room. Takumi stopped in the middle of the room. "Shadow shield," he said, covering his body in his shadow arms. He still had the two arms holding photon revolvers shooting in random directions. Takumi pressed the release on his magazines to his CRFFs, dropping them. Two more shadow arms grabbed new magazines and reloaded his CRFFs. "Hydra's Wrath!" Takumi yelled as his arms shot out in every direction. Some of the arms hit nothing, and others stabbed into the cover of the enemy.

Takumi threw all of them aside and shot at everything he could. He struck into the ceiling again to get out of the way of some returned fire and blocked shots with his shadow arms. The room was pretty clear after all of this, just three guys left. One retreated further into the room while the other two charged Takumi. Takumi leaped over them and gunned them down with all four of his weapons.

Strangely, Takumi noticed them fade away like a collapsing cloud of smoke. Then, Takumi noticed there were far fewer bodies lying on the ground than there should have been. "Only one left," said Emily as she and Ben ran into the room.

"That one might be a Deicended. Be careful," Takumi warned. They ran to the back of the room where the last one of their enemies stood before the backup generator. The man wore a long overcoat that covered his whole body and had a hood that made it difficult to see his face. "It's the Deicended that creates illusion," said Emily.

The rogue Deicended raised his hand, and a copy of himself appeared to run out of his body and headed towards Ben. "Not going to fall for this. It's going to go right through me," said Ben.

As the clone got close, it wound its hand back and swung at Ben, knocking him to the ground. "Owwww, this is the real one for sure," said Ben. Emily threw a dagger and stuck him in the side. Once hit, the man faded away in a cloud of smoke.

"What?! Since when could his illusions hurt us?" asked Ben.

"Hahaha, sounds like you met my brother. Don't worry! Unlike him, my tricks pack a punch," said the rogue Deicended. He sent out two more clones, and Takumi immediately shot them down.

"Bind," yelled Takumi. His shadow arm reached out, wrapped around the rogue Deicended, and lifted him in the air. He struggled, attempting to free himself, and his body appeared to be glitching out, attempting to make more clones.

"Okay, you got me," said the rogue Deicended. "I surrender. Just let me go, and I'll cooperate."

"Not a chance. You're staying with me," said Takumi.

"Can't blame a man for trying," said the rogue Deicended. Emily walked up to the generator and threw a few daggers into it. Then, she struck lightning to the daggers, killing the generator. She took a step back and thought about Anne. "We did our part. Don't mess this up, Tyr," Emily whispered to herself.

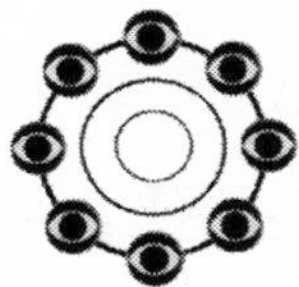

Before setting off across the uncovered ground to make for the hangar, Tyr turned to speak to Neith. "Neith, do you mind if I get your concussion pistol?" asked Tyr.

"Sure, I don't think I would get much use out of it anyways," replied Neith.

"Sorry, I should have picked one up myself," said Tyr.

They ran out of the room and to the next building. It appeared empty. Lucy went to a window and could see parts of the hanger. "Looks like they are prepping their ships to leave. I can also see a platoon worth of people running in our direction. We should probably stay clear of them. Don't want to waste too much time trying to fight through them," said Lucy.

"Let's head over to that building then. It connects to the back of the hanger," said Tyr. They ran out, and Tyr kept his armor up, planning on charging into whatever mess they came up against, to take whatever came at him. He bust down the door into the building after the bridge they just ran over. Tyr noticed six enemies. One was right in front of him and had no time to react. Tyr swung with the concussion pistol and blasted the guy, sending him flying into a table. The man bent backwards over the table in a manner that appeared to sever his spine. Four of the other enemies opened fire on Tyr, and one without a weapon attempted to flee. The one running was the first Lucy took out. She shot another one that was firing at Tyr, dropping him pretty quickly. Neith summoned four violet orbs and sent them flying at one of the enemies. Two of the orbs hit the enemy, dropping him behind cover.

Tyr charged the last man standing and used his concussion pistol. He was standing next to the wall, and the force of the pistol sent him flying through and onto the mountain side. Neith ran to the man she hit, her eyes and hands shined in a bright violet color as she got close to him. When she saw him, she could hear his clothes sizzle from where her orbs hit, but the man made no noise.

"Let's get moving," said Tyr. The group ran out of the room and onto the last bridge before the hangar. When they got to the door and opened it, they noticed the room filled with possibly fifty people, scrambling around and prepping the aircraft. "We can't engage them like this. There are too many of them," said Tyr.

"We could try to get close and ground whatever aircraft the Hawk tries to escape in. Honestly, we won't be able to get all these guys. Once the others kill the backup generator, they'll all try to escape, and we'll only have to fight the ones who don't flee quickly enough," said Neith.

The group agreed to the plan and moved up behind some crates relatively close to the aircraft. With Lucy concealing them, this time the enemy was too much in a panic to discover them. It wasn't long before the lights flickered for a second and went completely out. The enemy reacted quickly and scrambled to board their aircraft and fly off. The Hawk, accompanied by a few others, ran into the hangar, heading for an Owl.

"Now!" yelled Tyr. Lucy opened fire on the group while Tyr charged for them. The Hawk sent a massive gust that threw Tyr back and knocked away the crates that Lucy and Neith were using as cover. He kept the gust going constantly, really trying to knock the three off the hangar's main entrance that opened out over a cliffside. Tyr, after flying back a ways, stuck his dagger into the floor to keep himself in place. He held onto his pistol for dear life, expecting to rely on it in a few minutes. Lucy extended her arms to hang onto a piece of metal smelted to the ground. She dropped her rifle and lost it to the wind. Neith dropped her rifle as well, attempting to find anything to hold onto.

"Go, I'll hold them off and catch up," the Hawk said to his team. Neith was knocked off the edge. Below the platform, unaffected by the wind, she used her powers to stop herself in place. She reached for the edge of the platform but was just a foot away. "C'mon, c'mon."

"Up, just go up," she said to herself. Neith began to descend ever so slightly. She looked up to see the Owl transporting the Hawk's companions fly over her and out into the night. "No! This isn't my limit!" she shouted to herself. She stopped moving again, and her eyes glowed brighter than ever before. For the first time, she rose. It was only a centimeter, but it was progress. The harder she strained her abilities, the higher she rose until her hand grabbed hold of the ledge and she pulled herself up.

Once the Hawk noticed his allies were safe, he ended the gust. "Bunch of cocky fuckers, aren't you? Only three of you showed? Are the other ones dead already?" asked the Hawk.

Nobody responded. Instead, Tyr charged him. The Hawk leaped over Tyr with ease, and when he was directly above him, the Hawk created a blade of air that he flung down on Tyr. Tyr shot the blade with his concussion pistol, nullifying the attack. Lucy threw her arm with her dagger in its hand, aiming to stab the Hawk. It was heading for his back, yet he stepped aside, dodging the attack. Then, the

Hawk sliced Lucy's hand off. He went to follow up, throwing a blade of wind at Lucy. It was heading for Lucy's center mass, and she wasn't able to move out of the way in time. Lucy flinched, closing her eyes, ready for the attack to hit her. When she opened her eyes, she saw a violet shield protecting her. Tyr ran up and tried to stab the Hawk. He ducked under the attack and jabbed at Tyr with his dagger. The Hawk's dagger merely chipped at Tyr's hardened skin. Tyr went to use his concussion pistol, but the Hawk shoved it away before Tyr could pull the trigger.

The Hawk kicked Tyr in the abs, also using a force of wind to knock Tyr back and then changed his target. He went for Lucy, who had just picked her dagger back up after she grew her hand back. He sent two wind blades for her as he ran up. Lucy dodged both attacks and blocked the Hawk when he went to stab her. He swung his blade at her, and Lucy ducked under just to feel his knee slam into her face.

He attempted to strike her heart but was blocked by Neith's shield. The Hawk snapped his head to Neith and ran for her. Lucy sent three arms, extending them to block the Hawk from getting to Neith. In one swing, the Hawk cut all three limbs down. He then sent two wind blades for Neith.

At the same time, he sent a powerful gust for Lucy. Neith shielded herself from the attack, and Lucy was knocked back. The Hawk charged Neith again, constantly sending wind blades to keep her shield up and pinned down. He didn't notice Tyr running to intercept him. When he did notice Tyr, it was too late for him to react. Tyr hit him with the concussion pistol, sending him flying to the side. Lucy ran for him and thrust with the dagger in her right hand. The Hawk blocked the attack. She followed up with a right hook, and the Hawk blocked it as well. Lucy grew an arm under her right one and punched the Hawk in the gut, grinning with satisfaction at having landed a blow on him. She went to stab him again, but the Hawk shoved his dagger into that arm, stopping it in motion. Then, he took it out and swung it into her helmet, shattering her visor and swiping the blade across her nose. He created a shockwave of wind to knock her limp body back. Tyr had already started running for the Hawk. When he pushed Lucy's body away, he threw a wind blade at Tyr. Unable to dodge, Tyr put his arms in front of him. The wind cut into his hardened skin, but that was as far as it went. The Hawk leaped over Tyr, aiming his dagger at the back of his head.

When the Hawk thrust the dagger, it was blocked by Neith's shield. When he landed, he threw a wind blade at Neith, causing her to shield herself, and then, he pushed Tyr back with a gust. While the Hawk ran for Neith, she generated energy orbs and threw them at him one by one. The Hawk side stepped each orb, quickly closing in on Neith. He tossed a few more wind blades at her, but she blocked all of them with her shield.

Then, he waved his hand to the right, creating a strong breeze from behind the shield, knocking Neith to the ground and out of cover. Lucy attempted to interject by extending her leg to kick, but the Hawk shoved his dagger into her foot without even looking at her. He created a wind blade with his hand and sliced her foot off. Tyr caught up and stuck his hand out, freezing the Hawk in place with his powers. The masked man struggled, trying to free himself with no luck. Lucy grew her foot back and rushed him.

Even though he was unable to move, wind began to circulate around, becoming fiercer as Lucy got closer. She stopped progressing and was starting to lose her footing. Tyr was also being forced back but concentrated on holding the Hawk in place. The wind cut off suddenly when Neith put a bubble shield around the Hawk. Tyr let go of him and dropped to the ground, out of breath. The Hawk tried stabbing at the shield with no effect. He lifted his arms appearing to generate wind, but the shield was unaffected.

"Got him," said Neith.

"Can you hold him until backup gets here?" asked Tyr.

"Oh, yeah! I can hold this all day," said Neith.

Lucy walked up to the shield. "Hmph. I guess that's all you got," said Lucy, almost sounding disappointed.

The Hawk held out his dagger. It was unclear what he was trying to do with the strong violet tint obscuring everyone's vision. His clothes were rapidly moving as if a storm was brewing inside the shield. Then, the Hawk swung his dagger and shattered Neith's shield. Lucy, being the closest, was sent flying backwards from the force. Now, it appeared that the Hawk's dagger was one hundred little wind blades dancing around forming a sword. Tyr charged for him, and when the Hawk swung his wind sword, Tyr tried to block the attack with his left arm. Even with Tyr's armor, the sword cut through his forearm and through his shoulder. Tyr stumbled back, screaming in pain. He dropped to his knees, and the Hawk walked up to him.

He swung his sword for a finishing blow. In a last effort, Tyr shot his concussion pistol. It shattered the wind sword, generating another gust, and Tyr was knocked back a few meters. Lucy had grown two additional arms on each of her sides. In an instant, the Hawk formed the wind sword again. The Hawk swung his sword, and Lucy stopped his hand in the air. She used one of her arms to punch him in the gut again and another slammed into his mask. He created a pulse of wind, knocking Lucy back a few feet, but she stayed standing.

Then, the Hawk swung his blade downward at the three arms on her left. He cut through them like they were butter. Lucy tried to kick him, but he just lopped the leg off with the wind sword. She grabbed onto him before falling without the support of a second leg. The Hawk used another wind pulse and jumped back as a beam of violet energy missed him. The beam disintegrated two of the three remaining arms that Lucy had.

"That was mighty risky. If all three of you fought like that, you might have been able to get the upper hand on me," said the Hawk. He ran for Neith, and she put a bubble shield around herself. The Hawk swiped his sword across the shield, shattering it. He then stuck his hand out, creating a powerful force of wind that sent Neith flying and smacking into the wall. She tried to stand, but instead, coughed up blood and collapsed.

The Hawk looked at Lucy and noticed that none of her limbs were growing back. "Your healing abilities are quite outstanding, but you were foolish to allow yourself to reach your limits," said the Hawk.

All three of the Deicended couldn't move. Neith was barely holding onto her consciousness. Tyr was in too much pain from the loss of his arm and was drained from freezing the Hawk. Lucy had used her powers too much and didn't have enough limbs on her body to stand.

"So, tell me! What has George been saying lately. It tells you nothing but lies," said the Hawk.

Oh no! If he tells Lucy and Tyr what Cade told me, they might not be ready to hear it. If only I had more power, I could stop him, thought Neith.

"I'm so curious to find out which of you is the special one," said the Hawk. They could hear a mocking smile in his voice.

Is he talking about me? The one that Cade told his secrets to? thought Neith.

"You're the monster that attacked our school. You will pay for what you did to us!" yelled Tyr.

"Is that what you think? I'm some kind of monster?" asked the Hawk. He lifted the mask and revealed his face. He had a fair looking face, not looking older than thirty years. He had bright white hair that laid an inch above his shoulder line. "I'm no monster. I'm not the lie that George tries to portray. You don't have to join me, but you are not going to mischaracterize me. It knows my name. It's Serpico. I'm sure It left that part out in an attempt to dehumanize me."

"You can think whatever you want about yourself. We are going to kill you for what you did," Tyr said through gritted teeth.

"You're really not understanding what I'm saying about George lying, are you? You know, if I had to guess which of you the special one is," Serpico trailed off and looked at Lucy.

Lucy's eyes widened when he looked down at her. *I need to become a Primech,* she thought to herself.

The Hawk stepped closer to Lucy. "Yeah, with your powers, that would make sense," he said.

"You really need to learn to shut your mouth," said Lucy. She reached out with her last remaining arm, extending it with her powers. Her arm split into two, and each one, before Serpico could react, grabbed his wrists and held them apart. The arm split again into two more arms. One grabbed his white hair and raised him a few feet in the air. The other wrapped around his legs. Another arm grew from Lucy's body and grabbed her dagger from one of her arms that was cut off previously.

"No, you can't," Serpico pleaded. "I hel…" he was saying before Lucy shoved her dagger into the bottom of his jaw and through the top of his head. She dropped his limp body. Her arms retracted to her body, and she began to heal and regenerated her severed limbs.

"Lucy… you did it," said Tyr.

Neith limped over to Tyr and knelt to help him up. "No, I'm losing too much blood. I can't stand," said Tyr. Lucy walked over to him, "I can't use any more of my powers. I feel like my insides want to come out. I've never pushed my powers like this before."

"I think I can stop the bleeding," said Neith. She put her hand near Tyr's shoulder where his arm was missing. Her hand lit up with her energy. She burned the wound using her powers, and Tyr grunted in pain.

"Thanks, Neith," said Tyr. *I'll lose a thousand arms to have her take care of me like that,* he thought.

"I can't believe you did it," said Neith. "I thought you were at your limit, too. How did you manage that?"

"I figure we would never make any ground just trying to overpower him. He was obviously better and stronger than us, more experienced. I figured faking him out and taking him by surprise would be our only chance," said Lucy.

"I knew he would be strong, but I had no idea he would overpower us so easily. And you just took care of him in a second. You need to show me how you could access that type of power. I had nothing against him, and you took care of him in a flash," said Neith.

"I think it was just the surprise that got him honestly," said Lucy.

Emily, Takumi, and Ben sprinted into the hanger. "Are you guys okay? Did he get away?" asked Emily.

"We're okay for now, but no, he didn't get away. That's him, lying on the ground," said Tyr, wincing as he gestured with his remaining arm.

"With the white hair?" asked Ben. Tyr nodded his head. The three walked over to the Hawk's dead body. Neith noticed Serpico's dagger on the ground a couple of feet away from his body. She picked it up and noticed a hawk etched into the side of the dagger. It was the same exact dagger that all of the Deicended had. Making sure nobody else noticed, she hid the dagger in her cloak.

"I was supposed to be the one," said Emily.

"I think we all feel that way," said Takumi.

"Be glad it's done with. We all got our revenge," said Ben.

"Why doesn't it feel like it, then? I didn't even get a chance to fight him," said Emily.

"Even if you were the one to kill him, I don't think that would change your feelings. Killing him wouldn't change what he has already done," said Ben.

A fleet of Owl and Dove class aircraft arrived. Out of one of the Owls, Nicholas stepped out, taking in the scene and the corpse of the Hawk. He nodded and addressed them as a group. "Well done! You lot are more proficient than we could have expected," he said.

"What are we supposed to do now that we killed the Hawk?" asked Ben.

"He's not the only rogue Deicended, or did you forget about the threat out there? From what I can see, it looks like a lot of the Hawk's crew managed to escape," said Nicholas. He looked down again at the lifeless body of Serpico. When the Deicended saw his reaction, it took what little joy and relief they had from beating the Hawk. Though Nicholas often had an expressionless face, they were hoping for something to make them feel like this was a huge success. "The fight doesn't end once the king dies, it ends when the kingdom is destroyed."

20

Time and Silence

"Greetings, my young Deicended," said Cade. "I am aware that a lot has happened since you left the base, but we will need to debrief you before you can get some much-needed rest."

Only Tyr and Lucy held their heads high as they walked in. Tyr would have been proud whether or not they got the Hawk. His death was just a bonus to leading a successful mission. Lucy didn't look proud or anything, just neutral.

Tyr began to tell all of the details and covered everything up until the group split. "Takumi, would you mind telling the details of your group when we split?" asked Tyr.

"I… I don't know. I would leave too much out. Someone else should," Takumi said nervously.

Everyone looked at Emily, expecting her to volunteer, but, by the look on her face and her crossed arms, they could tell she didn't want to talk. So, everyone turned their heads to Ben. He gulped and stepped forward.

"So, we were going to run into the room like we had been, but then the enemy noticed us. So, we went back inside and ran from them. Oh, and Takumi did this sweet move called Shadow Train where Emily put some metal on his shadow arms. Then, Takumi just charged through the enemy like a mad man. Then, we were holding a position over the bridge when some dude tried to attack me. Of course, the dude couldn't handle the heat I was putting out and just dropped to the ground. You know, if I hadn't taken that guy out, this whole mission could have gone a different way." Everyone in the room rolled their eyes.

"So, we were about to retreat because the enemy had way too much firepower. Then, Takumi came in clutch again and started gunning down everyone with his photon revolvers hooked up to his shadow arms. Dude was a mad man, just taking out everyone in the room. That's when we noticed the rogue Deicended we captured. Guy can make copies I guess, and Takumi just wrapped the guy up with his ability like the guy was some kind of present. Then, we destroyed the generator, and that's kind of it. We met up with Lucy, Tyr, and Neith pretty much right after. So, I guess technically Takumi gets MVP of our squad, but I was a close second."

Emily slapped him in the back of the head and cracked a smile for the first time since that mission started. "Thank you, Benjamin, for that ah… description of events," said Cade. "Please, Tyr, continue with your squad's part after the split."

"Yes, sir. Once we split from the others, we noticed a large group of enemies heading towards us. So, we decided to take an alternate path from the most direct route. From there, we ran into a building with six enemies inside. We quickly took them out with no one exposing our position or harming anyone in the squad. We moved on from there to the hangar where we took a position near the aircraft in order to take them out if we needed to. Once the power to the base went out thanks to the efforts of Takumi, Emily, and Ben, the Hawk and the rest of his crew came out to the hangar to escape. We confronted him but were unable to prevent the others from getting away. After engaging the Hawk, we were overpowered at first, but then Lucy tricked him into believing she was out of power and caught him off guard. Shortly after that, the others arrived and so did the rest of George's fleet," Tyr reported professionally.

"Very well. So, the Hawk has been defeated. I have to say that I am quite surprised that this was the end of that one's story. You have redeemed George's great error in allowing your school to be defiled. Currently, we have a task force searching the base for any information. We still need to find out how he was able to bomb the school in the first place, and we are looking for clues to where the rest of the rogue Deicended may have gone," said Cade. "Lucy, you must know that Mercury has asked me about the details of your training, and Mars has asked to arrange a meeting with you. He is too large, as you know, to come to this base, so we will have to find some time in the schedule to bring you out to a more open area to have this meeting."

"Oh, yes! Could we just have the meeting over communications?" asked Lucy.

"Sadly, he requires it to be in person. Now, I know you want to be chosen as a Primech, but this might only be a meeting for the sake of acknowledging that he has noticed you," said Cade.

"Understood," Lucy said with a big smile on her face.

The Deicended went to leave the room, except Neith stayed back. When she was sure the others were gone, she drew the Hawk's dagger and shoved it into the table. "I understand that he has been training much longer than us, but how? How could he overpower us so easily? I couldn't do a single thing in that fight except slow him down a little. He didn't just have skill and experience. He had raw power, and not only him, Lucy beat him in a single move. I must be able to get more power through the Dawn Edge. Somehow, Lucy must have gripped more power from there or something. When she was pretending to be out of power, I had already thought she had gone past her limits. I think she got something more from the Dawn Edge," she said.

"This is completely possible… Though, from your suspicions, it makes me question whether you might have been hiding something from your trip to the Dawn Edge," said Cade.

"You're right. I didn't try out my powers, but I still felt the power. At first, I thought it was just a high from the drug, but then, I realized that I was feeling my true potential. I felt the essence of pure energy. I know with that power I could have wiped away the whole base by barely budging a finger," said Neith.

"It is very possible; that is true. That type of power is both our goal and our fear. That power was achieved by one before, and that was George's greatest mistake," said Cade.

"I thought the Hawk's bombing was George's greatest mistake," said Neith.

"My child, you have much to learn," said Cade.

"You lied to me," Neith stated.

"Lied? About what?" asked Cade.

"George never viewed Kathleen as a mistake. She was Its greatest step to learning about the true creation," said Neith.

"You are wise, my child. Thank you for keeping the details of the Hawk's past between us," said Cade as he grabbed the dagger.

"Certainly. Now, I think I'm owed a little in return," said Neith.

"Oh, do you?" asked Cade.

"Yes, I do and, don't worry, this will be mutually beneficial for both George and me," said Neith.

"Well then, tell me what it is that we can do for you," said Cade.

"I would like to go to the Dawn Edge. Today," said Neith.

"That is risky, and we are in short supply of the Flower of Eos," said Cade.

"Then my discretion is in short supply," responded Neith.

Cade cracked a smile. "I am sure we could spare some, but I stand by it being risky."

"We would have never reached the Moon or Mars if we didn't take risks. If the world was filled with overly cautious people, we would have died out in caves a long time ago," said Neith. Cade shook his head but was still smiling.

"You have convinced me. Let me get the Flower of Eos, and I want Lind to assist me in monitoring your trip," said Cade.

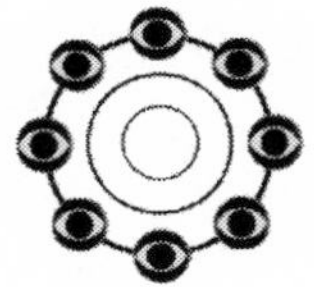

Neith swelled with success and walked into an observation room with nothing but a chair in the middle and a window with Cade and Lind standing behind it.

"Are you ready, Neith?" asked Lind.

"Of course," replied Neith.

Neith took a seat in the chair. Fumes began to rise over her, and Neith took in a deep breath as she closed her eyes. She let out a long exhale and opened her eyes. The room became grey. She felt like she was in an old black and white movie except a little color came from herself. The feeling of vibration overwhelmed her, bringing a strange peace. She looked down at her hand and made it glow with her powers. "Yes, this is the power I remember," she said. She held her hand out, and, with ease, a beam projected from her hand.

When it made contact with the wall, it seemed to just go through it. She walked up to the wall after she stopped trying to blow it down and touched it. She pushed a little and was stopped by it. She weirdly didn't feel the wall, though she could touch it. "I think I'm getting it. I'm in this parallel universe that overlaps my own. Those in this universe can only view ours. It's like being a ghost or something. My mind and powers are overlapping in this universe, but they are anchored to my body in my own universe. Are the Phosphorus ghosts or something?" Neith looked up to Cade, waiting for an answer, then realized they can't hear her as long as she is in the Dawn Edge. "I need to go outside. This is too limiting for research."

Neith went to go for the door to pantomime to Cade to let her out. When she stepped over, an octopus leaped from the floor and latched onto her leg. In a panic, Neith's eyes glowed, then her hands, and then her whole body gave off a violet aura. She ascended ten feet off the ground and floated. She blasted the head off of the octopus, and its tentacles let go of her and flopped on the ground. Then, she realized that she was in fact flying. Cade and Lind were looking right at her with amazement. "So, she can influence her body in some manner from the Dawn Edge," said Lind.

Next, Neith flew down to the door and pointed to it, signaling to Cade to let her out. Cade shook his head, no. Neith was getting a little worried that she wasn't going to be able to see the Phosphorus and was upset at how much she was being limited by Cade. *Maybe they aren't aware that I am here,* she thought. Neith raised her arm and launched a massive beam into the ceiling. *My power is probably going right through that, and at least a few of them should be able to see the signal.*

She waited around for a few minutes, experimenting with her new ability to fly. It didn't take long for her to get bored. *I didn't come here to just fly around. Where the hell are they?* she thought. Almost right after she finished her thought, she saw someone poke their head in. When that person noticed Neith, it walked in and was followed by another. It appeared to be a man and a woman. They were both narrow framed, fit, and light skinned. The man's hair was long, black, and in a ponytail. The woman's hair was white and fell past her shoulders. They looked like normal young people, except their eyes were white with no pupil or iris.

"Ahhh, Neith. Back again so soon?" the woman said with a smirk on her face. Neith turned away from the window and camera so that Cade and Lind couldn't read her lips.

"Last time I was here, you told me not to trust George," said Neith. "Why? Are you simply trying to manipulate me, like you do the Deicended that go rogue from George?"

"Hmmm, I do not think we are. Do you think we are?" the woman asked the man.

"Why, no. I do not believe so," said the man.

"Is that not the same question you already asked us before?" asked the woman.

"A lot has happened since then. Cade told me his secret, and I understand why he did what he did," said Neith.

"We gave advice already. We do not repeat ourselves. We were thinking that coming here was a waste of time, and it seems to be that way. I understand now why the others did not follow their curiosity to interact with you as we did," said the man. They turned around and started to walk away. Neith channeled her power and shot a beam of energy, cutting the two of them off from their path. The woman stopped for a second and left. The man turned around, smiling.

"You are a determined one. I will stay for a while and listen," said the man.

"What are you really? What is this place? What does it have to do with my universe?" asked Neith.

"Be careful not to insult me. I warned you once to not make me repeat myself. Those are the same questions you have already asked before. You have one more chance to ask me something worth my time or else I will take your ability to exist away," said the man, his face did not betray much emotion, but Neith was certain he would follow through on that.

Still floating above the man, Neith was unmoved by his threat. "How can I have this power in my own universe?" she asked.

The man's smile grew wider. "What an interesting question," he said.

All of a sudden, color returned to the room, and Neith's eyes widened as she realized the drug was wearing off. The glow around her faded away, and she fell to the ground, landing on her back. She groaned, started to get up, and looked around the room. She noticed everything looking normal except there was some sort of black liquid on the ground. It was in the same spot where she had killed the octopus. She got closer to take a look, and it wasn't like anything she had seen before. Lind zipped into the room and used one of its arms to suck up the liquid and put it in a tube.

"What is it?" asked Neith.

"We have no idea. We have never had anything like this happen in one of our studies. The better question would be to ask you what happened," said Cade.

"I killed an octopus right there. It attacked me, and I killed it. Could that have come from the octopus?" asked Neith.

"It is possible," said Cade.

"This would lend credence to our theory of death having a link to the Dawn Edge," said Lind.

"You've had this theory before?" asked Neith.

"Ah, yes. We have had that theory before, but we never went anywhere with it. It was not a theory worth pursuing since we had zero evidence validating such a theory," said Cade. He paused in deep thought, no doubt communing with George, then turned to Neith. "It is time you joined the others now. This trip has been well worthwhile, and I am glad you pushed us to do it. We will see what happens after we run some tests on this substance."

"Hold up. When are you going to let the others know about the secret that you have told me?" asked Neith.

"The truth will be revealed to them in due time. Kathleen is still a threat to us all. We will need to take care of her before we can reveal anything to the others. Please, continue to keep our secret until then," said Cade.

"Certainly, but when will that be?" asked Neith.

"Soon," Cade responded.

"Why don't we train longer, make sure that we are ready? The Hawk was hard enough for Tyr, Lucy, and I to defeat," said Neith.

"Trust me, I wish we could, but recently, before we laid siege to the Hawk's base, one of our Owls that patrols the outskirts of her domain was blown up unexpectedly. We have no recourse other than to believe it was her that had caused the incident. Though she has remained in the same place for years, we believe she may plan to attack us soon and is probing our strength. Though we are confident George can hold her back, we are not sure at what cost," said Cade.

"Does George not fear that we will become like her?" asked Neith.

"We can only hope that at least one of you gains the power of a god. However, doing so and then turning on George and his people, that fear is the price It is willing to pay for finding truth," said Cade.

21

Deus Vult

Four days after the death of Serpico, the Deicended were exercising in the gym when Cade called them into the strategy room.

"Thank you for joining me, Deicended. We have found information from the enemy's base that is vital to your next mission," said Cade.

"Does it have to do with the other Deicended turning rogue?" asked Takumi.

"No, we have found out that the Hawk was not the leader of their band," said Cade. Lucy tensed, along with most of the other Deicended, except Neith. Ben asked incredulously, "What do you mean? He was taking orders from someone else?"

"We've found correspondence with the Hawk's group and another. From the conversations, we've determined that the Hawk was indeed taking orders from the other person. This person seems to be the mastermind behind all of the Hawk's attacks," said Nicholas.

"Were there any details about the attack on our school?" asked Takumi.

"Sadly, no. There was no data older than a year," responded Nicholas. "We have determined the location of their base though."

"Is there another EMP on the base that is going to keep George's forces from helping?" asked Emily.

"No, there isn't. However, there may be something far more dangerous. We have already sent forces to the base's location. Every single fleet we sent has been destroyed. There seems to be a very powerful Deicended in the base. We haven't been able to get a single aircraft closer than one hundred miles before losing contact. We've tried satellite cameras to get information, but there is something blocking the camera's vision. We believe both what is destroying our aircraft and blocking the satellite's sight are related to a Deicended," said Nicholas.

"Do we know what destroyed the aircraft? Any idea what kind of power we are going up against?" asked Neith.

"From the footage we have seen, it appears that they have a Deicended that can create black holes," said Nicholas.

"Black holes?! How is that a power? That is way OP," said Ben.

"Yeah, seriously! You're not suggesting we go to take out this Deicended are you?" asked Emily.

"The only option is stealth. We have already sent multiple units of Primoids and Primechs and have received no sign of their success," said Nicholas.

"So much for the all-powerful George. First, It needed us to kill the Hawk, now this? You know what? I'm done with this. I'm not going on this mission," said Emily.

"I regret to say that I agree with Emily," said Tyr. "If there is a Deicended with such power, we should not take the fight to them. We should wait for them to come to us. Traveling over one hundred miles, trying to go unnoticed or else we die, is too big of a risk."

"You will not be alone this time. We will send you in with some Primechs as well," said Cade.

"What about any Arch Primoids?" asked Lucy.

"Not all of the Arch Primoids are built for stealth. Also, they are busy with George's tasks for them at the moment, and we have no idea how long you are going to stay in this location," said Cade.

"This seems too rushed. You can't even get information on the base. I think risking them running and hiding again is our better option," said Tyr.

"If we wait for them to attack us, they might have enough power to seriously harm George's people," said Nicholas.

"Oh, c'mon. That's not possible," said Ben.

"Anything is possible, Benjamin. We never expected there would be a Deicended that could create a black hole. We suspect that the only thing keeping them from directly attacking us is that they do not believe they could win. Though they would never be able to truly beat George, they could still harm our people and create a hundred more cases of school bombings like the one that happened to you," said Cade.

"We killed the Hawk, then we kill the next person for you. Who's after this one? I'm finished for real. I'm officially requesting to go to Australia with the rest of the free people," said Emily.

"Emily, no! You can't leave us!" said Ben.

"I'll be waiting in my bunk for an aircraft to get ready to take me to Australia," Emily said as she walked out of the room.

"I'll do whatever George needs of us, but I would like to request leave to see my family before deploying," said Takumi. "It's been years, and we haven't even been allowed to speak to them."

"This mission needs to start as soon as possible, we were going to send you guys back home before discovering this information, but we have to wait for that until you return from this mission," said Nicholas.

"I can't agree to go then. I'm going to the cafeteria. I'm sorry, but I have to see my family, it's been too long," said Takumi. He walked out of the room.

"I have to say, I am disappointed. I thought we had taught you all better. This is about the greater good. This risk is to ensure that thousands of possible deaths are prevented," said Cade.

"I apologize, sir, but I have to leave as well. I can't in good conscience take my team on such a risky mission, especially without the whole team together," Tyr said as he walked out of the room. Cade placed his hands on the briefing table and leaned against it, the only outward sign of his exasperation.

"Is there anyone else that would like to excuse themselves?" asked Cade.

"What about my meeting with Mars?" asked Lucy.

"You will have to see him after the mission. I know you are eager to become a Primech, but even if he does select you right now, we can't afford to lose your powers for the mission," said Nicholas.

"Even so, child, coming back from this mission will definitely ensure your selection to become a Primech," said Cade.

"You all agree to going on this mission, then?" asked Nicholas. The three Deicended left in the room nodded their heads yes.

"Very well. However, we do need the other three to go on this mission as well," said Nicholas. "You three need to convince the others to come."

"I'll go talk to Takumi," said Ben.

"You should talk to Emily first. Lucy, you should talk to Takumi. At least until Ben can come help." Cade suggested.

"If you think so," Ben said as he walked off to look for Emily. Lucy shrugged and walked out, looking for Takumi.

"Obviously, you would be best suited to speak to Tyr. He clearly holds you in special regard," Cade said to Neith. She looked at her feet to hide her reaction to that before looking up at Cade.

"Sure thing. Just one question. How is a Deicended blocking the sight from all of the satellites? Does it have anything to do with Kathleen?" asked Neith.

Nicholas' eyes widened, "How do you know about her?"

"Do not worry, Nicholas. I have informed her about Kathleen and the Hawk's connection to us. She can be trusted with the knowledge," said Cade.

"Very well. To tell you the truth, we are unsure why the cameras don't work. It looks like there is a fog covering the whole area. It looks too wide to be from a Deicended though, so we are unsure of the origin of it," said Nicholas.

"Hmmm, okay then. I'm sure I can convince Tyr to come along on this mission, but what happens after this?" asked Neith.

"We will still, possibly, have the threat of the random rogue Deicended. Though we will not need you for that. You will be allowed to go home as much as you want, and, if you want, you can work with George in the Dawn Edge research department," said Cade. Neith smiled.

"Sounds promising," she said and walked out of the room, looking for Tyr.

Neith walked around for a bit but eventually found him lying in his rack. "Hey, what was that about? Why aren't you coming with us?" she asked.

"You guys aren't going without all six of the Deicended anyway. Look, I can't, in good conscience, lead you guys into such a dangerous mission," said Tyr.

"That really is disappointing. We all know there is a high risk, but that doesn't matter. We're putting George's people, our people, first. I thought that would be something you would understand," said Neith.

"I don't feel good about this decision, but it feels right. This works too since, if I don't go, there's no way Cade is going to deploy you. So, you'll all be safe," said Tyr.

Neith sat in the bed next to him, very close to him. "I always thought that you were the most dutiful of all of us. I've always admired that about you." She placed her hand on his forearm.

"And you are a great leader, Tyr. If there is anyone who could lead us into this and get us out safely, it's you. Also, I'm sorry if I misread this, but I kind of got the impression that you would want to watch my back anywhere." She smiled, and he looked back at her, very obviously conflicted.

"I would. I mean, I will," said Tyr. His face had genuine concern on it.

"I feel like you're being selfish, abandoning us, and you're covering it up with an excuse," said Neith as she stood up and stepped away.

Tyr grabbed her arm, "I would never! I will follow you. I would never abandon you. But I also don't want to lose you in this dangerous mission," he said.

Neith grabbed Tyr's hand. "I can take care of myself. You're letting your personal feelings cloud your judgment. There is no safety for us while there is still this threat looming over us. If you would truly never abandon me, then come with us and do everything you can to help us succeed rather than depriving us of your power. You are so strong, Tyr. We need you."

"Okay. I'll go. I promise you I wasn't trying to be selfish," said Tyr.

Neith put her other hand on Tyr's cheek, and she smiled, "Your intent may have been in good conscience, but your decision wasn't. You can't let rash decisions cloud your head."

Tyr put his head down, "You're right. I'm sorry. I should never have put my feelings in front of my squad members."

Neith let go of Tyr and walked out of the room. Tyr followed.

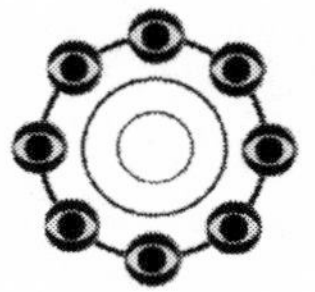

Lucy found Takumi eating a roast chicken with a side of rice in the mess hall.

"Hey, man. Feeling a little homesick?" asked Lucy. Takumi dropped his fork and looked up at her.

"A little? We haven't spoken to our families in years. I probably wouldn't even know my little sister if I passed her on the street," said Takumi. Lucy sat across from him and was quiet for a moment.

"My father… was more important to me than anyone else. I lost him. If I were in your situation, I would want to see my family more than anyone else. But we still have to take out the person responsible for what had happened to us. If we don't, then more will suffer like we have. I would give anything to be able to see my Daddy again, but I can't. I will never be able to see him again because of them. We have to end this," said Lucy. Takumi dropped his head and pushed his tray away.

"I know, I'm being selfish, but I can't risk never seeing my family again before we go on such a dangerous mission," said Takumi.

"Look, I wouldn't really care about you going, but Cade isn't going to send us unless you join us. I have a goal to become a Primech now. I don't have any family that I care about anymore, and now this goal is more important to me than anything else. You don't have to risk yourself; I can take care of everything myself. I took down the Hawk, and I'll take down this next obstacle," said Lucy. Takumi looked at her incredulously.

"Man, I thought I was being selfish. You might not have any biological family, but the Deicended are our family now. We've looked out for each other for years. I know you're strong, but what if you can't protect them?" asked Takumi.

"I'll try my best, and even if I can't take this rogue out before any of you get hurt, I can heal you. Or are you forgetting how easy it was for me to literally restart Ben's dead heart, years ago? We are all so much stronger now than we were back then, me included. I *will* get you all home to your families. Well, your *real* families." Lucy stared steadily into Takumi's eyes, unwavering. He returned her gaze with hesitation. Lucy threw her hands up in exasperation.

"Look," she continued. "Either you're coming or you're not. I don't really feel like wasting more of my time trying to convince you," He shook his head and looked over at her.

"You know what? I'm going, Lucy, but only because you are getting too overconfident after killing the Hawk. If you think this mission is going to play out exactly like the last one, then you're being ignorant. I'll go to keep my friends safe. That includes you, Lucy. You lost more than any of us in the bombing, except maybe Ben, so I can understand your drive. I care about you, and I want you to get justice for your dad. I am going only to look out for you all!" said Takumi.

"Good!" said Lucy, "Your skills will be helpful."

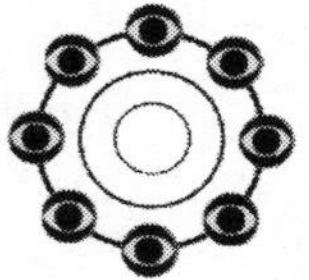

Ben found Emily in the hallway. She heard him coming and looked over her shoulder at him. "What do you want, Ben?"

"We need you," said Ben. She rolled her eyes.

"You already played this card with me," said Emily.

"Well, nothing has changed," said Ben.

"Yes, something has. The Hawk is dead! That was our goal. Our goal is now done, so we should move on," said Emily.

"Serpico was just the face of our problems. This person is the mastermind. It's not over until we kill the head," said Ben. Emily looked at him skeptically.

"You trust George too much," she said.

"Are you insinuating that George had something to do with that attack on our school?" asked Ben.

"No… I just feel like we're Its pawns, just taking out Its trash," responded Emily.

"Maybe you're right… but the Deicended have become my friends. We have to stick together. Whatever George's reasons for bringing us together and using us, we are a team now." Emily looked at him and exhaled. "Remember when we used to fight?" Ben asked her. She smiled.

"Yes, I do. You and Takumi used to gang up on me. That didn't last long though. Once training started, Takumi and I were the best; can't gang up on me when I can kick your ass," said Emily.

"Yeah, and you were nice to me. Well, for the most part. You had every right to put me down when I put you down," said Ben. He grabbed Emily by the hand. "I can't leave everyone else. I can't let them face this alone, and I can't let you leave us. If you leave, then our family will be split. I can't go through that again. Stay with us, please? Just this last time. Then, if you still want to leave, then I'll go with you." Emily started and looked at him, holding eye contact.

"Come with me now," she said.

Ben shook his head no, "We have to finish what we started. This is the person who killed my brother. We can't stop just short of the end."

Emily gritted her teeth, "I swear, I'm killing you again if anything goes wrong. And if you're already dead, then I'll have Lucy bring you back, so I can kill you a third time."

"Deal," Ben smiled as he hugged Emily.

22

Odyssey

The six Deicended boarded a stealth Owl. Nadin, Joe, and Cassandra joined them. Nadin was armed with a BRF 170, a photon revolver, and his vibro-katana. Joe had a BRF 184 with an extended magazine, a concussion rocket launcher, and his two long swords at his side. Cassandra had a BRF 172 with no scope and, at her side, her rapier. As the Owl took off there was a bit of a gloomy vibe in the aircraft. The Deicended took the extended flight time to go to sleep. After a couple of hours, the Primechs woke them up as they landed. As the ramp lowered, they disembarked and took in their surroundings. It was a quiet desert with nothing around them besides rocks and sand. The sunlight was blinding, and the heat was scorching.

A second Owl landed behind them, dropping off a Fox bike for each of the Deicended and the Primechs.

"Wait, is this really all that is going?" Emily asked Joe.

"Yes. This is a stealth mission," said Joe.

"Yeah, well, we can stealth with more. We don't even have an Arch Primoid with us. I was under the impression that this was the most important operation in the world right now," said Emily.

"This is. This is also not the only squad on this mission." Joe said. "We have others, surrounding this hundred-mile radius. The only information we have to go by for this place is old maps." He pulled out one of said maps and laid it on the ground for the whole team to see.

"This is the path we are taking. Hopefully, we meet up with the others. We believe this path will get us the farthest on the Fox bikes before we have to start walking," said Joe.

"Wouldn't we have a better chance to group up and fight together?" asked Ben.

"Normally, yes, but if we get spotted first, this rogue Deicended just needs to open up one black hole and we are all dead," said Nadin.

"We've discussed this enough; let's start moving," said Cassandra.

The group walked over to their Fox bikes. The Deicended's were equipped with their requested weaponry. Tyr's carried a BRF 170 and a plasma shotgun with a belt of plasma and HIDP rounds. He also had a lance rifle. Neith had a P2 pistol and a BRF 170. She also had an ABT rifle. Lucy had a photon carbine with a highly magnified scope. Ben had a BRF 170, a photon revolver, and a Lance rifle. Emily had a CRFF, a P2 pistol, and a belt of knives that she wrapped around her chest. Takumi took two CRFFs again, but this time, took six photon revolvers.

Joe led the convoy as the fox bikes rode out into the desert. The bikes were kicking up dust, making it difficult to see where they were going. They could see the person in front of them just fine though, forcing them to trust the person leading.

"Won't we be noticed in this wide, open desert?" Tyr asked, addressing the group through their in-helmet communications.

"We would have been if we were in the air, but there is no evidence of the enemy keeping an eye on this desert. We are approaching from the east since the fog doesn't seem to come out as far in this direction. Once we reach the fog, that's where we have to be careful on foot. Right over that mountain range is where it will begin," said Cassandra.

As they approached the mountains, they decreased the speed of their bikes. The landscape shifted drastically. The trees were tall but skinny, and even though there were many trees, at lower speeds the bikes were able to maneuver through them with ease. They were heading for the top of the mountain to hopefully get some intel on the area. The path they took was filled with rocks. It would have been challenging for a vehicle with wheels, but the bikes hovered over the obstacles with no issues. When they reached the top and looked down at the landscape, they saw nothing but fog and a mountain or two poking out above it. Joe put his hand to his head to radio in, "Can any unit read me?" No response followed. "HQ can you read me?"

"Yes, I can hear you, but you're cutting in and out," responded Nicholas.

"Roger. I believe we are going to be silent once we step down into this fog," said Joe.

"Good luck, over and out," said Nicholas.

The group began their descent; they left the bikes alone on top of the mountain. Tyr grabbed the pack for the ABT rifle that Neith was carrying. When they reached the fog line, they could see a few trees hiding in it. There was no way for this fog to be natural. The group stayed together as close as they could. The fog was so thick, they could barely see ten feet in front of themselves. They noticed that vegetation thickened significantly the farther they progressed. It was almost as if they were in a rainforest, but that would be impossible right next to a desert.

"Where are we going? We can't see anything. How are we supposed to find this base?" asked Neith.

"There is a big building that we were able to see rising above the fog that looked like it used to be a factory or something years ago. Our guess is that it has been repurposed as the enemies' new base," said Nadin.

The group focused on listening to their surroundings to remain alert to any potential enemies since their sight was almost useless now. Though, they weren't sure how useful their hearing was going to be since the forest was filled with the sounds of wildlife. The bugs sounded big and noisy, but the birds' squawking was probably the loudest.

The group halted after about thirty minutes. Joe, who was leading the way, announced that their path was blocked by something laying in their way. Everyone moved forward to see what he was referencing. It looked like a massive root to a, surely, even more massive tree. The root itself stood five feet high. Neith wished she could see the tree it was connected to. Looking both ways, it was not clear how far the root went. The group climbed over it, but there was something peculiar about it. They found a river soon after that was only about three feet wide; it was more of a stream.

"There were no rivers on the map. This doesn't make any sense," said Cassandra.

"This fog doesn't make any sense. I think the river is a little bit more believable," Emily said snarkily.

They continued, following the stream since it was flowing in the same direction as the facility they were heading to. The forest only thickened the farther they walked, slowing their progress. The stream led them to an old road. They decided to walk on the side of the road, figuring they could walk faster with the gap in the vegetation. Out of the fog appeared a building. It was a two-story building that looked like it could have been a home or a small business. It was difficult to tell with how rundown it was. It was practically ancient. From the outside in, the place appeared to be empty. Walking around the building, they noticed a few more buildings nearby. The place was like a ghost town except it was filled with the sounds of wildlife. For whatever reason, the fog seemed to be less thick between the buildings, allowing for a little more visibility.

"We must be getting close," said Tyr.

"Indeed. We should take shelter in one of these for the night. Visibility can only get worse. I doubt our night vision will help much," said Nadin.

"This building over here doesn't seem to have any windows on the second floor. We can use light in there," said Joe.

The first floor was open with few divided rooms, so sweeping the space didn't take long. The second floor, however, was a bit worrisome. There was a chance a group of enemies could be hiding in there. If they were to get into a firefight, which could alert the rogue Deicended to their presence, they would no doubt be swallowed up into a black hole. Lucy used her powers to turn invisible and slowly crept up the stairs to the second floor.

She came back down soon after, completely visible, and gave a thumbs up. The team walked up. It appeared to be a home for someone at some point. There were only two rooms. One was a bedroom, and the other was a living room with a kitchen attached. The bottom looked like some kind of store. Most likely, the owner was the one who stayed here. It was extremely dark upstairs, but at least the fog was even less dense there. Once they all found themselves a seat, they took off their helmets and took out a few lanterns.

Neith and Lucy walked straight for the dilapidated bed in what had surely been the bedroom and crashed. Tyr followed them, thinking back to the conversation he had with Neith back at the facility, about how she had touched his arm and pretty much acknowledged that she knew how he felt about her. *Maybe Neith wouldn't mind if I tried to lay in there too. Yeah, she would want that! No, wait; Lucy is there. That would be weird with her there. Actually, she probably just wants some sleep, and she wouldn't want me to snuggle up to her right now. Maybe, if I sleep next to the bed, she'll see how considerate I am,* Tyr thought. He laid down next to the bed's rusty frame and fell asleep. Neith had already been asleep the moment she got onto the bed.

Nadin and Joe went to the first floor to keep watch for any intruders. Takumi and Emily sat on a torn up old couch in the living room, staying awake for a bit to talk. "So, you are really heading to Australia when this is all done?" asked Takumi.

"Yeah. I keep saying, I'm done with all of this. I didn't choose to live under George. I never truly felt free in this world. I mean, I don't even feel like we had an option when it came to training as a Deicended," said Emily.

"I know how you feel, but I see this as a burden we have to bear, an obligation that we have to fulfill. I just didn't think I would have to be away from family for so long," said Takumi. "Aren't you going to miss your family while you're in Australia?"

"Not really. I never really cared for them. I'm sure my parents just wanted to look good in George's eyes when they gave me up. My brothers probably had a party. If anything, I'm going to miss you guys, especially you and Ben," said Emily.

"Ha ha! I know what you mean, you're like my second sister. Though, my real sister would probably get along with you, and I can't have my sisters ganging up on me," Takumi said, sending a gentle elbow her way. She laughed quietly.

"Thanks, Takumi, it means a lot to me. When this all started, I felt so alone. Now, I feel like I belong to something. I just wish it was without George's rule," said Emily.

"I don't know. I think Ben and I will be able to convince you before the end of this mission. We're family now, and in the end, you won't be able to leave us," said Takumi.

"Hm hm. We'll see. Speaking of Ben," her eyes wandered, searching for him, and saw him sitting with Cassandra by one of the lanterns. She felt an uncomfortable tightness in her chest. "Why is he over there talking to Cassandra?" asked Emily.

"I don't know," said Takumi.

"She's such a bitch. What is there even to talk about with a shell," said Emily.

"Hey, she's not a Primoid, but I'm pretty sure you can't call a Primech that either," said Takumi.

"Fine, maybe I'm being a little harsh. She was just always so mean to me. She reminded me of the kids I went to school with," said Emily, eyeing the elegant lines of Cassandra's designed body, wondering what she looked like when she was an actual human before she was able to just look however she wanted.

"You should probably go to sleep. You don't want to be tired tomorrow," Cassandra said to Ben.

"You're probably right, but I think I slept too long on the ride over here, so I'm going to wait a bit," Ben said.

"So, tell me how you guys took out the Hawk. I got briefed on the info, but I'm curious about what you have to say about it," said Cassandra.

"Well, I did part of the briefing. Anyways, all I did was help with shutting the lights off. Lucy was the one who took out the Hawk," said Ben. Cassandra chuckled.

"Oh, c'mon. that can't be all you did," said Cassandra.

Why is she so interested in what I have to say? I would have never had a girl this pretty talk to me when I was in high school, Ben thought. He shifted and cleared his throat. "Well, I did get into this fight with this one dude. It was when Emily, Takumi, and I split from the others. Emily and Takumi were distracted, and this guy attacked me. He kept trying to hit me, but I blocked all of his attacks, and I was giving off heat from my powers. Guess he couldn't handle it, passed out on the ground, and started tweaking out like this," he said as he imitated the enemy's seizure.

"Hahaha, is that really how he went out? How could you even tell he was having a heat stroke?" asked Cassandra, grinning and laughing at the thought.

"No doubt. His eyes rolled so far back in his head I thought he was being possessed, until I saw him flopping on the ground like a fish out of water," responded Ben.

"Haha, oh no, please stop! A fish out of water? Well, that's one of the most creative ways I've seen someone best their opponent," Cassandra said, giggling.

Ben rubbed the back of his head and blushed, "Well, to be honest, I didn't mean to use my powers. It just happened by instinct," said Ben.

"Well, I taught you guys to become proficient enough with your blades that fighting with it becomes instinct. I guess you just applied that concept to your powers as well. You all have come a long way from getting smacked with the side of a training blade. You're all effective agents that all of us Primechs who helped train you are really proud of," said Cassandra. Ben smiled back at her.

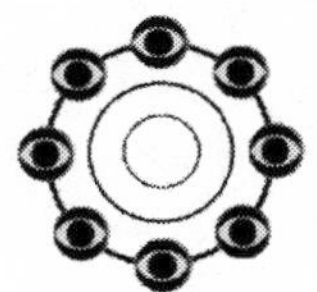

Outside, Joe leaned on the wall of the building as he was keeping a lookout, even though he wasn't worried about being found. Nadin walked up to Joe, coming out from the fog. "I've searched four nearby buildings and found no sign that anybody is here or has been here recently," said Nadin.

"Looks like the coast is clear," said Joe. "Too bad, would have loved some action."

"You're real cocky for the worst fighter of the Primechs," said Nadin.

Joe unsheathed his two longswords and went into an attack stance, grinning and facing Nadin, "You wanna put that theory to the test, small fry?" he said.

"Don't make me laugh. I'd say we need to keep quiet, but I doubt you would even have time to scream before I finished you," said Nadin.

Joe put back his swords, "You're not worth my time. I wouldn't waste my energy on you when I need to reserve it for an actual opponent," he said.

Nadin scoffed and walked into the building. Before the door closed, the two heard a loud thump. It was something big. The two drew their guns and kept them at the ready. They heard the sound again. It was coming from the street. Whatever it was, as the sound got louder, it was getting closer. The old shop had a counter, which the two hid behind, waiting to see something emerge out of the fog. Another thump, and it sounded too close for comfort.

First, they saw the leg of a creature, and then, the entire thing revealed itself. It looked humanoid, but it was twenty feet tall. It made an eerie growl or whimper of some kind. Its legs and one of its arms were too big for its body; it seemed to throw itself off and have difficulty walking because of it. This thing wore no clothes; its skin looked like layered scar tissue and had a bit of a yellowish-grey tint to it. Its face looked almost human, except its eyes were a dead black, and it had few teeth jutting out of its slack mouth. Its whole face seemed stretched and twisted. Joe thought that if he still had a human stomach, he might have thrown up.

Using their internal communications, "Cassandra, get everyone out here. We need to go and get away from this place," said Joe.

"What's going on out there?" asked Cassandra.

"You'll see once you get out here. Just be quiet," said Nadin.

Cassandra and the Deicended walked down the steps, and their eyes lit up from what they saw. "What in the world is that?" asked Neith.

"Your guess is as good as mine. Let's head to the back and get away from this thing," said Nadin.

While they sneaked out of the back of the building, something caught Ben's eyes, a magazine rack. The items on there were so dusty and old that he couldn't make out anything, except one. There was an animal on the cover of the magazine that Ben didn't recognize. It looked like some kind of small grey bear. It drove Ben's curiosity, but he had to ignore it and follow the others out the door.

They hurried through the thick of the woods for about half a mile. "Are we not going to talk about what the hell that thing was?" asked Ben.

"We told you already, we don't know," said Nadin.

"This place has been covered in this crazy fog, and you guys know more about the Deicended than we do," said Joe.

"Do you guys think that could have been a Deicended that could have been disfigured by not being able to control his powers?" asked Tyr.

"For all we know, it's possible," said Lucy. "Whatever that thing is, let's just stay away from it, and hopefully, we'll never have to see that thing again,"

"There's something really fishy about this place," said Takumi.

They continued to walk until they came across something blocking their path. It looked like another giant root. "I'm going to cut into it to see what the hell this thing is," said Neith.

Lucy grabbed her wrist as she took out her knife. "No, don't. I feel like that's a bad idea. I don't know why, but there is something off about it. We should just go over it and ignore it," she said.

"I agree. We have an objective; no reason to get sidetracked," said Nadin. Neith put back her knife, and the team crossed over the giant root. After traveling for a bit, they came across a gulley. The fog seemed to thicken towards the bottom. They continued down, and when they reached the bottom, it was slightly muddy, but there wasn't even a creek flowing through it. Barely able to see anything, they bumped into another giant root.

"Okay, we need to talk about these things. We really should get more intel before we head for the head honcho," said Neith.

"You know, I'm starting to think you are right," said Joe. "We should at least try to look for the other groups that have gone into the fog."

"Which…," Cassandra began saying something before hearing a grunt. It sounded like it was only ten feet away from them. They all looked at where the sound was coming from.

Suddenly, a creature emerged from the murk. I looked similar to the creature they had seen earlier, except this was only about six feet tall and slightly more bloated. It noticed them and started to growl, gradually getting louder.

"Shadow strike," Takumi whispered as a shadow reached out and pierced the creature in the chest. It wrestled the arm, trying to get free and growled louder. Then in a flash, Nadin jumped and thrust his katana into the creature's head. It stopped moving. Takumi retracted his shadow arm, and the creature fell to the ground.

Nadin was in the middle of sheathing his sword when they all heard another growl, then another growl, followed by another and another. They drew their guns, knowing they were surrounded. From every open direction, creatures similar to the thing they had just killed began to swarm them. The Deicended all faced their backs to the large root and began defending one side, forming a sort of triangle with the root. Nadin, Cassandra, Neith, Lucy, and Ben took one side. Tyr, Joe, Takumi, and Emily took the other side.

Lucy took point on her side and, looking over the top of her scope, which was useless in the fog, shot most of the creatures in the head. She was overwhelmed and missed a few shots or only hit the creatures in the chest which did not slow them down. For a while, Cassandra was able to pick off the ones Lucy missed. Nadin and Ben laid down supporting fire. Neith was launching random orbs of energy into the fog. Each one made a small explosion. Even if only a few of the ones she fired hit, it was still assisting majorly. If one got too close to her, she would fire a beam, slicing the creature in half like butter. Lucy, getting more overwhelmed, threw her rifle to the side. She grew four arms and engaged the enemy in close combat. All of her punches barely had any effect on the monsters, so she quickly got her dagger out and plunged it into their heads. She was tackled by one of the creatures; it stabbed its hand into Lucy's arm that was holding the dagger and ripped it off.

Before it could get another strike, Nadin came in and swung his katana. It sliced the top of the monster's head off, and he stopped the blade right before Lucy's face. Nadin then lunged to a new target and thrust his blade into one of the enemy's faces. His blade stuck, and he fought to get it free when another creature ran for him. Lucy extended one of her arms and wrapped it around the creature like a lasso. She reached out and grabbed her dagger off the ground as well. Then, she pulled the creature towards her and plunged her dagger through its eye.

"Quick, give me your daggers," Lucy said to Neith and Ben. They complied and tossed them over. Now with three daggers, Lucy was able to fend the creatures off much easier, her arms forming a whirling dance of blades.

Tyr blasted the rampaging creatures with his plasma shotgun. The shotgun was extremely effective and took the creatures down in one shot even if it was to the chest. Takumi and Emily backed him up with their CRFFs. Anything they couldn't handle was wiped out by Joe's BRF 184, shooting HIDP rounds that tore through the enemy. Unfortunately, the moment Tyr ran out of ammo, Joe did as well. Joe went to reload his gun as fast as he could, while Tyr didn't have the time and switched to his BRF 170. It wasn't enough firepower to hold the creatures off for long. "Neith, we need the ABT support!" Tyr shouted.

Neith drew the ABT rifle and aimed at the forces running for Tyr's team. When Neith pulled the trigger, drones fired out of Tyr's pack, shooting into the air and taking flight. It was unclear how high they went since they disappeared into the fog. The drones began to fire high powered laser targeted support on the creatures but fired on Tyr's position as well. At least one of the shots crashed on a creature and vaporized it. "Cut it off, Neith!" Tyr yelled in desperation. "The fog is screwing with the targeting," he said. Neith released the trigger and pressed a button that called the drones back to their pack.

After the barrage, Tyr held off the hoard for only a short time with his melee. None of the attacks the creature tried on Tyr could penetrate his hardened skin. It took four of the creatures to pile on him and take him down. The creatures started to head for Takumi next, and a few of them headed for Emily. She grabbed some knives off her belt and flung them at the creature closest to her. She used her magnetic powers to push it back ten feet. Two creatures were sprinting towards her still, and she magnetically pulled the daggers back from the other creature. They impaled the backs of the creatures running for her. They screeched but were still alive, so she continued to pull the daggers, making the creatures fly towards her. She swiftly slit their throats as they flew by her. Takumi had five creatures heading towards him, and, with a combination of shadow strikes and gunfire from his two CRFFs, he held them off long enough for Joe to reload. Joe shot off the creatures pinning Tyr down. With the firepower of Joe's BRF 184, they were able to hold off the enemy.

That was until a loud screech came from behind them. One of the creatures leaped down from the root at their back. Ben, being the closest, engaged by shooting it down. Five more came down, and Ben felt alone. He was the only one concentrated on them, and they were all concentrated on him. He felt his heart stop; he froze and watched the creatures running for him. "Shadow Strike," Ben heard as a shadow arm pierced the head of the creature in front of the group that was heading for him. Takumi gunned down two more that were heading for Ben and shadow struck another. Still, one more rushed for Ben, and he finally snapped back to reality. Ben drew his gun back up and started to fire at the creature. He hit it a few times in the chest but didn't stop it. It swiped away Ben's gun and grabbed onto his shoulder. Its long nails dug into him, and Ben's blood dripped down its fingers. Ben gritted his teeth in pain, shoved his hand into the creature's face, and used his heat powers. The creature's face started to melt slowly, but not fast enough. The creature tightened its grip, and Ben screamed in pain and desperation to conquer it. Ben screamed even louder, but this time, in pure determination. The creature's face started to melt faster until a flame burst from his palm and engulfed its head. The flame continued to burn until the creature let go and collapsed, revealing the creature's skull. It looked like a disfigured human skull.

Ben looked at his hand with amazement. "Finally, something cool," said Ben.

Ben looked around and only Takumi saw what he had done. The fighting seemed to end right after Ben burned the face off of the creature. The group was lowering their weapons with smoke rising from the barrels and fading into the fog around them. Lucy looked around for any wounded and saw that Ben had been the only one who was injured. She walked over to him and began healing his shoulder when Tyr addressed the group.

"Should we retreat out of the fog?" Tyr asked.

"We might run into trouble if we head out the way we came. You saw that giant thing. Might be tougher to take out then all these weird things," said Nadin.

"These things have me freaked out. What are they?" asked Takumi.

"Could this be some fucked up Deicended power?" asked Emily.

"Well, anything is possible with your weird powers. George doesn't even know what the limits of your powers are, so, yeah; it's kind of a guessing game," said Cassandra.

"We're close to the facility. We should at least trek a bit further before we decide to go back," said Joe.

"What if we end up in a worse situation than we are already in?" asked Takumi.

"There is a dangerous 'what if' whichever way we go. I say, we take our chances with the option that gets us closer to completing our mission," said Nadin.

Joe looked at the worried faces of the Deicended and stopped for a second. "Look, if you guys don't feel confident, we can head back. It won't be a problem if that's what you decide. This mission has already gone south bad," he said.

"I'm not speaking for everyone, but we took down the Hawk. We can handle whatever weird shit they throw at us," said Tyr. The rest of the Deicended also agreed with Tyr, nodding in determined unison. "We've already come this far, we should make it worth it," Takumi added.

When the group turned to head over the root and continue, there was another figure standing on top, obscured by the murk. When everyone aimed their weapons at the figure, branches and twigs shot out from the root and latched onto their weapons. The branches directed their weapons away from the mysterious figure.

"I am not your enemy. I have come here to negotiate with you," said the dark figure. The branches let go of their weapons, and the group lowered them. The man jumped down to reveal himself as the man with the Skull mask.

"Who are you, and what do you want?" asked Nadin.

"My name is John, and I've come to warn you against killing Kathleen," he said.

"Killing who?" asked Emily.

"The name of the person you seek," said John.

"And why would we trust you? You were reported to be working with the Hawk," said Joe.

"Serpico and I were friends many years ago, but we do not work together. I was there in his base to warn him against working with Kathleen," said John.

"Well, if you were warning him against working with Kathleen, why would you want us to not kill her?" asked Cassandra.

"I want her dead as well, but she has been warped by the Phosphorus and is not on the same level as us. If you fight her, you will die," said John.

"Coming from the guy who got beat by the Hawk. If you didn't know already, we killed him. I don't think you should be telling us where we stand in this," said Emily.

"Hmmm, you bested Serpico? I suppose that is possible. Maybe you are better than I believed. That doesn't change the fact that Kathleen will kill you if you face her," said John. "Serpico was powerful, but Kathleen possesses a power that has no right to exist in this world. There is a chance if you were to work with me towards that goal, but it cannot happen now. None of us are ready to face her."

"What? Do you think that we are stupid or something? We would never side with a rogue Deicended," said Tyr.

"As much as the Phosphorus are our enemy, George is as well. You truly need to see through the lies you have been taught," said John.

Lucy raised her rifle to John. "You need to see how arrogant you seem. Nothing is going to stand in our way today. You are clearly our enemy, now leave before we kill you."

Takumi looked worried about Lucy's aggression. "Lucy, we shouldn't threaten him; he's given us no reason to act harshly towards him,' he said.

"All we know for sure is that this guy was Serpico's friend. If we let our guard down, he'll take advantage of us. Now get the hell out of here," Lucy demanded.

"She's right. You should leave. We have no intention of listening to you," said Neith.

"Fair enough. I wish you luck in your venture. I'm sorry that I was unable to persuade you, and I truly hope that you survive this. When you see Kathleen's power, do the prudent thing and retreat. One last thing. Take this. Hopefully, when the time is right, it will show you the truth. It's only enough to last for a few minutes," John said as he handed Cassandra a bag and walked off into the fog. Cassandra looked at the bag and saw that it was a Flower of Eos. She showed everyone and then attached the bag to her belt. The group then climbed over the root and continued towards the facility.

Takumi walked up to Ben's side. "Dude! We need to talk about how awesome that was! I thought you were a goner, and all of a sudden you turned into a damn flamethrower!" Ben chuckled and thanked Takumi.

"I don't really know what happened. It was just like a survival instinct, like when I gave that guy a heatstroke," he explained. "I'm not even sure if I could do it again."

"Well, it seems like you can do it when it counts! Don't stress about it, you will totally be able to do it again. And, when you do, you gotta have a cool name for it! All badass moves like that need a name, man," Takumi enthused, adjusting his helmet that felt askew.

Ben thought for a moment and threw out, "Flamethrower? Mega Scorch? Incinerate?" Takumi nodded and thought as well. He lifted his head and smiled at Ben. "Phoenix Flame!"

Ben's mouth shaped into an o, and he jumped up and down slightly. "Dude, that's badass!" Takumi grinned and told Ben, "You have to use that, man!" Ben laughed.

After wandering around a bit, they came across another road. They traveled on the road for a time with no buildings to be seen along the side. Two miles down, they came across an old street sign that was clearly from another time and rusted around the edges that said Glenton Street.

"This is it," said Joe. "The facility is on this road."

"It should be a mile up," said Nadin.

They walked for twenty minutes, and Takumi noticed something on the ground. It was a flower. He took a closer look. It was a daisy, and immediately, he thought about his little sister. He felt tears threatening to fall. *I'll be with you again soon, Ichika,* he thought. He looked at the forest around him. *Even with all of this evil around us, there's a certain beauty to this place.* He snatched the flower and put it into his pocket.

They kept walking for another fifteen minutes until they heard familiar sounds of growls and screeches. They stopped and put their weapons to the ready position. They crept into the woods and walked out of the way a bit in hopes they could miss the crowd. After following this path for a short time, they turned to walk towards the facility again, keeping parallel with the road. They were careful not to make any sounds from walking through the trees, but soon after, they heard the sounds of the creatures again.

"Let's see if there is a way for us to sneak around them," said Nadin. The team got as close as they could to the swarm of creatures hidden behind some trees.

"There doesn't seem to be any way around them," said Ben.

"If we are fast, quiet, and efficient, then we can maybe sneak by. The fog could be our ticket past them," said Nadin.

"It's too risky though. If we shoot one round this close to the facility, then we might have signed our death warrants," said Cassandra.

"Well, I know I'll be fine, but this could be the true test of the Deicended training," Joe said sarcastically.

"Even if I were to walk over there alone using my camouflage, I doubt I would make it," said Lucy. "Maybe the fog will work better than we expect. If we crawl with our cloaks on and take out a few without the rest knowing, we could clear a path for the Primechs to make it over."

"There is way too much risk to this plan. It would be incredibly stupid for us to follow through with this," said Tyr.

"This is our only option," said Nadin.

"I hate to admit it, Tyr, but we don't have any other option. Even if we retreat at this point, we won't have anything else to throw into the mix to help us," said Joe.

"We beat the Hawk, something George wasn't able to do. If we can't pass through these creatures, then nobody else is going to be able to," said Neith.

"Okay. Maybe, with some help, I can clear a path," said Lucy.

"Only because this is our only option, I'll help clear the path," said Tyr.

"No, you're too big. I think Takumi and Emily should come with me," suggested Lucy.

"Do you guys agree?" asked Joe. Takumi and Emily nodded their heads.

Lucy walked forward first. She could see two creatures in front of her, a mound of dirt to the left, and a few boulders in the mix. Lucy, while invisible, snuck past the two and was able to see five more in front of her. "Takumi, help me kill these two, but the second they are dead, we are going to have to get the bodies out of sight of the others. Then, Emily, do what you can to get rid of the bodies in case more decide to stroll over here," she said.

Takumi crawled up to five feet away from one of the creatures. With his cloak camouflaging him in the fog, he went unnoticed. Lucy made a quick strike to the creature's throat and used her extending arms to push it towards Emily. Takumi wrapped his shadow arms around the other creature, drove his knife into its back, and pulled it up a foot before removing the knife. He then threw the dead creature towards Emily. As the creatures' bodies came towards Emily, she threw a knife into each and then magnetically pushed them into the woods, away from the rest of the hoard.

Next, were the five other creatures. Lucy could only see four now though. Two of them were turned away from the other two. She kept her eye out for the stray fifth one. Takumi swiftly bound the two on his side and stabbed one with his knife while Emily stabbed the other. Emily sent those two flying into the woods as well. The other two started to wander away from each other. Lucy sprinted towards the one nearest to a boulder and, as she stuck her dagger into the head of the creature, she found the fifth creature. It began to screech, so Lucy shoved her hand into the monster's mouth, muffling it. Lucy grew an arm to pull the creature towards her and used her other to drive her dagger into its mouth. Once the creature had dropped to the ground, Takumi had already killed the last creature in their sight. Emily gathered the bodies and sent them into the woods.

"I can't keep doing this, I only have so many knives," said Emily.

"Hopefully, we don't have too much farther," said Takumi.

The rest of the Deicended and Primechs walked up to their position. They found hiding places and waited for Lucy, Emily, and Takumi to clear more ground. Lucy crawled a bit further and found six more but feared that there were even more right next to them that she couldn't see. Lucy waited for a while to analyze the best course of action. "We'll have to strike those three then move on to the other three and hope there aren't any more near them. On my command, go in," said Lucy. She whipped her finger signaling the strike.

Lucy, Emily, and Takumi took out the first three in a flash. They sprinted quickly to take out their next targets. Emily and Lucy had no problem, but when Takumi went to stab his target in the back, the dagger slid off. Takumi realized his mistake and went to stab it again, but the dagger didn't penetrate. Takumi noticed that this creature's skin was covered in some sort of black substance. Then, as the creature turned around and looked at him, he realized its skin was similar to Tyr's black scales. The scaled creature let out a haunting scream.

Before Lucy and Emily could help Takumi, a shadow appeared in the fog and, out of it, emerged a swarm of creatures. The whole team fired at the incoming swarm with everything they had. Takumi was knocked to the ground by the scaled creature. He was able to bind its arms just barely. The creature overpowered Takumi's shadow arms and was able to swipe at him a couple of times. Takumi moved his head out of the way each time, barely dodging the creature. He grabbed onto its face, trying to stop it from biting him.

"Shadow Strike. Shadow Strike!" Takumi yelled, hitting the scaled creature with his shadow arms to no effect. The creature reached for Takumi's neck with its mouth. Takumi screamed, using all of his strength to hold the creature's face away. He began to gain some leverage as he felt even more adrenaline surge through his body. His fingers darkened and were swallowed by the same shadowy substance that composed his shadow arms. It was like a layer of armor around his hands and arms. Not only did he push the creature away, but the force of his new power caved in the scaled creature's face. Takumi threw the body to the side, stood up, and saw chaos.

Joe fired a concussion rocket into the crowd of creatures. None of them saw the impact of the rocket, but it blew away a large portion of the fog around them. They, then found out how dire the situation was. What they saw reminded Takumi of a nest of roaches. The fog began to quickly fill back in, but while it was dispersed, they saw a section of the facility on top of a hill. "Run for the facility! Run and don't stop!" Joe shouted.

As they ran, the massive hoard followed them. They didn't bother firing any guns at them. Rather, they saved their rounds for the creatures leaping at them from their sides and the ones that stood in their way. "Why aren't we dead yet?" asked Neith, as she covered the rear with her violet orbs. "I thought we would be sucked up by a black hole by now."

"Who gives a shit? We haven't, so just keep running and focus on making it to the facility," said Joe.

In front, a giant creature ran towards them. It was even bigger than the one they saw before in the ghost town. Tyr drew his lance rifle and fired it, impaling the massive creature. It barely flinched until the lance exploded, making a hole in its misshapen flesh. It was only stunned and hadn't fallen to the ground, so Joe loaded his concussion rocket and fired it at the giant creature. It hit above the lance rifle wound and separated its top half from its bottom.

The hoard in front of them was becoming too thick, and their progress to the facility was being halted. "We need more firepower up front," Tyr ordered.

"I got this!" Takumi replied. Six shadow arms reached out and each grabbed a photon revolver. He held a CRFF in each of his own hands. "Six Shooter, Six Shooter!" he yelled, firing all of his guns downrange and mowed the enemies down. He even blasted down some of the creatures rushing from the sides.

Another massive creature emerged from the fog. Joe fired his BRF 184 with HIDP rounds. Each shot took away a small chunk of the creature, but Joe ran out of ammo before he could do enough damage. Ben and Tyr took out their Lance rifles. Ben shot the giant creature in the hip and Tyr hit it in the shoulder. The lance rifles made big holes in the giant creature, but it wasn't down for the count. Joe, with no ammo in his BRF 184 or his concussion rocket launcher, drew his two long swords and charged the colossus. He drove one of his blades into its knee, and it howled in pain. The creature swung its arm down at Joe, and he stuck his other blade into its hand, preventing himself from being crushed. Joe then ripped his sword out of the creature's knee, causing it to collapse to its other knee. Joe then took his sword out of its hand, spun around, and sliced the top of the creature's head off where its eyes were once located.

From his flank, another massive creature popped out and swiped its hand, hitting Joe from the back and sending him flying out of the way. Takumi rushed it, using four photon revolvers to shoot it in the face, distracting it. He used the other two photon revolvers and CRFFs to shoot it in the right knee. When that knee buckled, Takumi leaped towards it. He used his shadow arms to pierce through its chest and climb to the top of it. Once on the back of its neck, Takumi took his dagger, shoved it into the back of the creature's head, and ripped it up and out. Then, he used two more shadow arms to crawl into the new wound and rip its skull outward, causing its face to fold in on itself.

The group made it to the part of the road that went up to the door of the facility. Only a few creatures were in their way now but were quickly disposed of. The massive hoard still followed them with an unknown number of creatures mixed in. The door to the facility was a large metal sliding door that looked like it could fit a small plane in it. Joe went to open the door. He tried his hardest, but it didn't budge.

"Where should we go now?" asked Emily.

"I don't know, but we don't have time to discuss it. Someone else, try to get this door open, while I hold them off," said Joe.

The only way to go now was back down the road, and it would be doubtful that they could cut through the whole hoard. Joe, Nadin, and Lucy took point on the road, chopping away at the front line of creatures. Emily, Ben, and Neith laid down supporting fire. Takumi and Tyr tried to open the door. Takumi tried to squeeze it with his shadow arms, but they weren't strong enough to move the door. With each second the door wasn't open, Joe, Nadin, and Lucy crept slowly towards it. They had already killed so many of the creatures that a pile was beginning to form in front of them. With every creature that they killed, the pile grew. The creatures simply climbed over the pile of lifeless flesh, hardly even slowing down as they continued to surge toward the Primechs and Deicended. Soon, they would be pinned against the door and overrun. Tyr used everything in his power to move the door, and it still didn't budge. The creatures were inching their way closer and closer.

"No! We're not done here," Tyr shouted. He grabbed the door handle and pulled for his life. Still, it didn't move. His muscles bulged out in his efforts. Tyr planted one of his feet on the wall next to the door and screamed as his arms and legs grew in size slightly. The door budged. Only an inch, but it was something. Tyr kept pulling, and Takumi helped, pulling with his shadow arms. Eventually, they were able to get it open almost two feet.

"It's not much, but it's enough. Everybody, get in!" yelled Tyr.

Neith created a force field between them and the creatures. Everyone ran inside except Joe. "What are you doing? Let's go already!" shouted Tyr.

"Neith, give me the ABT rifle," said Joe. Neith handed it to him.

"That thing is useless out here. Stop screwing around and let's go!" Tyr shouted. He threw his pack outside the door and felt a cold chill run down his spine as he saw Neith's shield begin to crack under the weight of the stacked monstrosities.

"No. I'm not using the drones," said Joe. "We have to slow down these creatures or else they'll get to you."

"No! What? Let's go before Neith's…" Tyr stopped for a second when Neith's shield cracked open. He could see her sweating from the effort of holding the horde back as they clawed and pounded relentlessly against her shield, screeching, and even throwing their own bodies against it. Joe smiled over his shoulder at Tyr and nodded. "Damn it!" Tyr shouted.

Tyr worked with the help of the others to slowly shut the door to the facility. Joe hit a switch on the ABT rifle to set it for the satellite targeting. Tyr watched Joe clash with the creatures. He saw him slice through multiple enemies with each swing of one of his longswords. Then, as there was only a crack of space left to see out of the door, Tyr saw Joe draw the ABT rifle and jump into the thick of the fog. Everyone stood silent in anticipation. A loud whistling noise could be heard from the sky, and a moment after, it was followed by the sound of an explosion that rang in their ears even behind the big metal door and shook the whole building.

23

Deicide

"It should have been me," Tyr whispered to himself. Everybody was silent for a moment.

"Let's get moving. We need to find and eliminate the target immediately," Nadin said.

Cassandra put her hand on Nadin's shoulder to stop him. "Look at them. Just give them a second."

"Fine," he replied.

The Deicended were quiet, trying to process what had happened to Joe. "Nadin is right. There is no time to waste. Let's go, everyone. We're going to finish this mission," said Tyr.

Emily shot up, "Let's kill that bitch!" she shouted.

The Deicended followed Tyr as he stormed down the hallway.

"I shouldn't have underestimated their fortitude," Cassandra said to Nadin.

"I'll admit, I'm a bit surprised myself. Although it annoyed the hell out of me, it looks like Joe's endless optimism and perseverance rubbed off on them a bit. This mission might even be a success," he responded.

The group was less worried about making noise now since they figured anyone would know they were there by now. Still, the enemy didn't know where they were in the building, so there was no reason to be too reckless. The facility looked pretty old and didn't seem like anyone had been living inside for years. Although, it didn't seem as old as the buildings out in the fog. They had no idea how large the building was and really had no idea where to go, but the hallway they were in only led in one direction.

At the end, there appeared to be an old security checkpoint. There was a locked double door with a call button to the side. Most likely, the only way to open the door was from the inside. Unlike the steel hangar door leading into the facility, this one was easy for Tyr to kick down. Past the door was another hallway with three creatures in it. Lucy, Emily, and Takumi swiftly took them out with their daggers before they could make any noise. They kept walking until the hallway split.

There were signs on the walls that seemed to be directions. They were badly worn though. One read 'Dining Hall' with an arrow pointing left. Another read 'Medical Bay' with an arrow pointing left. Nothing else was legible. They could see a 'Pr' and 'Tr', probably the beginning of words, but they were too faded to read. There were arrows pointing right for those letters, and they were most likely in the direction of the center of the facility. They decided to head that way.

"I guess they don't use the whole facility for their base of operation," said Ben.

"That would make sense. This facility is huge, and it wouldn't make sense for them to be hidden for so long without being caught by George if they were a large group of people," said Neith. "Something is off about this place though. I get using those creatures as guard dogs, but why wouldn't they support them, and why haven't we seen any guards inside?"

"I'm worried they fled when they heard us," said Takumi.

"Unlikely. We would have heard them trying to leave if that was the case," said Nadin.

"Is it possible they are already dead from these creatures?" asked Emily.

"No. It isn't possible that all of this could have happened both without George's knowledge and the help of rogue Deicended. Additionally, from what we know of Kathleen, she could wipe out the whole hoard with a snap of her finger," said Cassandra.

They heard growls coming from a separate corridor. The group decided to check it and found one creature wandering around. Emily threw five knives into it, and it dropped to the ground. As they went to walk around the creature and Emily picked her knives back up, arms reached out from the walls and swung about violently. The creatures growled and screamed like they did outside. The group realized that there were barred doors keeping them back; they were in prison cells.

"I have more questions now," said Emily.

"They can wait. Let's just be happy that we don't have to fight any of these," said Tyr.

"Should we kill them?" asked Ben.

"Not worth the effort," said Cassandra. "They don't seem to be attracting any unwanted guests. I suggest we keep moving and forget about them for now."

Everyone agreed and moved past the cells. The corridor was rather small for a prison, but there seemed to be other paths that lead to more prison cells. They walked down a few more hallways with still no sign of any legitimate base.

After a few more minutes of searching, they found a gaping hole in the wall that led to a crumbled room that was the size of a football field. It was bigger than the room they used in their training facility, but it looked like an explosion or something had torn down some of its surrounding walls. There were a bunch of creatures roaming around and six massive roots coming from the center of the room and leading out. In the center of the room, it looked like the roots were forming a pillar, like a stem to a flower without a bud. Although, as they cautiously approached it, Neith noticed that it had more of a skin like texture. It stood thirty feet tall, and it was barely moving, slightly expanding and contracting at a steady pace.

"Is that thing… breathing?" asked Ben.

"It appears so," said Nadin.

"Should we engage it or ignore it?" asked Takumi.

"Hmmm, if we take it now, we won't have to worry about it, but might waste time, or might aggravate something that would have otherwise been neutral. But, if we don't, it could end up being a bigger problem later," said Nadin.

"I think it might be best to ignore it for now," said Tyr.

"I'm not sure we should," said Neith. "There is something off about the fog and the roots and they all lead here. I think our best move would be to take this thing out."

"We would be risking a lot on that bet," said Tyr. "We could give our target more time to get away."

"We tried to play it safe when we faced the Hawk, and the plan still fell apart," said Neith.

"Okay… we'll have to do this quickly. Do we even have any firepower left?" asked Tyr.

"I have two shots with this Lance rifle," said Ben.

"Good, that should work. Okay, status report on everyone's supplies," Tyr ordered.

"I'm down to my Photon revolver and sword," said Nadin.

"I still have my photon carbine and rapier," said Cassandra.

"I'm down to my P2 pistol," said Neith.

"I'm pretty good on CRFF ammo, and I still have most of my knives," said Emily.

"172 still operational," said Lucy.

"Only enough ammo for one CRFF, but I still have the six photon revolvers I brought," said Takumi.

"I have one magazine left with my 170, a photon revolver, and you guys already know about the Lance rifle," said Ben.

"Alright, good. I still have some ammo with my BRF 170, but I'm drained on plasma rounds and HIDP rounds for my shotgun. Also, I have no lances left for my lance rifle," said Tyr. "Not that I don't think you could do this Ben, but I think Lucy should take the shot with the lance rifle."

"Fair enough," said Ben as he handed the lance rifle over to Lucy.

"Alright, everyone, get into position. After Lucy takes this thing down, we still have the other creatures wandering around to take out," said Tyr.

Everyone took up positions, and Lucy put the extra lance on the ground next to her, ready to load it quickly just in case. Lucy brought the buttstock up to her shoulder and aimed carefully, even though missing this thing would be challenging given its size. She exhaled and squeezed the trigger slowly to not jerk the rifle. *Click,* the lance fired out and pierced into the stem creature. After a second, it exploded, and the stem began to shake and growl. The creatures around it began to scream, looking around and finding the group in the crack of the wall. The creatures ran for them, and they opened fire. Lucy focused on reloading the rifle.

The stem shaped creature was actually four massive arms pressed together that was beginning to open and spread apart. This creature stood on its arms that were connected to its, now revealed, much smaller body, like a spider. It was a grotesque being with its mouth taking up most its head, with crooked teeth lining it all the way around. It had humanoid legs hanging down that looked atrophied and didn't seem to be working anymore. Its eyes looked like it came from a pupilless fish. Its hair was long, but it had only one strand every square inch. On top of its head were two horns that spiraled awkwardly a foot in length from its head.

Lucy shouldered the lance rifle again and aimed for the big mouth. She pulled the trigger, and the lance sprang from the rifle. Her aim was true, and it appeared that the creature was about to eat the lance when its legs twitched and sank its body to the ground. The lance fired over the creature's head and hit the wall.

"Oh, this isn't good," said Lucy.

"I'll slice the thing down," said Nadin as he unsheathed his katana and charged for the creature.

Tyr, Ben, Emily, and Takumi followed Nadin. Most of the smaller creatures were already wiped out in the room. Cassandra, Lucy, and Neith laid down supporting fire from the hole in the wall. Neith focused on creating as many violet orbs as possible to fling at the creature. None of the attacks seemed to do any damage.

"Six shoot, six shooter!" Takumi yelled as he grabbed his six photon revolvers with his shadow arms.

Ben and Takumi stopped charging once in mid-range and fired what they had at the creature. As they approached, the creature snarled and ripped its legs free of the connecting roots that buried themselves into the ground. Once they were close enough, the creature took one of its arms and went to crush Nadin, Tyr, or Emily. Nadin and Emily dived out of the way. Emily began throwing her knives, sticking them into the creature's frail body. Tyr tried to catch the arm as it came down on him but was smacked down into the ground by it. He wasn't hurt, but the creature picked him up and tried to crush him. The creature gave up after a second and dropped him.

While he was still in the air, the creature whipped around another arm and smacked it into Tyr, sending him flying across the room. Nadin and Emily were staggering the creature by stabbing into its arms that were planted on the ground. It screamed at them and launched itself into the air, going over Ben and Takumi. It landed next to the hole in the wall and punched at Neith, Lucy, and Cassandra. Neith projected a shield, blocking the punch. The creature punched again, not breaking the shield. It then changed its target to Takumi and Ben. Ben ran out of ammo for his BRF 170 and scrambled in a panic to get out his photon revolver.

The creature reached for Ben, and Takumi sent five of his shadow arms to wrap around the creature's arm. He managed to stop the arm, but, when the creature drew back its arm, it took Takumi with it and flung him away when he was unable to hold onto the creature's arm with his shadow arms. At the same time, another one of its four arms crashed into Ben, knocking him to the ground. Neith caught Takumi in the air with her power, slowing his descent.

"Group up!" Tyr yelled.

They all ran for Ben. When the monster tried to attack them, Neith put her shield up. Seeing they were all together now under Neith's shield, the creature backed up, a bit frustrated from not being able to penetrate Neith's shield. Ben went to stand up and couldn't see. He took his mask off and saw that it was completely destroyed with a wide crack running down the middle. He dropped it and drew his photon revolver and dagger.

"We can do this. If we use our powers together, we can take it down," said Tyr.

Neith put the shield down, and Nadin and Emily sprinted out. Emily used the connection she had with the knives stuck into the creature and shot lightning from her hand to the knives. The creature growled in pain and was stunned for a second. Nadin jumped over Emily, and she magnetically pushed Nadin's metallic body towards the creature. With a precise strike, Nadin sliced one of the arms off the creature where it connected to its body. Nadin landed on the ground, and the creature screamed in pain and stumbled backward.

"It's vulnerable now," Cassandra said while drawing her rapier.

The creature raised one of its three remaining arms into the air. Nadin, Cassandra, and the Deicended began to feel a pull. Then, small rocks and pieces of rubble lifted into the air and towards the creature. It appeared that there was nothing in the creature's hand, but something was pulling things around it. With each second, the pull became stronger. Then, light started to bend around it.

"It's a black hole!" Neith yelled, warning her team.

"That's Kathleen?!" Emily asked.

Lucy reached out to a pillar near the hole in the wall and wrapped her arm around it. She extended two more arms and wrapped one around Nadin and another around Tyr. Emily flung the knife attached to a rope that was wrapped around her arm around a different pillar and pulled herself towards it. Takumi used a shadow arm to grab onto a pillar. He then sent out more shadow arms to grab onto Ben, Neith, and Cassandra. The room was like a storm of wind, violently pulling them towards Kathleen. They held on for dear life. The pull was so strong they were lifted from the ground. The limp bodies of the foul creatures they had killed that were littered around the room began sliding towards Kathleen, eventually being picked up by the pull and sucked into the black hole. The pillar Takumi held onto was beginning to crack.

"I can't hold on forever!" yelled Takumi.

"What are we supposed to do?" asked Emily.

"Can we still kill the creature?" asked Nadin.

"If we get any closer, we'll be sucked into that thing," said Tyr.

"What else are we supposed to do? Close the black hole? That doesn't seem possible," said Emily.

"No, it is possible," said Neith.

"Technically speaking but is this really the time to start a class on black holes?" asked Nadin.

"If it eats enough energy, it should close," said Neith.

"Right, but there isn't enough energy in the world to do that," said Cassandra.

"Right… not in this one," said Neith.

"What is that supposed to mean?" asked Lucy.

"I have an idea, but I have no idea if it will work," said Neith.

"Is this the best time to try out an idea?" asked Emily.

"If you have any better solutions, I'm all ears," shouted Neith.

"Okay, just do it, we don't have much time," said Tyr.

"Cassandra, give me the Flower of Eos," said Neith. Takumi used his arms to pull them together. Cassandra handed the bag over to Neith. "Ben, I need you to burn these," she said.

Ben grabbed the flower and concentrated on heating it. Neith took her mask off, watching it sail away into the black hole, and put her face near the flower. Neith put a shield around her and Ben to keep the smoke from being dragged away. The flower lit on fire, and the smoke filled the shield. After a few seconds, the shield began to flicker and fade away. The smoke immediately pulled away into the black hole. Neith had entered the Dawn Edge. Ben was coughing and noticed that he too had been pulled into the Dawn Edge.

Neith looked around and saw the room was filled with Phosphorus. They were just sitting around and observing. Neith was tempted to talk to them but remembered that John said the flower would only take them to the Dawn Edge for a short time. Ben looked around and started to panic.

"What's wrong, Ben? We're in the Dawn Edge. It's going to be okay," said Neith.

"How can you say that when we are surrounded by these monsters?" said Ben. His breathing became uneasy. He looked at his friends and his eyes widened. He stopped breathing for a second, and his body went limp as he passed out.

Neith rolled her eyes and focused on the black hole. In the Dawn Edge, the black hole still seemed to be pulling things towards it. "This might just work," Neith thought. The violet aura around Neith shined brightly. She stuck her hand out and shot a beam of energy into the black hole. The beam bent as it was swallowed up. Neith concentrated, and the beam grew wider. She could hardly breathe from the exhilaration of so much power coursing through her body. She felt truly unlimited for the first time in her life and poured every ounce of it into the beam which had become blinding. It grew bigger and bigger until the pull from the black hole lessened and then stopped. Neith cut off her beam, and the black hole was gone. "I really do have the power of a god," she said.

Everyone except Neith and Ben jumped into action. Emily shocked Kathleen again. This time, Tyr grabbed Nadin and threw him at Kathleen. Nadin swung his katana, and as it was about to make contact with another one of Kathleen's arms, she moved quickly and chomped down on his body. She spat him onto the ground.

"Nadin!" Emily yelled.

"Doonn't worry about mme." It sounded like some of his circuits were shorting out. "Just take heerr out," Nadin ordered.

Tyr and Takumi charged Kathleen together. Lucy extended and wrapped her arms around one of Kathleen's arms. Kathleen pulled that arm back and spun it around. She crashed Lucy into Takumi. Tyr kept charging at Kathleen. She punched down at him, and he blocked her, standing his ground. She punched again, and Tyr still stood. She punched three more times, and Tyr's arms grew too tired to hold. Another punch came down, and Tyr collapsed into the ground. Emily sprinted for Kathleen, throwing as many knives as she could. When Kathleen turned towards her, Emily shot lightning to every knife she threw into her.

At first, Kathleen was stunned and shrieked from the pain, but this time, she pushed through the pain and lunged for Emily. She reached her arm towards Emily, but before it reached her, Cassandra stepped in and dug her rapier into the arm, stopping it in its path. Kathleen withdrew that arm and swung another around, slamming into both Cassandra and Emily. Cassandra stood back up but was twitching from the damage. When Emily stood, her arm fell limp. She looked down and noticed that she had broken her left arm.

"They need my powers," said Neith. The Phosphorus had faded from her sight. As she left the Dawn Edge, her powers no longer worked in it. But her powers still didn't work in her own world yet either.

Kathleen walked over to Tyr. He was conscious, but his black scales were gone. She raised an arm and slammed it toward Tyr. Tyr stuck his hand out and froze the arm in place. Kathleen fought it, and eventually, Tyr gave, letting the arm fall towards him. Takumi used eight shadow arms to grab on and stop the arm from crushing Tyr. Kathleen threw that arm into the air, taking Takumi with it. Then, she whipped that arm down, slamming Takumi down with it.

He tried to gasp as all of the air was forced out of his lungs. Then, Kathleen looked at Tyr again and raised her arm to kill Tyr. When the arm came down, it was stopped by Neith's shield. Kathleen turned her horrifying eyes on Neith and screamed in anger. Neith dropped to her knees.

"I'm completely drained," said Neith. Ben woke. He stumbled to get up and fell a few times trying. Kathleen began to run for the two of them. "You think you can do anything to stop her?" asked Neith.

"What happened?" Ben said, dazed and not fully aware of what was happening.

"Well, this is one way to go I guess," said Neith.

As Kathleen was running, Lucy wrapped her arm around one of Kathleen's, causing the grotesque woman to fall on her face. Kathleen tried to pull her arm back but couldn't. She got up and went to strike Lucy with a different arm. Lucy grew two arms and stopped the incoming attack.

Growing another arm and grabbing her dagger, Lucy sent it for Kathleen's body. Kathleen moved her body out of the way, but Lucy's arm came swinging around Kathleen's body. It wrapped around three times until Lucy stabbed the dagger into Kathleen. Then, Lucy retracted her arm with the dagger still stuck in. The dagger sliced completely around her, cutting her in half. Standing below Kathleen, Lucy was showered with her blood and gore. The room was silent except for the heavy thump as Kathleen's massive arms and remaining body slumped onto the ground.

"You did it!" said Neith. Everyone in the group limped over to where Lucy was standing, breathing heavily.

"First the Hawk and now Kathleen. Once Mars hears about this, he'll want to make you a Primech on the spot," Nadin said almost reverently while being carried by Tyr.

"Good. I worked so hard to become one," said Lucy.

"I'll radio Nicholas to send us some support. We just have to lay low for a bit, and this will all be done with," said Cassandra.

"It's strange. Why does it feel like your powers are on a completely different level than ours," Takumi said, looking at her suspiciously.

"I don't know about a different level, but who knows, maybe I just lucked out with the powers I was gifted," said Lucy.

Ben started to remember what he had seen in the Dawn Edge. The world around him started to spin. He dropped to his knees so he didn't pass out again. He rose slowly, his breathing uncontrollable. "Cassandra, can I see your rifle?" he asked.

"Sure. Are you okay though?" Cassandra asked while handing her photon carbine to Ben.

"Honestly, I'm not sure," said Ben. He backed up from everyone else and raised the photon carbine. He aimed it at Lucy.

"Woah, Ben! What are you doing?!" Emily asked.

"I'm sorry, but she's not like us. She's like those monsters in the Dawn Edge," said Ben. Lucy's jaw tightened as she stared down the barrel of Cassandra's gun.

"Ben, put the gun down! You're seeing things," said Tyr.

"No, I'm not. It's the same thing I saw when she woke me up when Emily shocked me. I'm not delusional," Ben pleaded.

"I'm your friend, Ben. How could you point a gun at me?" Lucy asked, her voice thick with emotion.

"I know what I saw. I'm not going to kill you, but we need to restrain her. She's up to something," said Ben.

"Is this really the thanks I get for saving y'all's rears," Lucy asked incredulously.

"Put down the weapon, Ben. Maybe we can look into what you are talking about, but we're not going to attack our team members," Nadin demanded.

Takumi shook his head, gritted his teeth, and sent two shadow arms out, binding Lucy's arms around her body with one and binding her legs with the other.

"What the hell, Takumi?!" Lucy shouted.

"I'm sorry, but I believe Ben. There has been something suspicious with you lately. I've had a feeling something wasn't right. Ben seems to know something we don't, and I think we need to have a serious look into you. I also have a feeling you won't go in willingly," said Takumi.

"Guys, stop it," demanded Tyr.

"I promise, we'll look into Lucy when we return, but we need to all relax," said Nadin.

"Look into me? But I've done nothing wrong!" said Lucy.

"I know, but just to put their minds at ease, we'll do a few tests, and this will be all over," said Nadin.

"Just because they are losing it doesn't mean I should be treated as a criminal. I expect to be made a Primech when we return," said Lucy.

"No need to rush," said Neith.

"No! I will not be tested! This is degrading!" yelled Lucy. "You! Get your filthy hands off of me!" she glared at Takumi.

"Takumi, I give you my word, I have just sent a message to George about this. It has confirmed that we will look into her once we get you all back to the safety of the facility, just let her go." Nadin spoke, trying to diffuse the situation. Takumi could feel Lucy trembling in his shadow arms.

"I'm not letting go until we get to the bottom of this," said Takumi.

"I just killed my own mother. I don't think you'll be able to stop me," Lucy said as one of her hands extended out of Takumi's grasp and grabbed her dagger. Her arm then extended to Takumi with the intent to kill.

Ben shot the photon carbine, but it jammed. He threw it to the side and stuck his hand out. *C'mon, shoot fire like you did before,* he thought to himself. He focused, and heat radiated from his hand, but no flame emerged. *Now! I need to do this now!* He focused harder, but no flame erupted.

The dagger in Lucy's hand flew closer, and right before it struck through Takumi's throat, he put his own dagger up to block. Lucy's dagger clashed with Takumi's. Her dagger shattered Takumi's dagger, breaking off the tip, and continued. Takumi wrapped a shadow arm around his neck, blocking the dagger. *Now!* Ben thought. He concentrated and put everything into making a flame. He took his hand back and threw it forward to ignite… nothing. Nothing shot from his hand.

Lucy whipped her hand back around and drove her dagger through the back of Takumi's head. The point of her dagger stuck out from Takumi's helmet, dripping with blood. His shadow arms faded away and Lucy was freed.

Ben dropped to the ground, barely feeling the impact of his knees hitting the ground. "I failed again," he said.

"No!" Emily screamed at the sight of her friend. She drew her CRFF and unloaded the entire magazine into Lucy.

Lucy twitched with every shot that hit her, but she never fell. Her head was lowered, but she picked it up after Emily was done firing. She had a big smile across her face. The expression was maniacal, and Lucy was hardly recognizable. She grew ten feet tall and began to grow arms all over her body. Her eyes faded to white, and blood started to drip from her brow. The blood fell all over her head, a bleeding halo.

"I guess I'll have to be the only survivor of this mission," said Lucy. Tyr, Neith, Emily, Ben, and even Cassandra and Nadin stared up in horror. Those of them who still had blood felt it run cold.

Right as Lucy was about to make her first move, a winding noise echoed through the chamber. It sounded like a chainsaw. Lucy looked up to see a claymore, with a chainsaw as a blade, cutting through the middle of her head. John dragged the blade all the way through her. Separated into two pieces, Lucy flopped to the ground. He turned around to the dumbstruck group, his eyes resting on Takumi's limp body, and sighed.

"This will only stop her for a few seconds. Come with me now," John demanded. An Owl class aircraft flew down from a hole in the ceiling. The back of the Owl opened up, and seeing Lucy's body still squirming around, the group complied and rushed towards the aircraft.

Emily stopped next to Takumi's body and knelt down. She took his hand with her good arm and let her tears flow freely as she cried. Tyr stopped next to her and put his hand on her shoulder. "We have to go, Emily," Tyr shouted over the sound of the Owl's engine. She grabbed Takumi's broken dagger and headed into the Owl. The aircraft took off, out of the fog, into the skies, and away from the facility.

24

Chasm

Silence rang in the Owl. Tyr gripped his dagger, worried about what was to come. Tension filled the space. Nadin, barely able to move, laid down. Beside John, there was a massive person, hidden in a brown cloak. It appeared to be a Primoid since one red light could be seen from the hood. Then, there was a woman that was smaller in stature and geared up in old military armor, holding a rifle at the ready. Last, there was a tall and well-built man with short, dirty blonde hair. He wore similar armor as John; it had a medieval armor look to it, but he didn't wear anything on his head.

Ben didn't care to look at anyone. He walked past everyone and took a seat near the cockpit. He kept his head down, not crying. He didn't blink either. His eyes just had a dead look to them.

"We have no intentions to harm you," said John.

"What are your intentions then?" asked Nadin.

"I was going to leave you after I found you all in the fog. I tried to recruit you and failed. I went there in the hope to sway you to our side and avoid an eventual death. But then, as we were taking off, I heard a loud explosion. I expected to see one of Kathleen's black holes, but there was nothing. I needed to see what was going on for myself. I've had suspicions that her power has dwindled, but this was the first confirmation. When I arrived at the facility, I saw you fighting, and then you killed her. Then, I was going to leave again. No point in trying to recruit you all after insisting you would lose and you didn't. As I was stepping off, I saw that person you were with transform. That's when I dropped in to save you," said John.

"Well, what now?" asked Tyr.

"You can come with me, my offer still stands, or if you would like, I can drop you off outside the City. I assume you can summon a transport from there," said John. He walked off into the cockpit.

There was still an uneasy feeling in the air. Tyr took a seat next to Nadin. Emily took a seat on the other side, took her helmet off, dropping it to the floor of the transport, and covered her face with her hair. Neith stayed standing, tapping her foot. She looked as focused as if she was trying to solve a difficult math problem.

The tall man in the armor walked over to Ben, taking the empty seat next to him hesitantly. "Hey, I'm Leroy. It's nice to meet you. I'm not sure what just happened to you guys, but I'm sorry it happened," he said. Ben didn't acknowledge him. "If you want, I could look out for you. You look like you've been through a lot." Ben made the slightest glance at Leroy. "I'm sorry, I didn't mean to annoy you. I was just trying to help." Leroy stood up and stepped away.

I can't let John just go, Neith thought to herself. *He's a threat to George. I still have too much I need to learn from It, and I can't afford to let John get in the way in the future. I have to take my chance now. I need to get my teammates with me too.*

"I don't trust you all for a second. You're rogue Deicended. The Dawn Edge has twisted you to defect from George, just like Serpico and Kathleen," she said. "For all we know, you are just as dangerous as they are. You aren't taking us back to our people, are you? You're going to take us to your rogue base." She looked at Emily and Tyr. She tried to make eye contact with Ben, but he hadn't seemed to have registered that she was even speaking.

"Do you really believe that Deicended just go 'rogue' out of nowhere? You need to stop believing the lies you have been fed," said Leroy.

"Says the terrorist that blows up schools," said Neith. Her hand lit violet, and she threw a ball of energy at Leroy. A translucent, light blue shield appeared when the ball was about to hit him. It disappeared right after, and his armor glowed red in the center of his chest.

Tyr shot up and got beside Neith. "I've got your back," he said.

The soldier aimed her rifle and fired at Neith. Neith projected a shield, blocking the shot. It was a concussive round and, exploding inside the ship, threw everyone outside of Neith's shield back. The ship shook violently. Leroy fell back on a button that opened up the back ramp of the Owl. The aircraft was filled with the noise of wind blaring into their ears. Tyr, armored up and with his dagger out, charged for the woman holding the rifle. The Primoid's cloak lifted, revealing two arms, each the size of a heavy person's body. Flames burst from its right elbow. It was a rocket that propelled its arm forward, slamming its fist into Tyr's chest and sending him flying out of the aircraft. As Tyr plummeted through the air, his scales faded away and a blind terror gripped him.

Neith's eyes radiated violet. She started to form orbs of energy above her. "Neith, forget this!" Nadin shouted. "You have to get Tyr. If he is unconscious, he won't survive the fall. Cassandra and I will handle this." He drew his pistol and used his katana to try to stand.

Neith looked outside towards Tyr, whose figure was already shrinking as he descended rapidly towards the waters below. Then, she looked at Ben and Emily who were still sitting. *Damn, I'm outnumbered,* Neith thought. She turned around and jumped out of the Owl, using her power to guide her freefall and accelerate her towards Tyr.

Emily shot up. *What do I do? What do I do?* she thought.

"Emily, let me handle this," said Nadin. He went to go shoot his pistol and another concussive round exploded right next to him. Nadin fell out of the aircraft as it shook again.

Emily stabilized herself. "Ben! We have to go, Ben!" Emily shouted. *Do I jump? I don't know if I want to jump. But my friends are out there… But Ben is… I… What should….,"* she thought. "Ben! Please," Emily pleaded. She reached out and started to pull Ben's dagger magnetically in an attempt to pull him to her. He started to budge. Then, the dagger ripped away from its sheath. It flew into her hand, setting her off-balance. She wasn't even sure herself whether she stepped or slipped off the ramp when the dagger reached her hand, but she fell into the air off the Owl. She saw Ben reaching for her hand, wide-eyed and desperate, and then she saw only the sky above her. *I don't know if I made the right choice,* she thought.

As she fell, she couldn't hear anything but the wind. Out of the clouds, she saw the water of the ocean rushing to meet her until she was surrounded by Neith's shield, catching her in the air. She descended slowly to the water. Emily and the others floated in Neith's shield. She saw Tyr and Nadin with them.

"George has an aircraft on route to pick us up," said Nadin.

"Where are Ben and Cassandra?" asked Tyr.

Emily put her head down and muttered, "I don't know."

Back in the Owl, John walked back into the cabin. "I see we have had quite a commotion since I left ten seconds ago," said John. He looked down at Ben and then at Cassandra. "Will you two be staying with us then?" Ben kept silent, not sure why he hadn't jumped with his team or… what was left of his team.

"I am supposed to protect the Deicended. Nadin is with the others; I want to make sure Ben is okay, so I will stay with him," said Cassandra. Ben was surprised but didn't understand why she wouldn't have just made him jump with the rest.

"As long as that doesn't get in the way of our plans, you are more than welcome to join us," said John.

"How can you trust me like that? I'm a Primech," said Cassandra.

"You may be tethered to George in a way, but that does not mean you are not able to carve your own path under your own influence," said John. He turned to walk back into the cockpit and stopped and glanced at Ben. "You're the one who saw through your friend for what she was, weren't you? Good, I was hoping you would be joining us more than the others. We'll be counting on you."

Counting on me? Ben thought, confused by the statement. John offered no further clarification.

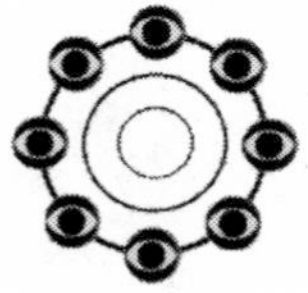

After a few more silent hours of flight, the Owl came over land again. They landed in a heavily forested area. When Ben and Cassandra got out of the aircraft, they found themselves in a small base. It was filled with humans, Primoids, and some Primechs. "How is this possible? How have you controlled all of these people?" asked Cassandra.

"Who said anything about control?" asked the woman that was in the Owl with them. They walked over to a massive Owl class aircraft that could almost be a small Swan class. It was strange looking as it didn't appear aerodynamic at all.

"Hey, man! You're really going to enjoy it here, I promise," Leroy said to Ben.

"It doesn't matter," said Ben. "I'm useless." Leroy's smile faltered for a moment, then rallied.

"Sounds like you've hit rock bottom. Well, good thing about that is you can only go up from there," Leroy responded cheerfully.

Ben cringed from what he said, but at least it was a feeling, something different from the hollowness he'd felt since Takumi died.

"Speaking of Rock… Where is that guy?" said Leroy. "Hey, Rock! Come here, boy." A beach ball-sized rock flew out from the trees. Leroy caught it and laughed as he pet it. "Oh, who's a good boy? Hey, Ben, right? This is Rock. Bet you can't guess why I named him that…. It's because he likes rocks." Leroy chuckled at his own joke, obviously very entertained by himself.

Of course, he's a Deicended who controls rocks. There's probably a bunch of us here, thought Ben. *Obviously, he's crazy though. A grown man with a pet rock that can also control rocks. Well, at least crazy ain't necessarily rogue. From what George taught us a rogue Deicended should be like, he doesn't seem to fit the profile. He's more like the profile of a guy who belongs in a straight jacket, which I guess is better.*

Every person and machine gathered their cargo and started to board the aircraft. "I don't know if I'm in the position to ask, but where are we going? We already seem to be in a secure base. Is there a more secure base?" asked Cassandra.

"There is," said John. "We're heading to a secret outpost… on Mars."

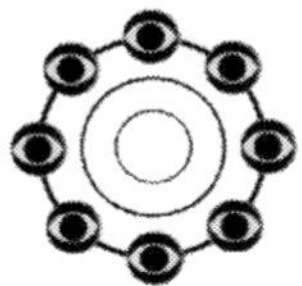

"The mission was a success, technically," said Nicholas.

"Who in their right mind would call that a success?" Tyr asked with his head in his hands.

"Either way, we have much to talk about," said Cade.

"I have nothing to talk about. I did this last mission, take me to the free people in Australia like you promised," Emily demanded.

"We need you more than ever, Emily. Now is not the time to make such a request," said Nicholas.

"You promised, and I expect you to fulfill that promise. I'm done with this. I'm done with George, and I'm done with the Deicended. We were not prepared for that disaster, I'm done being your expendable puppet," said Emily. The room was silent for a few moments.

"We did promise, and we will fulfill our promise, if necessary," said Cade. "Though, I must urge you to stay. Abandoning George at this time, when it is seemingly most detrimental for us, leaving us, would be most unwise."

"You always talked too much. I made up my mind a long time ago. Shut up and take me away," Emily demanded.

"So be it. There is an Owl outside, ready to take you," said Cade. Emily turned and walked towards the door. She stopped and walked over to Neith and Tyr. Neith could not believe that Emily would turn her back on George and offered her a cursory handshake. Tyr was torn. His squad had completely collapsed today. He had lost so much and did not want to lose Emily as well, but he couldn't force her to stay. When she stood in front of him, he gave her a hug.

"Take care of yourself, Emily. We'll miss you." She smiled up at him and looked back over at Neith, who was looking across the room, away from her. Tyr continued, "If you ever change your mind, please come back."

Emily sighed and shook her head. "Thanks, Tyr. You're a good squad leader, but I can't do this anymore." He nodded, and she walked out into the hallway to head for her transport.

"Tyr, you appear tired. This is unusual for you to show," said Cade.

"I've been unable to sleep. I can't shut my eyes for some reason," said Tyr.

"We don't have to do this debrief now. You can come back when you are well-rested," said Nicholas.

"I'll be fine. I can handle a few more hours," said Tyr.

"We would prefer you to sleep to give a more accurate recollection of what occurred. Your mind is no use to anyone if it is burnt out. We can have a Primoid sent up and administer something for you to aid you in sleeping," said Cade.

"Okay, then. I'll try. I'm sure, once I can close my eyes, I'll be able to rest," Tyr said and walked out of the room. Once Neith could no longer hear Tyr's receding footsteps, she turned on Cade.

"What the hell was that, Cade?! I thought there would be no more lies between us," Neith shouted. "What is Lucy?"

"I have not the slightest idea. Believe me, we had no idea. This is an embarrassment. The Phosphorus had turned Kathleen on us years ago, but we thought we had fixed that this time," said Cade.

"Fix it? What do you mean by that?" asked Neith.

"Well, first, I must reveal the last secret we withheld from you," said Cade.

"Last secret?! I thought we were past that. How am I supposed to trust what you say if you still lied even after supposedly revealing everything to me?" Neith stepped forward as she spoke, and the accusatory tone in her voice rose.

"We plan to have you work directly with us from now on," said Nicholas.

"We will introduce you to Sun, and you would have been made a Primech of Prudence, but because of recent events, we cannot afford to do that," said Cade. "Lucy's main goal was to become a Primech. She was not subtle about that, so we have to assume that the Phosphorus plan something that requires a Deicended to become a Primech. We do not know how, but why else would she want to become a Primech so badly? If that was the case, we cannot allow any Deicended to undergo that process until we have more information."

"I understand; it's a necessary precaution," said Neith. *I plan to become something greater with these powers anyways,* she thought.

"Good. Well, first, we must tell you the truth of your origins. You were not born… the conventional way. It is more like you were manufactured by George." He waited to see if Neith would have a reaction to this, but she only leaned forward with her hands on the table and stared at him intensely. Cade continued. "When we discovered the Dawn-Edge, Deicended had already been popping up in the City. Obviously, we needed a way to combat these Deicended since they did pose a threat to George and Its people. At the same time, we could run tests and learn about the Dawn-Edge. We discovered that the adult human mind and emotions battle the powers in their body. So, we took unborn fetuses and accelerated their growth. Once old enough, we released them with memories that we manipulated. Though mostly randomized, by controlling certain aspects, we could test with different personality types to see the results. You, Tyr, Lucy, Emily, Ben and Takumi were the first that we made sure had a proper motive that would give you drive to properly harness your powers. With a motive and purpose, we could hope to eliminate the chances of another incident like the one we had with Kathleen," Cade explained.

Neith's eyes brightened. Her right hand glowed with anger. "My childhood was a lie?" she said, gritting her teeth.

"All for the purpose of discovery!" pleaded Cade. "It was vital that we gain an understanding of the Dawn Edge and how it is impacting our world, and this was the only way that we could see to move forward.

"Why?! How could you see a benefit to this lie? You could have just influenced our personality by raising us like normal people. Why create this false narrative in our memories?" said Neith.

"You were shown a different world. I am sure you heard Emily's story about her experiences on the day your school was 'bombed'. She felt abandoned and isolated from the world. The world we showed her was a world with less restriction than George really enforces. You were bullied in your other memories as well. George's rules do not allow for this. As pleasant as it would have been to 'raise you like normal people', that would have left room for too many variables. George needed to ensure that, much like a Primoid, you were all engineered precisely to suit your purposes, to understand why George is necessary for the betterment of mankind and to have the proper motivation to do whatever it would take to reach your highest potential in Its service. Humans are far more complex than an average Primoid though, you Deicended really are one of George's greatest masterpieces of engineering," Cade expounded. She stared at him with a million thoughts running through her head.

After a few moments, Neith's energy calmed. "I'm sorry. I understand the reasoning for this. Sometimes, ridiculous measures are needed in order to discover the truth. I guess my past was pointless anyways, a means to learn, and I kept the knowledge I obtained over that fake time. That is the really important part," she said. "So, if the Hawk didn't bomb our supposed school, then what was he doing that made him an enemy of George?"

"Well, he did attack George, just not in the way you thought. He bombed this facility. We had assumed that he just wanted to disrupt our operations. We used him as the motivation for you Deicended. Now, because of recent events, our assumption might have been our greatest failing. I think there is no coincidence that a bombing occurred while we were creating you, then Lucy turns out to be some great evil force. They must have manipulated her somehow, introduced some corruption, but it almost still does not make sense. Even with the power they possessed, we would have found out if Lucy had been tampered with," said Cade. Neith thought for a moment, then looked up at Cade.

"When Lucy revealed herself, she called Kathleen her mother. Is it possible that they switched her baby with the one you were creating? It would explain how she too had immeasurable powers," said Neith. Cade shook his head in disbelief.

"No. From our tests, the power of the Deicended is not inherited, and we would have detected her. The Hawk and company alone did not possess the ability to trick George like this," Cade said, frustrated from trying to figure out the answer.

"Then, if she really is Kathleen's daughter and somehow was able to inherit her power, the real question is, what is Lucy?" asked Neith. Cade looked at her for a moment, letting the silence stretch out before responding. "A god among us."

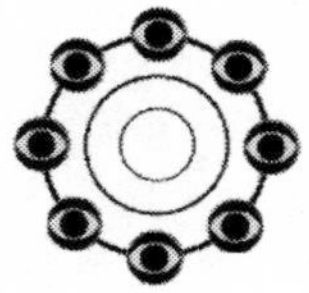

From a puddle of blood, muscles weaved together, connecting bones and ligaments. When the last bit of skin sealed, Lucy was formed and whole again.

"How pitiful, bested by mere humans," a voice said.

"Being bound to this body in this world limits me," Lucy said. "I hate every moment of it."

"What will we do now to kill George?" asked another voice.

"We could just continue having 'Lucy' disrupt the abomination's 'order'. That would be fun. You could just do that until the end of time," said a third voice.

"I would prefer to be rid of this anchor before I keep fighting for a millennium," said Lucy.

"Well, let's not be hasty. I doubt that we will be able to have another Deicended become a Primech under our control," said the second voice.

"George's weakness is Its illusion of omnipotence. We may already have a human that desires more than this world can give," said Lucy. "I'm sure we can find a way to use that."

Epilogue

It was a shorter trip than Emily had imagined. She could hear the engines start to wind down as the aircraft descended. *I figured there would be at least a few people on the Owl with me. I'm pretty capable on my own anyway. I'll just be glad to be away from George,* thought Emily. She was the only human on the aircraft, but there were two peacekeeping Primoids on board. They landed, and the bay door opened.

Emily walked out, and the sun stung her eyes. When her eyes adjusted, she noticed a massive building in front of her. She looked around, and she was surrounded by cement like she was in some sort of massive parking lot. The two Primoids stood behind her. "Why are you guys bothering to get off the Owl?" asked Emily.

Emily turned back to the facility and saw Lind floating before her. "Lind, what the hell are you doing in Australia?" asked Emily.

"Amusing. You still believe you've been sent to Australia. Ironic how you were just there too," said Lind.

The Primoids behind Emily grabbed onto her and secured her arms. "Get off me!" she shouted. She tried to use her powers to force them off, but they barely shook. "How?" she asked.

"They're made of plastic except for their wiring, of course. There isn't enough metal for you to push around I see. Excellent," said Lind.

Emily screamed and tried her hardest to push them magnetically. All they did was shake except the one on her right; its eyes flickered ever so slightly. "Where the hell am I?" asked Emily.

Lind responded in one of its inhuman voices. "Haha, ironic. You're at the Four Circles Prison. Welcome. The warden, Moon, has been eager to meet you."

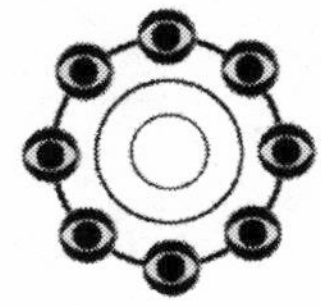

Made in the USA
Columbia, SC
02 February 2022